A PORTRAIT OF THE ARTIST
AS A YOUNG MAN

A PORTRAIT OF THE ARTIST AS A YOUNG MAN

◆

James Joyce

Introduction and Notes by
DR JACQUELINE BELANGER

WORDSWORTH CLASSICS

In loving memory of
MICHAEL TRAYLER
the founder of Wordsworth Editions

11

Readers who are interested in other titles from
Wordsworth Editions are invited to visit our website at
www.wordsworth-editions.com

For our latest list and a full mail-order service contact
Bibliophile Books, 5 Thomas Road, London E14 7BN
TEL: +44 (0) 207 515 9222 FAX: +44 (0) 207 538 4115
E-MAIL: orders@bibliophilebooks.com

This edition published 1992 by Wordsworth Editions Limited
8B East Street, Ware, Hertfordshire SG12 9ET
New Introduction and Notes added 2001

ISBN 978-1-85326-006-3

Typeset by Antony Gray
Printed and bound in Great Britain by
Clays Ltd, St Ives plc

FSC

Mixed Sources
Product group from well-managed
forests and other controlled sources

Cert no. SGS - COC - 2061
www.fsc.org
© 1996 Forest Stewardship Council

GENERAL INTRODUCTION

Wordsworth Classics are inexpensive editions designed to appeal to the general reader and students. We commissioned teachers and specialists to write wide ranging, jargon-free introductions and to provide notes that would assist the understanding of our readers rather than interpret the stories for them. In the same spirit, because the pleasures of reading are inseparable from the surprises, secrets and revelations that all narratives contain, we strongly advise you to enjoy this book before turning to the Introduction.

General Adviser
KEITH CARABINE
Rutherford College
University of Kent at Canterbury

INTRODUCTION

1 *Publishing background and biography*

In 1904 James Joyce submitted an essay entitled 'A Portrait of the Artist' to the Irish journal *Dana*. The piece was rejected, but out of this essay grew the novel *Stephen Hero*. Joyce revised *Stephen Hero* over the period 1907 to 1914, but in 1911 – frustrated by the failure of a business venture and difficulties in publishing his collection of short stories, *Dubliners* – Joyce threw the manuscript of the novel that had become *A Portrait of the Artist as a Young Man* into the fire. Although rescued by Joyce's sister Eileen, this was not the end of the troubles for the novel; initially serialised in the London journal the *Egoist*, the book form of the novel was rejected by a number of English publishers before being brought out by the American publisher B. W. Huebsch in 1916. It is perhaps fitting that *A Portrait of the Artist as a Young Man* – a novel whose organising principle, according to Richard Ellmann, is the 'gestation of a soul' – should itself have had such a long and slow gestation period.[1]

James Joyce (1882–1941) was born in Dublin into a middle-class Catholic family, one whose social and economic status slowly declined during Joyce's youth and adolescence. While Joyce's mother was a devout Catholic, his father was 'anti-clerical' (Jeffares, p. 219), a man who fiercely objected to the interference of the Catholic clergy in Irish politics and whose attitudes to the church and politics Joyce himself would inherit. From 1888 to 1891 Joyce attended the prestigious Jesuit school Clongowes Wood College, but was forced to leave Clongowes when his family fell upon increasing economic hardship. Joyce was briefly a pupil at a Christian Brothers school but returned to another Jesuit institution, Belvedere College, from 1893 to 1898. Joyce attended University College Dublin from 1899 to 1902, where he studied modern European languages. He left Ireland for Paris in 1902 but returned to Dublin the following year after receiving the news that his mother was dying. He taught in a secondary school for a time in Dublin, but left Ireland permanently for the continent in October 1904. Joyce visited Ireland for the last time in 1912.

Joyce was unique in rooting his works in his own urban, Catholic background and experiences. This was in contrast to some of his Anglo-Irish Protestant contemporaries such as William Butler Yeats and J. M. Synge, whose writings centre on attempts to connect Ireland's Protestant ruling class with an idealised rural Ireland. Joyce saw both the Irish Literary and Gaelic Revivals as restrictive and in the service of a narrow-gauge nationalism, and it is perhaps this perceived lack of literary choices or models open to Joyce in early-twentieth-century Ireland that led him to pursue a writing career abroad, as fellow Irish authors Oscar Wilde and George Bernard Shaw had done before him. Rather than following Wilde and Shaw to England, however, Joyce chose continental Europe for his self-imposed exile, living in Trieste, Paris, and Zurich (where he died in January 1941). From his earliest writings as a university student, Joyce indicated that he drew his artistic and intellectual influences from a wider European literary tradition (he was, for example, heavily influenced by the Norwegian dramatist Henrik Ibsen), and indeed his objection to late-nineteenth- and early-twentieth-century Irish cultural nationalism was that it was inward-looking rather than European-oriented.

1 Richard Ellmann, p. 297. For full bibliographic details of this and other references, please see the Works Cited list at the end of this Introduction.

However, although Joyce left Ireland permanently in 1904, Ireland was the central subject of his mature writing. His collection of short stories, *Dubliners* (published in 1914, the same year as *Portrait* began appearing in the *Egoist*), was meant, as Joyce remarked, to reveal the 'paralysis' at the heart of Irish society, and each of the fifteen stories deals with a different aspect of Dublin life, following a structural progression from childhood to adolescence, adulthood and public life. It was also in 1914 that Joyce began his second novel, *Ulysses*, a novel that begins with Stephen Dedalus's return to Ireland after the departure for Paris that closes *Portrait*.[2] Both *Ulysses* and Joyce's final work, *Finnegan's Wake* (1939), are remarkable for their stylistic, narrative and linguistic innovations – each section of *Ulysses*, for example, has its own particular style, ranging from the form of a drama in one episode to the question-and-answer pattern of the Catechism in another. The formal and narrative innovations of Joyce's later work in particular have led many critics to read his works in terms of an early-twentieth-century movement in Western art and literature that has come to be known as modernism, and which includes the work of Ezra Pound, Virginia Woolf and T. S. Eliot. Characterised by an experimental and self-reflexive approach to form and language, modernist literature is often thought of as anti-realist, distinguished by a loss of any belief that a stable 'real' world can be unproblematically depicted in representational language.

In many ways *Portrait* stands on the cusp between the naturalism of *Dubliners* and the formal experimentation of the later works. The often experimental nature of the novel is signalled from the very first page, which establishes *Portrait* as a work that breaks with strict conventions of novelistic realism in favour of a more impressionistic rendering of the significant events in the protagonist's development. This emerges even more fully when *Portrait* is compared to its earlier incarnation, *Stephen Hero*. In the revision process, *Stephen Hero* was cut from its original 900 pages, divided into twenty-five chapters focusing largely on Stephen's experiences at university, to the five chapters of *Portrait*. While in *Stephen Hero* the characters of Emma Clery and members of Stephen's family are fully realised, these characters become shadowy in *Portrait*, defined only in terms of Stephen's perception of and relation to them (Emma Clery becomes merely E— C— in *Portrait*, for example). Only those most essential elements relating to the development of Stephen

2 *Ulysses* was published in England in 1922 but was not published in the United States until 1934, after a court ruled that the novel was not pornographic.

Dedalus remain in the revised text, so that characterisation of other figures in the novel becomes less a matter of representing them as actual individuals and more a matter of showing how encounters with them relate to Stephen himself.

2   *Language, structure, imagery*

While many critics have noted the parallels between the life and experiences of Joyce and those of his young protagonist Stephen Dedalus (Stephen also attends Clongowes Wood College and University College Dublin, for example), the shift in focus that takes place between *Stephen Hero* and *Portrait* – the intense concentration on Stephen's psychological, spiritual and artistic development exhibited in *Portrait* – makes these autobiographical parallels between Joyce and Stephen less important than they might at first seem. More important than the actual facts of Stephen's environment and experiences is the effect these have on his growing awareness of himself and his place in the world. In its fictional tracing of an individual's development, *Portrait* is an example of a type of novel termed a *Bildungsroman*, a novel 'that has as its main themes the formative years or spiritual education of one person' (*OED*). More precisely, however, the novel is a *Künstlerroman*, which takes as its focus the spiritual and emotional formation of the artist. *Portrait* details the development of Stephen Dedalus from his first moments of childhood consciousness of the world around him to the moment when he is ready to leave Ireland to pursue his calling as an artist, with Stephen's fitful journey towards maturity rendered not only in terms of plot and basic description, but also through subtle changes in the narrative and stylistic techniques employed by Joyce.

The first chapter is composed of Stephen's earliest childhood memories, his experiences as a schoolboy at Clongowes Wood College and his first encounters with the world of Irish politics. The chapter largely represents Stephen's responses to the sensory stimulations of the external world and is characterised by a loose associational style that links seemingly unconnected thoughts and images. Stephen's thoughts on the first page of the novel jump, for example, from the oilsheet that 'had the queer smell' to 'His mother had a nicer smell than his father' (p. 3), the sense of smell associating seemingly disparate ideas and also enabling Stephen to make tentative steps towards understanding the difference between his father and mother. This, in turn, leads him to distinguish between his family and another: 'The Vances lived in number seven. They had a different father and mother.

They were Eileen's father and mother' (p. 3). This first chapter sees Stephen gradually situating himself in relation to the world around him, developing an identity largely through a recognition of the differences between himself and others.

It is through *language* that Stephen begins to understand his relationship to others, and throughout the novel language is for Stephen the primary mode of negotiating and shaping the world around him and finding his own place within it. In the novel, according to Seamus Deane, 'we see a young mind coming to grips with his world through an increasing mastery of language . . . Stephen begins by receiving the language of his world – nursery rhymes, Latin tags, political arguments . . . hell-fire sermons, literary models. He ends by supplanting these forms of language with his own, so that the subject of the book becomes, in a formal sense, its author' (p. 182). The novel as a whole traces the shift from Stephen as passive receiver of language to the 'author' of the diary that closes the novel; however, this shift is signalled even on the first page, as Stephen first passively hears the story of 'baby tuckoo', then realises that 'He was baby tuckoo' (p. 3), becoming the subject and the centre of the story told to him. Likewise, the song initially sung to him by his father becomes 'his song' and is given in Stephen's voice, thereby marking the first attempts to appropriate the language of his father to make it his own. As Hugh Kenner remarks, the first two pages of the novel 'enact the entire action in microcosm' (p. 126), establishing many of *Portrait*'s dominant themes and images, not least of which is the concern with how Stephen's identity is fundamentally shaped *in* and *through* language.

As Stephen matures, his attempts to understand the meanings of words and the connections between words and things continue, the ideas with which he grapples – and the language used to express these ideas – becoming more abstract as the chapter and novel progress. Stephen's confusion about whether it is right to kiss his mother after being teased by older boys at Clongowes Wood sees him struggling not only to understand the right answer and most socially acceptable behaviour, but also leads him to wonder about the meaning of the word 'kiss' itself: 'What did that mean, to kiss? You put your face up like that to say good night and then his mother put her face down. That was to kiss. His mother put her lips on his cheek; her lips were soft and they wetted his cheek; and they made a tiny little noise: kiss. Why did people do that with their two faces?' (p. 9). Not only does Stephen try to decipher why a kiss is called a 'kiss' (is it because of the noise it makes?) but also the social meaning attached to certain behaviour (why

do people say good-night by placing their lips on each other's cheeks?).
Rather than simply making associations between sensory impressions,
Stephen now attempts to understand what words such as 'kiss', 'belt',
and 'suck' mean and *why* they mean what they do. By Chapter 5, the
question of whether it is right to kiss one's mother has evolved from a
linguistic and social issue to a theological concern that expresses
Stephen's ambivalence about the demands placed upon him by family
and nation.

If Chapter 1 centres on Stephen's efforts to situate himself in relation
to his surroundings and to others, in Chapter 2 Stephen begins both to
impose his own vision on to the world around him, in order to shape
his environment, and to intellectualise his experiences, appropriating
the language of texts such as *The Count of Monte Cristo* to structure his
own reactions to the world. These attempts to use literature to
understand the world become for Stephen a characteristic way of
approaching life, and by Chapter 5 many of his experiences are filtered
almost entirely through his reading. At the start of Chapter 5, Stephen
is confronted with the squalid physical realities of life in the Dedalus
home, and in response, he takes refuge in literature, seeing (or perhaps
not seeing) Dublin through the medium of literary texts: 'His morning
walk across the city had begun, and he foreknew that as he passed the
sloblands of Fairview he would think of the cloistral silver-veined prose
of Newman . . . that as he went by Baird's stonecutting works in Talbot
Place the spirit of Ibsen would blow through him like a keen wind, a
spirit of wayward boyish beauty' (pp. 135–6).

In the course of the novel, Stephen's efforts to steer a path between
everyday existence and a vision of life that is above worldly or material
concerns take a variety of forms, such as the strict religious observances
of Chapter 4, the poetic attempts of Chapters 2 and 5 and the rigid
aesthetic theories expressed in Chapter 5. These are, however, endeav-
ours that begin in earnest in Chapter 2, with his family's steady social
and economic decline. In response to the disconcerting changes in his
external environment, Stephen attempts both to introduce a semblance
of order into his own life and, by using money from a school prize, to
provide structure for the increasingly chaotic Dedalus household: 'He
had tried to build a breakwater of order and elegance against the sordid
tide of life without him and to dam up, by rules of conduct and active
interests and new filial relations, the powerful recurrence of the tides
within him. Useless. From without as from within the waters had
flowed over his barriers: their tides began once more to jostle fiercely
above the crumbled mole' (p. 74). Throughout *Portrait*, Stephen

vacillates between embracing the sensual and the material aspects of life and retreating from them, and the rhythm of the novel itself follows his alternating indulgence (Chapters 2 and 4) and denial (Chapter 3) of the 'tides within him', tides of dissatisfaction with the world around him and of adolescent sexual desire.

While such futile moves to impose order on to his life can be seen as very tangible reactions to his family's humiliating change of fortune and to his own seemingly uncontrollable sexual urges, they also, perhaps ironically, represent a flight from the reality of experience that Stephen claims he wishes to encounter. Significantly, Stephen's efforts to master the 'tides' both within and without him find expression in Chapter 2 in one of his first poetic attempts – one of only two actually seen in *Portrait* (both for the young woman E— C—). In both these poems, all 'reality' is written out of the finished products, which, while perhaps technically accomplished, are coldly formal in their denial of emotion and sexual desire. In composing the poem in Chapter 2, for example, 'all those elements which he deemed common and insignificant fell out of the scene. There remained no trace of the tram itself nor of the tram-men nor of the horses: nor did he and she appear vividly. The verses told only of the night and the balmy breeze and the maiden lustre of the moon' (p. 53). Similarly, the villanelle of Chapter 5 transforms E— C— from innocent young woman into the figure of the 'temptress' and the representative of her 'race'. Art, therefore, becomes for Stephen a way of rewriting his experiences and anaesthetising his encounters with women, who become, in both poems, the 'depersonalised' products of Stephen's creative processes (Henke, p. 62).

Religion represents another mode of retreat (this time a literal one) from the world of sensual experience. After his experiences with the Dublin prostitutes at the close of Chapter 2 and the start of Chapter 3, the sermons of Chapter 3 have a profound effect on Stephen, prompting in him intense feelings of sin and guilt and a desire for confession and redemption. His actual embrace of sexual desire with the prostitutes is thus followed by a counter-movement into the spiritual realm, although the vision of hell presented in Father Arnall's powerful sermon is decidedly one of the senses, where the torture meted out to sinners is described in gruesome detail. Stephen egocentrically reacts to the sermon by feeling an intense sense of his own fallen state: 'Every word of it was for him. Against his sin, foul and secret, the whole wrath of God was aimed' (p. 88). Much as he had responded to his desire for E— C— in Chapter 2 with a poem that transfigured actual experience into something purely aesthetic,

Stephen responds to these sermons and to his own guilt by conflating at various moments the figures of the Virgin Mary, E— C— and Dante Alighieri's spiritual guide Beatrice, in order to transform women from physical beings into angelic guides who can lead him towards spiritual renewal and intercede with God for his salvation.

While Chapter 3 closes with Stephen's sense of rebirth after confessing his sins, Chapter 4 opens with a dry relation of the formal religious observances around which he has structured his life in the wake of his confession – as is consistent with the structural pattern of the novel as a whole, Stephen's moment of spiritual elation is thus followed by a fall back into earthly realities. This rigorous schedule of devotion and prayer is predictably short-lived and ends with Stephen's realisation that his acts of piety are intellectual and superficial, without substance or feeling: 'To merge his life in the common tide of other lives was harder for him than any fasting or prayer and it was his constant failure to do this to his own satisfaction which caused in his soul at last a sensation of spiritual dryness together with a growth of doubts and scruples. His soul traversed a period of desolation in which the sacraments themselves seemed to have turned into dried-up sources' (p. 116). This 'spiritual dryness' comes to be representative of religion in general for Stephen, and Roman Catholicism in particular is seen as a life-denying force that instils in its adherents a fear and loathing of sensual experience. Stephen rejects the prospect of a religious vocation for this very reason – 'The chill and order of the life repelled him' (p. 123) – and in so doing acknowledges that 'His destiny was to be elusive of social or religious orders. The wisdom of the priest's appeal did not touch him to the quick. He was destined to learn his own wisdom apart from others or to learn the wisdom of others himself wandering among the snares of the world. The snares of the world were its ways of sin. He would fall' (p. 124). Chapter 4 closes with Stephen's experience of the 'call of life to his soul' (p. 130) that accompanies the revelation of his artistic vocation – a call to life that is the 'fall' into the ways of the world.

After this realisation of his artistic calling, Chapter 5 – the longest chapter in the novel – represents Stephen's struggle to articulate the role of the artist and the nature of art and to reject those duties (demanded by family, church and nation) that would prevent him from realising his vocation. In wishing to escape from the demands made upon him by these institutions, Stephen again takes on the mantle of Lucifer in his declaration of *non serviam* ('I will not serve', p. 184). Stephen's severing of familial and social ties is inextricably bound up with his theory of artistic creation and the role of the artist, which similarly emphasises the need for distance and detachment: 'The artist, like the God of creation, remains within or behind or beyond or above his handiwork, invisible, refined out of existence, indifferent, pairing his fingernails' (p. 166). In making such claims, Stephen takes on the role not only of Lucifer, but also of God the Father and (in relation to Cranly's John the Baptist) of Jesus. For Stephen, the artist is thus both the rebellious intellect refusing to serve any master (whether that be the Catholic Church or Ireland) and the betrayed victim sacrificed by those who place worldly interests above any higher concerns.

Stephen's aesthetic theories synthesise a number of thematic strands at work in *Portrait*: for example, his belief in the need for exile in order to realise his artistic vocation and his sense of loneliness and difference from others are brought together in a view of art and the artist that emphasises detachment and social isolation. His argument that the highest form of art is 'impersonal' and that the beautiful is that which produces 'stasis' – feelings neither of desire nor of loathing (pp. 158–9) – represents the aesthetic resolution of his repeated attempts to negotiate his own feelings of desire and loathing throughout the course of the novel, and also justifies his sterile artistic efforts. Stephen's movement towards realising his destiny as an artist – of which the formulation of these aesthetic theories is a part – is further signalled in the shift from the third- to the first-person narrative voice (in the form of Stephen's diary) in the closing pages of the novel. As Grant Redford notes, in the shift from the third- to the first-person voice, Stephen 'is beginning to cross over from the passive recipient to the active maker, the artificer' (p. 110). At the close of the text, with the invocation of his artificer namesake 'Daedalus', Stephen begins to be the author-creator of his own story, just as on the first page of the novel Stephen became the subject of his father's story and then the 'author' of 'his' song. Where the first page had begun with the language of his father, the final page closes with Stephen's own writing and the choice of a new, mythical father to guide him through life.

Although *Portrait* traces the trajectory of Stephen's growth into a fledging young artist, what is perhaps most important in the novel is not the linear progression of narrative, but the formation of Stephen's consciousness. Joyce is therefore interested in selecting only those experiences most crucial to Stephen's development, and for this reason the novel has an episodic and seemingly disjointed narrative – jumping, in the first chapter, for example, from his infancy to Stephen's experiences at Clongowes to the Christmas dinner, with little transitional matter. The novel is held together instead by the recurrence of certain symbols and leitmotifs, the use of epiphanies (to be discussed more fully below) and the structural and thematic pattern of flight and fall. The first chapter establishes many of the recurring patterns of images that are at work in the text: the senses of cold, wet, damp, slime and water (Eileen's hands are cool and white; Stephen is made ill by being pushed into the cold slimy water of the ditch). These sensations are closely linked in Stephen's mind: 'He wondered whether the scullion's apron was damp too or whether all white things were cold and damp' (p. 7). Conversely, heat, warmth and colour are comforting sensations for Stephen, associated as they are with his mother: 'She had her feet on the fender and her jewelly slippers were so hot and they had such a lovely warm smell!' (p. 6). The 'jewelly' green and maroon velvet of Dante's brushes, however, also represents the heated world of Irish politics; the anger and dissent that ruin Christmas dinner oppose the comfort and safety of mother and home, despite both being represented by colour and warmth, a point that underlines William York Tindall's contention that symbols and images in *Portrait* 'are not signs with one fixed meaning' (p. 90).

As the novel progresses, there is an accretion of meanings to symbols, and the pattern of imagery – and the meanings attached to various images – becomes more complex and elaborate. While water imagery often carries with it negative associations for Stephen, Chapter 1 closes with an image of water that is emblematic both of Stephen's own development and of the progressively more complicated relation-ship between meanings and symbols in the text itself: 'pick, pack, pock, puck: like drops of water in a fountain falling softly in the brimming bowl' (p. 44).[3] The impossibility of differentiating the individual drops of water once they have fallen into the 'brimming bowl' thus mirrors the difficulty in ascribing one single meaning to any one symbol, or of disentangling one set of meanings from any other. In Chapter 5, the image of the 'brimming bowl' is given explicit articulation as a symbol of the soul in Stephen's flippant answer to the Dean's question 'You know Epictetus?': 'An old gentleman, said Stephen coarsely, who said that the soul is very like a bucketful of water' (p. 144). Stephen's 'conscience' develops out of the individual 'drops' of experience – the individual incidents in the text – that have meaning in and of themselves but take on further meaning once seen as part of the whole.

3 This phrase, with a slight variation, also appears on p. 30.

Likewise, the images of birds also carry with them a plurality of meanings in *Portrait*'s complex pattern of symbols. Established in the first pages of the first chapter, with the rhyme about the 'eagles' who will 'pull out his eyes' if he does not 'apologise' (p. 4), the association between the bird-like and the command to confess or apologise is echoed later in Chapter 2 with Stephen's memory of Heron and the other boys who punish Stephen's supposed heresy with the repeated commands to 'Admit', a memory itself prompted by Heron's admonishing of Stephen to 'admit' about E— C— (pp. 58–9, 62). If these avian voices demanding obedience and submission to family, nation and church are representative of all Stephen wishes to escape, birds are also central to his realisation of his destiny and vocation: the epiphany at the close of Chapter 4 involves the bird-like girl who is the symbol of his own soul's 'flight', and Stephen's own name, Dedalus, refers to the figure from Greek mythology who fashioned wings to enable him to escape imprisonment and exile. The possibility that images and symbols in *Portrait* can have a multiplicity of meanings is hinted at by Stephen himself in Chapter 5, when he questions whether the birds he observes are 'symbol[s] of departure or of loneliness?' (p. 174).

3   *Myth, epiphany, irony*

While 'flight' is an important recurring image in *Portrait*, a pattern of flight and fall also acts as a structural element in the text, one that is immediately established in the opening epigraph from Ovid alluding to the Greek myth of Icarus and Daedalus: 'Et ignotas dimittit in artes' – 'And he applies his mind to obscure arts.' The 'he' refers to Daedalus, whose name in Greek means 'cunning artificer' and who is the 'Old father, old artificer' Stephen invokes in his last journal entry of the novel. Providing an underlying structure for the novel, this myth details the story of Daedalus and his son Icarus, placed on an island as punishment for constructing the labyrinth that housed the Minotaur. Daedalus fashioned wings to enable himself and his son to fly in order to escape from the island; Icarus, however, despite his father's warning, flew too close to the sun, melting the wax on his wings and plunging him to his death in the sea. For Stephen, his name is a 'prophecy' and represents the powerful image of the artist soaring above the earth.

The elements of the myth relating both to Daedalus the father's triumphal flight and the fall to earth of Icarus the son are translated into the narrative structure of the novel itself: Stephen's moments of triumph and spiritual elevation are consistently followed by episodes of deflation, where his pride is wounded by his fall back to earth. While in

Chapter 1 Stephen experiences a triumph in successfully complaining to the rector of Clongowes of the unfair punishment he receives at the hands of Father Dolan, in Chapter 2 it is revealed that this incident was treated as a joke by the rector and the priest. Similarly, Stephen's transformative experience with a prostitute at the close of Chapter 2 is closely followed in Chapter 3 by a reminder of the grosser realities of bodily existence, and another such moment occurs after the vision of the bird-like girl at the close of Chapter 4. In this pattern of flight and fall, Stephen is both Daedalus and Icarus (just as he identifies himself, as an artist, with both God the Father and Jesus), as well as the rebellious angel Lucifer who, like Icarus, falls from Heaven. One of Stephen's main struggles in the novel is to become 'the father', soaring out of the shadow of his own father and of his 'Fatherland' to create his own identity and an identity for his 'race'.

These moments of flight can be most usefully understood in terms of the concept of the epiphany. While Stephen discusses his theory of the epiphany in *Stephen Hero*, any explicit reference to the term was omitted in the revision of *Hero* into *Portrait*; however, the epiphanic episodes themselves remain in *Portrait* as defining moments in Stephen's spiritual and artistic development. In *Stephen Hero*, Stephen explains the epiphany as 'a sudden spiritual manifestation, whether in the vulgarity of speech or of gesture or in a memorable phase of the mind itself' (p. 216). For Stephen and Joyce, the epiphany is the sudden 'revelation of the whatness of a thing' (Richard Ellmann, p. 83), 'an image, sensually apprehended and emotionally vibrant, which communicates instantaneously the meaning of experience' (Van Ghent, p. 65). As Dorothy Van Ghent observes, while 'minor epiphanies mark all the stages of Stephen's understanding' (such as when he sees the word 'foetus' carved into a school desk and understands it as an external manifestation and expression of his own feelings), 'major epiphanies, occurring at the end of each chapter, mark the chief revelations of the nature of his environment and of his destiny in it' (p. 65).

These moments of clarity and enlightenment can be prompted by the everyday or the mundane and represent a '*fusion* of objective fact and subjective consciousness' (Watson, p. 197) in which both the artistic consciousness and the perceived object are transfigured into something new. Perhaps the best example of such a moment is at the close of Chapter 4, where Stephen's witnessing of the girl wading in the sea gives rise to a moment of spiritual clarity that fills him with a sense of his artistic vocation. Just before seeing the girl, the call of his name prompts him to recognise the 'prophecy' his name holds for him and conjures up a vision of the mythic figure of Daedalus and of his own destiny:

> Now, at the name of the fabulous artificer, he seemed to hear the noise of dim waves and to see a winged form flying above the waves and slowly climbing the air. What did it mean? Was it a quaint device opening a page of some medieval book of prophecies and symbols, a hawk-like man flying sunward above the sea, a prophecy of the end he had been born to serve and had been following through the mists of childhood and boyhood, a symbol of the artist forging anew in his workshop out of the sluggish matter of the earth a new soaring impalpable imperishable being?   [p. 130]

Stephen then encounters the bird-like girl wading in the sea, and in this moment of epiphany – in the fusion of an 'object' in the external world with Stephen's subjective vision of that object – the girl becomes the outward manifestation of the call to life Stephen has just experienced:

> Her image had passed into his soul for ever and no word had broken the holy silence of his ecstasy. Her eyes had called him and his soul had leaped to the call. To live, to err, to fall, to triumph, to recreate life out of life! A wild angel had appeared to him, the angel of mortal youth and beauty, an envoy from the fair courts of life, to throw open before him in an instant of ecstasy the gates of all the ways of error and glory.   [p. 132]

This revelation is the certainty of his own destiny and artistic calling, and Stephen experiences a sense of power and freedom, the winged form of Daedalus becoming an image for Stephen of 'his soul . . . in flight' (p. 130).

However, even in this epiphanic moment on the beach – the climactic moment of the novel – the inflated language in which the revelation is expressed, and the gap between the external reality and Stephen's response to it, opens up the possibility that Stephen is being treated with a degree of irony in *Portrait*. As the feminist critic Suzette Henke notes in commenting on the above scene, rather than responding to the young woman with sexual desire, Stephen immediately retreats into a visionary mode that sublimates any physical longing into a quasi-religious revelation of his destiny: 'The young man catches sight of an attractive nubile form and immediately detaches himself from emotional participation in the scene. His reaction is self-consciously static, theoretically purged of desire and loathing. Once again, his leap into aesthetic fantasy quenches an initial impulse to approach the girl, to reach out and touch her, or to risk the possibility of social intercourse' (Henke, p. 74). While Stephen's reaction to the girl may represent an ironic retreat from sexual desire and the 'call to life' her very presence seems to inspire, this pivotal moment on the beach cannot be dismissed as entirely ironic as it does represent the culmination of the journey towards understanding his destiny that has occupied Stephen throughout the novel.

For many critics, the interpretative crux of the novel rests on this question of irony and the point of view adopted towards Stephen in the text. Hugh Kenner argues that the narrative tone in *Portrait* is heavily ironic, seeing the presentation of Stephen in the novel as almost entirely unsympathetic: 'The dark intensity of the first four chapters is moving enough, but our impulse on being confronted with the final edition of Stephen Dedalus is to laugh' (p. 149). For Kenner, then, the ironic rendering of Stephen as a humourless egocentric makes it impossible to read *Portrait* as anything but highly critical of the young man's pretensions to an artistic calling. Wayne Booth, on the other hand, argues that it is almost impossible to decide on the perspective we should adopt towards Stephen and sees this as a symptom of Joyce's own ambivalent attitude towards his protagonist, who is both a version of the author himself and a fictional character. For critics such as Patrick Parrinder, however, the ironic perspective on Stephen is the result of 'Joyce's balancing of the different points of view it is possible to adopt towards the young Stephen' (p. 72), that is, the very fact that we are asked both to see Stephen sympathetically and to judge him critically. This 'balance' largely arises from the use of free indirect speech – which enables an identification with Stephen's perspective – in conjunction with the third-person voice, which prevents a complete acceptance of this perspective and allows an ironic distance to emerge in the treatment of Stephen.

The question of how to judge the villanelle Stephen composes in Chapter 5 illustrates many of the problems involved in negotiating this 'double vision of Stephen as hero or as poseur' (Deane, p. 186). For Kenner, this villanelle marks out Stephen as an 'aesthete' who 'writes Frenchified verses in bed' (p. 124), someone who, despite having highly developed theories of beauty and art, produces few convincing examples of his own artistic abilities. In contrast, Wayne Booth points out that, without the sort of explicit guidance from the narrator that is available in *Stephen Hero* – in which Stephen is described as writing 'some pages of sorry verse' (p. 72) – it is truly impossible to decide whether to see the villanelle as a promising, if immature, artistic effort or as evidence of

Stephen's pretentious dilettantism. Crucially, in the final pages of the novel, Stephen does reveal an instance of self-irony: 'Talked rapidly of myself and my plans. In the midst of it unluckily I made a sudden gesture of a revolutionary nature. I must have looked like a fellow throwing a handful of peas into the air' (p. 195). In providing a glimpse of Stephen's potential to become self-aware and self-critical, Joyce holds out the possibility that Stephen may in future escape from the trap of his own egotism, and in so doing make the connections with others that are necessary if one is to become a fully developed artist.

4 *Historical, social, cultural context*

While it might be tempting to read Stephen's repudiation of the Catholic Church and Ireland as mirroring Joyce's own rejection of any real involvement with Irish political and religious issues, *A Portrait of the Artist* is a novel that is profoundly engaged with the cultural, social, and political events of late-nineteenth- and early-twentieth-century Ireland. Declan Kiberd argues that 'In Joyce's hands, the *Bildungsroman* was an instrument with which to investigate the Irish experience, and the ensuing self-understanding was a discovery of the real Ireland of the present' (p. 336). Thus, the development of Stephen's personal identity is inextricably linked to the desire to 'forge' in his own soul 'the uncreated conscience of [his] race' (p. 196), making the growth of the individual conscience – and consciousness – inseparable from that of the Irish nation. In recasting questions of Ireland's search for national identity in terms of Stephen's own painful road to maturity, Joyce rejects definitions of Irishness that are formulated by looking to the past, and instead embraces an Irish identity based on the realities of contemporary Ireland and its relation to Britain and the rest of Europe.

The Ireland Joyce left in 1904 was a country that had experienced, since the ninth century, successive waves of invasion – by the Danes, Normans and English. The Norman conquest that took place under Henry II (reigned 1154–89) was at times fitful and uneven, with many of the Norman settlers intermarrying with the native Irish population and assimilating into this native culture by adopting the Gaelic language and customs. Those who did assimilate into Gaelic culture came to be known as the 'Old English', to distinguish them from the new English arrivals who settled in Ireland during the Tudor period. While the Normans, and later the Tudors, attempted to use a mixture of diplomacy and military force to quell discontent amongst the native Irish population, it was under the reign of Elizabeth I that a policy of military subjugation of Ireland was fully enforced, and a new effort was made to establish plantation settlements of 'loyal' English subjects. This policy was pursued because both the Irish and many Old English settlers remained loyal to the Catholic Church after the Reformation and were therefore seen as potentially disloyal to the English crown – for much of post-Reformation Irish history, Roman Catholicism would be a rallying point for those resistant to English colonialism in Ireland.

It was with the defeat of Catholic James II by William of Orange in 1690 at the Battle of the Boyne that English power in Ireland was fully cemented. From this period, through military force and the enactment of penal laws against Catholics, the hegemony of 'new' Protestant English settlers (the Anglo-Irish, or, as they came to be called in the eighteenth century, the Protestant Ascendancy) was established. Catholics were prevented from owning large tracts of land, were denied access to education and were disenfranchised and prevented from participating in government unless they took an oath of loyalty to the British crown. The Catholic clergy were banned, and it became illegal to celebrate mass. Largely as a result of such measures, the Protestant Ascendancy controlled most of the land and wealth of Ireland up until the second half of the nineteenth century, despite the fact that they were a minority in Ireland.

Some of these penal laws began to be relaxed in the latter half of the eighteenth century, and Ireland also achieved some measure of parliamentary independence from Britain in 1782 with the establishment of the so-called 'patriot parliament' of Henry Grattan and Henry Flood m ntioned by Simon Dedalus in Chapter 2, when he and Stephen are standing in the former Irish House of Commons. However, the period that many identify as the height of Protestant power in Ireland came to an end in the aftermath of the United Irishmen uprising in 1798. Led by the Ulster Protestant Wolfe Tone, the United Irishmen sought a relaxation of the penal laws against Catholics and Irish independence from Britain. The rebellion was unsuccessful and led to the passing of the Act of Union of 1800, in which the Irish parliament was dissolved and the 'United Kingdom of Britain and Ireland' was formed. After 1800, the focus of much political activity was directed towards achieving Catholic Emancipation; under the leadership of Daniel O'Connell (the 'Liberator'), emancipation was achieved in 1829, and the focus of political activity then shifted to agitation for the repeal of the union. However, political agitation for independence was temporarily put on hold with the splintering of the Repeal Movement in the 1840s and, more importantly, the Great Famine of 1845 to 1849. With the dramatic decline in population that resulted from mass emigration and deaths through starvation and disease, the famine irrevocably altered Irish society. After the famine, the focus of Irish politics shifted to land reform and the issue of Home Rule for Ireland. While agitation for land reform was carried out by the Land League (established by Michael Davitt in 1879), the Irish Parliamentary Party, led by Charles Stuart Parnell, used its considerable influence at Westminster to negotiate for Irish Home Rule.

Charles Stuart Parnell was for Joyce – as well as for Stephen Dedalus – the single most important political figure in Ireland in the late nineteenth century. The son of Protestant landed gentry, Parnell became the most popular leader of his time in the struggle for Irish independence from Britain. Parnell, in alliance with William Gladstone's Liberal Party, was on the verge of achieving Irish Home Rule when he was implicated in a scandal involving his long-time mistress Katherine O'Shea. Parnell was named as co-respondent in the O'Shea divorce case and was consequently seen by the British Liberal Party as a political liability. He initially retained the support of his party, but was later asked to step down as leader of the Irish Parliamentary Party and was violently condemned by a number of prominent Irish Catholic clergymen. The parliamentary campaign for Home Rule collapsed, and Parnell died a broken man shortly after in 1891. For Joyce (and, again, for Stephen), this 'betrayal' of Parnell by the Irish people was but one more example of the continued pattern of Ireland's betrayal of its own leaders. As Stephen says to his nationalist friend Davin in Chapter 5, Ireland is 'the old sow that eats her farrow' (p. 157).

The divisiveness of the Parnell case is literally brought home to Stephen in the vividly realised scene in which Christmas dinner is ruined by the argument between Dante Riordan, Simon Dedalus and Mr Casey. In many ways the divisions in the Dedalus house at Christmas represent in microcosm the split the Parnell incident brought about in Irish society as a whole – a split between those who, like Dante, felt that Irish identity should be intertwined with Catholicism and that the Irish people should follow the lead of the Catholic clergy in denouncing Parnell, and those who, like Simon Dedalus and Mr Casey, believed that the Catholic Church had no place in Irish political life. The all-pervasiveness of this issue is signalled in Stephen's strange dream of Parnell and Dante while recovering from illness in the school infirmary. This dream, in which Stephen confuses a vision of his own funeral with that of Parnell, foreshadows the associations made later between the betrayed outcast Parnell and the artist Stephen.

With the collapse of the parliamentary campaign for Home Rule and the fall of Parnell, many turned to a version of nationalism centred on culture rather than on overtly political action. In the 1890s, two movements emerged – the Irish Literary Revival and the Gaelic Revival – that struggled not only to define the parameters of a truly 'national' Irish literature, but also what it meant to be Irish at a time in which Irishness had come to be seen by many as synonymous with Catholicism. By the 1880s, the Anglo-Irish Protestant class had largely ceased to dominate Irish political life and was faced with an increasingly militant Irish Catholic nationalism that turned itself against both the British government and those it believed were the representatives of British power in Ireland, the Protestant Ascendancy. Some critics have seen the Literary Revival – a movement predominately led by Protestant writers such as W. B. Yeats and Lady Gregory – as an attempt on the part of the Anglo-Irish to form a legitimate link to the Irish past and thus a place for itself in modern Ireland. Those involved with the Literary Revival wished to form a national Irish literature in the English language, and often in their writings harked back to an ancient, pagan, Celtic pre-colonial past in which Ireland had not yet been marked by the class and sectarian divisions that characterised it in the late nineteenth century.

There were, however, many who felt that Irish identity (and the literature that expressed that identity) should be defined in different terms: 'The doctrines of the Irish Ireland movement . . . insisted that Ireland's authentic cultural nationalist identity was unquestionably as a Gaelic and catholic nation, in which the Anglo-Irish English-speaking protestant could have no part' (Brown, p. 517). In the sphere of cultural nationalism, this attitude manifested itself in the formation of the Gaelic League in 1893, which sought to promote the use of the Irish language, and in the arguments of many who believed that a truly national Irish literature could not be written in the English language. The differing agendas of these two versions of cultural nationalism often clashed, as was the case with the performance of Yeats's play *The Countess Cathleen* in 1899. Many Catholic nationalists objected to the play's portrayal of an aristocratic Irish woman who sells her soul in order to save her starving tenants – for Stephen, who recalls his attendance at this performance in Chapter 5 of *Portrait*, the furore over the play represents Irish nationalism at its most narrow-minded.

Stephen's exchanges with the nationalist Davin in Chapter 5 highlight the language question that had emerged in the 1890s. While Stephen cannot fully accept the view that Gaelic should be a central aspect of Irish life and identity to the exclusion of English, he is also aware that

English is not the 'mother tongue' in Ireland. His discomfort with the English language is expressed in his encounter with the dean of studies of the university, where a moment of misunderstanding reveals some of the potential difficulties in communication between English and Irish subjects:

> The language in which we are speaking is his before it is mine. How different are the words *home, Christ, ale, master*, on his lips and on mine! I cannot speak or write these words without unrest of spirit. His language, so familiar and so foreign, will always be for me an acquired speech. I have not made or accepted its words. My voice holds them at bay. My soul frets in the shadow of his language.   [p. 146]

Stephen's impulse to create something new (the *'uncreated* conscience' of his race) partly emerges from the fact that neither identity, neither language – English nor Irish – fully expresses or explains his own experience of himself and of Ireland.

Despite his desire to speak to and for Ireland, Stephen remains ambivalent about the demands made upon him by family, church, and nation, especially where these demands might impinge on his own path to self-realisation:

> While his mind had been pursuing its intangible phantoms and turning in irresolution from such pursuits he had heard about him the constant voices of his father and of his masters, urging him to be a gentleman above all things and urging him to be a good catholic above all things. These voices had now come to be hollow-sounding in his ears. When the gymnasium had been opened he had heard another voice urging him to be strong and manly and healthy and when the movement towards national revival had begun to be felt in the college yet another voice had bidden him to be true to his country and help to raise up her language and tradition. In the profane world, as he foresaw, a worldly voice would bid him raise up his father's fallen state by his labours and, meanwhile, the voice of his school comrades urged him to be a decent fellow, to shield others from blame or to beg them off and to do his best to get free days for the school. And it was the din of all these hollow-sounding voices that made him halt irresolutely in the pursuit of phantoms. He gave them ear only for a time but he was happy only when he was far from them, beyond their call, alone or in the company of phantasmal comrades.   [p. 63]

These insistent 'voices' of the church, nation, and family become in Chapter 5 the 'nets' that Stephen must evade in order to realise his artistic vocation: 'When the soul of a man is born in this country there are nets flung at it to hold it back from flight. You talk to me of nationality, language, religion. I shall try to fly by those nets' (p. 157). For Stephen, the only way to escape such restrictive nets is through an uncompromising artistic and personal freedom, again expressed in terms that evoke the rebellious Satan's declaration of *non serviam*: 'I will tell you what I will do and what I will not do. I will not serve that in which I no longer believe, whether it call itself my home, my fatherland, or my church: and I will try to express myself in some mode of life or art as freely as I can and as wholly as I can, using for my defence the only arms I allow myself to use – silence, exile, and cunning' (p. 191). Instead of joining Davin and the other young men in the nationalist movement, Stephen chooses exile as the only means of eluding these constricting ready-made sources of identity, even if this exile means a life of loneliness and solitude.

In his essay 'The Day of the Rabblement' (October 1901), Joyce responds to the establishment of the Irish National Theatre by arguing for a more European-oriented theatre, rather than one that conformed to what he believed were narrow nationalist demands. The opening sentence of Joyce's essay, written when he was only nineteen, is illuminating when read alongside Stephen's declaration of artistic independence in *Portrait*: 'No man, said the Nolan, can be a lover of the true or the good unless he abhors the multitude; and the artist, though he may employ the crowd, is careful to isolate himself' (Joyce, *Critical Writings*, p. 69). The figure of the proud, betrayed heroic figure persecuted by or rejecting the demands of society surfaces continuously throughout *Portrait*: in the references to Edmund Dantes from *The Count of Monte Cristo*, who Stephen imagines leaves Mercedes with a 'proud gesture of refusal' (p. 47); in Stephen's praise of the quintessential artist-as-isolated-hero Byron; and, perhaps most importantly, in Parnell. Whether seeing himself as the betrayed Jesus or as the Lucifer who declares 'non serviam', Stephen's view of the role of the artist is of an individual who is 'careful to isolate himself' from others and from social, religious and political institutions. Stephen (and Joyce) see artistic independence as the only alternative to any art beholden to Irish nationalism.

However, the question of irony also affects how we understand Stephen's attempts to distance himself from the demands of family, church and nation in his bid for complete artistic independence. For all his assertions of the need for such independence, Stephen is ultimately shown to be a product of the very institutions he claims to despise. His vocation is expressed in 'quasi-religious language' (Jeffares, p. 222) in which Stephen presents the artist as 'a priest of the eternal imagination, transmuting the daily bread of experience into the radiant body of everliving life' (pp. 170–1). As his friend Cranly observes, Stephen's mind is 'supersaturated with the religion' in which he claims not to believe (p. 185). Stephen's artistic pretensions are thus shown to be the result of a Romantic myth of the artist as lonely hero, which makes Stephen believe that he can be independent of the society that has in fact produced him: 'Through him [Stephen], Joyce is able both to affirm the romantic myth of artistic genius, and to partially dissociate himself from the arrogance and self-conceit which follows from that myth' (Parrinder, p. 72). The ambivalence revealed in this attitude – which both affirms the need for independence from nation and church and ultimately shows this independence as an unattainable myth – points not only to the highly complex (and sometimes contradictory) nature of the pressures placed upon the young artist in an Ireland struggling to define its own identity, but also underscores the fact that Stephen's act of rejection and denial is in and of itself no guarantee of the freedom he so desires.

5 Critical perspectives

Critical responses to *Portrait* at the time of its appearance in 1917 were mixed and often focused on the dual aspects of the novel's realistically detailed rendering of Stephen's physical experiences and surroundings and the non-realist mode of the narrative itself. A number of critics agreed that the novel was technically brilliant, while objecting to its depictions of some of the grosser aspects of Stephen Dedalus's experiences and environment. An anonymous reviewer in the Irish *Freeman's Journal* (April 1917) complains that *Portrait* focuses too much on the 'ugliness' that surrounds Stephen and that 'Mr Joyce plunges and drags his readers after him into the slime of foul sewers.'[4] The reviewer in the *Irish Book Lover* praises Joyce only to bemoan his wasted talent and to say of *Portrait* that 'no clean minded person could possibly allow it to remain within reach of his wife, his sons and daughters'.[5]

In his review of *Portrait* for *The Nation*, H. G. Wells agrees with other reviewers that Joyce seems to have a 'cloacal obsession', but acknowledges that 'The value of Mr Joyce's book has little to do with

4 unsigned review, *Freeman's Journal*, 7 April 1917; in Deming, p. 98
5 unsigned review, *Irish Book Lover*, April–May 1917, Vol. 8; in Deming, p. 102

its incidental insanitary condition', going on to offer a reading of the
novel that recognises some of the novel's more important formal
innovations:

> Like some of the best novels in the world it is a story of an
> education . . . . It is a mosaic of jagged fragments that does
> altogether render with extreme completeness the growth of a
> rather secretive, imaginative boy in Dublin. The technique is
> startling, but on the whole it succeeds. Like so many Irish writers
> from Sterne to Shaw Mr Joyce is a bold experimentalist with
> paragraph and punctuation. He breaks away from scene to scene
> without a hint of the change of time and place; at the end he passes
> suddenly from the third person to the first . . . [6]

Similarly, a number of reviewers comment that *Portrait* defies many
formal conventions of the novel: 'A reader of novels will see at once
that he has never even thought of "plot" in the ordinary sense.' This
reviewer acknowledges that what is most important in *Portrait* is not a
conventional plot but the depiction of significant incidents in Stephen's
life and his reactions to them: 'What gives its intensity to the portrait is
the art Mr Joyce has mastered of communicating the incidents of
Stephen's career through the emotions they excited in him. We do not
perceive Stephen's father and mother by description. We get them by
the ebb and flood of Stephen's feeling . . .'[7]

Like Wells's commentary on *Portrait*, subsequent critical responses
have focused intensely on questions of structure and language in the
novel. This is particularly true of those critics working within 'New
Criticism', a strand of American literary criticism that emerged in the
1950s. 'New critics' such as William York Tindall concentrate on
revealing the internal unity of *Portrait* by highlighting patterns of
symbolism and imagery. Such criticism also focuses on the question of
irony and narrative point of view in *Portrait*. Perhaps one of the most
influential readings of *Portrait* to have emerged in the mid-twentieth
century, however, came not in the form of a work of literary criticism
but in Richard Ellmann's definitive biography of Joyce. In tracing the
details of Joyce's childhood and young adulthood, Ellmann makes a
convincing case for reading *Portrait* as a thinly-veiled autobiography of
Joyce's early life. Ellmann's work has served as a critical touchstone
since its first appearance in 1959, challenging critics and readers alike

6 H. G. Wells, *The Nation*, 1917; in Deming, pp. 86 and 87
7 Francis Hackett, *New Republic*, 1917; in Deming, p. 95

to decide just how much consideration should actually be given to Joyce's use of autobiographical details in *Portrait*.

More recently, *A Portrait of the Artist* has been analysed from a variety of theoretical positions, such as those represented by post-structuralist, feminist and postcolonial criticism. The poststructuralist theorists whose work appears in the important collection of essays entitled *Poststructuralist Joyce* resist attempts to reduce texts to one singular, unified meaning, but instead seek to open up a plurality of possible meanings that often work in opposition to one another. Thus, Stephen Heath's reading of *Portrait* highlights the ways in which the irony directed at Stephen in the text produces an instability that makes any single interpretation of Stephen (and Joyce's attitude towards Stephen) impossible: 'the writing of *A Portrait* proceeds not from the position of Stephen but, as it were, in the "between" of that position and its opposite. The strategies of hesitation place Joyce's writing not in some fixed outside (the illusion of "Reality") but within a continual process of fragmentation, destruction, hesitation' (Heath, p. 36). Poststructuralist readings not only highlight contradictions or discontinuities in the text, but also focus on the construction of Stephen's identity through language and on the contentious question of how individual identity is constituted. In her poststructuralist account of *Portrait*, Maud Ellmann argues that, rather than showing Stephen's development over the course of the narrative, the novel in fact demonstrates the impossibility of Stephen forming a coherent or stable sense of self through the unreliable medium of language.

Perhaps in reaction to poststructuralist readings that tend to con-centrate largely on the text itself, much recent criticism of *Portrait* has sought to place it firmly within its contemporary social, political and cultural contexts. Studies such as Vincent Cheng's *Joyce, Race, and Empire* and Emer Nolan's *Joyce and Nationalism* examine Joyce's work in terms of the history of Ireland's relationship to England, often using the framework of colonial/postcolonial theory. Vincent Cheng, for example, reads Stephen Dedalus's rejection of the 'narrow-minded provincialism' of certain aspects of the Irish nationalist movement as a response to 'the logic of a Celtic xenophobia constructed as a mirror image of English racial/national chauvinism' (p. 65). In other words, Stephen (and Joyce) object to the fact that some Irish nationalists 'demean anything English and glorify everything Irish' in what is a mere reversal of the strategies of English colonisers who consistently asserted a 'racial/national' superiority over the Irish. In order to escape the trap of assertion and counter-assertion of one nation's superiority over another, Stephen wishes to 'forge . . . the uncreated conscience of his race' by 'seeking a spiritual liberation for Ireland that looks to a wider internationalist perspective' (Cheng, p. 66). Joyce, in consistently looking to Europe for artistic influences, seeks to avoid the habit of many Irish nationalists in defining Irishness solely in terms of its relationship to Englishness.

Postcolonial studies of Joyce's work often overlap with criticism that focuses on the representation of gender in texts such as *Portrait*. C. L. Innes's *Woman and Nation* examines the representation of women in *Portrait* in a context in which 'Throughout the history of its colonisation, Ireland has been represented by British imperialists as well as Irish nationalists and artists as female' (p. 2). In Stephen's view that the 'soul' of the Irish nation is represented by the 'bat-like' (pp. 141 and 170) souls of women such as E— C— and the peasant woman who tempts Davin, Innes sees Stephen as part of the long tradition that has made women 'silent images and symbols' of Ireland itself (p. 64). For Innes, however, the ironic view taken of Stephen at points in the narrative indicates that Joyce is actually critical of this view of women as mere symbols of the Irish nation – a view connected to his generally sceptical attitude to certain aspects of Irish nationalism.

Feminist readings that are not immediately influenced by postcolonial theory have also drawn attention to Stephen's view of women as symbols of Ireland, and in addition have highlighted the silencing of women that occurs in *Portrait*. Suzette Henke, in *James Joyce and the Politics of Desire*, argues that, for Stephen, the women he encounters in the text have no life of their own but exist only as he perceives them and creates (or recreates) them. As Henke notes, 'Female characters are present everywhere and nowhere in *A Portrait of the Artist as a Young Man*. They pervade the novel, yet remain elusive . . . Like everything else in *A Portrait*, women are portrayed almost exclusively from Stephen's point of view' (p. 50). Feminist critics have generally reacted unfavourably to the representation of women in *Portrait*, not only because they have no voice of their own, but also because they appear to be categorised according to stereotypes that construct women as either virgins or whores. While this is undeniably true of Stephen's view of women in the novel, Henke – like Innes – sees the degree of irony directed at Stephen as crucial to an understanding that Stephen's views of women are not necessarily fully endorsed in the text.

However, as many feminist critics have noted, it is not merely that the potentially ironic view of Stephen problematises his view of women, but that his view of women actually generates much of the ironic perspective on Stephen in *Portrait*. Stephen believes he will be transfigured by a sexual experience he imagines as a 'holy encounter . . . at which weakness and timidity and inexperience were to fall from him' (p. 75), and, indeed, his experience with the prostitute that closes Chapter 2 is presented as a moment in which he is seemingly transformed: 'In her arms he felt that he had suddenly become strong and fearless and sure of himself' (p. 77). However, Stephen's passivity in the encounter – his 'surrendering himself' to the prostitute – subverts his fantasy of a 'holy encounter' that will enable him to become 'strong and fearless' rather than boyish and timid.

As Innes, Henke and many other critics have noted, before judging Stephen's artistic pretensions too harshly, we should take account of the title of the novel: <u>A</u> *Portrait of the Artist as a <u>Young Man</u>*. The indefinite article (<u>a</u> portrait) asks us to consider the possibility that the view of Stephen presented in the text is only one of many possible portraits that might have been given of the development of an individual 'conscience' from infancy to fledgling steps towards independence; that this is a portrait of a <u>young man</u> also warns us that Stephen's ideas of life and art remain largely untested and untempered by experience by the time he has chosen to try his wings and 'fly' from home and Ireland. In light of this, it is significant that the ending of *Portrait* is open – considered in terms of the conventions of the realist novel, it seems not much of an ending at all. In fact, readers must wait until *Ulysses* to discover that Stephen has returned to Ireland, frustrated in his attempts to escape the 'nets' of home, church and nation. However, the open ending of *A Portrait of the Artist as a Young Man* seems the most appropriate conclusion to a work whose primary concern is to trace the development of the mind and conscience of the artist. Ultimately, the end result of Stephen's development is less important than the documenting of the arduous journey to the point of being ready to encounter life.

DR JACQUELINE BELANGER

WORKS CITED

Booth, Wayne, 'The Problem of Distance in *A Portrait of the Artist*', in
Morris Beja (ed.), *James Joyce: 'Dubliners' and 'A Portrait of the Artist
as a Young Man'*, Casebook Series, Macmillan, London 1973

Brown, Terence, 'Cultural Nationalism 1880–1930', in Seamus Deane
(ed.), *Field Day Anthology of Irish Literature*, Vol. 2, Field Day
Publications, Derry 1991

Cheng, Vincent, *Joyce, Race, and Empire*, Cambridge University Press,
Cambridge 1995

Deane, Seamus, *A Short History of Irish Literature*, University of Notre
Dame Press, Indiana 1986

Deming, Robert H. (ed.), *James Joyce: The Critical Heritage, Vol. 1,
1902–1927*, Routledge and Kegan Paul, London 1970

Ellmann, Maud, 'Disremembering Dedalus: *A Portrait of the Artist as a
Young Man*', in Robert Young (ed.), *Untying the Text: A Post-
Structuralist Reader*, Routledge and Kegan Paul, London 1981

Ellmann, Richard, *James Joyce*, Oxford University Press, Oxford 1982
(revised edition)

Heath, Stephen, 'Amibiviolences: Notes for Reading Joyce', in Heath
and Daniel Ferrer (eds), *Poststructuralist Joyce: Essays from the
French*, Cambridge University Press, Cambridge 1984

Henke, Suzette, *James Joyce and the Politics of Desire*, Routledge,
London 1990

Innes, C. L., *Woman and Nation in Irish Literature and Society, 1880–
1935*, Harvester, London 1993

Jeffares, A. Norman, *Anglo-Irish Literature*, Macmillan, London 1982

Joyce, James, *Stephen Hero*, Jonathan Cape, London 1975 (revised
edition)

Joyce, James, 'The Day of the Rabblement', in Ellsworth Mason and
Richard Ellmann (eds), *The Critical Writings of James Joyce*, Cornell
University Press, Ithaca, New York 1989

Kenner, Hugh, 'The *Portrait* in Perspective', in Morris Beja (ed.),
James Joyce: 'Dubliners' and 'A Portrait of the Artist of a Young Man',
Casebook Series, Macmillan, London 1973

Kiberd, Declan, *Inventing Ireland*, Jonathan Cape, London 1995

Nolan, Emer, *James Joyce and Nationalism*, Routledge, London 1995

Parrinder, Patrick, *James Joyce*, Cambridge University Press, Cambridge 1984

Redford, Grant, 'The Role of Structure in Joyce's *Portrait*', in Thomas Connolly (ed.), *Joyce's Portrait: Criticisms and Critiques*, Appleton-Century-Crofts, New York 1962

Tindall, William York, *A Reader's Guide to James Joyce*, Noonday Press, New York 1959

Van Ghent, Dorothy, 'On *A Portrait of the Artist as a Young Man*', in Thomas Connolly (ed.), *Joyce's Portrait: Criticisms and Critiques*, Appleton-Century-Crofts, New York 1962

Watson, G. J., *Irish Identity and the Literary Revival: Synge, Yeats, Joyce and O'Casey*, Croom Helm, London 1979

BIBLIOGRAPHY

General

Attridge, Derek (ed.), *The Cambridge Companion to James Joyce*, Cambridge University Press, Cambridge 1990

Beja, Morris (ed.), *James Joyce: 'Dubliners' and 'A Portrait of the Artist as a Young Man'*, Casebook Series, Macmillan, London 1973

Connolly, Thomas (ed.), *Joyce's Portrait: Criticisms and Critiques*, Appleton-Century-Crofts, New York 1962

Ellmann, Richard, *James Joyce*, Oxford University Press, Oxford 1959 (revised edition, 1982)

Parrinder, Patrick, *James Joyce*, Cambridge University Press, Cambridge 1984

Reynolds, Mary T. (ed.), *James Joyce: A Collection of Critical Essays*, Prentice Hall, New Jersey 1993

Seed, David, *James Joyce's 'A Portrait of the Artist as a Young Man'*, Harvester, London 1992

Tindall, William York, *A Reader's Guide to James Joyce*, Noonday Press, New York 1959

Political and Historical Contexts

Brown, Richard, *James Joyce and Sexuality*, Cambridge University Press, Cambridge 1985

Deane, Seamus, 'Joyce and Stephen: The Provincial Intellectual' and 'Joyce and Nationalism', in *Celtic Revivals: Essays in Modern Irish Literature 1880–1980*, Faber and Faber, London 1985

Manganiello, Dominic, *Joyce's Politics*, Routledge and Kegan Paul, London 1980

Watson, G. J., *Irish Identity and the Literary Revival: Synge, Yeats, Joyce and O'Casey*, Croom Helm, London 1979

Critical Perspectives

Cheng, Vincent, *Joyce, Race, and Empire*, Cambridge University Press, Cambridge 1995

Ellmann, Maud, 'Disremembering Dedalus: *A Portrait of the Artist as a Young Man*', in Robert Young (ed.), *Untying the Text: A Post-Structuralist Reader*, Routledge and Kegan Paul, London 1981

Heath, Stephen and Ferrer, Daniel (eds.), *Poststructuralist Joyce: Essays from the French*, Cambridge University Press, Cambridge 1984

Henke, Suzette, *James Joyce and the Politics of Desire*, Routledge, London 1990

Innes, C. L., *Woman and Nation in Irish Literature and Society, 1880–1935*, Harvester, London 1993

MacCabe, Colin, *James Joyce and the Revolution of the Word*, Macmillan, London 1979

Nolan, Emer, *James Joyce and Nationalism*, Routledge, London 1995

Roughley, Alan, *James Joyce and Critical Theory: An Introduction*, Harvester, London 1991

A PORTRAIT OF THE ARTIST
AS A YOUNG MAN

Et ignotas animum dimittit in artes[1]

Ovid, *Metamorphosis* viii, 188

Chapter 1

ONCE UPON A TIME and a very good time it was there was a moocow coming down along the road and this moocow that was coming down along the road met a nicens little boy named baby tuckoo . . .

His father told him that story: his father looked at him through a glass: he had a hairy face.

He was baby tuckoo. The moocow came down the road where Betty Byrne lived: she sold lemon platt.[2]

> O, the wild rose blossoms
> On the little green place.

He sang that song. That was his song.

> O, the green wothe botheth.

When you wet the bed first it is warm then it gets cold. His mother put on the oilsheet. That had the queer smell.

His mother had a nicer smell than his father. She played on the piano the sailor's hornpipe for him to dance. He danced:

> Tralala lala,
> Tralala tralaladdy,
> Tralala lala,
> Tralala lala.

Uncle Charles and Dante clapped. They were older than his father and mother but uncle Charles was older than Dante.

Dante had two brushes in her press. The brush with the maroon velvet back was for Michael Davitt[3] and the brush with the green velvet back was for Parnell.[4] Dante gave him a cachou[5] every time he brought her a piece of tissue paper,

The Vances lived in number seven. They had a different father and mother. They were Eileen's father and mother. When they were grown up he was going to marry Eileen. He hid under the table. His mother said:

– O, Stephen will apologize.

Dante said:

– O, if not, the eagles will come and pull out his eyes. –

> *Pull out his eyes,*
> *Apologize,*
> *Apologize,*
> *Pull out his eyes.*
>
> *Apologize,*
> *Pull out his eyes,*
> *Pull out his eyes,*
> *Apologize.*[6]

The wide playgrounds were swarming with boys. All were shouting and the prefects urged them on with strong cries. The evening air was pale and chilly and after every charge and thud of the footballers the greasy leather orb flew like a heavy bird through the grey light. He kept on the fringe of his line, out of sight of his prefect, out of the reach of the rude feet, feigning to run now and then. He felt his body small and weak amid the throng of the players and his eyes were weak and watery. Rody Kickham was not like that: he would be captain of the third line all the fellows said.

Rody Kickham was a decent fellow but Nasty Roche was a stink. Rody Kickham had greaves in his number and a hamper in the refectory. Nasty Roche had big hands. He called the Friday pudding dog-in-the-blanket. And one day he had asked:

– What is your name?

Stephen had answered: Stephen Dedalus.[7]

Then Nasty Roche had said:

– What kind of a name is that?

And when Stephen had not been able to answer Nasty Roche had asked:

– What is your father?

Stephen had answered:

– A gentleman.

Then Nasty Roche had asked:

– Is he a magistrate?

He crept about from point to point on the fringe of his line, making little runs now and then. But his hands were bluish with cold. He kept his hands in the side pockets of his belted grey suit. That was a belt round his pocket. And belt was also to give a fellow a belt. One day a fellow said to Cantwell:

– I'd give you such a belt in a second.

Cantwell had answered:

– Go and fight your match. Give Cecil Thunder a belt. I'd like to see you. He'd give you a toe in the rump for yourself.

That was not a nice expression. His mother had told him not to speak with the rough boys in the college. Nice mother! The first day in the hall of the castle when she had said goodbye she had put up her veil double to her nose to kiss him: and her nose and eyes were red. But he had pretended not to see that she was going to cry. She was a nice mother but she was not so nice when she cried. And his father had given him two five-shilling pieces for pocket money. And his father had told him if he wanted anything to write home to him and, whatever he did, never to peach[8] on a fellow. Then at the door of the castle the rector had shaken hands with his father and mother, his soutane fluttering in the breeze, and the car had driven off with his father and mother on it. They had cried to him from the car, waving their hands:

– Goodbye, Stephen, goodbye!

– Goodbye, Stephen, goodbye!

He was caught in the whirl of a scrimmage and, fearful of the flashing eyes and muddy boots, bent down to look through the legs. The fellows were struggling and groaning and their legs were rubbing and kicking and stamping. Then Jack Lawton's yellow boots dodged out the ball and all the other boots and legs ran after. He ran after them a little way and then stopped. It was useless to run on. Soon they would be going home for the holidays. After supper in the study hall he would change the number pasted up inside his desk from seventy-seven to seventy-six.

It would be better to be in the study hall than out there in the cold. The sky was pale and cold but there were lights in the castle. He wondered from which window Hamilton Rowan[9] had thrown his hat on the ha-ha and had there been flowerbeds at that time under the windows. One day when he had been called to the castle the butler had shown him the marks of the soldiers' slugs in the wood of the door and had given him a piece of shortbread that the community ate. It was nice and warm to see the lights in the castle. It was like something in a book. Perhaps Leicester Abbey[10] was like that. And there were nice sentences in Doctor Cornwell's Spelling Book.[11] They were like poetry but they were only sentences to learn the spelling from.

> *Wolsey[12] died in Leicester Abbey*
> *Where the abbots buried him.*
> *Canker is a disease of plants,*
> *Cancer one of animals.*

It would be nice to lie on the hearthrug before the fire, leaning his head upon his hands, and think on those sentences. He shivered as if he had cold slimy water next his skin. That was mean of Wells to shoulder him into the square ditch[13] because he would not swop his little snuffbox for Wells's seasoned hacking chestnut,[14] the conqueror of forty. How cold and slimy the water had been! A fellow had once seen a big rat jump into the scum. Mother was sitting at the fire with Dante waiting for Brigid to bring in the tea. She had her feet on the fender and her jewelly slippers were so hot and they had such a lovely warm smell! Dante knew a lot of things. She had taught him where the Mozambique Channel was and what was the longest river in America and what was the name of the highest mountain in the moon. Father Arnall knew more than Dante because he was a priest but both his father and uncle Charles said that Dante was a clever woman and a well-read woman. And when Dante made that noise after dinner and then put up her hand to her mouth: that was heartburn.

A voice cried far out on the playground:

– All in!

Then other voices cried from the lower and third lines:

– All in! All in!

The players closed around, flushed and muddy, and he went among them, glad to go in. Rody Kickham held the ball by its greasy lace. A fellow asked him to give it one last: but he walked on without even answering the fellow. Simon Moonan told him not to because the prefect was looking. The fellow turned to Simon Moonan and said:

– We all know why you speak. You are McGlade's suck.[15]

Suck was a queer word. The fellow called Simon Moonan that name because Simon Moonan used to tie the prefect's false sleeves behind his back and the prefect used to let on to be angry. But the sound was ugly. Once he had washed his hands in the lavatory of the Wicklow Hotel[16] and his father pulled the stopper up by the chain after and the dirty water went down through the hole in the basin. And when it had all gone down slowly the hole in the basin had made a sound like that: suck. Only louder.

To remember that and the white look of the lavatory made him feel cold and then hot. There were two cocks that you turned and water came out: cold and hot. He felt cold and then a little hot: and he could see the names printed on the cocks. That was a very queer thing.

And the air in the corridor chilled him too. It was queer and wettish. But soon the gas would be lit and in burning it made a light noise like a little song. Always the same: and when the fellows stopped talking in the playroom you could hear it.

It was the hour for sums. Father Arnall wrote a hard sum on the board and then said:

– Now then, who will win? Go ahead, York! Go ahead, Lancaster![17]

Stephen tried his best, but the sum was too hard and he felt confused. The little silk badge with the white rose on it that was pinned on the breast of his jacket began to flutter. He was no good at sums, but he tried his best so that York might not lose. Father Arnall's face looked very black, but he was not in a wax:[18] he was laughing. Then Jack Lawton cracked his fingers and Father Arnall looked at his copybook and said:

– Right. Bravo Lancaster! The red rose wins. Come on now, York! Forge ahead!

Jack Lawton looked over from his side. The little silk badge with the red rose on it looked very rich because he had a blue sailor top on. Stephen felt his own face red too, thinking of all the bets about who would get first place in elements,[19] Jack Lawton or he. Some weeks Jack Lawton got the card for first and some weeks he got the card for first. His white silk badge fluttered and fluttered as he worked at the next sum and heard Father Arnall's voice. Then all his eagerness passed away and he felt his face quite cool. He thought his face must be white because it felt so cool. He could not get out the answer for the sum but it did not matter. White roses and red roses: those were beautiful colours to think of. And the cards for first place and second place and third place were beautiful colours too: pink and cream and lavender. Lavender and cream and pink roses were beautiful to think of. Perhaps a wild rose might be like those colours and he remembered the song about the wild rose blossoms on the little green place. But you could not have a green rose. But perhaps somewhere in the world you could.

The bell rang and then the classes began to file out of the rooms and along the corridors towards the refectory. He sat looking at the two prints of butter on his plate but could not eat the damp bread. The tablecloth was damp and limp. But he drank off the hot weak tea which the clumsy scullion, girt with a white apron, poured into his cup. He wondered whether the scullion's apron was damp too or whether all white things were cold and damp. Nasty Roche and Saurin drank cocoa that their people sent them in tins. They said they could not drink the tea; that it was hogwash. Their fathers were magistrates, the fellows said.

All the boys seemed to him very strange. They had all fathers and mothers and different clothes and voices. He longed to be at home and lay his head on his mother's lap. But he could not: and so he longed for the play and study and prayers to be over and to be in bed.

He drank another cup of hot tea and Fleming said:

– What's up? Have you a pain or what's up with you?

– I don't know, Stephen said.

– Sick in your breadbasket, Fleming said, because your face looks white. It will go away.

– O yes, Stephen said.

But he was not sick there. He thought that he was sick in his heart if you could be sick in that place. Fleming was very decent to ask him. He wanted to cry. He leaned his elbows on the table and shut and opened the flaps of his ears. Then he heard the noise of the refectory every time he opened the flaps of his ears It made a roar like a train at night. And when he closed the flaps the roar was shut off like a train going into a tunnel. That night at Dalkey[20] the train had roared like that and then, when it went into the tunnel, the roar stopped. He closed his eyes and the train went on, roaring and then stopping; roaring again, stopping. It was nice to hear it roar and stop and then roar out of the tunnel again and then stop.

Then the higher line fellows began to come down along the matting in the middle of the refectory, Paddy Rath and Jimmy Magee and the Spaniard who was allowed to smoke cigars and the little Portuguese who wore the woolly cap. And then the lower line tables and the tables of the third line. And every single fellow had a different way of walking.

He sat in a corner of the playroom pretending to watch a game of dominoes and once or twice he was able to hear for an instant the little song of the gas. The prefect was at the door with some boys and Simon Moonan was knotting his false sleeves. He was telling them something about Tullabeg.[21]

Then he went away from the door and Wells came over to Stephen and said:

– Tell us, Dedalus, do you kiss your mother before you go to bed?

Stephen answered:

– I do.

Wells turned to the other fellows and said:

– O, I say, here's a fellow says he kisses his mother every night before he goes to bed.

The other fellows stopped their game and turned round, laughing. Stephen blushed under their eyes and said:

– I do not.

Wells said:

– O, I say, here's a fellow says he doesn't kiss his mother before he goes to bed.

They all laughed again. Stephen tried to laugh with them. He felt his whole body hot and confused in a moment. What was the right answer to the question? He had given two and still Wells laughed. But Wells must know the right answer for he was in third of grammar. He tried to think of Wells's mother but he did not dare to raise his eyes to Wells's face. He did not like Wells's face. It was Wells who had shouldered him into the square ditch the day before because he would not swop his little snuffbox for Wells's seasoned hacking chestnut, the conqueror of forty. It was a mean thing to do; all the fellows said it was. And how cold and slimy the water had been! And a fellow had once seen a big rat jump plop into the scum.

The cold slime of the ditch covered his whole body; and, when the bell rang for study and the lines filed out of the playrooms, he felt the cold air of the corridor and staircase inside his clothes. He still tried to think what was the right answer. Was it right to kiss his mother or wrong to kiss his mother? What did that mean, to kiss? You put your face up like that to say good night and then his mother put her face down. That was to kiss. His mother put her lips on his cheek; her lips were soft and they wetted his cheek; and they made a tiny little noise: kiss. Why did people do that with their two faces?

Sitting in the study hall he opened the lid of his desk and changed the number pasted up inside from seventy-seven to seventy-six. But the Christmas vacation was very far away: but one time it would come because the earth moved round always.

There was a picture of the earth on the first page of his geography: a big ball in the middle of clouds. Fleming had a box of crayons and one night during free study he had coloured the earth green and the clouds maroon. That was like the two brushes in Dante's press, the brush with the green velvet back for Parnell and the brush with the maroon velvet back for Michael Davitt. But he had not told Fleming to colour them those colours. Fleming had done it himself.

He opened the geography to study the lesson; but he could not learn the names of places in America. Still they were all different places that had different names. They were all in different countries and the countries were in continents and the continents were in the world and the world was in the universe.

He turned to the flyleaf of the geography and read what he had written there: himself, his name and where he was.

Stephen Dedalus
Class of Elements

Clongowes Wood College[22]
Sallins
County Kildare[23]
Ireland
Europe
The World
The Universe

That was in his writing: and Fleming one night for a cod[24] had written on the opposite page:

Stephen Dedalus is my name,
Ireland is my nation.
Clongowes is my dwelling place
And heaven my expectation.

He read the verses backwards but then they were not poetry. Then he read the flyleaf from the bottom to the top till he came to his own name. That was he: and he read down the page again. What was after the universe? Nothing. But was there anything round the universe to show where it stopped before the nothing place began? It could not be a wall; but there could be a thin thin line there all round everything. It was very big to think about everything and everywhere. Only God could do that. He tried to think what a big thought that must be; but he could only think of God. God was God's name just as his name was Stephen. *Dieu* was the French for God and that was God's name too; and when anyone prayed to God and said *Dieu* then God knew at once that it was a French person that was praying. But, though there were different names for God in all the different languages in the world and God understood what all the people who prayed said in their different languages, still God remained always the same God and God's real name was God.

It made him very tired to think that way. It made him feel his head very big. He turned over the flyleaf and looked wearily at the green round earth in the middle of the maroon clouds. He wondered which was right, to be for the green or for the maroon, because Dante had ripped the green velvet back off the brush that was for Parnell one day with her scissors and had told him that Parnell was a bad man. He wondered if they were arguing at home about that. That was called politics. There were two sides in it: Dante was on one side and his father and Mr Casey were on the other side but his mother and uncle Charles were on no side. Every day there was something in the paper about it.

It pained him that he did not know well what politics meant and that he did not know where the universe ended. He felt small and weak. When would he be like the fellows in poetry and rhetoric? They had big voices and big boots and they studied trigonometry. That was very far away. First came the vacation and then the next term and then vacation again and then again another term and then again the vacation. It was like a train going in and out of tunnels and that was like the noise of the boys eating in the refectory when you opened and closed the flaps of the ears. Term, vacation; tunnel, out; noise, stop. How far away it was! It was better to go to bed to sleep. Only prayers in the chapel and then bed. He shivered and yawned. It would be lovely in bed after the sheets got a bit hot. First they were so cold to get into. He shivered to think how cold they were first. But then they got hot and then he could sleep. It was lovely to be tired. He yawned again. Night prayers and then bed: he shivered and wanted to yawn. It would be lovely in a few minutes. He felt a warm glow creeping up from the cold shivering sheets, warmer and warmer till he felt warm all over, ever so warm and yet he shivered a little and still wanted to yawn.

The bell rang for night prayers and he filed out of the study hall after the others and down the staircase and along the corridors to the chapel. The corridors were darkly lit and the chapel was darkly lit. Soon all would be dark and sleeping. There was cold night air in the chapel and the marbles were the colour the sea was at night. The sea was cold day and night: but it was colder at night. It was cold and dark under the seawall beside his father's house. But the kettle would be on the hob to make punch.

The prefect of the chapel prayed above his head and his memory knew the responses:

> *O Lord, open our lips*
> *And our mouths shall announce Thy praise.*
> *Incline unto our aid, O God!*
> *O Lord, make haste to help us!*[25]

There was a cold night smell in the chapel. But it was a holy smell. It was not like the smell of the old peasants who knelt at the back of the chapel at Sunday mass. That was a smell of air and rain and turf and corduroy. But they were very holy peasants. They breathed behind him on his neck and sighed as they prayed. They lived in Clane,[26] a fellow said: there were little cottages there and he had seen a woman standing at the half-door of a cottage with a child in her arms as the cars had come past from Sallins. It would be lovely to sleep for one night in that cottage before the fire of smoking turf, in the dark lit by the fire, in the warm dark, breathing the smell of the peasants, air and rain and turf and corduroy. But O, the road there between the trees was dark! You would be lost in the dark. It made him afraid to think of how it was.

He heard the voice of the prefect of the chapel saying the last prayer. He prayed it too against the dark outside under the trees.

> *Visit, we beseech Thee, O Lord, this habitation and drive away from it all the snares of the enemy. May Thy holy angels dwell herein to preserve us in peace and may Thy blessings be always upon us through Christ our Lord.*[27]
>
> *Amen.*

His fingers trembled as he undressed himself in the dormitory. He told his fingers to hurry up. He had to undress and then kneel and say his own prayers and be in bed before the gas was lowered so that he might not go to hell when he died. He rolled his stockings off and put on his nightshirt quickly and knelt trembling at his bedside and repeated his prayers quickly, fearing that the gas would go down. He felt his shoulders shaking as he murmured:

> *God bless my father and my mother and spare them to me!*
> *God bless my little brothers and sisters and spare them to me!*
> *God bless Dante and Uncle Charles and spare them to me!*

He blessed himself and climbed quickly into bed and, tucking the end of the nightshirt under his feet, curled himself together under the cold white sheets, shaking and trembling. But he would not go to hell when he died; and the shaking would stop. A voice bade the boys in the dormitory good night. He peered out for an instant over the coverlet and saw the yellow curtains round and before his bed that shut him off on all sides. The light was lowered quietly.

The prefect's shoes went away. Where? Down the staircase and along the corridors or to his room at the end? He saw the dark. Was it true about the black dog that walked there at night with eyes as big as carriage-lamps? They said it was the ghost of a murderer. A long shiver of fear flowed over his body. He saw the dark entrance hall of the castle. Old servants in old dress were in the ironing-room above the staircase. It was long ago. The old servants were quiet. There was a fire there, but the hall was still dark. A figure came up the staircase from the hall. He wore the white cloak of a marshal; his face was pale and strange; he held his hand pressed to his side. He looked out of strange eyes at the old servants. They looked at him and saw their master's face and cloak and knew that he had received his death-wound. But only the dark was where they looked: only dark silent air. Their master had received his death-wound on the battlefield of Prague far away over the sea. He was standing on the field; his hand was pressed to his side; his face was pale and strange and he wore the white cloak of a marshal.[28]

O how cold and strange it was to think of that! All the dark was cold and strange. There were pale strange faces there, great eyes like carriage-lamps. They were the ghosts of murderers, the figures of marshals who had received their death-wound on battlefields far away over the sea. What did they wish to say that their faces were so strange?

Visit, we beseech Thee, O Lord, this habitation and drive away from it all . . .

Going home for the holidays! That would be lovely: the fellows had told him. Getting up on the cars in the early wintry morning outside the door of the castle. The cars were rolling on the gravel. Cheers for the rector!

Hurray! Hurray! Hurray!

The cars drove past the chapel and all caps were raised. They drove merrily along the country roads. The drivers pointed with their whips to Bodenstown.[29] The fellows cheered. They passed the farmhouse of the Jolly Farmer. Cheer after cheer after cheer. Through Clane they drove, cheering and cheered. The peasant women stood at the half-doors, the men stood here and there. The lovely smell there was in the wintry air: the smell of Clane: rain and wintry air and turf smouldering and corduroy.

The train was full of fellows: a long long chocolate train with cream facings. The guards went to and fro opening, closing, locking, unlocking the doors. They were men in dark blue and silver; they had silvery whistles and their keys made a quick music: click, click: click, click.

And the train raced on over the flat lands and past the Hill of Allen.[30] The telegraph poles were passing, passing. The train went on and on. It knew. There were lanterns in the hall of his father's house and ropes of green branches. There were holly and ivy round the pierglass and holly and ivy, green and red, twined round the chandeliers. There were red holly and green ivy round the old portraits on the walls. Holly and ivy for him and for Christmas.

Lovely . . .

All the people. Welcome home, Stephen! Noises of welcome. His mother kissed him. Was that right? His father was a marshal now: higher than a magistrate. Welcome home, Stephen!

Noises . . .

There was a noise of curtain-rings running back along the rods, of water being splashed in the basins. There was a noise of rising and dressing and washing in the dormitory: a noise of clapping of hands as the prefect went up and down telling the fellows to look sharp. A pale sunlight showed the yellow curtains drawn back, the tossed beds. His bed was very hot and his face and body were very hot.

He got up and sat on the side of his bed. He was weak. He tried to pull on his stocking. It had a horrid rough feel. The sunlight was queer and cold.

Fleming said:

– Are you not well?

He did not know; and Fleming said:

– Get back into bed. I'll tell McGlade you're not well.

– He's sick.

– Who is?

– Tell McGlade.

– Get back into bed.

– Is he sick?

A fellow held his arms while he loosened the stocking clinging to his foot and climbed back into the hot bed.

He crouched down between the sheets, glad of their tepid glow. He heard the fellows talk among themselves about him as they dressed for mass. It was a mean thing to do, to shoulder him into the square ditch, they were saying.

Then their voices ceased; they had gone. A voice at his bed said:

– Dedalus, don't spy on us, sure you won't?

Wells's face was there. He looked at it and saw that Wells was afraid.

– I didn't mean to. Sure you won't?

His father had told him, whatever he did, never to peach on a fellow. He shook his head and answered no and felt glad.

Wells said:

– I didn't mean to, honour bright. It was only for cod. I'm sorry.

The face and the voice went away. Sorry because he was afraid. Afraid that it was some disease. Canker was a disease of plants and cancer one of animals: or another different. That was a long time ago then out on the playgrounds in the evening light, creeping from point to point on the fringe of his line, a heavy bird flying low through the grey light. Leicester Abbey lit up. Wolsey died there. The abbots buried him themselves.

It was not Wells's face, it was the prefect's. He was not foxing.[31] No, no: he was sick really. He was not foxing. And he felt the prefect's hand on his forehead; and he felt his forehead warm and damp against the prefect's cold damp hand. That was the way a rat felt, slimy and damp and cold. Every rat had two eyes to look out of. Sleek slimy coats, little little feet tucked up to jump, black slimy eyes to look out of. They could understand how to jump. But the minds of rats could not understand trigonometry. When they were dead they lay on their sides. Their coats dried then. They were only dead things.

The prefect was there again and it was his voice that was saying that he was to get up, that Father Minister had said he was to get up and dress and go to the infirmary. And while he was dressing himself as quickly as he could the prefect said:

– We must pack off to Brother Michael[32] because we have the collywobbles!

He was very decent to say that. That was all to make him laugh. But he could not laugh because his cheeks and lips were all shivery: and then the prefect had to laugh by himself.

The prefect cried:

– Quick march! Hayfoot! Strawfoot![33]

They went together down the staircase and along the corridor and past the bath. As he passed the door he remembered with a vague fear the warm turf-coloured bogwater, the warm moist air, the noise of plunges, the smell of the towels, like medicine.

Brother Michael was standing at the door of the infirmary and from the door of the dark cabinet on his right came a smell like medicine. That came from the bottles on the shelves. The prefect spoke to Brother Michael and Brother Michael answered and called the prefect sir. He had reddish hair mixed with grey and a queer look. It was queer that he would always be a brother. It was queer too that you could not call him sir because he was a brother and had a different kind of look. Was he not holy enough or why could he not catch up on the others?

There were two beds in the room and in one bed there was a fellow: and when they went in he called out:

– Hello! It's young Dedalus! What's up?

– The sky is up, Brother Michael said.

He was a fellow out of the third of grammar and, while Stephen was undressing, he asked Brother Michael to bring him a round of buttered toast.

– Ah, do! he said.

– Butter you up! said Brother Michael. You'll get your walking papers in the morning when the doctor comes.

– Will I? the fellow said. I'm not well yet.

Brother Michael repeated:

– You'll get your walking papers. I tell you.

He bent down to rake the fire. He had a long back like the long back of a tramhorse. He shook the poker gravely and nodded his head at the fellow out of third of grammar

Then Brother Michael went away and after a while the fellow out of third of grammar turned in towards the wall and fell asleep.

That was the infirmary. He was sick then. Had they written home to tell his mother and father? But it would be quicker for one of the priests to go himself to tell them. Or he would write a letter for the priest to bring.

> Dear Mother,
>   I am sick. I want to go home. Please come and take me home. I am in the infirmary.
>   Your fond son,
>
>   Stephen

How far away they were! There was cold sunlight outside the window. He wondered if he would die. You could die just the same on a sunny day. He might die before his mother came. Then he would have a dead mass in the chapel like the way the fellows had told him it was when Little had died. All the fellows would be at the mass, dressed in black, all with sad faces. Wells too would be there but no fellow would look at him. The rector would be there in a cope of black and gold and there would be tall yellow candles on the altar and round the catafalque.[34] And they would carry the coffin out of the chapel slowly and he would be buried in the little graveyard of the community off the main avenue of limes. And Wells would be sorry then for what he had done. And the bell would toll slowly.

He could hear the tolling. He said over to himself the song that Brigid had taught him.

> *Dingdong! The castle bell!*
> *Farewell my mother!*
> *Bury me in the old churchyard*
> *Beside my oldest brother.*
> *My coffin shall be black,*

> *Six angels at my back,*
> *Two to sing and two to pray*
> *And two to carry my soul away.*[35]

How beautiful and sad that was! How beautiful the words were where they said *Bury me in the old churchyard!* A tremor passed over his body. How sad and how beautiful! He wanted to cry quietly but not for himself: for the words, so beautiful and sad, like music. The bell! The bell! Farewell! O farewell!

The cold sunlight was weaker and Brother Michael was standing at his bedside with a bowl of beef-tea. He was glad for his mouth was hot and dry. He could hear them playing in the playgrounds. And the day was going on in the college just as if he were there.

Then Brother Michael was going away and the fellow out of the third of grammar told him to be sure and come back and tell him all the news in the paper. He told Stephen that his name was Athy[36] and that his father kept a lot of racehorses that were spiffing jumpers and that his father would give a good tip to Brother Michael any time he wanted it because Brother Michael was very decent and always told him the news out of the paper they got every day up in the castle. There was every kind of news in the paper: accidents, shipwrecks, sports, and politics.

– Now it is all about politics in the papers, he said. Do your people talk about that too?

– Yes, Stephen said.

– Mine too, he said.

Then he thought for a moment and said:

– You have a queer name, Dedalus, and I have a queer name too, Athy. My name is the name of a town. Your name is like Latin.

Then he asked:

– Are you good at riddles?

Stephen answered:

– Not very good.

Then he said:

– Can you answer me this one? Why is the county of Kildare like the leg of a fellow's breeches?

Stephen thought what could be the answer and then said:

– I give it up.

– Because there is a thigh in it, he said. Do you see the joke? Athy is the town in the county Kildare and a thigh is the other thigh.

– Oh, I see, Stephen said.

– That's an old riddle, he said.

After a moment he said:

– I say!

– What? asked Stephen.

– You know, he said, you can ask that riddle another way.

– Can you? said Stephen.

– The same riddle, he said. Do you know the other was to ask it?

– No, said Stephen.

– Can you not think of the other way? he said.

He looked at Stephen over the bedclothes as he spoke. Then he lay back on the pillow and said:

– There is another way but I won't tell you what it is.

Why did he not tell it? His father, who kept the racehorses, must be a magistrate too like Saurin's father and Nasty Roche's father. He thought of his own father, of how he sang songs while his mother played and of how he always gave him a shilling when he asked for sixpence and he felt sorry for him that he was not a magistrate like the other boys' fathers. Then why was he sent to that place with them? But his father had told him that he would be no stranger there because his granduncle had presented an address to the liberator[37] there fifty years before. You could know the people of that time by their old dress. It seemed to him a solemn time: and he wondered if that was the time when the fellows in Clongowes wore blue coats with brass buttons and yellow waistcoats and caps of rabbit-skin and drank beer like grownup people and kept greyhounds of their own to course the hares with.

He looked at the window and saw that the daylight had grown weaker. There would be cloudy grey light over the playgrounds. There was no noise on the playgrounds. The class must be doing the themes or perhaps Father Arnall was reading out of the book.

It was queer that they had not given him any medicine. Perhaps Brother Michael would bring it back when he came. They said you got stinking stuff to drink when you were in the infirmary. But he felt better now than before. It would be nice getting better slowly. You could get a book then. There was a book in the library about Holland. There were lovely foreign names in it and pictures of strange looking cities and ships. It made you feel so happy.

How pale the light was at the window! But that was nice. The fire rose and fell on the wall. It was like waves. Someone had put coal on and he heard voices. They were talking. It was the noise of the waves. Or the waves were talking among themselves as they rose and fell.

He saw the sea of waves, long dark waves rising and falling, dark under the moonless night. A tiny light twinkled at the pierhead where the ship was entering: and he saw a multitude of people gathered by the waters' edge to see the ship that was entering their harbour. A tall man stood on the deck, looking out towards the flat dark land: and by the light at the pierhead he saw his face, the sorrowful face of Brother Michael.

He saw him lift his hand towards the people and heard him say in a loud voice of sorrow over the waters:

– He is dead. We saw him lying upon the catafalque.

A wail of sorrow went up from the people.

– Parnell! Parnell! He is dead!

They fell upon their knees, moaning in sorrow.

And he saw Dante in a maroon velvet dress and with a green velvet mantle hanging from her shoulders walking proudly and silently past the people who knelt by the water's edge.

A great fire, banked high and red, flamed in the grate and under the ivy-twined branches of the chandelier the Christmas table was spread. They had come home a little late and still dinner was not ready: but it would be ready in a jiffy his mother had said. They were waiting for the door to open and for the servants to come in, holding the big dishes covered with their heavy metal covers.

All were waiting: uncle Charles, who sat far away in the shadow of the window, Dante and Mr Casey who sat in the easy-chairs at either side of the hearth, Stephen, seated on a chair between them, his feet resting on the toasted boss.[38] Mr Dedalus looked at himself in the pierglass above the mantelpiece, waxed out his moustache ends and then, parting his coat-tails, stood with his back to the glowing fire: and still from time to time he withdrew a hand from his coat-tail to wax out one of his moustache ends. Mr Casey leaned his head to one side and, smiling, tapped the gland of his neck with his fingers. And Stephen smiled too for he knew now that it was not true that Mr Casey had a purse of silver in his throat. He smiled to think how the silvery noise which Mr Casey used to make had deceived him. And when he had tried to open Mr Casey's hand to see if the purse of silver was hidden there he had seen that the fingers could not be straightened out: and Mr Casey had told him that he had got those three cramped fingers making a birthday present for Queen Victoria.[39] Mr Casey tapped the gland of his neck and smiled at Stephen with sleepy eyes: and Mr Dedalus said to him:

– Yes. Well now, that's all right. O, we had a good walk, hadn't we, John? Yes . . . I wonder if there's any likelihood of dinner this evening. Yes . . . O, well now, we got a good breath of ozone round the Head[40] today. Ay, bedad.

He turned to Dante and said:

– You didn't stir out at all, Mrs Riordan?

Dante frowned and said shortly:

– No.

Mr Dedalus dropped his coat-tails and went over to the sideboard. He brought forth a great stone jar of whisky from the locker and filled the decanter slowly, bending now and then to see how much he had poured in. Then replacing the jar in the locker he poured a little of the whisky into two glasses, added a little water and came back with them to the fireplace.

– A thimbleful, John, he said, just to whet your appetite.

Mr Casey took the glass, drank, and placed it near him on the mantelpiece. Then he said:

– Well, I can't help thinking of our friend Christopher manufacturing . . .

He broke into a fit of laughter and coughing and added:

– . . . manufacturing that champagne[41] for those fellows.

Mr Dedalus laughed loudly.

– Is it Christy? he said. There's more cunning in one of those warts on his bald head than in a pack of jack foxes.

He inclined his head, closed his eyes, and, licking his lips profusely, began to speak with the voice of the hotel keeper.

– And he has such a soft mouth when he's speaking to you, don't you know. He's very moist and watery about the dewlaps,[42] God bless him.

Mr Casey was still struggling through his fit of coughing and laughter. Stephen, seeing and hearing the hotel keeper through his father's face and voice, laughed.

Mr Dedalus put up his eyeglass and, staring down at him, said quietly and kindly:

– What are you laughing at, you little puppy, you?

The servants entered and placed the dishes on the table. Mrs Dedalus followed and the places were arranged.

– Sit over, she said.

Mr Dedalus went to the end of the table and said:

– Now, Mrs Riordan, sit over. John, sit you down, my hearty.

He looked round to where uncle Charles sat and said:

– Now then, sir, there's a bird here waiting for you.

When all had taken their seats he laid his hand on the cover and then said quickly, withdrawing it:

– Now, Stephen.

Stephen stood up in his place to say the grace before meals:

Bless us, O Lord, and these Thy gifts which through Thy bounty we are about to receive through Christ our Lord. Amen.[43]

All blessed themselves and Mr Dedalus with a sigh of pleasure lifted from the dish the heavy cover pearled around the edge with glistening drops.

Stephen looked at the plump turkey which had lain, trussed and skewered, on the kitchen table. He knew that his father had paid a guinea for it in Dunn's of D'Olier Street[44] and that the man had prodded it often at the breastbone to show how good it was: and he remembered the man's voice when he had said:

– Take that one, sir. That's the real Ally Daly.[45]

Why did Mr Barrett in Clongowes call his pandybat[46] a turkey? But Clongowes was far away: and the warm heavy smell of turkey and ham and celery rose from the plates and dishes and the great fire was banked high and red in the grate and the green ivy and red holly made you feel so happy and when dinner was ended the big plum pudding would be carried in, studded with peeled almonds and sprigs of holly, with bluish fire running around it and a little green flag flying from the top.

It was his first Christmas dinner and he thought of his little brothers and sisters who were waiting in the nursery, as he had often waited, till the pudding came. The deep low collar and the Eton jacket[47] made him feel queer and oldish: and that morning when his mother had brought him down to the parlour, dressed for mass, his father had cried. That was because he was thinking of his own father. And uncle Charles had said so too.

Mr Dedalus covered the dish and began to eat hungrily. Then he said:

– Poor old Christy, he's nearly lopsided now with roguery.

– Simon, said Mrs Dedalus, you haven't given Mrs Riordan any sauce.

Mr Dedalus seized the sauceboat.

– Haven't I? he cried. Mrs Riordan, pity the poor blind.

Dante covered her plate with her hands and said:

– No, thanks.

Mr Dedalus turned to uncle Charles.

– How are you off, sir?

– Right as the mail, Simon.

– You, John?

– I'm all right. Go on yourself.

– Mary? Here, Stephen, here's something to make your hair curl.

He poured sauce freely over Stephen's plate and set the boat again on the table. Then he asked uncle Charles was it tender. Uncle Charles could not speak because his mouth was full; but he nodded that it was.

– That was a good answer our friend made to the canon. What? said Mr Dedalus.

– I didn't think he had that much in him, said Mr Casey.

– *I'll pay your dues, father, when you cease turning the house of God into a polling-booth.*[48]

– A nice answer, said Dante, for any man calling himself a catholic to give to his priest.

– They have only themselves to blame, said Mr Dedalus suavely. If they took a fool's advice they would confine their attention to religion.

– It is religion, Dante said. They are doing their duty in warning the people.

– We go to the house of God, Mr Casey said, in all humility to pray to our Maker and not to hear election addresses.

– It is religion, Dante said again. They are right. They must direct their flocks.

– And preach politics from the altar, is it? asked Mr Dedalus.

– Certainly, said Dante. It is a question of public morality. A priest would not be a priest if he did not tell his flock what is right and what is wrong.

Mrs Dedalus bid down her knife and fork, saying:

– For pity sake and for pity sake let us have no political discussion on this day of all days in the year.

– Quite right, ma'am, said uncle Charles. Now, Simon, that's quite enough now. Not another word now.

– Yes, yes, said Mr Dedalus quickly.

He uncovered the dish boldly and said:

– Now then, who's for more turkey?

Nobody answered. Dante said:

– Nice language for any catholic to use!

– Mrs Riordan, I appeal to you, said Mrs Dedalus, to let the matter drop now.

Dante turned on her and said:

– And am I to sit here and listen to the pastors of my church being flouted?

– Nobody is saying a word against them, said Mr Dedalus, so long as they don't meddle in politics.

– The bishops and priests of Ireland have spoken, said Dante, and they must be obeyed.

– Let them leave politics alone, said Mr Casey, or the people may leave their church alone.

– You hear? said Dante, turning to Mrs Dedalus.

– Mr Casey! Simon! said Mrs Dedalus, let it end now.

– Too bad! Too bad! said uncle Charles.

– What? cried Mr Dedalus. Were we to desert him at the bidding of the English people?[49]

– He was no longer worthy to lead, said Dante. He was a public sinner.

– We are all sinners and black sinners, said Mr Casey coldly.

– *Woe be to the man by whom the scandal cometh!* said Mrs Riordan. *It would be better for him that a millstone were tied about his neck and that he were cast into the depths of the sea rather than that he should scandalize one of these, my least little ones.* That is the language of the Holy Ghost.[50]

– And very bad language if you ask me, said Mr Dedalus coolly.

– Simon! Simon! said uncle Charles. The boy.

– Yes, yes, said Mr Dedalus. I meant about the . . . I was thinking about the bad language of the railway porter. Well now, that's all right. Here, Stephen, show me your plate, old chap. Eat away now. Here.

He heaped up the food on Stephen's plate and served uncle Charles and Mr Casey to large pieces of turkey and splashes of sauce. Mrs Dedalus was eating little and Dante sat with her hands in her lap. She was red in the face. Mr Dedalus rooted with the carvers at the end of the dish and said:

– There's a tasty bit here we call the pope's nose.[51] If any lady or gentleman . . .

He held a piece of fowl up on the prong of the carving-fork. Nobody spoke. He put it on his own plate, saying:

– Well, you can't say but you were asked. I think I had better eat it myself because I'm not well in my health lately.

He winked at Stephen and, replacing the dish-cover, began to eat again.

There was a silence while he ate. Then he said:

– Well now, the day kept up fine after all. There were plenty of strangers down too.

Nobody spoke. He said again:

– I think there were more strangers down than last Christmas.

He looked round at the others whose faces were bent towards their plates and, receiving no reply, waited for a moment and said bitterly:

– Well, my Christmas dinner has been spoiled anyhow.

– There could be neither luck nor grace, Dante said, in a house where there is no respect for the pastors of the church.

Mr Dedalus threw his knife and fork noisily on his plate.

– Respect! he said. Is it for Billy with the lip or for the tub of guts up in Armagh?[52] Respect!

– Princes of the church, said Mr Casey with slow scorn.

– Lord Leitrim's coachman,[53] yes, said Mr Dedalus.

– They are the Lord's anointed, Dante said. They are an honour to their country.

– Tub of guts, said Mr Dedalus coarsely. He has a handsome face, mind you, in repose. You should see that fellow lapping up his bacon and cabbage of a cold winter's day. O Johnny!

He twisted his features into a grimace of heavy bestiality and made a lapping noise with his lips.

– Really, Simon, you should not speak that way before Stephen. It's not right.

– O, he'll remember all this when he grows up, said Dante hotly – the language he heard against God and religion and priests in his own home.

– Let him remember too, cried Mr Casey to her from across the table, the language with which the priests and the priests' pawns broke Parnell's heart and hounded him into his grave. Let him remember that too when he grows up.

– Sons of bitches! cried Mr Dedalus. When he was down they turned on him to betray him and rend him like rats in a sewer. Low-lived dogs! And they look it! By Christ, they look it!

– They behaved rightly, cried Dante. They obeyed their bishops and their priests. Honour to them!

– Well, it is perfectly dreadful to say that not even for one day in the year, said Mrs Dedalus, can we be free from these dreadful disputes!

Uncle Charles raised his hands mildly and said:

– Come now, come now, come now! Can we not have our opinions whatever they are without this bad temper and this bad language? It is too bad surely.

Mrs Dedalus spoke to Dante in a low voice but Dante said loudly:

– I will not say nothing. I will defend my church and my religion when it is insulted and spit on by renegade catholics.

Mr Casey pushed his plate rudely into the middle of the table and, resting his elbows before him, said in a hoarse voice to his host:

– Tell me, did I tell you that story about a very famous spit?

– You did not, John, said Mr Dedalus.

– Why then, said Mr Casey, it is a most instructive story. It happened not long ago in the County Wicklow[54] where we are now.

He broke off and, turning towards Dante, said with quiet indignation:

– And I may tell you, ma'am, that I, if you mean me, am no renegade catholic. I am a catholic as my father was and his father before him and his father before him again, when we gave up our lives rather than sell our faith.

– The more shame to you now, Dante said, to speak as you do.

– The story, John, said Mr Dedalus smiling. Let us have the story anyhow.

– Catholic indeed! repeated Dante ironically. The blackest protestant in the land would not speak the language I have heard this evening

Mr Dedalus began to sway his head to and fro, crooning like a country singer.

– I am no protestant, I tell you again, said Mr Casey, flushing. Mr Dedalus, still crooning and swaying his head, began to sing in a grunting nasal tone:

> *O, come all you Roman catholics*
> *That never went to mass.*

He took up his knife and fork again in good humour and set to eating, saying to Mr Casey:

– Let us have the story, John. It will help us to digest.

Stephen looked with affection at Mr Casey's face which stared across the table over his joined hands. He liked to sit near him at the fire, looking up at his dark fierce face. But his dark eyes were never fierce and his slow voice was good to listen to. But why was he then against the priests? Because Dante must be right then. But he had heard his father say that she was a spoiled nun and that she had come out of the convent in the Alleghanies[55] when her brother had got the money from the savages for the trinkets and the chainies.[56] Perhaps that made her severe against Parnell. And she did not like him to play with Eileen because Eileen was a protestant and when she was young she knew children that used to play with protestants and the protestants used to make fun of the litany of the Blessed Virgin. *Tower of Ivory*, they used to say, *House of Gold!*[57] How could a woman be a tower of ivory or a house of gold? Who was right then? And he remembered the evening in the infirmary in Clongowes, the dark waters, the light at the pierhead and the moan of sorrow from the people when they had heard.

Eileen had long white hands. One evening when playing tig[58] she had put her hands over his eyes: long and white and thin and cold and soft. That was ivory: a cold white thing. That was the meaning of *Tower of Ivory*.

– The story is very short and sweet, Mr Casey said. It was one day down in Arklow,[59] a cold bitter day, not long before the chief[60] died. May God have mercy on him!

He closed his eyes wearily and paused. Mr Dedalus took a bone from his plate and tore some meat from it with his teeth, saying:

– Before he was killed, you mean.

Mr Casey opened his eyes, sighed and went on:

– It was down in Arklow one day. We were down there at a meeting and after the meeting was over we had to make our way to the railway station through the crowd. Such booing and baaing, man, you never heard. They called us all the names in the world. Well there was one old lady, and a drunken old harridan she was surely, that paid all her attention to me. She kept dancing along beside me in the mud bawling and screaming into my face: *Priest-hunter!*[61] *The Paris Funds! Mr Fox! Kitty O'Shea!*[62]

– And what did you do, John? asked Mr Dedalus.

– I let her bawl away, said Mr Casey. It was a cold day and to keep up my heart I had (saving your presence, ma'am) a quid of Tullamore[63] in my mouth and sure I couldn't say a word in any case because my mouth was full of tobacco juice.

– Well, John?

– Well. I let her bawl away, to her heart's content, *Kitty O'Shea* and the rest of it till at last she called that lady a name that I won't sully this Christmas board nor your ears, ma'am, nor my own lips by repeating.

He paused. Mr Dedalus, lifting his head from the bone, asked:

– And what did you do, John?

– Do! said Mr Casey. She stuck her ugly old face up at me when she said it and I had my mouth full of tobacco juice. I bent down to her and *Phth!* says I to her like that.

He turned aside and made the act of spitting.

– *Phth!* says I to her like that, right into her eye.

He clapped his hand to his eye and gave a hoarse scream of pain.

– *O Jesus, Mary and Joseph!* says she. *I'm blinded! I'm blinded and drownded!*

He stopped in a fit of coughing and laughter, repeating:

– *I'm blinded entirely.*

Mr Dedalus laughed loudly and lay back in his chair while uncle Charles swayed his head to and fro.

Dante looked terribly angry and repeated while they laughed:

– Very nice! Ha! Very nice!

It was not nice about the spit in the woman's eye.

But what was the name the woman had called Kitty O'Shea that Mr Casey would not repeat? He thought of Mr Casey walking through the crowds of people and making speeches from a wagonette. That was what he had been in prison for and he remembered that one night Sergeant O'Neill had come to the house and had stood in the hall, talking in a low voice with his father and chewing nervously at the chinstrap of his cap. And that night Mr Casey had not gone to Dublin by tram but a car had come to the door and he had heard his father say something about the Cabinteely road.[64]

He was for Ireland and Parnell and so was his father: and so was Dante too for one night at the band on the esplanade she had hit a gentleman on the head with her umbrella because he had taken off his hat when the band played *God save the Queen* at the end.

Mr Dedalus gave a snort of contempt.

– Ah, John, he said. It is true for them. We are an unfortunate priest-ridden race and always were and always will be till the end of the chapter.

Uncle Charles shook his head, saying:

– A bad business! A bad business!

Mr Dedalus repeated:

– A priestridden Godforsaken race!

He pointed to the portrait of his grandfather on the wall to his right.

– Do you see that old chap up there, John? he said. He was a good Irishman when there was no money in the job. He was condemned to death as a whiteboy.[65] But he had a saying about our clerical friends, that he would never let one of them put his two feet under his mahogany.[66]

Dante broke in angrily:

– If we are a priestridden race we ought to be proud of it! They are the apple of God's eye. *Touch them not*, says Christ, *for they are the apple of My eye.*[67]

– And can we not love our country then? asked Mr Casey. Are we not to follow the man that was born to lead us?

– A traitor to his country! replied Dante. A traitor, an adulterer! The priests were right to abandon him. The priests were always the true friends of Ireland.

– Were they, faith? said Mr Casey.

He threw his fist on the table and, frowning angrily, protruded one finger after another.

– Didn't the bishops of Ireland betray us in the time of the union when Bishop Lanigan presented an address of loyalty to the Marquess Cornwallis?[68] Didn't the bishops and priests sell the aspirations of their country in 1829 in return for catholic emancipation?[69] Didn't they denounce the fenian movement from the pulpit and in the confession box?[70] And didn't they dishonour the ashes of Terence Bellew MacManus?[71]

His face was glowing with anger and Stephen felt the glow rise to his own cheek as the spoken words thrilled him. Mr Dedalus uttered a guffaw of coarse scorn.

– O, by God, he cried, I forgot little old Paul Cullen![72] Another apple of God's eye!

Dante bent across the table and cried to Mr Casey:

– Right! Right! They were always right! God and morality and religion come first.

Mrs Dedalus, seeing her excitement, said to her:

– Mrs Riordan, don't excite yourself answering them.

– God and religion before everything! Dante cried. God and religion before the world.

Mr Casey raised his clenched fist and brought it down on the table with a crash.

– Very well then, he shouted hoarsely, if it comes to that, no God for Ireland!

– John! John! cried Mr Dedalus, seizing his guest by the coat sleeve.

Dante stared across the table, her cheeks shaking. Mr Casey struggled up from his chair and bent across the table towards her, scraping the air from before his eyes with one hand as though he were tearing aside a cobweb.

– No God for Ireland! he cried. We have had too much God in Ireland. Away with God!

– Blasphemer! Devil! screamed Dante, starting to her feet and almost spitting in his face.

Uncle Charles and Mr Dedalus pulled Mr Casey back into his chair again, talking to him from both sides reasonably. He stared before him out of his dark flaming eyes, repeating:

– Away with God, I say!

Dante shoved her chair violently aside and left the table, upsetting her napkin-ring which rolled slowly along the carpet and came to rest against the foot of an easy-chair. Mr Dedalus rose quickly and followed

her towards the door. At the door Dante turned round violently and
shouted down the room, her cheeks flushed and quivering with rage:

– Devil out of hell! We won! We crushed him to death! Fiend!

The door slammed behind her.

Mr Casey, freeing his arms from his holders, suddenly bowed his
head on his hands with a sob of pain.

– Poor Parnell! he cried loudly. My dead king!

He sobbed loudly and bitterly.

Stephen, raising his terror-stricken face, saw that his father's eyes
were full of tears.

The fellows talked together in little groups.

One fellow said:

– They were caught near the Hill of Lyons.[73]

– Who caught them?

– Mr Gleeson and the minister. They were on a car.

The same fellow added:

– A fellow in the higher line told me.

Fleming asked:

– But why did they run away, tell us?

– I know why, Cecil Thunder said. Because they had fecked cash[74]
out of the rector's room.

– Who fecked it?

– Kickham's brother. And they all went shares in it.

– But that was stealing. How could they have done that?

– A fat lot you know about it, Thunder! Wells said. I know why they
scut.

– Tell us why.

– I was told not to, Wells said.

– O, go on, Wells, all said. You might tell us. We won't let it out.

Stephen bent forward his head to hear. Wells looked round to see if
anyone was coming. Then he said secretly:

– You know the altar wine they keep in the press in the sacristy?[75]

– Yes.

– Well, they drank that and it was found out who did it by the smell.
And that's why they ran away, if you want to know.

And the fellow who had spoken first said:

– Yes, that's what I heard too from the fellow in the higher line.

The fellows all were silent. Stephen stood among them, afraid to
speak, listening. A faint sickness of awe made him feel weak. How
could they have done that? He thought of the dark silent sacristy.

There were dark wooden presses there where the crimped surplices lay quietly folded. It was not the chapel but still you had to speak under your breath. It was a holy place. He remembered the summer evening he had been there to be dressed as boatbearer, the evening of the procession to the little altar in the wood.[76] A strange and holy place. The boy that held the censer had swung it lifted by the middle chain to keep the coals lighting. That was called charcoal: and it had burned quietly as the fellow had swung it gently and had given off a weak sour smell. And then when all were vested he had stood holding out the boat to the rector and the rector had put a spoonful of incense in it and it had hissed on the red coals.

The fellows were talking together in little groups here and there on the playground. The fellows seemed to him to have grown smaller: that was because a sprinter[77] had knocked him down the day before, a fellow out of second of grammar. He had been thrown by the fellow's machine lightly on the cinder path and his spectacles had been broken in three pieces and some of the grit of the cinders had gone into his mouth.

That was why the fellows seemed to him smaller and farther away and the goalposts so thin and far and the soft grey sky so high up. But there was no play on the football grounds for cricket was coming: and some said that Barnes would be prof[78] and some said it would be Flowers. And all over the playgrounds they were playing rounders and bowling twisters and lobs.[79] And from here and from there came the sounds of the cricket bats through the soft grey air. They said: pick, pack, pock, puck: little drops of water in a fountain slowly falling in the brimming bowl.

Athy, who had been silent, said quietly:

– You are all wrong.

All turned towards him eagerly.

– Why?

– Do you know?

– Who told you?

– Tell us, Athy.

Athy pointed across the playground to where Simon Moonan was walking by himself kicking a stone before him.

– Ask him, he said.

The fellows looked there and then said:

– Why him?

– Is he in it?

Athy lowered his voice and said:

– Do you know why those fellows scut? I will tell you but you must not let on you know.

– Tell us, Athy. Go on. You might if you know.

He paused for a moment and then said mysteriously:

– They were caught with Simon Moonan and Tusker Boyle in the square one night.

The fellows looked at him and asked:

– Caught?

– What doing?

Athy said:

– Smugging.[80]

All the fellows were silent: and Athy said:

– And that's why.

Stephen looked at the faces of the fellows but they were all looking across the playground. He wanted to ask somebody about it. What did that mean about the smugging in the square? Why did the five fellows out of the higher line run away for that? It was a joke, he thought. Simon Moonan had nice clothes and one night he had shown him a ball of creamy sweets that the fellows of the football fifteen had rolled down to him along the carpet in the middle of the refectory when he was at the door. It was the night of the match against the Bective Rangers;[81] and the ball was made just like a red and green apple only it opened and it was full of the creamy sweets. And one day Boyle had said that an elephant had two tuskers instead of two tusks and that was why he was called Tusker Boyle but some fellows called him Lady Boyle because he was always at his nails, paring them.

Eileen had long thin cool white hands too because she was a girl. They were like ivory; only soft. That was the meaning of *Tower of Ivory* but protestants could not understand it and made fun of it. One day he had stood beside her looking into the hotel grounds. A waiter was running up a trail of bunting on the flagstaff and a fox terrier was scampering to and fro on the sunny lawn. She had put her hand into his pocket where his hand was and he had felt how cool and thin and soft her hand was. She had said that pockets were funny things to have: and then all of a sudden she had broken away and had run laughing down the sloping curve of the path. Her fair hair had streamed out behind her like gold in the sun. *Tower of Ivory. House of Gold.* By thinking of things you could understand them.

But why in the square? You went there when you wanted to do something. It was all thick slabs of slate and water trickled all day out of tiny pinholes and there was a queer smell of stale water there. And behind the door of one of the closets there was a drawing in red pencil of a bearded man in a Roman dress with a brick in each hand and underneath was the name of the drawing:

Balbus was building a wall.[82]

Some fellow had drawn it there for a cod. It had a funny face but it was very like a man with a beard. And on the wall of another closet there was written in backhand in beautiful writing:

Julius Caesar wrote The Calico Belly[83]

Perhaps that was why they were there because it was a place where some fellows wrote things for cod. But all the same it was queer what Athy said and the way he said it. It was not a cod because they had run away. He looked with others across the playground and began to feel afraid.

At last Fleming said:

– And we are all to be punished for what other fellows did?

– I won't come back, see if I do, Cecil Thunder said. Three days' silence in the refectory and sending us up for six and eight every minute.[84]

– Yes, said Wells. And old Barrett has a new way of twisting the note so that you can't open it and fold it again to see how many ferulae[85] you are to get. I won't come back too.

– Yes, said Cecil Thunder, and the prefect of studies was in second of grammar this morning.

– Let us get up a rebellion, Fleming said. Will we?

All the fellows were silent. The air was very silent and you could hear the cricket bats but more slowly than before: pick, pock.

Wells asked:

– What is going to be done to them?

– Simon Moonan and Tusker are going to be flogged, Athy said, and the fellows in the higher line got their choice of flogging or being expelled.

– And which are they taking? asked the fellow who had spoke first.

– All are taking expulsion except Corrigan, Athy answered. He's going to be flogged by Mr Gleeson.

– I know why, Cecil Thunder said. He is right and the other fellows are wrong because a flogging wears off after a bit but a fellow that has been expelled from college is known all his life on account of it. Besides Gleeson won't flog him hard.

– It's best of his play not to, Fleming said.

– I wouldn't like to be Simon Moonan and Tusker Cecil Thunder said. But I don't believe they will be flogged. Perhaps they will be sent up for twice nine.[86]

– No, no, said Athy. They'll both get it on the vital spot.

Wells rubbed himself and said in a crying voice:

– Please, sir, let me off!

Athy grinned and turned up the sleeves of his jacket, saying:

> It can't be helped;
> It must be done.
> So down with your breeches
> And out with your bum.

The fellows laughed; but he felt that they were a little afraid. In the silence of the soft grey air he heard the cricket bats from here and from there: pock. That was a sound to hear but if you were hit then you would feel a pain. The pandybat made a sound too but not like that. The fellows said it was made of whalebone and leather with lead inside: and he wondered what was the pain like. There were different kinds of sounds. A long thin cane would have a high whistling sound and he wondered what was that pain like. It made him shivery to think of it and cold: and what Athy said too. But what was there to laugh at in it? It made him shivery: but that was because you always felt like a shiver when you let down your trousers. It was the same in the bath when you undressed yourself. He wondered who had to let them down, the master or the boy himself. O how could they laugh about it that way?

He looked at Athy's rolled-up sleeves and knuckly inky hands. He had rolled up his sleeves to show how Mr Gleeson would roll up his sleeves. But Mr Gleeson had round shiny cuffs and clean white wrists and fattish white hands and the nails of them were long and pointed. Perhaps he pared them too like Lady Boyle. But they were terribly long and pointed nails. So long and cruel they were, though the white fattish hands were not cruel but gentle. And though he trembled with cold and fright to think of the cruel long nails and of the high whistling sound of the cane and of the chill you felt at the end of your shirt when you undressed yourself yet he felt a feeling of queer quiet pleasure inside him to think of the white fattish hands, clean and strong and gentle. And he thought of what Cecil Thunder had said: that Mr Gleeson would not flog Corrigan hard. And Fleming had said he would not because it was best of his play not to. But that was not why.

A voice from far out on the playground cried:

– All in!

And other voices cried:

– All in! All in!

During the writing lesson he sat with his arms folded, listening to the slow scraping of the pens. Mr Harford went to and fro making little signs in red pencil and sometimes sitting beside the boy to show him how to hold his pen. He had tried to spell out the headline for himself though he knew already what it was for it was the last of the book. *Zeal without prudence is like a ship adrift.* But the lines of the letters were like fine invisible threads and it was only by closing his right eye tight and staring out of the left eye that he could make out the full curves of the capital.

But Mr Harford was very decent and never got into a wax. All the other masters got into dreadful waxes. But why were they to suffer for what fellows in the higher line did? Wells had said that they had drunk some of the altar wine out of the press the sacristy and that it had been found out who had done it by the smell. Perhaps they had stolen a monstrance[87] to run away with and sell it somewhere. That must have been a terrible sin, to go in there quietly at night, to open the dark press and steal the flashing gold thing into which God was put on the altar in the middle of flowers and candles at benediction while the incense went up in clouds at both sides as the fellow swung the censer and Dominic Kelly sang the first part by himself in the choir. But God was not in it of course when they stole it. But still it was a strange and a great sin even to touch it. He thought of it with deep awe; a terrible and strange sin: it thrilled him to think of it in the silence when the pens scraped lightly. But to drink the altar wine out of the press and be found out by the smell was a sin too: but it was not terrible and strange. It only made you feel a little sickish on account of the smell of the wine. Because on the day when he had made his first holy communion in the chapel he had shut his eyes and opened his mouth and put out his tongue a little: and when the rector had stooped down to give him the holy communion he had smelt a faint winy smell off the rector's breath after the wine of the mass. The word was beautiful: wine. It made you think of dark purple because the grapes were dark purple that grew in Greece outside houses like white temples. But the faint smell of the rector's breath had made him feel a sick feeling on the morning of his first communion. The day of your first communion was the happiest day of your life. And once a lot of generals had asked Napoleon what was the happiest day of his life. They thought he would say the day he won some great battle or the day he was made an emperor. But he said:

– Gentlemen, the happiest day of my life was the day on which I made my first holy communion.

Father Arnall came in and the Latin lesson began and he remained still, leaning on the desk with his arms folded. Father Arnall gave out the theme-books and he said that they were scandalous and that they were all to be written out again with the corrections at once. But the worst of all was Fleming's theme because the pages were stuck together by a blot: and Father Arnall held it up by a corner and said it was an insult to any master to send him up such a theme. Then he asked Jack Lawton to decline the noun *mare*[88] and Jack Lawton stopped at the ablative singular and could not go on with the plural.

– You should be ashamed of yourself, said Father Arnall sternly. You, the leader of the class!

Then he asked the next boy and the next and the next. Nobody knew. Father Arnall became very quiet, more and more quiet as each boy tried to answer it and could not. But his face was black-looking and his eyes were staring though his voice was so quiet. Then he asked Fleming and Fleming said that the word had no plural. Father Arnall suddenly shut the book and shouted at him:

– Kneel out there in the middle of the class. You are one of the idlest boys I ever met. Copy out your themes again the rest of you.

Fleming moved heavily out of his place and knelt between the two last benches. The other boys bent over their theme-books and began to write. A silence filled the classroom and Stephen, glancing timidly at Father Arnall's dark face, saw that it was a little red from the wax he was in.

Was that a sin for Father Arnall to be in a wax or was he allowed to get into a wax when the boys were idle because that made them study better or was he only letting on to be in a wax? It was because he was allowed, because a priest would know what a sin was and would not do it. But if he did it one time by mistake what would he do to go to confession? Perhaps he would go to confession to the minister. And if the minister did it he would go to the rector: and the rector to the provincial: and the provincial to the general[89] of the jesuits. That was called the order: and he had heard his father say that they were all clever men. They could all have become high-up people in the world if they had not become jesuits. And he wondered what Father Arnall and Paddy Barrett would have become and what Mr McGlade and Mr Gleeson would have become if they had not become jesuits. It was hard to think what because you would have to think of them in a different way with different coloured coats and trousers and with beards and moustaches and different kinds of hats.

The door opened quietly and closed. A quick whisper ran through the class: the prefect of studies. There was an instant of dead silence and then the loud crack of a pandybat on the last desk. Stephen's heart leapt up in fear.

– Any boys want flogging here, Father Arnall? cried the prefect of studies. Any lazy idle loafers that want flogging in this class?

He came to the middle of the class and saw Fleming on his knees.

– Hoho! he cried. Who is this boy? Why is he on his knees? What is your name, boy?

– Fleming, sir.

– Hoho, Fleming! An idler of course. I can see it in your eye. Why is he on his knees, Father Arnall?

– He wrote a bad Latin theme, Father Arnall said, and he missed all the questions in grammar.

– Of course he did! cried the prefect of studies, of course he did! A born idler! I can see it in the corner of his eye.

He banged his pandybat down on the desk and cried:

– Up, Fleming! Up, my boy!

Fleming stood up slowly.

– Hold out! cried the prefect of studies.

Fleming held out his hand. The pandybat came down on it with a loud smacking sound: one, two, three, four, five, six.

– Other hand!

The pandybat came down again in six loud quick smacks.

– Kneel down! cried the prefect of studies.

Fleming knelt down, squeezing his hands under his armpits, his face contorted with pain; but Stephen knew how hard his hands were because Fleming was always rubbing rosin into them. But perhaps he was in great pain for the noise of the pandybat was terrible. Stephen's heart was beating and fluttering.

– At your work, all of you! shouted the prefect of studies. We want no lazy idle loafers here, lazy idle little schemers. At your work, I tell you. Father Dolan will be in to see you every day. Father Dolan will be in tomorrow.

He poked one of the boys in the side with his pandybat, saying:

– You, boy! When will Father Dolan be in again?

– Tomorrow, sir, said Tom Furlong's voice.

– Tomorrow and tomorrow and tomorrow,[90] said the prefect of studies. Make up your minds for that. Every day Father Dolan. Write away. You, boy, who are you?

Stephen's heart jumped suddenly.

– Dedalus, sir.

– Why are you not writing like the others?

– I . . . my . . .

He could not speak with fright.

– Why is he not writing, Father Arnall?

– He broke his glasses, said Father Arnall, and I exempted him from work.

– Broke? What is this I hear? What is this your name is! said the prefect of studies.

– Dedalus, sir.

– Out here, Dedalus. Lazy little schemer. I see schemer in your face. Where did you break your glasses?

Stephen stumbled into the middle of the class, blinded by fear and haste.

– Where did you break your glasses? repeated the prefect of studies.

– The cinder-path, sir.

– Hoho! The cinder-path! cried the prefect of studies. I know that trick.

Stephen lifted his eyes in wonder and saw for a moment Father Dolan's white-grey not young face, his baldy white-grey head with fluff at the sides of it, the steel rims of his spectacles and his no-coloured eyes looking through the glasses. Why did he say he knew that trick?

– Lazy idle little loafer! cried the prefect of studies. Broke my glasses! An old schoolboy trick! Out with your hand this moment!

Stephen closed his eyes and held out in the air his trembling hand with the palm upwards. He felt the prefect of studies touch it for a moment at the fingers to straighten it and then the swish of the sleeve of the soutane as the pandybat was lifted to strike. A hot burning stinging tingling blow like the loud crack of a broken stick made his trembling hand crumple together like a leaf in the fire: and at the sound and the pain scalding tears were driven into his eyes. His whole body was shaking with fright, his arm was shaking and his crumpled burning livid hand shook like a loose leaf in the air. A cry sprang to his lips, a prayer to be let off. But though the tears scalded his eyes and his limbs quivered with pain and fright he held back the hot tears and the cry that scalded his throat.

– Other hand! shouted the prefect of studies.

Stephen drew back his maimed and quivering right arm and held out his left hand. The soutane sleeve swished again as the pandybat was lifted and a loud crashing sound and a fierce maddening tingling burning pain made his hand shrink together with the palms and fingers in a livid quivering mass. The scalding water burst forth from his eyes and, burning with shame and agony and fear, he drew back his shaking arm in terror and burst out into a whine of pain. His body shook with a palsy of fright and in shame and rage he felt the scalding cry come from his throat and the scalding tears falling out of his eyes and down his flaming cheeks.

– Kneel down, cried the prefect of studies.

Stephen knelt down quickly pressing his beaten hands to his sides. To think of them beaten and swollen with pain all in a moment made him feel so sorry for them as if they were not his own but someone else's that he felt sorry for. And as he knelt, calming the last sobs in his throat and feeling the burning tingling pain pressed into his sides, he thought of the hands which he had held out in the air with the palms up and of the firm touch of the prefect of studies when he had steadied the shaking fingers and of the beaten swollen reddened mass of palm and fingers that shook helplessly in the air.

– Get at your work, all of you, cried the prefect of studies from the door. Father Dolan will be in every day to see if any boy, any lazy idle little loafer wants flogging. Every day. Every day.

The door closed behind him.

The hushed class continued to copy out the themes. Father Arnall rose from his seat and went among them, helping the boys with gentle words and telling them the mistakes they had made. His voice was very gentle and soft. Then he returned to his seat and said to Fleming and Stephen:

– You may return to your places, you two.

Fleming and Stephen rose and, walking to their seats, sat down. Stephen, scarlet with shame, opened a book quickly with one weak hand and bent down upon it, his face close to the page.

It was unfair and cruel because the doctor had told him not to read without glasses and he had written home to his father that morning to send him a new pair. And Father Arnall had said that he need not study till the new glasses came. Then to be called a schemer before the class and to be pandied when he always got the card for first or second and was the leader of the Yorkists! How could the prefect of studies know that it was a trick? He felt the touch of the prefect's fingers as they had steadied his hand and at first he had thought he was going to shake hands with him because the fingers were soft and firm: but then in an instant he had heard the swish of the soutane sleeve and the crash. It was cruel and unfair to make him kneel in the middle of the class then: and Father Arnall had told them both that they might return to their places without making any difference between them. He listened to Father Arnall's low and gentle voice as he corrected the themes. Perhaps he was sorry now and wanted to be decent. But it was unfair and cruel. The prefect of studies was a priest but that was cruel and unfair. And his white-grey face and the no-coloured eyes behind the steel-rimmed spectacles were cruel looking because he had steadied the hand first with his firm soft fingers and that was to hit it better and louder.

– It's a stinking mean thing, that's what it is, said Fleming in the corridor as the classes were passing out in file to the refectory, to pandy a fellow for what is not his fault.

– You really broke your glasses by accident, didn't you? Nasty Roche asked.

Stephen felt his heart filled by Fleming's words and did not answer.

– Of course he did! said Fleming. I wouldn't stand it. I'd go up and tell the rector on him.

– Yes, said Cecil Thunder eagerly, and I saw him lift the pandybat over his shoulder and he's not allowed to do that.

– Did they hurt you much? Nasty Roche asked.

– Very much, Stephen said.

– I wouldn't stand it, Fleming repeated, from Baldyhead or any other Baldyhead. It's a stinking mean low trick, that's what it is. I'd go straight up to the rector and tell him about it after dinner.

– Yes, do. Yes, do, said Cecil Thunder.

– Yes, do. Yes, go up and tell the rector on him, Dedalus, said Nasty Roche, because he said that he'd come in tomorrow again and pandy you.

– Yes, yes. Tell the rector, all said.

And there were some fellows out of second of grammar listening and one of them said:

– The senate and the Roman people[91] declared that Dedalus had been wrongly punished.

It was wrong; it was unfair and cruel; and, as he sat in the refectory, he suffered time after time in memory the same humiliation until he began to wonder whether it might not really be that there was something in his face which made him look like a schemer and he wished he had a little mirror to see. But there could not be; and it was unjust and cruel and unfair.

He could not eat the blackish fish fritters they got on Wednesdays in lent and one of his potatoes had the mark of the spade in it. Yes, he would do what the fellows had told him. He would go up and tell the rector that he had been wrongly punished. A thing like that had been done before by somebody in history, by some great person whose head was in the books of history And the rector would declare that he had been wrongly punished because the senate and the Roman people always declared that the men who did that had been wrongly punished. Those were the great men whose names were in Richmal Magnall's Questions.[92] History was all about those men and what they did and that was what Peter Parley's Tales about Greece and Rome[93] were all about. Peter Parley himself was on the first page in a picture. There was a road over a heath with grass at the side and little bushes: and Peter Parley had a broad hat like a protestant minister and a big stick and he was walking fast along the road to Greece and Rome.

It was easy what he had to do. All he had to do was when the dinner was over and he came out in his turn to go on walking but not out to the corridor but up the staircase on the right that led to the castle. He had nothing to do but that: to turn to the right and walk fast up the staircase and in half a minute he would be in the low dark narrow corridor that led through the castle to the rector's room. And every fellow had said that it was unfair, even the fellow out of second of grammar who had said that about the senate and the Roman people.

What would happen?

He heard the fellows of the higher line stand up at the top of the refectory and heard their steps as they came down the matting: Paddy Rath and Jimmy Magee and the Spaniard and the Portuguese and the fifth was big Corrigan who was going to be flogged by Mr Gleeson. That was why the prefect of studies had called him a schemer and pandied him for nothing: and, straining his weak eyes, tired with the tears, he watched big Corrigan's broad shoulders and big hanging black head passing in the file. But he had done something and besides Mr Gleeson would not flog him hard: and he remembered how big Corrigan looked in the bath. He had skin the same colour as the turf coloured bogwater in the shallow end of the bath and when he walked along the side his feet slapped loudly on the wet tiles and at every step his thighs shook a little because he was fat.

The refectory was half empty and the fellows were still passing out in file. He could go up the staircase because there was never a priest or a prefect outside the refectory door. But he could not go. The rector would side with the prefect of studies and think it was a schoolboy trick and then the prefect of studies would come in every day the same, only it would be worse because he would be dreadfully waxy at any fellow going up to the rector about him. The fellows had told him to go but they would not go themselves. They had forgotten all about it. No, it was best to forget all about it and perhaps the prefect of studies had only said he would come in. No, it was best to hide out of the way because when you were small and young you could often escape that way.

The fellows at his table stood up. He stood up and passed out among them in the file. He had to decide. He was coming near the door. If he went on with the fellows he could never go up to the rector because he could not leave the playground for that. And if he went and was pandied all the same all the fellows would make fun and talk about young Dedalus going up to the rector to tell on the prefect of studies.

He was walking down along the matting and he saw the door before him. It was impossible: he could not. He thought of the baldy head of the prefect of studies with the cruel no-coloured eyes looking at him and he heard the voice of the prefect of studies asking him twice what his name was. Why could he not remember the name when he was told the first time? Was he not listening the first time or was it to make fun out of the name? The great men in the history had names like that and nobody made fun of them. It was his own name that he should have made fun of if he wanted to make fun. Dolan: it was like the name of a woman who washed clothes.

He had reached the door and, turning quickly up to the right, walked up the stairs and, before he could make up his mind to come back, he had entered the low dark narrow corridor that led to the castle. And as he crossed the threshold of the door of the corridor he saw, without turning his head to look, that all the fellows were looking after him as they went filing by.

He passed along the narrow dark corridor, passing little doors that were the doors of the rooms of the community. He peered in front of him and right and left through the gloom and thought that those must be portraits. It was dark and silent and his eyes were weak and tired with tears so that he could not see. But he thought they were the portraits of the saints and great men of the order who were looking down on him silently as he passed: saint Ignatius Loyola[94] holding an open book and pointing to the words *Ad Majorem Dei Gloriam*[95] in it; saint Francis Xavier pointing to his chest;[96] Lorenzo Ricci with his berretta on his head [97]like one of the prefects of the lines, the three patrons of holy youth – saint Stanislaus Kostka, saint Aloysius Gonzaga, and Blessed John Berchmans,[98] all with young faces because they died when they were young, and Father Peter Kenny[99] sitting in a chair wrapped in a big cloak.

He came out on the landing above the entrance hall and looked about him. That was where Hamilton Rowan had passed and the marks of the soldiers' slugs were there. And it was there that the old servants had seen the ghost in the white cloak of a marshal.

An old servant was sweeping at the end of the landing. He asked him where was the rector's room and the old servant pointed to the door at the far end and looked after him as he went on to it and knocked.

There was no answer. He knocked again more loudly and his heart jumped when he heard a muffled voice say:

– Come in!

He turned the handle and opened the door and fumbled for the handle of the green baize door inside. He found it and pushed it open and went in.

He saw the rector sitting at a desk writing. There was a skull on the desk[100] and a strange solemn smell in the room like the old leather of chairs.

His heart was beating fast on account of the solemn place he was in and the silence of the room: and he looked at the skull and at the rector's kind-looking face.

– Well, my little man, said the rector, what is it?

Stephen swallowed down the thing in his throat and said:

– I broke my glasses, sir.

The rector opened his mouth and said:

– O!

Then he smiled and said:

– Well, if we broke our glasses we must write home for a new pair.

– I wrote home, sir, said Stephen, and Father Arnall said I am not to study till they come.

– Quite right! said the rector.

Stephen swallowed down the thing again and tried to keep his legs and his voice from shaking.

– But, sir?

– Yes?

– Father Dolan came in today and pandied me because I was not writing my theme.

The rector looked at him in silence and he could feel the blood rising to his face and the tears about to rise to his eyes.

The rector said:

– Your name is Dedalus, isn't it?

– Yes, sir . . .

– And where did you break your glasses?

– On the cinder-path, sir. A fellow was coming out of the bicycle house and I fell and they got broken. I don't know the fellow's name.

The rector looked at him again in silence. Then he smiled and said:

– O, well, it was a mistake; I am sure Father Dolan did not know.

– But I told him I broke them, sir, and he pandied me.

– Did you tell him that you had written home for a new pair? the rector asked.

– No, sir.

– O well then, said the rector, Father Dolan did not understand. You can say that I excuse you from your lessons for a few days.

Stephen said quickly for fear his trembling would prevent him:

– Yes, sir, but Father Dolan said he will come in tomorrow to pandy me again for it.

– Very well, the rector said, it is a mistake and I shall speak to Father Dolan myself. Will that do now?

Stephen felt the tears wetting his eyes and murmured:

– O yes sir, thanks.

The rector held his hand across the side of the desk where the skull was and Stephen, placing his hand in it for a moment, felt a cool moist palm.

– Good day now, said the rector, withdrawing his hand and bowing.

– Good day, sir, said Stephen.

He bowed and walked quietly out of the room, closing the doors carefully and slowly.

But when he had passed the old servant on the landing and was again in the low narrow dark corridor he began to walk faster and faster. Faster and faster he hurried on through the gloom excitedly. He bumped his elbow against the door at the end and, hurrying down the staircase, walked quickly through the two corridors and out into the air.

He could hear the cries of the fellows on the playgrounds. He broke into a run and, running quicker and quicker, ran across the cinder-path and reached the third line playground, panting.

The fellows had seen him running. They closed round him in a ring, pushing one against another to hear.

– Tell us! Tell us!

– What did he say?

– Did you go in?

– What did he say?

– Tell us! Tell us!

He told them what he had said and what the rector had said and, when he had told them, all the fellows flung their caps spinning up into the air and cried:

– Hurroo!

They caught their caps and sent them up again spinning sky-high and cried again:

– Hurroo! Hurroo!

They made a cradle of their locked hands and hoisted him up among them and carried him along till he struggled to get free. And when he had escaped from them they broke away in all directions, flinging their caps again into the air and whistling as they went spinning up and crying:

– Hurroo!

And they gave three groans for Baldyhead Dolan and three cheers for Conmee and they said he was the decentest rector that was ever in Clongowes.

The cheers died away in the soft grey air. He was alone. He was happy and free; but he would not be anyway proud with Father Dolan. He would be very quiet and obedient: and he wished that he could do something kind for him to show him that he was not proud.

The air was soft and grey and mild and evening was coming. There was the smell of evening in the air, the smell of the fields in the country where they digged up turnips to peel them and eat them when they went out for a walk to Major Barton's,[101] the smell there was in the little wood beyond the pavilion where the gallnuts[102] were.

The fellows were practising long shies and bowling lobs and slow twisters. In the soft grey silence he could hear the bump of the balls: and from here and from there through the quiet air the sound of the cricket bats: pick, pack, pock, puck: like drops of water in a fountain falling softly in the brimming bowl.

Chapter 2

UNCLE CHARLES SMOKED such black twist[103] that at last his nephew suggested to him to enjoy his morning smoke in a little outhouse at the end of the garden.

– Very good, Simon. All serene, Simon, said the old man tranquilly. Anywhere you like. The outhouse will do me nicely: it will be more salubrious.

– Damn me, said Mr Dedalus frankly, if I know how you can smoke such villainous awful tobacco. It's like gunpowder, by God.

– It's very nice, Simon, replied the old man. Very cool and mollifying.

Every morning, therefore, uncle Charles repaired to his outhouse but not before he had greased and brushed scrupulously his back hair and brushed and put on his tall hat. While he smoked the brim of his tall hat and the bowl of his pipe were just visible beyond the jambs of the outhouse door. His arbour, as he called the reeking outhouse which he shared with the cat and the garden tools, served him also as a sounding-box: and every morning he hummed contentedly one of his favourite songs: O, *twine me a bower* or *Blue Eyes and Golden Hair* or *The Groves of Blarney*[104] while the grey and blue coils of smoke rose slowly from his pipe and vanished in the pure air.

During the first part of the summer in Blackrock[105] uncle Charles was Stephen's constant companion. Uncle Charles was a hale old man with a well tanned skin, rugged features and white side whiskers. On week days he did messages between the house in Carysfort Avenue and those shops in the main street of the town with which the family dealt. Stephen was glad to go with him on these errands for uncle Charles helped him very liberally to handfuls of whatever was exposed in open boxes and barrels outside the counter. He would seize a handful of grapes and sawdust or three or four American apples and thrust them generously into his grandnephew's hand while the shopman smiled uneasily; and, on Stephen's feigning reluctance to take them, he would frown and say:

– Take them, sir. Do you hear me, sir? They're good for your bowels.

When the order list had been booked the two would go on to the park where an old friend of Stephen's father, Mike Flynn, would be found seated on a bench, waiting for them. Then would begin

Stephen's run round the park. Mike Flynn would stand at the gate near the railway station, watch in hand, while Stephen ran round the track in the style Mike Flynn favoured, his head high lifted, his knees well lifted and his hands held straight down by his sides. When the morning practice was over the trainer would make his comments and sometimes illustrate them by shuffling along for a yard or so comically in an old pair of blue canvas shoes. A small ring of wonderstruck children and nursemaids would gather to watch him and linger even when he and uncle Charles had sat down again and were talking athletics and politics. Though he had heard his father say that Mike Flynn had put some of the best runners of modern times through his hands Stephen often glanced at his trainer's flabby stubble covered face, as it bent over the long stained fingers through which he rolled his cigarette, and with pity at the mild lustreless blue eyes which would look up suddenly from the task and gaze vaguely into the blue distance while the long swollen fingers ceased their rolling and grains and fibres of tobacco fell back into the pouch.

On the way home uncle Charles would often pay a visit to the chapel and, as the font was above Stephen's reach, the old man would dip his hand and then sprinkle the water briskly about Stephen's clothes and on the floor of the porch.[106] While he prayed he knelt on his red handkerchief and read above his breath from a thumb blackened prayer book wherein catchwords were printed at the foot of every page. Stephen knelt at his side respecting, though he did not share, his piety. He often wondered what his grand-uncle prayed for so seriously. Perhaps he prayed for the souls in purgatory or for the grace of a happy death or perhaps he prayed that God might send him back a part of the big fortune he had squandered in Cork.[107]

On Sundays Stephen with his father and his grand-uncle took their constitutional. The old man was a nimble walker in spite of his corns and often ten or twelve miles of the road were covered. The little village of Stillorgan was the parting of the ways. Either they went to the left towards the Dublin mountains or along the Goatstown road and thence into Dundrum, coming home by Sandyford.[108] Trudging along the road or standing in some grimy wayside public house his elders spoke constantly of the subjects nearer their hearts, of Irish politics, of Munster[109] and of the legends of their own family, to all of which Stephen lent an avid ear. Words which he did not understand he said over and over to himself till he had learnt them by heart: and through them he had glimpses of the real world about them. The hour when he too would take part in the life of that world seemed drawing near and in secret he began to make ready for the great part which he felt awaited him the nature of which he only dimly apprehended.

His evenings were his own; and he pored over a ragged translation of *The Count of Monte Cristo*.[110] The figure of that dark avenger stood forth in his mind for whatever he had heard or divined in childhood of the strange and terrible. At night he built up on the parlour table an image of the wonderful island cave[111] out of transfers and paper flowers and coloured tissue paper and strips of the silver and golden paper in which chocolate is wrapped. When he had broken up this scenery, weary of its tinsel, there would come to his mind the bright picture of Marseille, of sunny trellises, and of Mercedes.[112]

Outside Blackrock, on the road that led to the mountains, stood a small whitewashed house in the garden of which grew many rosebushes: and in this house, he told himself, another Mercedes lived. Both on the outward and on the homeward journey he measured distance by this landmark: and in his imagination he lived through a long train of adventures, marvellous as those in the book itself, towards the close of which there appeared an image of himself, grown older and sadder, standing in a moonlit garden with Mercedes who had so many years before slighted his love, and with a sadly proud gesture of refusal, saying:

– Madam, I never eat muscatel grapes.[113]

He became the ally of a boy named Aubrey Mills and founded with him a gang of adventurers in the avenue. Aubrey carried a whistle dangling from his buttonhole and a bicycle lamp attached to his belt while the others had short sticks thrust daggerwise through theirs. Stephen, who had read of Napoleon's plain style of dress, chose to remain unadorned and thereby heightened for himself the pleasure of taking counsel with his lieutenant before giving orders. The gang made forays into the gardens of old maids or went down to the castle[114] and fought a battle on the shaggy weed-grown rocks, coming home after it weary stragglers with the stale odours of the foreshore in their nostrils and the rank oils of the seawrack[115] upon their hands and in their hair.

Aubrey and Stephen had a common milkman and often they drove out in the milk-car to Carrickmines where the cows were at grass. While the men were milking the boys would take turns in riding the tractable mare round the field. But when autumn came the cows were driven home from the grass: and the first sight of the filthy cowyard at Stradbrook[116] with its foul green puddles and clots of liquid dung and steaming bran troughs, sickened Stephen's heart. The cattle which had seemed so beautiful in the country on sunny days revolted him and he could not even look at the milk they yielded.

The coming of September did not trouble him this year for he was not to be sent back to Clongowes. The practice in the park came to an end when Mike Flynn went into hospital. Aubrey was at school and had only an hour or two free in the evening. The gang fell asunder and there were no more nightly forays or battles on the rocks. Stephen sometimes went round with the car which delivered the evening milk and these chilly drives blew away his memory of the filth of the cowyard and he felt no repugnance at seeing the cow hairs and hayseeds on the milkman's coat. Whenever the car drew up before a house he waited to catch a glimpse of a well scrubbed kitchen or of a softly lighted hall and to see how the servant would hold the jug and how she would close the door. He thought it should be a pleasant life enough, driving along the roads every evening to deliver milk, if he had warm gloves and a fat bag of gingernuts in his pocket to eat from. But the same foreknowledge which had sickened his heart and made his legs sag suddenly as he raced round the park, the same intuition which had made him glance with mistrust at his trainer's flabby stubble-covered face as it bent heavily over his long stained fingers, dissipated any vision of the future. In a vague way he understood that his father was in trouble and that this was the reason why he himself had not been sent back to Clongowes. For some time he had felt the slight change in his house; and those changes in what he had deemed unchangeable were so many slight shocks to his boyish conception of the world. The ambition which he felt astir at times in the darkness of his soul sought no outlet. A dusk like that of the outer world obscured his mind as he heard the mare's hoofs clattering along the tramtrack on the Rock Road and the great can swaying and rattling behind him.

He returned to Mercedes and, as he brooded upon her image, a strange unrest crept into his blood. Sometimes a fever gathered within him and led him to rove alone in the evening along the quiet avenue. The peace of the gardens and the kindly lights in the windows poured a tender influence into his restless heart. The noise of children at play annoyed him and their silly voices made him feel, even more keenly than he had felt at Clongowes, that he was different from others. He did not want to play. He wanted to meet in the real world the unsubstantial image which his soul so constantly beheld. He did not know where to seek it or how, but a premonition which led him on told him that this image would, without any overt act of his, encounter him. They would meet quietly as if they had known each other and had made their tryst, perhaps at one of the gates or in some more secret place. They would be alone, surrounded by darkness and silence: and in that moment of supreme tenderness he would be transfigured. He would fade into something impalpable under her eyes and then in a moment he would be transfigured. Weakness and timidity and inexperience would fall from him in that magic moment.

Two great yellow caravans had halted one morning before the door and men had come tramping into the house to dismantle it. The furniture had been hustled out through the front garden which was strewn with wisps of straw and rope ends and into the huge vans at the gate. When all had been safely stowed the vans had set off noisily down the avenue: and from the window of the railway carriage, in which he had sat with his red-eyed mother, Stephen had seen them lumbering along the Merrion Road.[117]

The parlour fire would not draw that evening and Mr Dedalus rested the poker against the bars of the grate to attract the flame. Uncle Charles dozed in a corner of the half furnished uncarpeted room and near him the family portraits leaned against the wall. The lamp on the table shed a weak light over the boarded floor, muddied by the feet of the van-men. Stephen sat on a footstool beside his father listening to a long and incoherent monologue. He understood little or nothing of it at first but he became slowly aware that his father had enemies and that some fight was going to take place. He felt, too, that he was being enlisted for the fight, that some duty was being laid upon his shoulders. The sudden flight from the comfort and revery of Blackrock, the passage through the gloomy foggy city, the thought of the bare cheerless house in which they were now to live made his heart heavy, and again an intuition, a foreknowledge of the future came to him. He understood also why the servants had often whispered together in the hall and why his father had often stood on the hearthrug with his back to the fire, talking loudly to uncle Charles who urged him to sit down and eat his dinner.

– There's a crack of the whip left in me yet, Stephen, old chap, said Mr Dedalus, poking at the dull fire with fierce energy. We're not dead yet, sonny. No, by the Lord Jesus (God forgive me) not half dead.

Dublin was a new and complex sensation. Uncle Charles had grown so witless that he could no longer be sent out on errands and the disorder in settling in the new house left Stephen freer than he had been in Blackrock. In the beginning he contented himself with circling timidly round the neighbouring square or, at most, going half way down one of the side streets but when he had made a skeleton map of the city in his mind he followed boldly one of its central lines until he reached the custom-house.[118] He passed unchallenged among the docks and along the quays wondering at the multitude of corks that lay bobbing on the surface of the water in a thick yellow scum, at the crowds of quay porters and the rumbling carts and the ill-dressed bearded policeman. The vastness and strangeness of the life suggested to him by the bales of merchandise stocked along the walls or swung aloft out of the holds of steamers wakened again in him the unrest which had sent him wandering in the evening from garden to garden in search of Mercedes. And amid this new bustling life he might have fancied himself in another Marseille but that he missed the bright sky and the sun-warmed trellises of the wineshops. A vague dissatisfaction grew up within him as he looked on the quays and on the river and on the lowering skies and yet he continued to wander up and down day after day as if he really sought someone that eluded him.

He went once or twice with his mother to visit their relatives: and though they passed a jovial array of shops lit up and adorned for Christmas his mood of embittered silence did not leave him. The causes of his embitterment were many, remote and near. He was angry with himself for being young and the prey of restless foolish impulses, angry also with the change of fortune which was reshaping the world about him into a vision of squalor and insincerity. Yet his anger lent nothing to the vision. He chronicled with patience what he saw, detaching himself from it and tasting its mortifying flavour in secret.

He was sitting on the backless chair in his aunt's kitchen. A lamp with a reflector hung on the japanned wall of the fireplace and by its light his aunt was reading the evening paper that lay on her knees. She looked a long time at a smiling picture that was set in it and said musingly:

– The beautiful Mabel Hunter![119]

A ringletted girl stood on tiptoe to peer at the picture and said softly:

– What is she in, mud?

– In a pantomime, love.

The child leaned her ringletted head against her mother's sleeve, gazing on the picture, and murmured as if fascinated:

– The beautiful Mabel Hunter!

As if fascinated, her eyes rested long upon those demurely taunting eyes and she murmured devotedly:

– Isn't she an exquisite creature?

And the boy who came in from the street, stamping crookedly under his stone of coal, heard her words. He dropped his load promptly on the floor and hurried to her side to see. He mauled the edges of the paper with his reddened and blackened hands, shouldering her aside and complaining that he could not see.

He was sitting in the narrow breakfast room high up in the old dark-windowed house. The firelight flickered on the wall and beyond the window a spectral dusk was gathering upon the river. Before the fire an old woman was busy making tea and, as she bustled at the task, she told in a low voice of what the priest and the doctor had said. She told too of certain changes they had seen in her of late and of her odd ways and sayings. He sat listening to the words and following the ways of adventure that lay open in the coals, arches and vaults and winding galleries and jagged caverns.

Suddenly he became aware of something in the doorway. A skull appeared suspended in the gloom of the doorway. A feeble creature like a monkey was there, drawn thither by the sound of voices at the fire. A whining voice came from the door asking:

– Is that Josephine?

The old bustling woman answered cheerily from the fireplace:

– No, Ellen, it's Stephen.

– O . . . O, good evening, Stephen.

He answered the greeting and saw a silly smile break over the face in the doorway.

– Do you want anything, Ellen? asked the old woman at the fire.

But she did not answer the question and said:

– I thought it was Josephine. I thought you were Josephine, Stephen.

And, repeating this several times, she fell to laughing feebly.

He was sitting in the midst of a children's party at Harold's Cross.[120] His silent watchful manner had grown upon him and he took little part in the games. The children, wearing the spoils of their crackers, danced and romped noisily and, though he tried to share their merriment, he felt himself a gloomy figure amid the gay cocked hats and sunbonnets.

But when he had sung his song and withdrawn into a snug corner of the room he began to taste the joy of his loneliness. The mirth, which in the beginning of the evening had seemed to him false and trivial, was like a soothing air to him, passing gaily by his senses, hiding from other eyes the feverish agitation of his blood while through the circling of the dancers and amid the music and laughter her glance travelled to his corner, flattering, taunting, searching, exciting his heart.

In the hall the children who had stayed latest were putting on their things: the party was over. She had thrown a shawl about her and, as they went together towards the tram, sprays of her fresh warm breath flew gaily above her cowled head and her shoes tapped blithely on the glassy road.

It was the last tram. The lank brown horses knew it and shook their bells to the clear night in admonition. The conductor talked with the driver, both nodding often in the green light of the lamp. On the empty seats of the tram were scattered a few coloured tickets. No sound of footsteps came up or down the road. No sound broke the peace of the night save when the lank brown horses rubbed their noses together and shook their bells.

They seemed to listen, he on the upper step and she on the lower. She came up to his step many times and went down to hers again between their phrases and once or twice stood close beside him for some moments on the upper step, forgetting to go down, and then went down. His heart danced upon her movements like a cork upon a tide. He heard what her eyes said to him from beneath their cowl and knew that in some dim past, whether in life or revery, he had heard their tale before. He saw her urge her vanities, her fine dress and sash and long black stocking, and knew that he had yielded to them a thousand times. Yet a voice within him spoke above the noise of his dancing heart, asking him would he take her gift to which he had only to stretch out his hand. And he remembered the day when he and Eileen had stood looking into the hotel grounds, watching the waiters running up a trail of bunting on the flagstaff and the fox terrier scampering to and fro on the sunny lawn and how, all of a sudden, she had broken out into a peal of laughter and had run down the sloping curve of the path. Now, as then, he stood listlessly in his place, seemingly a tranquil watcher of the scene before him.

– She too wants me to catch hold of her, he thought. That's why she came with me to the tram. I could easily catch hold of her when she comes up to my step: nobody is looking. I could hold her and kiss her.

But he did neither: and, when he was sitting alone in the deserted tram, he tore his ticket into shreds and stared gloomily at the corrugated footboard.

The next day he sat at his table in the bare upper room for many hours. Before him lay a new pen, a new bottle of ink and a new emerald exercise. From force of habit he had written at the top of the first page the initial letters of the jesuit motto: A.M.D.G.[121] On the first line of the page appeared the title of the verses he was trying to write: To E— C—.[122] He knew it was right to begin so for he had seen similar titles in the collected poems of Lord Byron.[123] When he had written this title and drawn an ornamental line underneath he fell into a daydream and began to draw diagrams on the cover of the book. He saw himself sitting at his table in Bray the morning after the discussion at the Christmas dinner table, trying to write a poem about Parnell on the back of one of his father's second moiety notices.[124] But his brain had then refused to grapple with the theme and, desisting, he had covered the page with the names and addresses of certain of his classmates:

> Roderick Kickham
> John Lawton
> Anthony MacSwiney
> Simon Moonan

Now it seemed as if he would fail again but, by dint of brooding on the incident, he thought himself into confidence. During this process all those elements which he deemed common and insignificant fell out of the scene. There remained no trace of the tram itself nor of the tram-men nor of the horses: nor did he and she appear vividly. The verses told only of the night and the balmy breeze and the maiden lustre of the moon. Some undefined sorrow was hidden in the hearts of the protagonists as they stood in silence beneath the leafless trees and when the moment of farewell had come the kiss, which had been withheld by one, was given by both. After this the letters L. D. S.[125] were written at the foot of the page, and, having hidden the book, he went into his mother's bedroom and gazed at his face for a long time in the mirror of her dressing-table.

But his long spell of leisure and liberty was drawing to its end. One evening his father came home full of news which kept his tongue busy all through dinner. Stephen had been awaiting his father's return for there had been mutton hash that day and he knew that his father would make him dip his bread in the gravy. But he did not relish the hash for the mention of Clongowes had coated his palate with a scum of disgust.

– I walked bang into him, said Mr Dedalus for the fourth time, just at the corner of the square.

– Then I suppose, said Mrs Dedalus, he will be able to arrange it. I mean about Belvedere.[126]

– Of course he will, said Mr Dedalus. Don't I tell you he's provincial of the order now?

– I never liked the idea of sending him to the Christian brothers[127] myself, said Mrs Dedalus.

– Christian brothers be damned! said Mr Dedalus. Is it with Paddy

Stink and Micky Mud? No, let him stick to the jesuits in God's name since he began with them. They'll be of service to him in after years. Those are the fellows that can get you a position.

– And they're a very rich order, aren't they, Simon?

– Rather. They live well, I tell you. You saw their table at Clongowes. Fed up, by God, like gamecocks.

Mr Dedalus pushed his plate over to Stephen and bade him finish what was on it.

– Now then, Stephen, he said, you must put your shoulder to the wheel, old chap. You've had a fine long holiday.

– O, I'm sure he'll work very hard now, said Mrs Dedalus, especially when he has Maurice with him.

– O, Holy Paul, I forgot about Maurice, said Mr Dedalus. Here, Maurice! Come here, you thick-headed ruffian! Do you know I'm going to send you to a college where they'll teach you to spell c.a.t. cat. And I'll buy you a nice little penny handkerchief to keep your nose dry. Won't that be grand fun?

Maurice grinned at his father and then at his brother.

Mr Dedalus screwed his glass into his eye and stared hard at both his sons. Stephen mumbled his bread without answering his father's gaze.

– By the bye, said Mr Dedalus at length, the rector, or provincial rather, was telling me that story about you and Father Dolan. You're an impudent thief, he said.

– O, he didn't, Simon!

– Not he! said Mr Dedalus. But he gave me a great account of the whole affair. We were chatting, you know, and one word borrowed another. And, by the way, who do you think he told me will get that job in the corporation?[128] But I'll tell you that after. Well, as I was saying, we were chatting away quite friendly and he asked me did our friend here wear glasses still, and then he told me the whole story.

– And was he annoyed, Simon?

– Annoyed? Not he! *Manly little chap!* he said.

Mr Dedalus imitated the mincing nasal tone of the provincial.

Father Dolan and I, when I told them all at dinner about it, Father Dolan and I had a great laugh over it. *You better mind yourself, Father Dolan*, said I, *or young Dedalus will send you up for twice nine*. We had a famous laugh together over it. Ha! Ha! Ha!

Mr Dedalus turned to his wife and interjected in his natural voice:

– Shows you the spirit in which they take the boys there. O, a jesuit for your life, for diplomacy!

He reassumed the provincial's voice and repeated:

– I told them all at dinner about it and Father Dolan and I and all of us we had a hearty laugh together over it. Ha! Ha! Ha!

The night of the Whitsuntide[129] play had come and Stephen from the window of the dressing-room looked out on the small grass-plot across which lines of Chinese lanterns were stretched. He watched the visitors come down the steps from the house and pass into the theatre. Stewards in evening dress, old Belvedereans, loitered in groups about the entrance to the theatre and ushered in the visitors with ceremony. Under the sudden glow of a lantern he could recognize the smiling face of a priest.

The Blessed Sacrament had been removed[130] from the tabernacle and the first benches had been driven back so as to leave the dais of the altar and the space before it free. Against the walls stood companies of barbells and Indian clubs;[131] the dumbbells were piled in one corner: and in the midst of countless hillocks of gymnasium shoes and sweaters and singlets in untidy brown parcels there stood the stout leather-jacketed vaulting horse waiting its turn to be carried up on the stage and set in the middle of the winning team at the end of the gymnastic display.

Stephen, though in deference to his reputation for essay writing he had been elected secretary to the gymnasium, had had no part in the first section of the programme but in the play which formed the second section he had the chief part, that of a farcical pedagogue. He had been cast for it on account of his stature and grave manners for he was now at the end of his second year at Belvedere and in number two.

A score of the younger boys in white knickers and singlets came pattering down from the stage, through the vestry and into the chapel. The vestry and chapel were peopled with eager masters and boys. The plump bald sergeant major was testing with his foot the springboard of the vaulting horse. The lean young man in a long overcoat, who was to give a special display of intricate club swinging, stood near watching with interest, his silver-coated clubs peeping out of his deep sidepockets. The hollow rattle of the wooden dumbbells was heard as another team made ready to go up on the stage: and in another moment the excited prefect was hustling the boys through the vestry like a flock of geese, flapping the wings of his soutane nervously and crying to the laggards to make haste. A little troop of Neapolitan peasants were practising their steps at the end of the chapel, some circling their arms above their heads, some swaying their baskets of paper violets and curtsying. In a dark corner of the chapel at the gospel side of the altar a stout old lady knelt amid her copious black skirts. When she stood up a pink-dressed figure, wearing a curly golden wig and an old-fashioned straw sunbonnet, with black pencilled eyebrows and cheeks delicately rouged and powdered, was discovered. A low murmur of curiosity ran round the chapel at the discovery of this girlish figure. One of the prefects, smiling and nodding his head, approached the dark corner and, having bowed to the stout old lady, said pleasantly:

– Is this a beautiful young lady or a doll that you have here, Mr Tallon?

Then, bending down to peer at the smiling painted face under the leaf of the bonnet, he exclaimed:

– No! Upon my word I believe it's little Bertie Tallon after all!

Stephen at his post by the window heard the old lady and the priest laugh together and heard the boys' murmurs of admiration behind him as they passed forward to see the little boy who had to dance the sunbonnet dance by himself. A movement of impatience escaped him. He let the edge of the blind fall and, stepping down from the bench on which he had been standing, walked out of the chapel.

He passed out of the schoolhouse and halted under the shed that flanked the garden. From the theatre opposite came the muffled noise of the audience and sudden brazen clashes of the soldiers' band. The light spread upwards from the glass roof making the theatre seem a festive ark, anchored among the hulks of houses, her frail cables of lanterns looping her to her moorings. A side door of the theatre opened suddenly and a shaft of light flew across the grass plots. A sudden burst of music issued from the ark, the prelude of a waltz: and when the side door closed again the listener could hear the faint rhythm of the music. The sentiment of the opening bars, their languor and supple movement, evoked the incommunicable emotion which had been the cause of all his day's unrest and of his impatient movement of a moment before. His unrest issued from him like a wave of sound: and on the tide of flowing music the ark was journeying, trailing her cables of lanterns in her wake. Then a noise like dwarf artillery broke the movement. It was the clapping that greeted the entry of the dumbbell team on the stage.

At the far end of the shed near the street a speck of pink light showed in the darkness and as he walked towards it he became aware of a faint aromatic odour. Two boys were standing in the shelter of a doorway, smoking, and before he reached them he had recognized Heron by his voice.

– Here comes the noble Dedalus! cried a high throaty voice. Welcome to our trusty friend!

This welcome ended in a soft peal of mirthless laughter as Heron salaamed and then began to poke the ground with his cane.

– Here I am, said Stephen, halting and glancing from Heron to his friend.

The latter was a stranger to him but in the darkness, by the aid of the glowing cigarette tips, he could make out a pale dandyish face over which a smile was travelling slowly, a tall overcoated figure and a hard hat. Heron did not trouble himself about an introduction but said instead:

– I was just telling my friend Wallis what a lark it would be tonight if you took off the rector in the part of the schoolmaster. It would be a ripping good joke.

Heron made a poor attempt to imitate for his friend Wallis the rector's pedantic bass and then, laughing at his failure, asked Stephen to do it.

– Go on, Dedalus, he urged, you can take him off rippingly. *He that will not hear the churcha let him be to theea as the heathena and the publicana.*[132]

The imitation was prevented by a mild expression of anger from Wallis in whose mouthpiece the cigarette had become too tightly wedged.

– Damn this blankety blank holder, he said, taking it from his mouth and smiling and frowning upon it tolerantly. It's always getting stuck like that. Do you use a holder?

– I don't smoke, answered Stephen.

– No, said Heron, Dedalus is a model youth. He doesn't smoke and he doesn't go to bazaars and he doesn't flirt and he doesn't damn anything or damn all.

Stephen shook his head and smiled in his rival's flushed and mobile face, beaked like a bird's. He had often thought it strange that Vincent Heron had a bird's face as well as a bird's name. A shock of pale hair lay on the forehead like a ruffled crest: the forehead was narrow and bony and a thin hooked nose stood out between the close-set prominent eyes which were light and inexpressive. The rivals were school friends. They sat together in class, knelt together in the chapel, talked together after beads[133] over their lunches. As the fellows in number one were undistinguished dullards, Stephen and Heron had been during the year the virtual heads of the school. It was they who went up to the rector together to ask for a free day or to get a fellow off.

– O by the way, said Heron suddenly, I saw your governor going in.

The smile waned on Stephen's face. Any allusion made to his father by a fellow or by a master put his calm to rout in a moment. He waited in timorous silence to hear what Heron might say next. Heron, however, nudged him expressively with his elbow and said:

– You're a sly dog.

– Why so? said Stephen.

– You'd think butter wouldn't melt in your mouth, said Heron. But I'm afraid you're a sly dog.

– Might I ask you what you are talking about? said Stephen urbanely.

– Indeed you might, answered Heron. We saw her, Wallis, didn't we? And deucedly pretty she is too. And inquisitive! *And what part does Stephen take, Mr Dedalus? And will Stephen not sing, Mr Dedalus?* Your governor was staring at her through that eyeglass of his for all he was worth so that I think the old man has found you out too. I wouldn't care a bit, by Jove. She's ripping, isn't she, Wallis?

– Not half bad, answered Wallis quietly as he placed his holder once more in a corner of his mouth.

A shaft of momentary anger flew through Stephen's mind at these indelicate allusions in the hearing of a stranger. For him there was nothing amusing in a girl's interest and regard. All day he had thought of nothing but their leave-taking on the steps of the tram at Harold's Cross, the stream of moody emotions it had made to course through him and the poem he had written about it. All day he had imagined a new meeting with her for he knew that she was to come to the play. The old restless moodiness had again filled his breast as it had done on the night of the party, but had not found an outlet in verse. The growth and knowledge of two years of boyhood stood between then and now, forbidding such an outlet: and all day the stream of gloomy tenderness within him had started forth and returned upon itself in dark courses and eddies, wearying him in the end until the pleasantry of the perfect and the painted little boy had drawn from him a movement of impatience.

– So you may as well admit, Heron went on, that we've fairly found you out this time. You can't play the saint on me any more, that's one sure five.[134]

A soft peal of mirthless laughter escaped from his lips and, bending down as before, he struck Stephen lightly across the calf of the leg with his cane, as if in jesting reproof.

Stephen's moment of anger had already passed. He was neither flattered nor confused, but simply wished the banter to end. He scarcely resented what had seemed to him a silly indelicateness for he knew that the adventure in his mind stood in no danger from these words: and his face mirrored his rival's false smile.

– Admit! repeated Heron, striking him again with his cane across the calf of the leg.

The stroke was playful but not so lightly given as the first one had been. Stephen felt the skin tingle and glow slightly and almost painlessly; and, bowing submissively, as if to meet his companion's jesting mood, began to recite the *Confiteor*.[135] The episode ended well, for both Heron and Wallis laughed indulgently at the irreverence.

The confession came only from Stephen's lips and, while they spoke the words, a sudden memory had carried him to another scene called up, as if by magic, at the moment when he had noted the faint cruel dimples at the corners of Heron's smiling lips and had felt the familiar stroke of the cane against his calf and had heard the familiar word of admonition:

– Admit.

It was towards the close of his first term in the college when he was in number six. His sensitive nature was still smarting under the lashes of an undivined and squalid way of life. His soul was still disquieted and cast down by the dull phenomenon of Dublin. He had emerged from a two years' spell of revery to find himself in the midst of a new scene, every event and figure of which affected him intimately, disheartened him or allured and, whether alluring or disheartening, filled him always with unrest and bitter thoughts. All the leisure which his school life left him was passed in the company of subversive writers whose jibes and violence of speech set up a ferment in his brain before they passed out of it into his crude writings.

The essay was for him the chief labour of his week and every Tuesday, as he marched from home to the school, he read his fate in the incidents of the way, pitting himself against some figure ahead of him and quickening his pace to outstrip it before a certain goal was reached or planting his steps scrupulously in the spaces of the patch-work of the pathway and telling himself that he would be first and not first in the weekly essay.

On a certain Tuesday the course of his triumphs was rudely broken. Mr Tate, the English master, pointed his finger at him and said bluntly:

– This fellow has heresy in his essay.

A hush fell on the class. Mr Tate did not break it but dug with his hand between his thighs while his heavily starched linen creaked about his neck and wrists. Stephen did not look up. It was a raw spring morning and his eyes were still smarting and weak. He was conscious of failure and of detection, of the squalor of his own mind and home, and felt against his neck the raw edge of his turned and jagged collar.

A short loud laugh from Mr Tate set the class more at ease.

– Perhaps you didn't know that, he said.

– Where? asked Stephen.

Mr Tate withdrew his delving hand and spread out the essay.

– Here. It's about the Creator and the soul. Rrm . . . rrm . . . rrm . . . Ah! *without a possibility of ever approaching nearer.* That's heresy.

Stephen murmured:

– I meant *without a possibility of ever reaching.*[136]

It was a submission and Mr Tate, appeased, folded up the essay and passed it across to him, saying:

– O . . . Ah! *ever reaching.* That's another story.

But the class was not so soon appeased. Though nobody spoke to him of the affair after class he could feel about him a vague general malignant joy.

A few nights after this public chiding he was walking with a letter along the Drumcondra Road when he heard a voice cry:

– Halt!

He turned and saw three boys of his own class coming towards him in the dusk. It was Heron who had called out and, as he marched forward between his two attendants, he cleft the air before him with a thin cane in time to their steps. Boland, his friend, marched beside him, a large grin on his face, while Nash came on a few steps behind, blowing from the pace and wagging his great red head.

As soon as the boys had turned into Clonliffe Road together they began to speak about books and writers, saying what books they were reading and how many books there were in their fathers' bookcases at home. Stephen listened to them in some wonderment for Boland was the dunce and Nash the idler of the class. In fact, after some talk about their favourite writers, Nash declared for Captain Marryat[137] who, he said, was the greatest writer.

– Fudge! said Heron. Ask Dedalus. Who is the greatest writer, Dedalus?

Stephen noted the mockery in the question and said:

– Of prose do you mean?

– Yes.

– Newman, I think.

– Is it Cardinal Newman? asked Boland.

– Yes, answered Stephen.

The grin broadened on Nash's freckled face as he turned to Stephen and said:

– And do you like Cardinal Newman,[138] Dedalus?

– O, many say that Newman has the best prose style, Heron said to the other two in explanation, of course he's not a poet.

– And who is the best poet, Heron? asked Boland.

– Lord Tennyson, of course, answered Heron.

– O, yes, Lord Tennyson,[139] said Nash. We have all his poetry at home in a book.

At this Stephen forgot the silent vows he had been making and burst out:

– Tennyson a poet! Why, he's only a rhymester!

– O, get out! said Heron. Everyone knows that Tennyson is the greatest poet.

– And who do you think is the greatest poet? asked Boland, nudging his neighbour.

– Byron, of course, answered Stephen.

Heron gave the lead and all three joined in a scornful laugh.

– What are you laughing at? asked Stephen.

– You, said Heron. Byron the greatest poet! He's only a poet for uneducated people.

– He must be a fine poet! said Boland.

– You may keep your mouth shut, said Stephen, turning on him boldly. All you know about poetry is what you wrote up on the slates in the yard and were going to be sent to the loft for.

Boland, in fact, was said to have written on the slates in the yard a couplet about a classmate of his who often rode home from the college on a pony:

> *As Tyson was riding into Jerusalem*
> *He fell and hurt his Alec Kafoozelum.*[140]

This thrust put the two lieutenants to silence but Heron went on:

– In any case Byron was a heretic and immoral too.

– I don't care what he was, cried Stephen hotly.

– You don't care whether he was a heretic or not? said Nash.

– What do you know about it? shouted Stephen. You never read a line of anything in your life except a trans,[141] or Boland either.

– I know that Byron was a bad man, said Boland.

– Here, catch hold of this heretic, Heron called out.

In a moment Stephen was a prisoner.

– Tate made you buck up the other day, Heron went on, about the heresy in your essay.

– I'll tell him tomorrow, said Boland.

– Will you? said Stephen. You'd be afraid to open your lips.

– Afraid?

– Ay. Afraid of your life.

– Behave yourself! cried Heron, cutting at Stephen's legs with his cane.

It was the signal for their onset. Nash pinioned his arms behind while Boland seized a long cabbage stump which was lying in the gutter. Struggling and kicking under the cuts of the cane and the blows of the knotty stump Stephen was borne back against a barbed wire fence.

– Admit that Byron was no good.

– No.

– Admit.

– No.

– Admit.

– No. No.

At last after a fury of plunges he wrenched himself free. His tormentors set off towards Jones's Road, laughing and jeering at him, while he, half blinded with tears, stumbled on, clenching his fists madly and sobbing.

While he was still repeating the *Confiteor* amid the indulgent laughter of his hearers and while the scenes of that malignant episode were still passing sharply and swiftly before his mind he wondered why he bore no malice now to those who had tormented him. He had not forgotten a whit of their cowardice and cruelty but the memory of it called forth no anger from him. All the descriptions of fierce love and hatred which he had met in books had seemed to him therefore unreal. Even that night as he stumbled homewards along Jones's Road he had felt that some power was divesting him of that sudden-woven anger as easily as a fruit is divested of its soft ripe peel.

He remained standing with his two companions at the end of the shed listening idly to their talk or to the bursts of applause in the theatre. She was sitting there among the others perhaps waiting for him to appear. He tried to recall her appearance but could not. He could remember only that she had worn a shawl about her head like a cowl and that her dark eyes had invited and unnerved him. He wondered had he been in her thoughts as she had been in his. Then in the dark and unseen by the other two he rested the tips of the fingers of one hand upon the palm of the other hand, scarcely touching it lightly. But the pressure of her fingers had been lighter and steadier: and suddenly the memory of their touch traversed his brain and body like an invisible wave.

A boy came towards them, running along under the shed. He was excited and breathless.

– O, Dedalus, he cried, Doyle is in a great bake about you. You're to go in at once and get dressed for the play. Hurry up, you better.

– He's coming now, said Heron to the messenger with a haughty drawl, when he wants to.

The boy turned to Heron and repeated:

– But Doyle is in an awful bake.

– Will you tell Doyle with my best compliments that I damned his eyes? answered Heron.

– Well, I must go now, said Stephen, who cared little for such points of honour.

– I wouldn't, said Heron, damn me if I would. That's no way to send for one of the senior boys. In a bake, indeed! I think it's quite enough that you're taking a part in his bally old play.

This spirit of quarrelsome comradeship which he had observed lately in his rival had not seduced Stephen from his habits of quiet obedience. He mistrusted the turbulence and doubted the sincerity of such comradeship which seemed to him a sorry anticipation of manhood. The question of honour here raised was, like all such questions, trivial to him. While his mind had been pursuing its intangible phantoms and turning in irresolution from such pursuit he had heard about him the constant voices of his father and of his masters, urging him to be a gentleman above all things and urging him to be a good catholic above all things. These voices had now come to be hollow-sounding in his ears. When the gymnasium had been opened he had heard another voice urging him to be strong and manly and healthy and when the movement towards national revival[142] had begun to be felt in the college yet another voice had bidden him be true to his country and help to raise up her language and tradition. In the profane world, as he foresaw, a worldly voice would bid him raise up his father's fallen state by his labours and, meanwhile, the voice of his school comrades urged him to be a decent fellow, to shield others from blame or to beg them off and to do his best to get free days for the school. And it was the din of all these hollow-sounding voices that made him halt irresolutely in the pursuit of phantoms. He gave them ear only for a time but he was happy only when he was far from them, beyond their call, alone or in the company of phantasmal comrades.

In the vestry a plump fresh-faced jesuit and an elderly man, in shabby blue clothes, were dabbling in a case of paints and chalks. The boys who had been painted walked about or stood still awkwardly, touching their faces in a gingerly fashion with their furtive fingertips. In the middle of the vestry a young jesuit, who was then on a visit to the college, stood rocking himself rhythmically from the tips of his toes to his heels and back again, his hands thrust well forward into his side-pockets. His small head set off with glossy red curls and his newly shaven face agreed well with the spotless decency of his soutane and with his spotless shoes.

As he watched this swaying form and tried to read for himself the legend of the priest's mocking smile there came into Stephen's memory a saying which he had heard from his father before he had been sent to Clongowes, that you could always tell a jesuit by the style of his clothes. At the same moment he thought he saw a likeness between his father's mind and that of this smiling well-dressed priest: and he was aware of some desecration of the priest's office or of the vestry itself whose silence was now routed by loud talk and joking and its air pungent with the smells of the gas-jets and the grease.

While his forehead was being wrinkled and his jaws painted black and blue by the elderly man, he listened distractedly to the voice of the plump young jesuit which bade him speak up and make his points clearly. He could hear the band playing *The Lily of Killarney*[143] and knew that in a few moments the curtain would go up. He felt no stage fright but the thought of the part he had to play humiliated him. A remembrance of some of his lines made a sudden flush rise to his painted cheeks. He saw her serious alluring eyes watching him from among the audience and their image at once swept away his scruples, leaving his will compact. Another nature seemed to have been lent him: the infection of the excitement and youth about him entered into and transformed his moody mistrustfulness. For one rare moment he seemed to be clothed in the real apparel of boyhood: and, as he stood in the wings among the other players, he shared the common mirth amid which the drop scene was hauled upwards by two able-bodied priests with violent jerks and all awry.

A few moments after he found himself on the stage amid the garish gas and the dim scenery, acting before the innumerable faces of the void. It surprised him to see that the play which he had known at rehearsals for a disjointed lifeless thing had suddenly assumed a life of its own. It seemed now to play itself, he and his fellow actors aiding it with their parts. When the curtain fell on the last scene he heard the void filled with applause and, through a rift in a side scene, saw the simple body before which he had acted magically deformed, the void of faces breaking at all points and falling asunder into busy groups. He left the stage quickly and rid himself of his mummery and passed out through the chapel into the college garden. Now that the play was over his nerves cried for some further adventure. He hurried onwards as if to overtake it. The doors of the theatre were all open and the audience had emptied out. On the lines which he had fancied the moorings of an ark a few lanterns swung in the night breeze, flickering cheerlessly. He mounted the steps from the garden in haste, eager that some prey should not elude him, and forced his way through the crowd in the hall and past the two jesuits who stood watching the exodus and bowing and shaking hands with the visitors. He pushed onward nervously, feigning a still greater haste and faintly conscious of the smiles and stares and nudges which his powdered head left in its wake.

When he came out on the steps he saw his family waiting for him at the first lamp. In a glance he noted that every figure of the group was familiar and ran down the steps angrily.

– I have to leave a message down in George's Street, he said to his father quickly. I'll be home after you.

Without waiting for his father's questions he ran across the road and began to walk at breakneck speed down the hill. He hardly knew where he was walking. Pride and hope and desire like crushed herbs in his heart sent up vapours of maddening incense before the eyes of his mind. He strode down the hill amid the tumult of sudden-risen vapours of wounded pride and fallen hope and baffled desire. They streamed upwards before his anguished eyes in dense and maddening fumes and passed away above him till at last the air was clear and cold again.

A film still veiled his eyes but they burned no longer. A power, akin to that which had often made anger or resentment fall from him, brought his steps to rest. He stood still and gazed up at the sombre porch of the morgue and from that to the dark cobbled laneway at its side. He saw the word *Lotts* on the wall of the lane and breathed slowly the rank heavy air.

– That is horse piss and rotted straw, he thought. It is a good odour to breathe. It will calm my heart. My heart is quite calm now. I will go back.

Stephen was once again seated beside his father in the corner of a railway carriage at Kingsbridge.[144] He was travelling with his father by the night mail to Cork. As the train steamed out of the station he recalled his childish wonder of years before and every event of his first day at Clongowes. But he felt no wonder now. He saw the darkening lands slipping away past him, the silent telegraph-poles passing his window swiftly every four seconds, the little glimmering stations, manned by a few silent sentries, flung by the mail behind her and twinkling for a moment in the darkness like fiery grains flung backwards by a runner.

He listened without sympathy to his father's evocation of Cork and of scenes of his youth, a tale broken by sighs or draughts from his pocket flask whenever the image of some dead friend appeared in it or whenever the evoker remembered suddenly the purpose of his actual visit. Stephen heard but could feel no pity. The images of the dead were all strangers to him save that of uncle Charles, an image which had lately been fading out of memory. He knew, however, that his father's property was going to be sold by auction, and in the manner of his own dispossession he felt the world give the lie rudely to his phantasy.

At Maryborough he fell asleep. When he awoke-the train had passed out of Mallow[145] and his father was stretched asleep on the other seat. The cold light of the dawn lay over the country, over the unpeopled fields and the closed cottages. The terror of sleep fascinated his mind as he watched the silent country or heard from time to time his father's deep breath or sudden sleepy movement. The neighbourhood of unseen sleepers filled him with strange dread, as though they could harm him, and he prayed that the day might come quickly. His prayer, addressed neither to God nor saint, began with a shiver, as the chilly morning breeze crept through the chink of the carriage door to his feet, and ended in a trail of foolish words which he made to fit the insistent rhythm of the train; and silently, at intervals of four seconds, the telegraph-poles held the galloping notes of the music between punctual bars. This furious music allayed his dread and, leaning against the windowledge, he let his eyelids close again.

They drove in a jingle[146] across Cork while it was still early morning and Stephen finished his sleep in a bedroom of the Victoria Hotel.[147] The bright warm sunlight was streaming through the window and he could hear the din of traffic. His father was standing before the dressing-table, examining his hair and face and moustache with great care, craning his neck across the water jug and drawing it back sideways to see the better. While he did so he sang softly to himself with quaint accent and phrasing:

        ' 'Tis youth and folly
        Makes young men marry,
        So here, my love, I'll

No longer stay.
What can't be cured, sure,
Must be injured, sure,
So I'll go to
    Amerikay.

'My love she's handsome,
My love she's bony:
She's like good whisky
    When it is new;
But when 'tis old
And growing cold
It fades and dies like
    The mountain dew.'[148]

The consciousness of the warm sunny city outside his window and the tender tremors with which his father's voice festooned the strange sad happy air, drove off all the mists of the night's ill humour from Stephen's brain. He got up quickly to dress and, when the song had ended, said:

– That's much prettier than any of your other *come-all-yous*.[149]

– Do you think so? asked Mr Dedalus.

– I like it, said Stephen.

– It's a pretty old air, said Mr Dedalus, twirling the points of his moustache. Ah, but you should have heard Mick Lacy sing it! Poor Mick Lacy! He had little turns for it, grace notes that he used to put in that I haven't got. That was the boy who could sing a *come-all-you*, if you like.

Mr Dedalus had ordered drisheens[150] for breakfast and during the meal he cross-examined the waiter for local news. For the most part they spoke at cross purposes when a name was mentioned, the waiter having in mind the present holder and Mr Dedalus his father or perhaps his grandfather.

– Well, I hope they haven't moved the Queen's College[151] anyhow, said Mr Dedalus, for I want to show it to this youngster of mine.

Along the Mardyke[152] the trees were in bloom. They entered the grounds of the college and were led by the garrulous porter across the quadrangle. But their progress across the gravel was brought to a halt after every dozen or so paces by some reply of the porter's.

– Ah, do you tell me so? And is poor Pottlebelly dead?

– Yes, sir. Dead, sir.

During these halts Stephen stood awkwardly behind the two men, weary of the subject and waiting restlessly for the slow march to begin again. By the time they had crossed the quadrangle his restlessness had risen to fever. He wondered how his father, whom he knew for a shrewd suspicious man, could be duped by the servile manners of the porter; and the lively southern speech which had entertained him all the morning now irritated his ears.

They passed into the anatomy theatre where Mr Dedalus, the porter aiding him, searched the desks for his initials. Stephen remained in the background, depressed more than ever by the darkness and silence of the theatre and by the air it wore of jaded and formal study. On the desk he read the word *Foetus* cut several times in the dark stained wood. The sudden legend startled his blood: he seemed to feel the absent students of the college about him and to shrink from their company. A vision of their life, which his father's words had been powerless to evoke, sprang up before him out of the word cut in the desk. A broad-shouldered student with a moustache was cutting in the letters with a jack-knife, seriously. Other students stood or sat near him laughing at his handiwork. One jogged his elbow. The big student turned on him, frowning. He was dressed in loose grey clothes and had tan boots.

Stephen's name was called. He hurried down the steps of the theatre so as to be as far away from the vision as he could be and, peering closely at his father's initials, hid his flushed face.

But the word and the vision capered before his eyes as he walked back across the quadrangle and towards the college gate. It shocked him to find in the outer world a trace of what he had deemed till then a brutish and individual malady of his own mind. His monstrous reveries came thronging into his memory. They too had sprung up before him, suddenly and furiously, out of mere words. He had soon given in to them and allowed them to sweep across and abase his intellect, wondering always where they came from, from what den of monstrous images, and always weak and humble towards others, restless and sickened of himself when they had swept over him.

– Ay, bedad! And there's the Groceries[153] sure enough! cried Mr Dedalus. You often heard me speak of the Groceries, didn't you, Stephen. Many's the time we went down there when our names had been marked, a crowd of us, Harry Peard and little Jack Mountain and Bob Dyas and Maurice Moriarty, the French man, and Tom O'Grady and Mick Lacy that I told you of this morning and Joey Corbet and poor little good-hearted Johnny Keevers of the Tantiles.

The leaves of the trees along the Mardyke were astir and whispering in the sunlight. A team of cricketers passed, agile young men in flannels and blazers, one of them carrying the long green wicket-bag. In a quiet bystreet a German band of five players in faded uniforms and with battered brass instruments was playing to an audience of street arabs[154] and leisurely messenger boys. A maid in a white cap and apron was watering a box of plants on a sill which shone like a slab of limestone in the warm glare. From another window open to the air came the sound of a piano, scale after scale rising into the treble.

Stephen walked on at his father's side, listening to stories he had heard before, hearing again the names of the scattered and dead revellers who had been the companions of his father's youth. And a faint sickness sighed in his heart. He recalled his own equivocal position in Belvedere, a free boy, a leader afraid of his own authority, proud and sensitive and suspicious, battling against the squalor of his life and against the riot of his mind. The letters cut in the stained wood of the desk stared upon him, mocking his bodily weakness and futile enthusiasms and making him loathe himself for his own mad and filthy orgies. The spittle in his throat grew bitter and foul to swallow and the faint sickness climbed to his brain so that for a moment he closed his eyes and walked on in darkness.

He could still hear his father's voice

– When you kick out for yourself, Stephen – as I daresay you will one of these days – remember, whatever you do, to mix with gentlemen. When I was a young fellow I tell you I enjoyed myself. I mixed with fine decent fellows. Everyone of us could do something. One fellow had a good voice, another fellow was a good actor, another could sing a good comic song, another was a good oarsman or a good racket player, another could tell a good story and so on. We kept the ball rolling anyhow and enjoyed ourselves and saw a bit of life and we were none the worse of it either. But we were all gentlemen, Stephen – at least I hope we were – and bloody good honest Irishmen too. That's the kind of fellows I want you to associate with, fellows of the right kidney. I'm talking to you as a friend, Stephen. I don't believe a son should be afraid of his father. No, I treat you as your grandfather treated me when I was a young chap. We were more like brothers than father and son. I'll never forget the first day he caught me smoking. I was standing at the end of the South Terrace one day with some maneens[155] like myself and sure we thought we were grand fellows because we had pipes stuck in the corners of our mouths. Suddenly the governor passed. He didn't say a word, or stop even. But the next day, Sunday, we were out for a walk together and when we were coming home he took out his cigar case and said:

– By the by, Simon, I didn't know you smoked, or something like that.

– Of course I tried to carry it off as best I could.

– If you want a good smoke, he said, try one of these cigars. An American captain made me a present of them last night in Queenstown.

Stephen heard his father's voice break into a laugh which was almost a sob.

– He was the handsomest man in Cork at that time, by God he was! The women used to stand to look after him in the street.

He heard the sob passing loudly down his father's throat and opened his eyes with a nervous impulse. The sunlight breaking suddenly on his sight turned the sky and clouds into a fantastic world of sombre masses with lakelike spaces of dark rosy light. His very brain was sick and powerless. He could scarcely interpret the letters of the signboards of the shops. By his monstrous way of life he seemed to have put himself beyond the limits of reality. Nothing moved him or spoke to him from the real world unless he heard in it an echo of the infuriated cries within him. He could respond to no earthly or human appeal, dumb and insensible to the call of summer and gladness and companionship, wearied and dejected by his father's voice. He could scarcely recognize as his own thoughts, and repeated slowly to himself:

– I am Stephen Dedalus. I am walking beside my father whose name is Simon Dedalus. We are in Cork, in Ireland. Cork is a city. Our room is in the Victoria Hotel. Victoria and Stephen and Simon. Simon and Stephen and Victoria. Names.

The memory of his childhood suddenly grew dim. He tried to call forth some of its vivid moments but could not. He recalled only names. Dante, Parnell, Clane, Clongowes. A little boy had been taught geography by an old woman who kept two brushes in her wardrobe. Then he had been sent away from home to a college, he had made his first communion and eaten slim jim[156] out of his cricket cap and watched the firelight leaping and dancing on the wall of a little bedroom in the infirmary and dreamed of being dead, of mass being said for him by the rector in a black and gold cope, of being buried then in the little graveyard of the community off the main avenue of limes. But he had not died then. Parnell had died. There had been no mass for the dead in the chapel and no procession. He had not died but he had faded out like a film in the sun. He had been lost or had wandered out of existence for he no longer existed. How strange to think of him passing out of existence in such a way, not by death but by fading out in the sun or by being lost and forgotten somewhere in the universe! It was strange to see his small body appear again for a moment: a little boy in a grey belted suit. His hands were in his side-pockets and his trousers were tucked in at the knees by elastic bands.

On the evening of the day on which the property was sold Stephen followed his father meekly about the city from bar to bar. To the sellers in the market, to the barmen and barmaids, to the beggars who importuned him for a lob[157] Mr Dedalus told the same tale – that he was an old Corkonian, that he had been trying for thirty years to get rid of his Cork accent up in Dublin and that Peter Pickackafax beside him was his eldest son but that he was only a Dublin jackeen.[158]

They had set out early in the morning from Newcombe's coffee-house, where Mr Dedalus's cup had rattled noisily against its saucer, and Stephen had tried to cover that shameful sign of his father's drinking bout of the night before by moving his chin and coughing. One humiliation had succeeded another – the false smiles of the market sellers, the curvetings and oglings of the barmaids with whom his father flirted, the compliments and encouraging words of his father's friends. They had told him that he had a great look of his grandfather and Mr Dedalus had agreed that he was an ugly likeness. They had unearthed traces of a Cork accent in his speech and made him admit that the Lee[159] was a much finer river than the Liffey. One of them, in order to put his Latin to the proof, had made him translate short passages from Dilectus[160] and asked him whether it was correct to say: *Tempora mutantur nos et mutamur in illis* or *Tempora mutantur et nos mutamur in illis*.[161] Another, a brisk old man, whom Mr Dedalus called Johnny Cashman, had covered him with confusion by asking him to say which were prettier, the Dublin girls or the Cork girls.

– He's not that way built, said Mr Dedalus. Leave him alone. He's a level-headed thinking boy who doesn't bother his head about that kind of nonsense.

– Then he's not his father's son, said the little old man.

– I don't know, I'm sure, said Mr Dedalus, smiling complacently.

– Your father, said the little old man to Stephen, was the boldest flirt in the city of Cork in his day. Do you know that?

Stephen looked down and studied the tiled floor of the bar into which they had drifted.

– Now don't be putting ideas into his head, said Mr Dedalus. Leave him to his Maker.

– Yerra, sure I wouldn't put any ideas into his head. I'm old enough to be his grandfather. And I am a grandfather, said the little old man to Stephen. Do you know that?

– Are you? asked Stephen.

– Bedad I am, said the little old man. I have two bouncing grand-children out at Sunday's Well.[162] Now, then! What age do you think I am? And I remember seeing your grandfather in his red coat riding out to hounds. That was before you were born.

– Ay, or thought of, said Mr Dedalus.

– Bedad I did, repeated the little old man. And, more than that, I can remember even your greatgrandfather, old John Stephen Dedalus, and a fierce old fire-eater he was. Now, then! There's a memory for you!

– That's three generations – four generations, said another of the company. Why, Johnny Cashman, you must be nearing the century.

– Well, I'll tell you the truth, said the little old man. I'm just twenty-seven years of age.

– We're as old as we feel, Johnny, said Mr Dedalus. And just finish what you have there and we'll have another. Here, Tim or Tom or whatever your name is, give us the same again here. By God, I don't feel more than eighteen myself. There's that son of mine there not half my age and I'm a better man than he is any day of the week.

– Draw it mild now, Dedalus. I think it's time for you to take a back seat, said the gentleman who had spoken before.

– No, by God! asserted Mr Dedalus. I'll sing at tenor song against him or I'll vault a five-barred gate against him or I'll run with him after the hounds across the country as I did thirty years ago along with the Kerry Boy[163] and the best man for it.

– But he'll beat you here, said the little old man, tapping his forehead and raising his glass to drain it.

– Well, I hope he'll be as good a man as his father. That's all I can say, said Mr Dedalus.

– If he is, he'll do, said the little old man.

– And thanks be to God, Johnny, said Mr Dedalus, that we lived so long and did so little harm.

– But did so much good, Simon, said the little old man gravely. Thanks be to God we lived so long and did so much good.

Stephen watched the three glasses being raised from the counter as his father and his two cronies drank to the memory of their past. An abyss of fortune or of temperament sundered him from them. His mind seemed older than theirs: it shone coldly on their strifes and happiness and regrets like a moon upon a younger earth. No life or youth stirred in him as it had stirred in them. He had known neither the pleasure of companionship with others nor the vigour of rude male health nor filial piety. Nothing stirred within his soul but a cold and cruel and loveless lust. His childhood was dead or lost and with it his soul capable of simple joys and he was drifting amid life like the barren shell of the moon.

> *Art thou pale for weariness*
> *Of climbing heaven and gazing on the earth,*
> *Wandering companionless . . . ?*[164]

He repeated to himself the lines of Shelley's fragment. Its alternation of sad human ineffectiveness with vast inhuman cycles of activity chilled him and he forgot his own human and ineffectual grieving.

Stephen's mother and his brother and one of his cousins waited at the corner of quiet Foster Place while he and his father went up the steps and along the colonnade where the Highland sentry was parading. When they had passed into the great hall and stood at the counter Stephen drew forth his orders on the governor of the bank of Ireland for thirty and three pounds; and these sums, the moneys of his exhibition and essay prize, were paid over to him rapidly by the teller in notes and in coin respectively. He bestowed them in his pockets with feigned composure and suffered the friendly teller, to whom his father chatted, to take his hand across the broad counter and wish him a brilliant career in after life. He was impatient of their voices and could not keep his feet at rest. But the teller still deferred the serving of others to say he was living in changed times and that there was nothing like giving a boy the best education that money could buy. Mr Dedalus lingered in the hall gazing about him· and up at the roof and telling Stephen, who urged him to come out, that they were standing in the house of commons of the old Irish parliament.[165]

– God help us! he said piously, to think of the men of those times, Stephen, Hely Hutchinson and Flood and Henry Grattan and Charles Kendal Bushe,[166] and the noblemen we have now, leaders of the Irish people at home and abroad. Why, by God, they wouldn't be seen dead in a ten-acre field with them. No, Stephen, old chap, I'm sorry to say that they are only as I roved out one fine May morning in the merry month of sweet July.[167]

A keen October wind was blowing round the bank. The three figures standing at the edge of the muddy path had pinched cheeks and watery eyes. Stephen looked at his thinly clad mother and remembered that a few days before he had seen a mantle priced at twenty guineas in the windows of Barnardo's.[168]

– Well that's done, said Mr Dedalus.

– We had better go to dinner, said Stephen. Where?

– Dinner? said Mr Dedalus. Well, I suppose we had better, what?

– Some place that's not too dear, said Mrs Dedalus.

– Underdone's?[169]

– Yes. Some quiet place.

– Come along, said Stephen quickly. It doesn't matter about the dearness.

He walked on before them with short nervous steps, smiling. They tried to keep up with him, smiling also at his eagerness.

– Take it easy like a good young fellow, said his father. We're not out for the half mile, are we?

For a swift season of merrymaking the money of his prizes ran through Stephen's fingers. Great parcels of groceries and delicacies and dried fruits arrived from the city. Every day he drew up a bill of fare for the family and every night led a party of three or four to the theatre to see *Ingomar* or *The Lady of Lyons*.[170] In his coat pockets he carried squares of Vienna chocolate for his guests while his trousers' pocket bulged with masses of silver and copper coins. He bought presents for everyone, overhauled his room, wrote out resolutions, marshalled his books up and down their shelves, pored upon all kinds of price lists, drew up a form of commonwealth for the household by which every member of it held some office, opened a loan bank for his family and pressed loans on willing borrowers so that he might have the pleasure of making out receipts and reckoning the interests on the sums lent. When he could do no more he drove up and down the city in trams. Then the season of pleasure came to an end. The pot of pink enamel paint gave out and the wainscot of his bedroom remained with its unfinished and ill-plastered coat.

His household returned to its usual way of life. His mother had no further occasion to upbraid him for squandering his money. He too returned to his old life at school and all his novel enterprises fell to pieces. The commonwealth fell, the loan bank closed its coffers and its books on a sensible loss, the rules of life which he had drawn about himself fell into desuetude.

How foolish his aim had been! He had tried to build a breakwater of order and elegance against the sordid tide of life without him and to dam up, by rules of conduct and active interests and new filial relations, the powerful recurrence of the tides within him. Useless. From without as from within the waters had flowed over his barriers: their tides began once more to jostle fiercely above the crumbled mole.

He saw clearly too his own futile isolation. He had not gone one step nearer the lives he had sought to approach nor bridged the restless shame and rancour that had divided him from mother and brother and sister. He felt that he was hardly of the one blood with them but stood to them rather in the mystical kinship of fosterage, fosterchild and fosterbrother.

He turned to appease the fierce longings of his heart before which everything else was idle and alien. He cared little that he was in mortal sin, that his life had grown to be a tissue of subterfuge and falsehood. Beside the savage desire within him to realize the enormities which he brooded on nothing was sacred. He bore cynically with the shameful details of his secret riots in which he exulted to defile with patience whatever image had attracted his eyes. By day and by night he moved among distorted images of the outer world. A figure that had seemed to him by day demure and innocent came towards him by night through the winding darkness of sleep, her face transfigured by a lecherous cunning, her eyes bright with brutish joy. Only the morning pained him with its dim memory of dark orgiastic riot, its keen and humiliating sense of transgression.

He returned to his wanderings. The veiled autumnal evenings led him from street to street as they had led him years before along the quiet avenues of Blackrock. But no vision of trim front gardens or of kindly lights in the windows poured a tender influence upon him now. Only at times, in the pauses of his desire, when the luxury that was wasting him gave room to a softer languor, the image of Mercedes traversed the background of his memory. He saw again the small white house and the garden of rose-bushes on the road that led to the mountains and he remembered the sadly proud gesture of refusal which he was to make there, standing with her in the moonlit garden after years of estrangement and adventure. At those moments the soft speeches of Claude Melnotte[171] rose to his lips and eased his unrest. A tender premonition touched him of the tryst he had then looked forward to and, in spite of the horrible reality which lay between his hope of then and now, of the holy encounter he had then imagined at which weakness and timidity and inexperience were to fall from him.

Such moments passed and the wasting fires of lust sprang up again. The verses passed from his lips and the inarticulate cries and the unspoken brutal words rushed forth from his brain to force a passage. His blood was in revolt. He wandered up and down the dark slimy streets peering into the gloom of lanes and doorways, listening eagerly for any sound. He moaned to himself like some baffled prowling beast.

He wanted to sin with another of his kind, to force another being to sin with him and to exult with her in sin. He felt some dark presence moving irresistibly upon him from the darkness, a presence subtle and murmurous as a flood filling him wholly with itself. Its murmur besieged his ears like the murmur of some multitude in sleep; its subtle streams penetrated his being. His hands clenched convulsively and his teeth set together as he suffered the agony of its penetration. He stretched out his arms in the street to hold fast the frail swooning form that eluded him and incited him: and the cry that he had strangled for so long in his throat issued from his lips. It broke from him like a wail of despair from a hell of sufferers and died in a wail of furious entreaty, a cry for an iniquitous abandonment, a cry which was but the echo of an obscene scrawl which he had read on the oozing wall of a urinal.

He had wandered into a maze of narrow and dirty streets. From the foul laneways he heard bursts of hoarse riot and wrangling and the drawling of drunken singers. He walked onward, dismayed, wondering whether he had strayed into the quarter of the Jews. Women and girls dressed in long vivid gowns traversed the street from house to house. They were leisurely and perfumed. A trembling seized him and his eyes grew dim. The yellow gas-flames arose before his troubled vision against the vapoury sky, burning as if before an altar. Before the doors and in the lighted halls groups were gathered arrayed as for some rite. He was in another world: he had awakened from a slumber of centuries.

He stood still in the middle of the roadway, his heart clamouring against his bosom in a tumult. A young woman dressed in a long pink gown laid her hand on his arm to detain him and gazed into his face. She said gaily:

– Good night, Willie dear!

Her room was warm and lightsome. A huge doll sat with her legs apart in the copious easy-chair beside the bed. He tried to bid his tongue speak that he might seem at ease, watching her as she undid her gown, noting the proud conscious movements of her perfumed head.

As he stood silent in the middle of the room she came over to him and embraced him gaily and gravely. Her round arms held him firmly to her and he, seeing her face lifted to him in serious calm and feeling the warm calm rise and fall of her breast, all but burst into hysterical weeping. Tears of joy and relief shone in his delighted eyes and his lips parted though they would not speak.

She passed her tinkling hand through his hair, calling him a little rascal.

– Give me a kiss, she said.

His lips would not bend to kiss her. He wanted to be held firmly in her arms, to be caressed slowly, slowly, slowly. In her arms he felt that he had suddenly become strong and fearless and sure of himself. But his lips would not bend to kiss her.

With a sudden movement she bowed his head and joined her lips to his and he read the meaning of her movements in her frank uplifted eyes. It was too much for him. He closed his eyes, surrendering himself to her, body and mind, conscious of nothing in the world but the dark pressure of her softly parting lips. They pressed upon his brain as upon his lips as though they were the vehicle of a vague speech; and between them he felt an unknown and timid pressure, darker than the swoon of sin, softer than sound or odour.

Chapter 3

THE SWIFT DECEMBER DUSK had come tumbling clownishly after its dull day and, as he stared through the dull square of the window of the schoolroom, he felt his belly crave for its food. He hoped there would be stew for dinner, turnips and carrots and bruised potatoes and fat mutton pieces to be ladled out in thick peppered flour-fattened sauce. Stuff it into you, his belly counselled him.

It would be a gloomy secret night. After early nightfall the yellow lamps would light up, here and there, the squalid quarter of the brothels. He would follow a devious course up and down the streets, circling always nearer and nearer in a tremor of fear and joy, until his feet led him suddenly round a dark corner. The whores would be just coming out of their houses making ready for the night, yawning lazily after their sleep and settling the hairpins in their clusters of hair. He would pass by them calmly waiting for a sudden movement of his own will or a sudden call to his sin-loving soul from their soft perfumed flesh. Yet as he prowled in quest of that call, his senses, stultified only by his desire, would note keenly all that wounded or shamed them; his eyes, a ring of porter froth on clothless table or a photograph of two soldiers standing to attention or a gaudy playbill; his ears, the drawling jargon of greeting:

– Hello, Bertie, any good in your mind?
– Is that you, pigeon?
– Number ten. Fresh Nelly is waiting on you.
– Good night, husband! Coming in to have a short time?

The equation on the page of his scribbler began to spread out a widening tail, eyed and starred like a peacock's; and, when the eyes and stars of its indices had been eliminated, began slowly to fold itself together again. The indices appearing and disappearing were eyes opening and closing; the eyes opening and closing were stars being born and being quenched. The vast cycle of starry life bore his weary mind outward to its verge and inward to its centre, a distant music accompanying him outward and inward. What music? The music came nearer and he recalled the words, the words of Shelley's fragment upon the moon wandering companionless, pale for weariness.[172] The stars began to crumble and a cloud of fine stardust fell through space.

The dull light fell more faintly upon the page whereon another equation began to unfold itself slowly and to spread abroad its widening tail. It was his own soul going forth to experience, unfolding itself sin by sin, spreading abroad the bale-fire of its burning stars and folding back upon itself, fading slowly, quenching its own lights and fires. They were quenched: and the cold darkness filled chaos.

A cold lucid indifference reigned in his soul. At his first violent sin he had felt a wave of vitality pass out of him and had feared to find his body or his soul maimed by the excess. Instead the vital wave had carried him on its bosom out of himself and back again when it receded: and no part of body or soul had been maimed but a dark peace had been established between them. The chaos in which his ardour extinguished itself was a cold indifferent knowledge of himself. He had sinned mortally not once but many times and he knew that, while he stood in danger of eternal damnation for the first sin alone, by every succeeding sin he multiplied his guilt and his punishment. His days and works and thoughts could make no atonement for him, the fountains of sanctifying grace having ceased to refresh his soul. At most, by an alms given to a beggar whose blessing he fled from, he might hope wearily to win for himself some measure of actual grace.[173] Devotion had gone by the board. What did it avail to pray when he knew that his soul lusted after its own destruction? A certain pride, a certain awe, withheld him from offering to God even one prayer at night, though he knew it was in God's power to take away his life while he slept and hurl his soul hellward ere he could beg for mercy. His pride in his own sin, his loveless awe of God, told him that his offence was too grievous to be atoned for in whole or in part by a false homage to the All-seeing and All-knowing.

– Well now, Ennis, I declare you have a head and so has my stick! Do you mean to say that you are not able to tell me what a surd is?

The blundering answer stirred the embers of his contempt of his fellows. Towards others he felt neither shame nor fear. On Sunday mornings as he passed the church door he glanced coldly at the worshippers who stood bareheaded, four deep, outside the church, morally present at the mass which they could neither see nor hear.[174] Their dull piety and the sickly smell of the cheap hair-oil with which they had anointed their heads repelled him from the altar they prayed at. He stooped to the evil of hypocrisy with others, sceptical of their innocence which he could cajole so easily.

On the wall of his bedroom hung an illuminated scroll, the certificate of his prefecture in the college of the sodality of the Blessed

Virgin Mary.[175] On Saturday mornings when the sodality met in the chapel to recite the little office[176] his place was a cushioned kneeling-desk at the right of the altar from which he led his wing of boys through the responses. The falsehood of his position did not pain him. If at moments he felt an impulse to rise from his post of honour and, confessing before them all his unworthiness, to leave the chapel, a glance at their faces restrained him. The imagery of the psalms of prophecy[177] soothed his barren pride. The glories of Mary held his soul captive: spikenard and myrrh and frankincense, symbolising her royal lineage, her emblems, the late-flowering plant and late-blossoming tree, symbolising the age-long gradual growth of her cultus among men. When it fell to him to read the lesson towards the close of the office he read it in a veiled voice, lulling his conscience to its music.

> *Quasi cedrus exaltata sum in Libanon et quasi cupressus in monte Sion.*
> *Quasi palma exaltata sum in Gades et quasi plantatio rosae in Jericho.*
> *Quasi uliva speciosa in campis et quasi platanus exaltata sum juxta*
> *aquam in plateis. Sicut cinnamomum et balsamum aromatizans odorem*
> *dedi et quasi myrrha electa dedi suavitatem odoris.*[178]

His sin, which had covered him from the sight of God, had led him nearer to the refuge of sinners. Her eyes seemed to regard him with mild pity; her holiness, a strange light glowing faintly upon her frail flesh, did not humiliate the sinner who approached her. If ever he was impelled to cast sin from him and to repent the impulse that moved him was the wish to be her knight. If ever his soul, re-entering her dwelling shyly after the frenzy of his body's lust had spent itself, was turned towards her whose emblem is the morning star, *bright and musical, telling of heaven and infusing peace,*[179] it was when her names were murmured softly by lips whereon there still lingered foul and shameful words, the savour itself of a lewd kiss.

That was strange. He tried to think how it could be. But the dusk, deepening in the schoolroom, covered over his thoughts. The bell rang. The master marked the sums and cuts[180] to be done for the next lesson and went out. Heron, beside Stephen, began to hum tunelessly.

> *My excellent friend Bombados.*[181]

Ennis, who had gone to the yard, came back, saying:
– The boy from the house is coming up for the rector.
A tall boy behind Stephen rubbed his hands and said:
– That's game ball. We can scut[182] the whole hour. He won't be in

till after half two. Then you can ask him questions on the catechism, Dedalus.

Stephen, leaning back and drawing idly on his scribbler, listened to the talk about him which Heron checked from time to time by saying:

– Shut up, will you. Don't make such a bally racket![183]

It was strange too that he found an arid pleasure in following up to the end the rigid lines of the doctrines of the church and penetrating into obscure silences only to hear and feel the more deeply his own condemnation. The sentence of saint James which says that he who offends against one commandment becomes guilty of all,[184] had seemed to him first a swollen phrase until he had begun to grope in the darkness of his own state. From the evil seed of lust all other deadly sins had sprung forth: pride in himself and contempt of others, covetousness in using money for the purchase of unlawful pleasures, envy of those whose vices he could not reach to and calumnious murmuring against the pious, gluttonous enjoyment of food, the dull glowering anger amid which he brooded upon his longing, the swamp of spiritual and bodily sloth in which his whole being had sunk.

As he sat in his bench gazing calmly at the rector's shrewd harsh face, his mind wound itself in and out of the curious questions proposed to it. If a man had stolen a pound in his youth and had used that pound to amass a huge fortune how much was he obliged to give back, the pound he had stolen only or the pound together with the compound interest accruing upon it or all his huge fortune? If a layman in giving baptism pour the water before saying the words is the child baptized? Is baptism with a mineral water valid? How comes it that while the first beatitude promises the kingdom of heaven to the poor of heart the second beatitude promises also to the meek that they shall possess the land? Why was the sacrament of the eucharist instituted under the two species of bread and wine if Jesus Christ be present body and blood, soul and divinity, in the bread alone and in the wine alone? Does a tiny particle of the consecrated bread contain all the body and blood of Jesus Christ or a part only of the body and blood? If the wine change into vinegar and the host crumble into corruption after they have been consecrated, is Jesus Christ still present under their species as God and as man?

– Here he is! Here he is!

A boy from his post at the window had seen the rector come from the house. All the catechisms were opened and all heads bent upon them silently. The rector entered and took his seat on the dais. A gentle kick from the tall boy in the bench behind urged Stephen to ask a difficult question.

The rector did not ask for a catechism to hear the lesson from. He clasped his hands on the desk and said:

– The retreat will begin on Wednesday afternoon in honour of saint Francis Xavier whose feast day is Saturday.[185] The retreat will go on from Wednesday to Friday. On Friday confession will be heard all the afternoon after beads. If any boys have special confessors perhaps it will be better for them not to change. Mass will be on Saturday morning at nine o'clock and general communion for the whole college. Saturday will be a free day. But Saturday and Sunday being free days some boys might be inclined to think that Monday is a free day also. Beware of making that mistake. I think you, Lawless, are likely to make that mistake.

– I sir? Why, sir?

A little wave of quiet mirth broke forth over the class of boys from the rector's grim smile. Stephen's heart began slowly to fold and fade with fear like a withering flower.

The rector went on gravely:

– You are all familiar with the story of the life of saint Francis Xavier, I suppose, the patron of your college. He came of an old and illustrious Spanish family and you remember that he was one of the first followers of saint Ignatius.[186] They met in Paris where Francis Xavier was professor of philosophy at the university. This young and brilliant nobleman and man of letters entered heart and soul into the ideas of our glorious founder and you know that he, at his own desire, was sent by saint Ignatius to preach to the Indians. He is called, as you know, the apostle of the Indies. He went from country to country in the east, from Africa to India, from India to Japan, baptising the people. He is said to have baptized as many as ten thousand idolaters in one month. It is said that his right arm had grown powerless from having been raised so often over the heads of those whom he baptized. He wished then to go to China to win still more souls for God but he died of over on the island of Sancian. A great saint, saint Francis Xavier! A great soldier of God!

The rector paused and then, shaking his clasped hands before him, went on:

– He had the faith in him that moves mountains. Ten thousand souls won for God in a single month! That is a true conqueror, true to the motto of our order: *ad majorem Dei gloriam!* A saint who has great power in heaven, remember: power to intercede for us in our grief; power to obtain whatever we pray for if it be for the good of our souls; power above all to obtain for us the grace to repent if we be in sin. A great saint, saint Francis Xavier! A great fisher of souls![187]

He ceased to shake his clasped hands and, resting them against his forehead, looked right and left of them keenly at his listeners out of his dark stern eyes.

In the silence their dark fire kindled the dusk into a tawny glow. Stephen's heart had withered up like a flower of the desert that feels the simoom coming from afar.

– *Remember only thy last things and thou shalt not sin for ever* – words taken, my dear little brothers in Christ, from the book of Ecclesiastes, seventh chapter, fortieth verse.[188] In the name of the Father and of the Son and of the Holy Ghost. Amen.

Stephen sat in the front bench of the chapel. Father Arnall sat at a table to the left of the altar. He wore about his shoulders a heavy cloak; his pale face was drawn and his voice broken with rheum. The figure of his old master, so strangely re-arisen, brought back to Stephen's mind his life at Clongowes: the wide playgrounds, swarming with boys; the square ditch; the little cemetery off the main avenue of limes where he had dreamed of being buried; the firelight on the wall of the infirmary where he lay sick; the sorrowful face of Brother Michael. His soul, as these memories came back to him, became again a child's soul.

– We are assembled here today, my dear little brothers in Christ, for one brief moment far away from the busy bustle of the outer world to celebrate and to honour one of the greatest of saints, the apostle of the Indies, the patron saint also of your college, saint Francis Xavier. Year after year, for much longer than any of you, my dear little boys, can remember or than I can remember, the boys of this college have met in this very chapel to make their annual retreat before the feast day of their patron saint. Time has gone on and brought with it its changes. Even in the last few years what changes can most of you not remember? Many of the boys who sat in those front benches a few years ago are perhaps now in distant lands, in the burning tropics, or immersed in professional duties or in seminaries, or voyaging over the vast expanse of the deep or, it may be, already called by the great God to another life and to the rendering up of their stewardship. And still as the years roll by, bringing with them changes for good and bad, the memory of the great saint is honoured by the boys of this college who make every year their annual retreat on the days preceding the feast day set apart by our Holy Mother the Church to transmit to all the ages the name and fame of one of the greatest sons of catholic Spain.

– Now what is the meaning of this word *retreat* and why is it allowed on all hands to be a most salutary practice for all who desire to lead before God and in the eyes of men a truly christian life? A retreat, my dear boys, signifies a withdrawal for awhile from the cares of our life, the cares of this workaday world, in order to examine the state of our conscience, to reflect on the mysteries of holy religion and to understand better why we are here in this world. During these few days I intend to put before you some thoughts concerning the four last things. They are, as you know from your catechism, death, judgement, hell, and heaven. We shall try to understand them fully during these few days so that we may derive from the understanding of them a lasting benefit to our souls. And remember, my dear boys, that we have been sent into this world for one thing and for one thing alone: to do God's holy will and to save our immortal souls. All else is worthless. One thing alone is needful, the salvation of one's soul. What doth it profit a man to gain the whole world if he suffer the loss of his immortal soul?[189] Ah, my dear boys, believe me there is nothing in this wretched world that can make up for such a loss.

– I will ask you, therefore, my dear boys, to put away from your minds during these few days all worldly thoughts, whether of study or pleasure or ambition, and to give all your attention to the state of your souls. I need hardly remind you that during the days of the retreat all boys are expected to preserve a quiet and pious demeanour and to shun all loud unseemly pleasure. The elder boys, of course, will see that this custom is not infringed and I look especially to the prefects and officers of the sodality of Our Blessed Lady and of the sodality of the holy angels to set a good example to their fellow-students.

– Let us try, therefore, to make this retreat in honour of saint Francis with our whole heart and our whole mind. God's blessing will then be upon all your year's studies. But, above and beyond all, let this retreat be one to which you can look back in after years when maybe you are far from this college and among very different surroundings, to which you can look back with joy and thankfulness and give thanks to God for having granted you this occasion of laying the first foundation of a pious honourable zealous christian life. And if, as may so happen, there be at this moment in these benches any poor soul who has had the unutterable misfortune to lose God's holy grace and to fall into grievous sin, I fervently trust and pray that this retreat may be the turning point in the life of that soul. I pray to God through the merits of His zealous servant Francis Xavier, that such a soul may be led to sincere repentance and that the holy communion on saint Francis's day of this year may be a lasting covenant between God and that soul. For just and unjust, for saint and sinner alike, may this retreat be a memorable one.

– Help me, my dear little brothers in Christ. Help me by your pious attention, by your own devotion, by your outward demeanour. Banish from your minds all worldly thoughts and think only of the last things, death, judgement, hell, and heaven. He who remembers these things, says Ecclesiastes, shall not sin for ever.[190] He who remembers the last things will act and think with them always before his eyes. He will live a good life and die a good death, believing and knowing that, if he has sacrificed much in this earthly life, it will be given to him a hundredfold and a thousandfold more in the life to come, in the kingdom without end – a blessing, my dear boys, which I wish you from my heart, one and all, in the name of the Father and of the Son and of the Holy Ghost. Amen!

As he walked home with silent companions, a thick fog seemed to compass his mind. He waited in stupor of mind till it should lift and reveal what it had hidden. He ate his dinner with surly appetite and when the meal was over and the grease-strewn plates lay abandoned on the table, he rose and went to the window, clearing the thick scum from his mouth with his tongue and licking it from his lips. So he had sunk to the state of a beast that licks his chaps after meat. This was the end; and a faint glimmer of fear began to pierce the fog of his mind. He pressed his face against the pane of the window and gazed out into the darkening street. Forms passed this way and that through the dull light. And that was life. The letters of the name of Dublin lay heavily upon his mind, pushing one another surlily hither and thither with slow boorish insistence. His soul was fattening and congealing into a gross grease, plunging ever deeper in its dull fear into a sombre threatening dusk while the body that was his stood, listless and dishonoured, gazing out of darkened eyes, helpless, perturbed, and human for a bovine god[191] to stare upon.

The next day brought death and judgement, stirring his soul slowly from its listless despair. The faint glimmer of fear became a terror of spirit as the hoarse voice of the preacher blew death into his soul. He suffered its agony. He felt the death chill touch the extremities and creep onward towards the heart, the film of death veiling the eyes, the bright centres of the brain extinguished one by one like lamps, the last sweat oozing upon the skin, the powerlessness of the dying limbs, the speech thickening and wandering and failing, the heart throbbing faintly and more faintly, all but vanquished, the breath, the poor breath, the poor helpless human spirit, sobbing and sighing, gurgling and rattling in the throat. No help! No help! He – he himself – his body to which he had yielded was dying. Into the grave with it. Nail it down into a wooden box, the corpse. Carry it out of the house on the shoulders of hirelings. Thrust it out of men's sight into a long hole in the ground, into the grave, to rot, to feed the masses of its creeping worms and to be devoured by scuttling plump-bellied rats.

And while the friends were still standing in tears by the bedside the soul of the sinner was judged. At the last moment of consciousness the whole earthly life passed before the vision of the soul and, ere it had time to reflect, the body had died and the soul stood terrified before the judgement seat. God, who had long been merciful, would then be just. He had long been patient, pleading with the sinful soul, giving it time to repent, sparing it yet awhile. But that time had gone. Time was to sin and to enjoy, time was to scoff at God and at the warnings of His holy church, time was to defy His majesty, to disobey His commands, to hoodwink one's fellow men, to commit sin after sin and to hide one's corruption from the sight of men. But that time was over. Now it was God's turn: and He was not to be hoodwinked or deceived. Every sin would then come forth from its lurking place, the most rebellious against the divine will and the most degrading to our poor corrupt nature, the tiniest imperfection and the most heinous atrocity. What did it avail then to have been a great emperor, a great general, a marvellous inventor, the most learned of the learned? All were as one before the judgement seat of God. He would reward the good and punish the wicked. One single instant was enough for the trial of a man's soul. One single instant after the body's death, the soul had been weighed in the balance. The particular judgment was over and the soul had passed to the abode of bliss or to the prison of purgatory or had been hurled howling into hell.

Nor was that all. God's justice had still to be vindicated before men: after the particular there still remained the general judgment.[192] The last day had come. The doomsday was at hand. The stars of heaven were falling upon the earth like the figs cast by the fig-tree which the wind has shaken. The sun, the great luminary of the universe, had become as sackcloth of hair. The moon was blood-red. The firmament was as a scroll rolled away.[193] The archangel Michael, the prince of the heavenly host, appeared glorious and terrible against the sky. With one foot on the sea and one foot on the land he blew from the arch-angelical trumpet the brazen death of time.[194] The three blasts of the angel filled all the universe. Time is, time was, but time shall be no more. At the last blast the souls of universal humanity throng towards the valley of Jehoshaphat,[195] rich and poor, gentle and simple, wise and foolish, good and wicked. The soul of every human being that has ever existed, the souls of all those who shall yet be born, all the sons and daughters of Adam, all are assembled on that supreme day. And lo, the supreme judge is coming! No longer the lowly Lamb of God, no longer the meek Jesus of Nazareth, no longer the Man of Sorrows, no longer the Good Shepherd, He is seen now coming upon the clouds, in great power and majesty, attended by nine choirs of angels, angels and archangels, principalities, powers and virtues, thrones and dominations, cherubim and seraphim, God Omnipotent, God Everlasting.[196] He speaks: and His voice is heard even at the farthest limits of space, even in the bottomless abyss. Supreme Judge, from His sentence there will be and can be no appeal. He calls the just to His side, bidding them enter into the kingdom, the eternity of bliss prepared for them. The unjust He casts from Him, crying in His offended majesty: *Depart from me, ye cursed, into everlasting fire which was prepared for the devil and his angels.*[197] O, what agony then for the miserable sinners! Friend is torn apart from friend, children are torn from their parents, husbands from their wives. The poor sinner holds out his arms to those who were dear to him in this earthly world, to those whose simple piety perhaps he made a mock of, to those who counselled him and tried to lead him on the right path, to a kind brother, to a loving sister, to the mother and father who loved him so dearly. But it is too late: the just turn away from the wretched damned souls which now appear before the eyes of all in their hideous and evil character. O you hypocrites, O, you whited sepulchres,[198] O you who present a smooth smiling face to the world while your soul within is a foul swamp of sin, how will it fare with you in that terrible day?

And this day will come, shall come, must come: the day of death and the day of judgment. It is appointed unto man to die and after death the judgment. Death is certain. The time and manner are uncertain, whether from long disease or from some unexpected accident: the Son of God cometh at an hour when you little expect Him. Be therefore ready every moment, seeing that you may die at any moment. Death is the end of us all. Death and judgment, brought into the world by the sin of our first parents, are the dark portals that close our earthly existence, the portals that open into the unknown and the unseen, portals through which every soul must pass, alone, unaided save by its good works, without friend or brother or parent or master to help it, alone and trembling. Let that thought be ever before our minds and then we cannot sin. Death, a cause of terror to the sinner, is a blessed moment for him who has walked in the right path, fulfilling the duties of his station in life, attending to his morning and evening prayers, approaching the holy sacrament frequently and performing good and merciful works. For the pious and believing catholic, for the just man, death is no cause of terror. Was it not Addison, the great English writer, who, when on his deathbed, sent for the wicked young earl of Warwick[199] to let him see how a christian can meet his end? He it is and he alone, the pious and believing-christian, who can say in his heart:

> *O grave, where is thy victory?*
> *O death, where is thy sting?*[200]

Every word of it was for him. Against his sin, foul and secret, the whole wrath of God was aimed. The preacher's knife had probed deeply into his disclosed conscience and he felt now that his soul was festering in sin. Yes, the preacher was right. God's turn had come. Like a beast in its lair his soul had lain down in its own filth but the blasts of the angel's trumpet had driven him forth from the darkness of sin into the light. The words of doom cried by the angel shattered in an instant his presumptuous peace. The wind of the last day blew through his mind, his sins, the jewel-eyed harlots of his imagination, fled before the hurricane, squeaking like mice in their terror and huddled under a mane of hair.

As he crossed the square, walking homeward, the light laughter of a girl reached his burning ear. The frail gay sound smote his heart more strongly than a trumpet blast, and, not daring to lift his eyes, he turned aside and gazed, as he walked, into the shadow of the tangled shrubs. Shame rose from his smitten heart and flooded his whole being. The image of Emma appeared before him, and under her eyes the flood of shame rushed forth anew from his heart. If she knew to what his mind had subjected her or how his brute-like lust had torn and trampled upon her innocence! Was that boyish love? Was that chivalry? Was that poetry? The sordid details of his orgies stank under his very nostrils. The soot-coated packet of pictures which he had hidden in the flue of the fireplace and in the presence of whose shameless or bashful wantonness he lay for hours sinning in thought and deed; his monstrous dreams, peopled by ape-like creatures and by harlots with gleaming jewel eyes; the foul long letters he had written in the joy of guilty confession and carried secretly for days and days only to throw them under cover of night among the grass in the corner of a field or beneath some hingeless door in some niche in the hedges where a girl might come upon them as she walked by and read them secretly. Mad! Mad! Was it possible he had done these things? A cold sweat broke out upon his forehead as the foul memories condensed within his brain.

When the agony of shame had passed from him he tried to raise his soul from its abject powerlessness. God and the Blessed Virgin were too far from him: God was too great and stern and the Blessed Virgin too pure and holy. But he imagined that he stood near Emma in a wide land and, humbly and in tears, bent and kissed the elbow of her sleeve.

In the wide land under a tender lucid evening sky, a cloud drifting westward amid a pale green sea of heaven, they stood together, children that had erred. Their error had offended deeply God's majesty though it was the error of two children; but it had not offended her whose beauty *is not like earthly beauty, dangerous to look upon, but like the morning star which is its emblem, bright and musical*.[201] The eyes were not offended which she turned upon him nor reproachful. She placed their hands together, hand in hand, and said, speaking to their hearts:

– Take hands, Stephen and Emma. It is a beautiful evening now in heaven. You have erred but you are always my children. It is one heart that loves another heart. Take hands together, my dear children, and you will be happy together and your hearts will love each other.

The chapel was flooded by the dull scarlet light that filtered through the lowered blinds; and through the fissure between the last blind and the sash a shaft of wan light entered like a spear and touched the embossed brasses of the candlestick upon the altar that gleamed like the battle worn mail armour of angels.

Rain was falling on the chapel, on the garden, on the college. It would rain for ever, noiselessly. The water would rise inch by inch, covering the grass and shrubs, covering the trees and houses, covering the monuments and the mountain tops. All life would be choked off, noiselessly: birds, men, elephants, pigs, children: noiselessly floating corpses amid the litter of the wreckage of the world. Forty days and forty nights[202] the rain would fall till the waters covered the face of the earth.

It might be. Why not?

– *Hell has enlarged its soul and opened its mouth without any limits* – words taken, my dear little brothers in Christ Jesus, from the book of Isaias, fifth chapter, fourteenth verse.[203] In the name of the Father and of the Son and of the Holy Ghost. Amen.

The preacher took a chainless watch from a pocket within his soutane and, having considered its dial for a moment in silence, placed it silently before him on the table.

He began to speak in a quiet tone.

– Adam and Eve, my dear boys, were, as you know, our first parents, and you will remember that they were created by God in order that the seats in heaven left vacant by the fall of Lucifer and his rebellious angels might be filled again. Lucifer, we are told, was a son of the morning,[204] a radiant and mighty angel; yet he fell: he fell and there fell with him a third part of the host of heaven: he fell and was hurled with his rebellious angels into hell. What his sin was we cannot say. Theologians consider that it was the sin of pride, the sinful thought conceived in an instant: *non serviam: I will not serve*.[205] That instant was his ruin.

He offended the majesty of God by the sinful thought of one instant and God cast him out of heaven into hell for ever.

– Adam and Eve were then created by God and placed in Eden, in the plain of Damascus, that lovely garden resplendent with sunlight and colour, teaming with luxuriant vegetation. The fruitful earth gave them her bounty: beasts and birds were their willing servants: they knew not the ills our flesh is heir to, disease and poverty and death: all that a great and generous God could do for them was done. But there was one condition imposed on them by God: obedience to His word. They were not to eat of the fruit of the forbidden tree.

– Alas, my dear little boys, they too fell. The devil, once a shining angel, a son of the morning, now a foul fiend came in the shape of a serpent, the subtlest of all the beasts of the field.[206] He envied them. He, the fallen great one, could not bear to think that man, a being of clay, should possess the inheritance which he by his sin had forfeited for ever. He came to the woman, the weaker vessel,[207] and poured the poison of his eloquence into her ear, promising her – O, the blasphemy of that promise! – that if she and Adam ate of the forbidden fruit they would become as gods, nay as God Himself. Eve yielded to the wiles of the archtempter. She ate the apple and gave it also to Adam who had not the moral courage to resist her. The poison tongue of Satan had done its work. They fell.

– And then the voice of God was heard in that garden, calling His creature man to account: and Michael, prince of the heavenly host, with a sword of flame in his hand, appeared before the guilty pair and drove them forth from Eden into the world, the world of sickness and striving, of cruelty and disappointment, of labour and hardship, to earn their bread in the sweat of their brow. But even then how merciful was God! He took pity on our poor degraded parents and promised that in the fullness of time He would send down from heaven One who would redeem them, make them once more children of God and heirs to the kingdom of heaven: and that One, that Redeemer of fallen man, was to be God's only begotten Son, the Second Person of the Most Blessed Trinity, the Eternal Word.

– He came. He was born of a virgin pure, Mary the virgin mother. He was born in a poor cowhouse in Judea[208] and lived as a humble carpenter for thirty years until the hour of His mission had come. And then, filled with love for men, He went forth and called to men to hear the new gospel.[209]

– Did they listen? Yes, they listened but would not hear. He was seized and bound like a common criminal, mocked at as a fool, set aside to give place to a public robber, scourged with five thousand lashes, crowned with a crown of thorns, hustled through the streets by the jewish rabble and the Roman soldiery, stripped of His garments and hanged upon a gibbet and His side was pierced with a lance and from the wounded body of our Lord water and blood issued continually.[210]

– Yet even then, in that hour of supreme agony, Our Merciful Redeemer had pity for mankind. Yet even there, on the hill of Calvary,[211] He founded the holy catholic church[212] against which, it is promised, the gates of hell shall not prevail. He founded it upon the rock of ages,[213] and endowed it with His grace, with sacraments and sacrifice, and promised that if men would obey the word of His church they would still enter into eternal life; but if, after all that had been done for them, they still persisted in their wickedness, there remained for them an eternity of torment: hell.

The preacher's voice sank. He paused, joined his palms for an instant, parted them. Then he resumed:

– Now let us try for a moment to realize, as far as we can, the nature of that abode of the damned which the justice of an offended God has called into existence for the eternal punishment of sinners. Hell is a strait and dark and foul-smelling prison, an abode of demons and lost souls, filled with fire and smoke. The straitness of this prison house is expressly designed by God to punish those who refused to be bound by His laws. In earthly prisons the poor captive had at least some liberty of movement, were it only within the four walls of his cell or is the gloomy yard of his prison. Not so in hell. There, by reason of the great number of the damned, the prisoners are heaped together in their awful prison, the walls of which are said to be four thousand miles thick: and the damned are so utterly bound and helpless that, as a blessed saint, saint Anselm, writes in his book on similitudes,[214] they are not even able to remove from the eye a worm that gnaws it.

– They lie in exterior darkness. For, remember, the fire of hell gives forth no light. As, at the command of God, the fire of the Babylonian furnace[215] lost its heat but not its light, so, at the command of God, the fire of hell, while retaining the intensity of its heat, burns eternally in darkness. It is a never ending storm of darkness, dark flames and dark smoke of burning brimstone, amid which the bodies are heaped one upon another without even a glimpse of air. Of all the plagues with which the land of the Pharaohs were smitten one plague alone, that of darkness, was called horrible.[216] What name, then, shall we give to the darkness of hell which is to last not for three days alone but for all eternity?

– The horror of this strait and dark prison is increased by its awful stench. All the filth of the world, all the offal and scum of the world, we are told, shall run there as to a vast reeking sewer when the terrible conflagration of the last day has purged the world. The brimstone, too, which burns there in such prodigious quantity fills all hell with its intolerable stench; and the bodies of the damned themselves exhale such a pestilential odour that, as saint Bonaventure[217] says, one of them alone would suffice to infect the whole world. The very air of this world, that pure element, becomes foul and unbreathable when it has been long enclosed. Consider then what must be the foulness of the air of hell. Imagine some foul and putrid corpse that has lain rotting and decomposing in the grave, a jelly-like mass of liquid corruption. Imagine such a corpse a prey to flames, devoured by the fire of burning brimstone and giving off dense choking fumes of nauseous loathsome decomposition. And then imagine this sickening stench, multiplied a millionfold and a millionfold again from the millions upon millions of fetid carcasses massed together in the reeking darkness, a huge and rotting human fungus. Imagine all this, and you will have some idea of the horror of the stench of hell.

– But this stench is not, horrible though it is, the greatest physical torment to which the damned are subjected. The torment of fire is the greatest torment to which the tyrant has ever subjected his fellow creatures. Place your finger for a moment in the flame of a candle and you will feel the pain of fire. But our earthly fire was created by God for the benefit of man, to maintain in him the spark of life and to help him in the useful arts, whereas the fire of hell is of another quality and was created by God to torture and punish the unrepentant sinner. Our earthly fire also consumes more or less rapidly according as the object which it attacks is more or less combustible, so that human ingenuity has even succeeded in inventing chemical preparations to check or frustrate its action. But the sulphurous brimstone which burns in hell is a substance which is specially designed to burn for ever and for ever with unspeakable fury. Moreover, our earthly fire destroys at the same time as it burns, so that the more intense it is the shorter is its duration; but the fire of hell has this property, that it preserves that which it burns, and, though it rages with incredible intensity, it rages for ever.

– Our earthly fire again, no matter how fierce or widespread it may be, is always of a limited extent; but the lake of fire in hell is boundless, shoreless and bottomless. It is on record that the devil himself, when asked the question by a certain soldier, was obliged to confess that if a whole mountain were thrown into the burning ocean of hell it would be burned up in an instant like a piece of wax. And this terrible fire will not afflict the bodies of the damned only from without, but each lost soul will be a hell unto itself, the boundless fire raging in its very vitals. O, how terrible is the lot of those wretched beings! The blood seethes and boils in the veins, the brains are boiling in the skull, the heart in the breast glowing and bursting, the bowels a red-hot mass of burning pulp, the tender eyes flaming like molten balls.

– And yet what I have said as to the strength and quality and boundlessness of this fire is as nothing when compared to its intensity, an intensity which it has as being the instrument chosen by divine design for the punishment of soul and body alike. It is a fire which proceeds directly from the ire of God, working not of its own activity but as an instrument of Divine vengeance. As the waters of baptism cleanse the soul with the body, so do the fires of punishment torture the spirit with the flesh. Every sense of the flesh is tortured and every faculty of the soul therewith: the eyes with impenetrable utter darkness, the nose with noisome odours, the ears with yells and howls and execrations, the taste with foul matter, leprous corruption, nameless suffocating filth, the touch with red-hot goads and spikes, with cruel tongues of flame. And through the several torments of the senses the immortal soul is tortured eternally in its very essence amid the leagues upon leagues of glowing fires kindled in the abyss by the offended majesty of the Omnipotent God and fanned into everlasting and ever-increasing fury by the breath of the anger of the God-head.

– Consider finally that the torment of this infernal prison is increased by the company of the damned themselves. Evil company on earth is so noxious that the plants, as if by instinct, withdraw from the company of whatsoever is deadly or hurtful to them. In hell all laws are overturned – there is no thought of family or country, of ties, of relationships. The damned howl and scream at one another, their torture and rage intensified by the presence of beings tortured and raging like themselves. All sense of humanity is forgotten. The yells of the suffering sinners fill the remotest corners of the vast abyss. The mouths of the damned are full of blasphemies against God and of hatred for their fellow sufferers and of curses against those which were their accomplices in sin. In olden times it was the custom to punish the parricide, the man who had raised his murderous hand against his father, by casting him into the depths of the sea in a sack in which were placed a cock, a monkey, and a serpent.[218] The intention of those law-givers who framed such a law, which seems cruel in our times, was to punish the criminal by the company of hurtful and hateful beasts. But what is the fury of those dumb beasts compared with the fury of execration which bursts from the parched lips and aching throats of the damned in hell when they behold in their companions in misery those who aided and abetted them in sin, those whose words sowed the first seeds of evil thinking and evil living in their minds, those whose immodest suggestions led them on to sin, those whose eyes tempted and allured them from the path of virtue. They turn upon those accomplices and upbraid them and curse them. But they are helpless and hopeless: it is too late now for repentance.

– Last of all consider the frightful torment to those damned souls, tempters and tempted alike, of the company of the devils. These devils will afflict the damned in two ways, by their presence and by their reproaches. We can have no idea of how horrible these devils are. Saint Catherine of Siena once saw a devil[219] and she has written that, rather than look again for one single instant on such a frightful monster, she would prefer to walk until the end of her life along a track of red coals. These devils, who were once beautiful angels, have become as hideous and ugly as they once were beautiful. They mock and jeer at the lost souls whom they dragged down to ruin. It is they, the foul demons, who are made in hell the voices of conscience. Why did you sin? Why did you lend an ear to the temptings of friends? Why did you turn aside from your pious practices and good works? Why did you not shun the occasions of sin? Why did you not leave that evil companion? Why did you not give up that lewd habit, that impure habit? Why did you not listen to the counsels of your confessor? Why did you not, even after you had fallen the first or the second or the third or the fourth or the hundredth time, repent of your evil ways and turn to God who only waited for your repentance to absolve you of your sins? Now the time for repentance has gone by. Time is, time was, but time shall be no more! Time was to sin in secrecy, to indulge in that sloth and pride, to covet the unlawful, to yield to the promptings of your lower nature, to live like the beasts of the field, nay worse than the beasts of the field, for they, at least, are but brutes and have no reason to guide them: time was, but time shall be no more. God spoke to you by so many voices, but you would not hear. You would not crush out that pride and anger in your heart, you would not restore those ill-gotten goods, you would not obey the precepts of your holy church nor attend to your religious duties, you would not abandon those wicked companions, you would not avoid those dangerous temptations. Such is the language of those fiendish tormentors, words of taunting and of reproach, of hatred and of disgust. Of disgust, yes! For even they, the very devils, when they sinned, sinned by such a sin as alone was compatible with such angelical natures, a rebellion of the intellect: and they, even they, the foul devils must turn away, revolted and disgusted, from the contemplation of those unspeakable sins by which degraded man outrages and defiles the temple of the Holy Ghost, defiles and pollutes himself.

– O, my dear little brothers in Christ, may it never be our lot to hear that language! May it never be our lot, I say! In the last day of terrible reckoning I pray fequently to God that not a single soul of those who are in this chapel today may be found among those miserable beings whom the Great Judge shall command to depart for ever from His sight, that not one of us may ever hear ringing in his ears the awful sentence of rejection: *Depart from me, ye cursed, into everlasting fire which was prepared for the devil and his angels!*[220]

He came down the aisle of the chapel, his legs shaking and the scalp of his head trembling as though it had been touched by ghostly fingers. He passed up the staircase and into the corridor along the walls of which the overcoats and waterproofs hung like gibbeted malefactors, headless and dripping and shapeless. And at every step he feared that he had already died, that his soul had been wrenched forth of the sheath of his body, that he was plunging headlong through space.

He could not grip the floor with his feet and sat heavily at his desk, opening one of his books at random and poring over it. Every word for him. It was true. God was almighty. God could call him now, call him as he sat at his desk, before he had time to be conscious of the summons. God had called him. Yes? What? Yes? His flesh shrank together as it felt the approach of the ravenous tongues of flames, dried up as it felt about it the swirl of stifling air. He had died. Yes. He was judged. A wave of fire swept through his body: the first. Again a wave. His brain began to glow. Another. His brain was simmering and bubbling within the cracking tenement of the skull. Flames burst forth from his skull like a corolla, shrieking like voices: –Hell! Hell! Hell! Hell! Hell!

Voices spoke near him:

– On hell.

– I suppose he rubbed it into you well.

– You bet he did. He put us all into a blue funk.[221]

– That's what you fellows want: and plenty of it to make you work.

He leaned back weakly in his desk. He had not died. God had spared him still. He was still in the familiar world of the school. Mr Tate and Vincent Heron stood at the window, talking, jesting, gazing out at the bleak rain, moving their heads.

– I wish it would clear up. I had arranged to go for a spin on the bike with some fellows out by Malahide.[222] But the roads must be knee-deep.

– It might clear up, sir.

The voices that he knew so well, the common words, the quiet of the classroom when the voices paused and the silence was filled by the sound of softly browsing cattle as the other boys munched their lunches tranquilly, lulled his aching soul.

There was still time. O Mary, refuge of sinners, intercede for him! O Virgin Undefiled, save him from the gulf of death!

The English lesson began with the hearing of the history. Royal persons, favourites, intriguers, bishops, passed like mute phantoms behind their veil of names. All had died: all had been judged. What did it profit a man to gain the whole world if he lost his soul? At last he had understood: and human life lay around him, a plain of peace whereon ant-like men laboured in brotherhood, their dead sleeping under quiet mounds. The elbow of his companion touched him and his heart was touched: and when he spoke to answer a question of his master he heard his own voice full of the quietude of humility and contrition.

His soul sank back deeper into depths of contrite peace, no longer able to suffer the pain of dread, and sending forth, as he sank, a faint prayer. Ah yes, he would still be spared; he would repent in his heart and be forgiven; and then those above, those in heaven, would see what he would do to make up for the past: a whole life, every hour of life. Only wait.

– All, God! All, all!

A messenger came to the door to say that confessions were being heard in the chapel. Four boys left the room; and he heard others passing down the corridor. A tremulous chill blew round his heart, no stronger than a little wind, and yet, listening and suffering silently, he seemed to have laid an ear against the muscle of his own heart, feeling it close and quail, listening to the flutter of its ventricles.

No escape. He had to confess, to speak out in words what he had done and thought, sin after sin. How? How?

– Father, I . . .

The thought slid like a cold shining rapier into his tender flesh: confession. But not there in the chapel of the college. He would confess all, every sin of deed and thought, sincerely; but not there among his school companions. Far away from there in some dark place he would murmur out his own shame; and he besought God humbly not to be offended with him if he did not dare to confess in the college chapel and in utter abjection of spirit he craved forgiveness mutely of the boyish hearts about him.

Time passed.

He sat again in the front bench of the chapel. The daylight without was already failing and, as it fell slowly through the dull red blinds, it seemed that the sun of the last day was going down and that all souls were being gathered for the judgment. – *I am cast away from the sight of Thine eyes:* words taken, my dear little brothers in Christ, from the Book of Psalms, thirtieth chapter, twenty-third verse.[223] In the name of the Father and of the Son and of the Holy Ghost. Amen.

The preacher began to speak in a quiet friendly tone. His face was kind and he joined gently the fingers of each hand, forming a frail cage by the union of their tips.

– This morning we endeavoured, in our reflection upon hell, to make what our holy founder calls in his book of spiritual exercises, the composition of place.[224] We endeavoured, that is, to imagine with the senses of the mind, in our imagination, the material character of that awful place and of the physical torments which all who are in hell endure. This evening we shall consider for a few moments the nature of the spiritual torments of hell.

– Sin, remember, is a twofold enormity. It is a base consent to the promptings of our corrupt nature to the lower instincts, to that which is gross and beast-like; and it is also a turning away from the counsel of our higher nature, from all that is pure and holy, from the Holy God Himself. For this reason mortal sin is punished in hell by two different forms of punishment, physical and spiritual.

Now of all these spiritual pains by far the greatest is the pain of loss, so great, in fact, that in itself it is a torment greater than all the others. Saint Thomas, the greatest doctor of the church, the angelic doctor,[225] as he is called, says that the worst damnation consists in this, that the understanding of man is totally deprived of divine light and his affection obstinately turned away from the goodness of God. God, remember, is a being infinitely good, and therefore the loss of such a being must be a loss infinitely painful. In this life we have not a very clear idea of what such a loss must be, but the damned in hell, for their greater torment, have a full understanding of that which they have lost, and understand that they have lost it through their own sins and have lost it for ever. At the very instant of death the bonds of the flesh are broken asunder and the soul at once flies towards God as towards the centre of her existence. Remember, my dear little boys, our souls long to be with God. We come from God, we live by God, we belong to God: we are His, inalienably His. God loves with a divine love every human soul, and every human soul lives in that love. How could it be otherwise? Every breath that we draw, every thought of our brain, every instant of life proceeds from God's inexhaustible goodness. And if it be pain for a mother to be parted from her child, for a man to be exiled from hearth and home, for friend to be sundered from friend, O think what pains what anguish it must be for the poor soul to be spurned from the presence of the supremely good and loving Creator Who has called that soul into existence from nothingness and sustained it in life and loved it with an immeasurable love. This, then, to be separated for ever from its greatest good, from God, and to feel the anguish of that separation, knowing full well that it is unchangeable: this is the greatest torment which the created soul is capable of bearing, *poena damni*, the pain of loss.[226]

The second pain which will afflict the souls of the damned in hell is the pain of conscience. Just as in dead bodies worms are engendered by putrefaction, so in the souls of the lost there arises a perpetual remorse from the putrefaction of sin, the sting of conscience, the worm, as Pope Innocent the Third calls it, of the triple sting.[227] The first sting inflicted by this cruel worm will be the memory of past pleasures. O what a dreadful memory will that be! In the lake of all-devouring flame the proud king will remember the pomps of his court, the wise but wicked man his libraries and instruments of research, the lover of artistic pleasures his marbles and pictures and other art treasures, he who delighted in the pleasures of the table his gorgeous feasts, his dishes prepared with such delicacy, his choice wines; the miser will remember his hoard of gold, the robber his ill-gotten wealth, the angry and revengeful and merciless murderers their deeds of blood and violence in which they revelled, the impure and adulterous the unspeakable and filthy pleasures in which they delighted. They will remember all this and loathe themselves and their sins. For how miserable will all those pleasures seem to the soul condemned to suffer in hellfire for ages and ages. How they will rage and fume to think that they have lost the bliss of heaven for the dross of earth, for a few pieces of metal, for vain honours, for bodily comforts, for a tingling of the nerves. They will repent indeed: and this is the second sting of the worm of conscience, a late and fruitless sorrow for sins committed. Divine justice insists that the understanding of those miserable wretches be fixed continually on the sins of which they were guilty, and moreover, as saint Augustine[228] points out, God will impart to them His own knowledge of sin, so that sin will appear to them in all its hideous malice as it appears to the eyes of God Himself. They will behold their sins in all their foulness and repent but it will be too late and then they will bewail the good occasions which they neglected. This is the last and deepest and most cruel sting of the worm of conscience. The conscience will say: You had time and opportunity to repent and would not. You were brought up religiously by your parents. You had the sacraments and grace and indulgences of the church to aid you. You had the minister of God to preach to you, to call you back when you had strayed, to forgive you your sins, no matter how many, how abominable, if only you had confessed and repented. No. You would not. You flouted the ministers of holy religion, you turned your back on the confessional, you wallowed deeper and deeper in the mire of sin. God appealed to you, threatened you, entreated you to return to Him. O, what shame, what misery! The Ruler of the universe entreated you, a creature of clay, to love Him Who made you and to keep His law. No. You would not. And now, though you were to flood all hell with your tears if you could still weep, all that sea of repentance would not gain for you what a single tear of true repentance shed during your mortal life would have gained for you. You implore now a moment of earthly life wherein to repent: in vain. That time is gone: gone for ever.

– Such is the threefold sting of conscience, the viper which gnaws the very heart's core of the wretches in hell, so that filled with hellish fury they curse themselves for their folly and curse the evil companions who have brought them to such ruin and curse the devils who tempted them in life and now mock them in eternity and even revile and curse the Supreme Being Whose goodness and patience they scorned and slighted but Whose justice and power they cannot evade.

– The next spiritual pain to which the damned are subjected is the pain of extension. Man, in this earthly life, though he be capable of many evils, is not capable of them all at once, in as much as one evil corrects and counteracts another just as one poison frequently corrects another. In hell, on the contrary, one torment, instead of counteracting another, lends it still greater force: and, moreover, as the internal faculties are more perfect than the external senses, so are they more capable of suffering. Just as every sense is afflicted with a fitting torment, so is every spiritual faculty; the fancy with horrible images, the sensitive faculty with alternate longing and rage, the mind and understanding with an interior darkness more terrible even than the exterior darkness which reigns in that dreadful prison. The malice, impotent though it be, which possesses these demon souls is an evil of boundless extension, of limitless duration, a frightful state of wickedness which we can scarcely realize unless we bear in mind the enormity of sin and the hatred God bears to it.

– Opposed to this pain of extension and yet coexistent with it we have the pain of intensity. Hell is the centre of evils and, as you know, things are more intense at their centres than at their remotest points. There are no contraries or admixtures of any kind to temper or soften in the least the pains of hell. Nay, things which are good in themselves become evil in hell. Company, elsewhere a source of comfort to the afflicted, will be there a continual torment: knowledge, so much longed for as the chief good of the intellect, will there be hated worse than ignorance: light, so much coveted by all creatures from the lord of creation down to the humblest plant in the forest, will be loathed intensely. In this life our sorrows are either not very long or not very great because nature either overcomes them by habits or puts an end to them by sinking under their weight. But in hell the torments cannot be overcome by habit, for while they are of terrible intensity they are at the same time of continual variety, each pain, so to speak, taking fire from another and re-endowing that which has enkindled it with a still fiercer flame. Nor can nature escape from these intense and various tortures by succumbing to them for the soul is sustained and maintained in evil so that its suffering may be the greater. Boundless extension of torment, incredible intensity of suffering, unceasing variety of torture – this is what the divine majesty, so outraged by sinners, demands; this is what the holiness of heaven, slighted and set aside for the lustful and low pleasures of the corrupt flesh, requires; this is what the blood of the innocent Lamb of God, shed for the redemption of sinners, trampled upon by the vilest of the vile, insists upon.

– Last and crowning torture of all the tortures of that awful place is the eternity of hell. Eternity! O, dread and dire word. Eternity! What mind of man can understand it? And remember, it is an eternity of pain. Even though the pains of hell were not so terrible as they are, yet they would become infinite, as they are destined to last for ever. But while they are everlasting they are at the same time, as you know, intolerably intense, unbearably extensive. To bear even the sting of an insect for all eternity would be a dreadful torment. What must it be, then, to bear the manifold tortures of hell for ever? For ever! For all eternity! Not for a year or for an age but for ever. Try to imagine the awful meaning of this. You have often seen the sand on the seashore. How fine are its tiny grains! And how many of those tiny little grains go to make up the small handful which a child grasps in its play. Now imagine a mountain of that sand, a million miles high, reaching from the earth to the farthest heavens, and a million miles broad, extending to remotest space, and a million miles in thickness; and imagine such an enormous mass of countless particles of sand multiplied as often as there are leaves in the forest, drops of water in the mighty ocean, feathers on birds, scales on fish, hairs on animals, atoms in the vast expanse of the air: and imagine that at the end of every million years a little bird came to that mountain and carried away in its beak a tiny grain of that sand. How many millions upon millions of centuries would pass before that bird had carried away even a square foot of that mountain, how many eons upon eons of ages before it had carried away all? Yet at the end of that immense stretch of time not even one instant of eternity could be said to have ended. At the end of all those billions and trillions of years eternity would have scarcely begun. And if that mountain rose again after it had been all carried away, and if the bird came again and carried it all away again grain by grain, and if it so rose and sank as many times as there are stars in the sky, atoms in the air, drops of water in the sea, leaves on the trees, feathers upon birds, scales upon fish, hairs upon animals, at the end of all those innumerable risings and sinkings of that immeasurably vast mountain not one single instant of eternity could be said to have ended; even then, at the end of such a period, after that eon of time the mere thought of which makes our very brain reel dizzily, eternity would scarcely have begun.

– A holy saint (one of our own fathers I believe it was) was once vouchsafed a vision of hell. It seemed to him that he stood in the midst of a great hall, dark and silent save for the ticking of a great clock. The ticking went on unceasingly; and it seemed to this saint that the sound of the ticking was the ceaseless repetition of the words – ever, never; ever, never. Ever to be in hell, never to be in heaven; ever to be shut off from the presence of God, never to enjoy the beatific vision; ever to be eaten with flames, gnawed by vermin, goaded with burning spikes, never to be free from those pains; ever to have the conscience upbraid one, the memory enrage, the mind filled with darkness and despair, never to escape; ever to curse and revile the foul demons who gloat fiendishly over the misery of their dupes, never to behold the shining raiment of the blessed spirits; ever to cry out of the abyss of fire to God for an instant, a single instant, of respite from such awful agony, never to receive, even for an instant, God's pardon; ever to suffer, never to enjoy; ever to be damned, never to be saved; ever, never; ever, never. O, what a dreadful punishment! An eternity of endless agony, of endless bodily and spiritual torment, without one ray of hope, without one moment of cessation, of agony limitless in intensity, of torment infinitely varied, of torture that sustains eternally that which it eternally devours, of anguish that everlastingly preys upon the spirit while it racks the flesh, an eternity, every instant of which is itself an eternity of woe. Such is the terrible punishment decreed for those who die in mortal sin by an almighty and a just God.

– Yes, a just God! Men, reasoning always as men, are astonished that God should mete out an everlasting and infinite punishment in the fires of hell for a single grievous sin. They reason thus because, blinded by the gross illusion of the flesh and the darkness of human understanding, they are unable to comprehend the hideous malice of mortal sin. They reason thus because they are unable to comprehend that even venial sin[229] is of such a foul and hideous nature that even if the omnipotent Creator could end all the evil and misery in the world, the wars, the diseases, the robberies, the crimes, the deaths, the murders, on condition that he allowed a single venial sin to pass unpunished, a single venial sin, a lie, an angry look, a moment of wilful sloth, He, the great omnipotent God could not do so because sin, be it in thought or deeds is a transgression of His law and God would not be God if He did not punish the transgressor.

– A sin, an instant of rebellious pride of the intellect, made Lucifer and a third part of the cohort of angels fall from their glory.[230] A sin, an instant of folly and weakness, drove Adam and Eve out of Eden and brought death and suffering into the world. To retrieve the consequences of that sin the Only Begotten Son of God came down to earth, lived and suffered and died a most painful death, hanging for three hours on the cross.[231]

– O, my dear little brethren in Christ Jesus, will we then offend that good Redeemer and provoke His anger? Will we trample again upon that torn and mangled corpse? Will we spit upon that face so full of sorrow and love? Will we too, like the cruel jews and the brutal soldiers, mock that gentle and compassionate Saviour Who trod alone for our sake the awful winepress of sorrow? Every word of sin is a wound in His tender side. Every sinful act is a thorn piercing His head. Every impure thought, deliberately yielded to, is a keen lance transfixing that sacred and loving heart. No, no. It is impossible for any human being to do that which offends so deeply the divine majesty, that which is punished by an eternity of agony, that which crucifies again the Son of God and makes a mockery of Him.

– I pray to God that my poor words may have availed today to confirm in holiness those who are in a state of grace, to strengthen the wavering, to lead back to the state of grace the poor soul that has strayed if any such be among you. I pray to God, and do you pray with me, that we may repent of our sins. I will ask you now, all of you, to repeat after me the act of contrition,[232] kneeling here in this humble chapel in the presence of God. He is there in the tabernacle burning with love for mankind, ready to comfort the afflicted. Be not afraid. No matter how many or how foul the sins if you only repent of them they will be forgiven you. Let no worldly shame hold you back. God is still the merciful Lord who wishes not the eternal death of the sinner but rather that he be converted and live.

– He calls you to Him. You are His. He made you out of nothing. He loved you as only a God can love. His arms are open to receive you even though you have sinned against Him. Come to Him, poor sinner, poor vain and erring sinner. Now is the acceptable time. Now is the hour.

The priest rose and, turning towards the altar, knelt upon the step before the tabernacle in the fallen gloom. He waited till all in the chapel had knelt and every least noise was still. Then, raising his head, he repeated the act of contrition, phrase by phrase, with fervour. The boys answered him phrase by phrase. Stephen, his tongue cleaving to his palate, bowed his head, praying with his heart.

> – *O my God!* –
> – *O my God!* –
> – *I am heartily sorry* –
> – *I am heartily sorry* –
> – *for having offended Thee* –
> – *for having offended Thee* –
> – *and I detest my sins* –
> – *and I detest my sins* –
> – *above every other evil* –

– above every other evil –
– because they displease Thee, my God –
– because they displease Thee, my God –
– Who art so deserving –
– Who art so deserving –
– of all my love –
– of all my love –
– and I firmly purpose –
– and I firmly purpose –
– by Thy holy grace –
– by Thy holy grace –
– never more to offend Thee –
– never more to offend Thee –
– and to amend my life –
– and to amend my life –

He went up to his room after dinner in order to be alone with his soul, and at every step his soul seemed to sigh; at every step his soul mounted with his feet, sighing in the ascent, through a region of viscid gloom.

He halted on the landing before the door and then, grasping the porcelain knob, opened the door quickly. He waited in fear, his soul pining within him, praying silently that death might not touch his brow as he passed over the threshold, that the fiends that inhabit darkness might not be given power over him. He waited still at the threshold as at the entrance to some dark cave. Faces were there; eyes: they waited and watched.

– We knew perfectly well of course that though it was bound to come to the light he would find considerable difficulty in endeavouring to try to induce himself to try to endeavour to ascertain the spiritual plenipotentiary and so we knew of course perfectly well –

Murmuring faces waited and watched; murmurous voices filled the dark shell of the cave. He feared intensely in spirit and in flesh but, raising his head bravely, he strode into the room firmly. A doorway, a room, the same room, same window. He told himself calmly that those words had absolutely no sense which had seemed to rise murmurously from the dark. He told himself that it was simply his room with the door open.

He closed the door and, walking swiftly to the bed, knelt beside it and covered his face with his hands. His hands were cold and damp and his limbs ached with chill. Bodily unrest and chill and weariness beset him, routing his thoughts. Why was he kneeling there like a child saying his evening prayers? To be alone with his soul, to examine his conscience, to meet his sins face to face, to recall their times and manners and circumstances, to weep over them. He could not weep. He could not summon them to his memory. He felt only an ache of soul and body, his whole being, memory, will, understanding, flesh, benumbed and weary.

That was the work of devils, to scatter his thoughts and overcloud his conscience, assailing him at the gates of the cowardly and sin-corrupted flesh: and, praying God timidly to forgive him his weakness, he crawled up on to the bed and, wrapping the blankets closely about him, covered his face again with his hands. He had sinned. He had sinned so deeply against heaven and before God that he was not worthy to be called God's child.

Could it be that he, Stephen Dedalus, had done those things? His conscience sighed in answer. Yes, he had done them, secretly, filthily, time after time, and, hardened in sinful impenitence, he had dared to wear the mask of holiness before the tabernacle itself while his soul within was a living mass of corruption. How came it that God had not struck him dead? The leprous company of his sins closed about him, breathing upon him, bending over him from all sides. He strove to forget them in an act of prayer, huddling his limbs closer together and binding down his eyelids: but the senses of his soul would not be bound and, though his eyes were shut fast, he saw the places where he had sinned and, though his ears were tightly covered, he heard. He desired with all his will not to hear or see. He desired till his frame shook under the strain of his desire and until the senses of his soul closed. They closed for an instant and then opened. He saw.

A field of stiff weeds and thistles and tufted nettle-bunches. Thick among the tufts of rank stiff growth lay battered canisters and clots and coils of solid excrement. A faint marshlight struggling upwards from all the ordure through the bristling grey-green weeds. An evil smell, faint and foul as the light, curled upwards sluggishly out of the canisters and from the stale crusted dung.

Creatures were in the field: one, three, six: creatures were moving in the field, hither and thither. Goatish creatures with human faces, hornybrowed, lightly bearded and grey as india-rubber. The malice of evil glittered in their hard eyes, as they moved hither and thither, trailing their long tails behind them. A rictus of cruel malignity lit up greyly their old bony faces. One was clasping about his ribs a torn flannel waistcoat, another complained monotonously as his beard stuck in the tufted weeds. Soft language issued from their spittleless lips as they swished in slow circles round and round the field, winding hither and thither through the weeds, dragging their long tails amid the rattling canisters. They moved in slow circles, circling closer and closer to enclose, to enclose, soft language issuing from their lips, their long swishing tails besmeared with stale shite, thrusting upwards their terrific faces . . .

Help!

He flung the blankets from him madly to free his face and neck. That was his hell. God had allowed him to see the hell reserved for his sins: stinking, bestial, malignant, a hell of lecherous goatish fiends. For him! For him!

He sprang from the bed, the reeking odour pouring down his throat, clogging and revolting his entrails. Air! The air of heaven! He stumbled towards the window, groaning and almost fainting with sickness. At the washstand a convulsion seized him within; and, clasping his cold forehead wildly, he vomited profusely in agony.

When the fit had spent itself he walked weakly to the window and, lifting the sash, sat in a corner of the embrasure and leaned his elbow upon the sill. The rain had drawn off; and amid the moving vapours from point to point of light the city was spinning about herself a soft cocoon of yellowish haze. Heaven was still and faintly luminous and the air sweet to breathe, as in a thicket drenched with showers; and amid peace and shimmering lights and quiet fragrance he made a covenant with his heart.

He prayed:

> – He once had meant to come on earth in heavenly glory but we sinned; and then He could not safely visit us but with a shrouded majesty and a bedimmed radiance for He was God. So He came Himself in weakness not in power and He sent thee, a creature in His stead, with a creature's comeliness and lustre suited to our state. And now thy very face and form, dear mother, speak to us of the Eternal; not like earthly beauty, dangerous to look upon, but like the morning star which is thy emblem, bright and musical, breathing purity, telling of heaven and infusing peace. O harbinger of day! O light of the pilgrim! Lead us still as thou hast led. In the dark night, across the bleak wilderness guide us on to our Lord Jesus, guide us home.[233]

His eyes were dimmed with tears and, looking humbly up to heaven, he wept for the innocence he had lost.

When evening had fallen he left the house, and the first touch of the damp dark air and the noise of the door as it closed behind him made ache again his conscience, lulled by prayer and tears. Confess! Confess! It was not enough to lull the conscience with a tear and a prayer. He had to kneel before the minister of the Holy Ghost and tell over his hidden sins truly and repentantly. Before he heard again the footboard of the housedoor trail over the threshold as it opened to let him in, before he saw again the table in the kitchen set for supper he would have knelt and confessed. It was quite simple.

The ache of conscience ceased and he walked onward swiftly through the dark streets. There were so many flagstones on the footpath of that street and so many streets in that city and so many cities in the world. Yet eternity had no end. He was in mortal sin. Even once was a mortal sin. It could happen in an instant. But how so quickly? By seeing or by thinking of seeing. The eyes see the thing, without having wished first to see. Then in an instant it happens. But does that part of the body understand or what? The serpent, the most subtle beast of the field. It must understand when it desires in one instant and then prolongs its own desire instant after instant, sinfully. It feels and understands and desires. What a horrible thing! Who made it to be like that, a bestial part of the body able to understand bestially and desire bestially? Was that then he or an inhuman thing moved by a lower soul? His soul sickened at the thought of a torpid snaky life feeding itself out of the tender marrow of his life and fattening upon the slime of lust. O why was that so? O why?

He cowered in the shadow of the thought, abasing himself in the awe of God Who had made all things and all men. Madness. Who could think such a thought? And, cowering in darkness and abject, he prayed mutely to his guardian angel to drive away with his sword the demon that was whispering to his brain.

The whisper ceased and he knew then clearly that his own soul had sinned in thought and word and deed wilfully through his own body. Confess! He had to confess every sin. How could he utter in words to the priest what he had done? Must, must. Or how could he explain without dying of shame? Or how could he have done such things without shame? A madman! Confess! O he would indeed to be free and sinless again! Perhaps the priest would know. O dear God!

He walked on and on through ill-lit streets, fearing to stand still for a moment lest it might seem that he held back from what awaited him, fearing to arrive at that towards which he still turned with longing. How beautiful must be a soul in the state of grace when God looked upon it with love!

Frowsy girls sat along the curbstones before their baskets. Their dank hair hung trailed over their brows. They were not beautiful to see as they crouched in the mire. But their souls were seen by God; and if their souls were in a state of grace they were radiant to see: and God loved them, seeing them.

A wasting breath of humiliation blew bleakly over his soul to think of how he had fallen, to feel that those souls were dearer to God than his. The wind blew over him and passed on to the myriads and myriads of other souls on whom God's favour shone now more and now less, stars now brighter and now dimmer sustained and failing. And the glimmering souls passed away, sustained and failing, merged in a moving breath. One soul was lost; a tiny soul: his. It flickered once and went out, forgotten, lost. The end: black, cold, void waste.

Consciousness of place came ebbing back to him slowly over a vast tract of time unlit, unfelt, unlived. The squalid scene composed itself around him; the common accents, the burning gas-jets in the shops, odours of fish and spirits and wet sawdust, moving men and women. An old woman was about to cross the street, an oilcan in her hand. He bent down and asked her was there a chapel near.

– A chapel, sir? Yes, sir. Church Street chapel.[234]

– Church?

She shifted the can to her other hand and directed him; and, as she held out her reeking withered right hand under its fringe of shawl, he bent lower towards her, saddened and soothed by her voice.

– Thank you.

– You are quite welcome, sir.

The candles on the high altar had been extinguished but the fragrance of incense still floated down the dim nave. Bearded workmen with pious faces were guiding a canopy out through a side door, the sacristan aiding them with quiet gestures and words. A few of the faithful still lingered praying before one of the side-altars or kneeling in the benches near the confessionals. He approached timidly and knelt at the last bench in the body, thankful for the peace and silence and fragrant shadow of the church. The board on which he knelt was narrow and worn and those who knelt near him were humble followers of Jesus. Jesus too had been born in poverty and had worked in the shop of a carpenter, cutting boards and planing them, and had first spoken of the kingdom of God to poor fishermen, teaching all men to be meek and humble of heart.

He bowed his head upon his hands, bidding his heart be meek and humble that he might be like those who knelt beside him and his prayer as acceptable as theirs. He prayed beside them but it was hard. His soul was foul with sin and he dared not ask forgiveness with the simple trust of those whom Jesus, in the mysterious ways of God, had called first to His side, the carpenters, the fishermen, poor and simple people following a lowly trade, handling and shaping the wood of trees, mending their nets with patience.

A tall figure came down the aisle and the penitents stirred; and at the last moment, glancing up swiftly, he saw a long grey beard and the brown habit of a capuchin.[235] The priest entered the box and was hidden. Two penitents rose and entered the confessional at either side. The wooden slide was drawn back and the faint murmur of a voice troubled the silence.

His blood began to murmur in his veins, murmuring like a sinful city summoned from its sleep to hear its doom. Little flakes of fire fell and powdery ashes fell softly, alighting on the houses of men. They stirred, waking from sleep, troubled by the heated air.

The slide was shot back. The penitent emerged from the side of the box. The farther side was drawn. A woman entered quietly and deftly where the first penitent had knelt. The faint murmur began again.

He could still leave the chapel. He could stand up, put one foot before the other and walk out softly and then run, run, run swiftly through the dark streets. He could still escape from the shame. Had it been any terrible crime but that one sin! Had it been murder! Little fiery flakes fell and touched him at all points, shameful thoughts, shameful words, shameful acts. Shame covered him wholly like fine glowing ashes falling continually. To say it in words! His soul, stifling and helpless, would cease to be.

The slide was shot back. A penitent emerged from the farther side of the box. The near slide was drawn. A penitent entered where the other penitent had come out. A soft whispering noise floated in vaporous cloudlets out of the box. It was the woman: soft whispering cloudlets, soft whispering vapour, whispering and vanishing.

He beat his breast with his fist humbly, secretly under cover of the wooden armrest. He would be at one with others and with God. He would love his neighbour. He would love God who had made and loved him. He would kneel and pray with others and be happy. God would look down on him and on them and would love them all.

It was easy to be good. God's yoke was sweet and light.[236] It was better never to have sinned, to have remained always a child, for God loved little children and suffered them to come to Him.[237] It was a terrible and a sad thing to sin. But God was merciful to poor sinners who were truly sorry. How true that was! That was indeed goodness.

The slide was shot to suddenly. The penitent came out. He was next. He stood up in terror and walked blindly into the box.

At last it had come. He knelt in the silent gloom and raised his eyes to the white crucifix suspended above him. God could see that he was sorry. He would tell all his sins. His confession would be long, long. Everybody in the chapel would know then what a sinner he had been. Let them know. It was true. But God had promised to forgive him if he was sorry. He was sorry. He clasped his hands and raised them towards the white form, praying with his darkened eyes, praying with all his trembling body, swaying his head to and fro like a lost creature, praying with whimpering lips.

– Sorry! Sorry! O sorry!

The slide clicked back and his heart bounded in his breast. The face of an old priest was at the grating, averted from him, leaning upon a hand. He made the sign of the cross and prayed of the priest to bless him for he had sinned. Then, bowing his head, he repeated the *Confiteor* in fright. At the words *my most grievous fault* he ceased, breathless.

– How long is it since your last confession, my child?

– A long time, father.

– A month, my child?

– Longer, father.

– Three months, my child?

– Longer, father.

– Six months?

– Eight months, father.

He had begun. The priest asked:

– And what do you remember since that time?

He began to confess his sins: masses missed, prayers not said, lies.

– Anything else, my child?

Sins of anger, envy of others, gluttony, vanity, disobedience.

– Anything else, my child?

There was no help. He murmured:

– I . . . committed sins of impurity, father.

The priest did not turn his head.

– With yourself, my child?

– And . . . with others.

– With women, my child?

– Yes, father.

– Were they married women, my child?

He did not know. His sins trickled from his lips, one by one, trickled in shameful drops from his soul, festering and oozing like a sore, a squalid stream of vice. The last sins oozed forth, sluggish, filthy. There was no more to tell. He bowed his head, overcome.

The priest was silent. Then he asked:

– How old are you, my child?

– Sixteen, father.

The priest passed his hand several times over his face. Then, resting his forehead against his hand, he leaned towards the grating and, with eyes still averted, spoke slowly. His voice was weary and old.

– You are very young, my child, he said, and let me implore of you to give up that sin. It is a terrible sin. It kills the body and it kills the soul. It is the cause of many crimes and misfortunes. Give it up, my child, for God's sake. It is dishonourable and unmanly. You cannot know where that wretched habit will lead you or where it will come against you. As long as you commit that sin, my poor child, you will never be worth one farthing to God. Pray to our mother Mary to help you. She will help you, my child. Pray to Our Blessed Lady when that sin comes into your mind. I am sure you will do that, will you not? You repent of all those sins. I am sure you do. And you will promise God now that by His holy grace you will never offend Him any more by that wicked sin. You will make that solemn promise to God, will you not?

– Yes, father.

The old and weary voice fell like sweet rain upon his quaking parching heart. How sweet and sad!

– Do so, my poor child. The devil has led you astray. Drive him back to hell when he tempts you to dishonour your body in that way – the foul spirit who hates our Lord. Promise God now that you will give up that sin, that wretched wretched sin.

Blinded by his tears and by the light of God's mercifulness he bent his head and heard the grave words of absolution spoken and saw the priest's hand raised above him in token of forgiveness.

– God bless you, my child. Pray for me.

He knelt to say his penance, praying in a corner of the dark nave; and his prayers ascended to heaven from his purified heart like perfume streaming upwards from a heart of white rose.

The muddy streets were gay. He strode homeward, conscious of an invisible grace pervading and making light his limbs. In spite of all he had done it. He had confessed and God had pardoned him. His soul was made fair and holy once more, holy and happy.

It would be beautiful to die if God so willed. It was beautiful to live in grace a life of peace and virtue and forbearance with others.

He sat by the fire in the kitchen, not daring to speak for happiness. Till that moment he had not known how beautiful and peaceful life could be. The green square of paper pinned round the lamp cast down a tender shade. On the dresser was a plate of sausages and white pudding and on the shelf there were eggs. They would be for the breakfast in the morning after the communion in the college chapel. White pudding and eggs and sausages and cups of tea. How simple and beautiful was life after all! And life lay all before him.

In a dream he fell asleep. In a dream he rose and saw that it was morning. In a waking dream he went through the quiet morning towards the college.

The boys were all there, kneeling in their places. He knelt among them, happy and shy. The altar was heaped with fragrant masses of white flowers; and in the morning light the pale flames of the candles among the white flowers were clear and silent as his own soul.

He knelt before the altar with his classmates, holding the altar cloth with them over a living rail of hands. His hands were trembling and his soul trembled as he heard the priest pass with the ciborium[238] from communicant to communicant.

– *Corpus Domini nostri.*

Could it be? He knelt there sinless and timid; and he would hold upon his tongue the host and God would enter his purified body.

– *In vitam eternam. Amen.*[239]

Another life! A life of grace and virtue and happiness! It was true. It was not a dream from which he would wake. The past was past.

– *Corpus Domini nostri.*

The ciborium had come to him.

Chapter 4

SUNDAY WAS DEDICATED to the mystery of the Holy Trinity, Monday to the Holy Ghost, Tuesday to the Guardian Angels, Wednesday to saint Joseph, Thursday to the Most Blessed Sacrament of the Altar, Friday to the Suffering Jesus, Saturday to the Blessed Virgin Mary.[240]

Every morning he hallowed himself anew in the presence of some holy image or mystery. His day began with an heroic offering of its every moment of thought or action for the intentions of the sovereign pontiff[241] and with an early mass. The raw morning air whetted his resolute piety; and often as he knelt among the few worshippers at the side-altar, following with his interleaved prayer-book[242] the murmur of the priest, he glanced up for an instant towards the vested figure standing in the gloom between the two candles, which were the old and the new testaments,[243] and imagined that he was kneeling at mass in the catacombs.[244]

His daily life was laid out in devotional areas. By means of ejaculations and prayers he stored up ungrudgingly for the souls in purgatory centuries of days and quarantines and years: yet the spiritual triumph which he felt in achieving with ease so many fabulous ages of canonical penances[245] did not wholly reward his zeal of prayer, since he could never know how much temporal punishment he had remitted by way of suffrage for the agonising soul; and, fearful lest in the midst of the purgatorial fire, which differed from the infernal only in that it was not everlasting, his penance might avail no more than a drop of moisture, he drove his soul daily through an increasing circle of works of supererogation.[246]

Every part of his day, divided by what he regarded now as the duties of his station in life, circled about its own centre of spiritual energy. His life seemed to have drawn near to eternity; every thought, word, and deed, every instance of consciousness could be made to revibrate radiantly in heaven; and at times his sense of such immediate repercussion was so lively that he seemed to feel his soul in devotion pressing like fingers the keyboard of a great cash register and to see the amount of his purchase start forth immediately in heaven, not as a number but as a frail column of incense or as a slender flower.

The rosaries, too, which he said constantly – for he carried his beads loose in his trousers' pockets that he might tell them as he walked the streets – transformed themselves into coronals of flowers of such vague unearthly texture that they seemed to him as hueless and odourless as they were nameless. He offered up each of his three daily chaplets that his soul might grow strong in each of the three theological virtues, in faith in the Father Who had created him, in hope in the Son Who had redeemed him and in love of the Holy Ghost Who had sanctified him;[247] and this thrice triple prayer he offered to the Three Persons through Mary in the name of her joyful and sorrowful and glorious mysteries.

On each of the seven days of the week he further prayed that one of the seven gifts of the Holy Ghost[248] might descend upon his soul and drive out of it day by day the seven deadly sins which had defiled it in the past; and he prayed for each gift on its appointed day, confident that it would descend upon him, though it seemed strange to him at times that wisdom and understanding and knowledge were so distinct in their nature that each should be prayed for apart from the others. Yet he believed that at some future stage of his spiritual progress this difficulty would be removed when his sinful soul had been raised up from its weakness and enlightened by the Third Person of the Most Blessed Trinity. He believed this all the more, and with trepidation, because of the divine gloom and silence wherein dwelt the unseen Paraclete, Whose symbols were a dove and a mighty wind, to sin against Whom was a sin beyond forgiveness, the eternal mysterious secret Being to Whom, as God, the priests offered up mass once a year,[249] robed in the scarlet of the tongues of fire.

The imagery through which the nature and kinship of the Three Persons of the Trinity were darkly shadowed forth in the books of devotion which he read – the Father contemplating from all eternity as in a mirror His Divine Perfections and thereby begetting eternally the Eternal Son and the Holy Spirit proceeding out of Father and Son from all eternity – were easier of acceptance by his mind by reason of their august incomprehensibility than was the simple fact that God had loved his soul from all eternity, for ages before he had been born into the world, for ages before the world itself had existed.

He had heard the names of the passions of love and hate pronounced solemnly on the stage and in the pulpit, had found them set forth solemnly in books and had wondered why his soul was unable to harbour them for any time or to force his lips to utter their names with conviction. A brief anger had often invested him but he had never been able to make it an abiding passion and had always felt himself passing out of it as if his very body were being divested with ease of some outer skin or peel. He had felt a subtle, dark, and murmurous presence penetrate his being and fire him with a brief iniquitous lust: it, too, had slipped beyond his grasp leaving his mind lucid and indifferent. This, it seemed, was the only love and that the only hate his soul would harbour.

But he could no longer disbelieve in the reality of love, since God Himself had loved his individual soul with divine love from all eternity. Gradually, as his soul was enriched with spiritual knowledge, he saw the whole world forming one vast symmetrical expression of God's power and love. Life became a divine gift for every moment and sensation of which, were it even the sight of a single leaf hanging on the twig of a tree, his soul should praise and thank the Giver. The world for all its solid substance and complexity no longer existed for his soul save as a theorem of divine power and love and universality. So entire and unquestionable was this sense of the divine meaning in all nature granted to his soul that he could scarcely understand why it was in any way necessary that he should continue to live. Yet that was part of the divine purpose and he dared not question its use, he above all others who had sinned so deeply and so foully against the divine purpose. Meek and abased by this consciousness of the one eternal omnipresent perfect reality his soul took up again her burden of pieties, masses and prayers and sacraments and mortifications, and only then for the first time since he had brooded on the great mystery of love did he feel within him a warm movement like that of some newly born life or virtue of the soul itself. The attitude of rapture in sacred art, the raised and parted hands, the parted lips and eyes as of one about to swoon, became for him an image of the soul in prayer, humiliated and faint before her Creator.

But he had been forewarned of the dangers of spiritual exaltation and did not allow himself to desist from even the least or lowliest devotion, striving also by constant mortification to undo the sinful past rather than to achieve a saintliness fraught with peril. Each of his senses was brought under a rigorous discipline. In order to mortify the sense of sight he made it his rule to walk in the street with downcast eyes, glancing neither to right nor left and never behind him. His eyes shunned every encounter with the eyes of women. From time to time also he balked them by a sudden effort of the will, as by lifting them suddenly in the middle of an unfinished sentence and closing the book. To mortify his hearing he exerted no control over his voice which was then breaking, neither sang nor whistled, and made no attempt to flee from noises which caused him painful nervous irritation such as the sharpening of knives on the knifeboard, the gathering of cinders on the fire-shovel and the twigging[250] of the carpet. To mortify his smell was more difficult as he found in himself no instinctive repugnance to bad odours whether they were the odours of the outdoor world, such as those of dung or tar, or the odours of his own person among which he had made many curious comparisons and experiments. He found in the end that the only odour against which his sense of smell revolted was a certain stale fishy stink like that of longstanding urine; and whenever it was possible he subjected himself to this unpleasant odour. To mortify the taste he practised strict habits at table, observed to the letter all the fasts of the church and sought by distraction to divert his mind from the savours of different foods. But it was to the mortification of touch he brought the most assiduous ingenuity of inventiveness. He never consciously changed his position in bed, sat in the most uncomfortable positions, suffered patiently every itch and pain, kept away from the fire, remained on his knees all through the mass except at the gospels, left part of his neck and face undried so that air might sting them and, whenever he was not saying his beads, carried his arms stiffly at his sides like a runner and never in his pockets or clasped behind him.

He had no temptations to sin mortally. It surprised him however to find that at the end of his course of intricate piety and self-restraint he was so easily at the mercy of childish and unworthy imperfections. His prayers and fasts availed him little for the suppression of anger at hearing his mother sneeze or at being disturbed in his devotions. It needed an immense effort of his will to master the impulse which urged him to give outlet to such irritation. Images of the outbursts of trivial anger which he had often noted among his masters, their twitching mouths, close-shut lips and flushed cheeks, recurred to his memory, discouraging him, for all his practice of humility, by the comparison. To merge his life in the common tide of other lives was harder for him than any fasting or prayer and it was his constant failure to do this to his own satisfaction which caused in his soul at last a sensation of spiritual dryness together with a growth of doubts and scruples. His soul traversed a period of desolation in which the sacraments themselves seemed to have turned into dried-up sources. His confession became a channel for the escape of scrupulous and unrepented imperfections. His actual reception of the eucharist did not bring him the same dissolving moments of virginal self-surrender as did those spiritual communions made by him sometimes at the close of some visit to the Blessed Sacrament.[251] The book which he used for these visits was an old neglected book written by saint Alphonsus Liguori,[252] with fading characters and sere foxpapered leaves. A faded world of fervent love and virginal responses seemed to be evoked for his soul by the reading of its pages in which the imagery of the canticles[253] was interwoven with the communicant's prayers. An inaudible voice seemed to caress the soul, telling her names and glories, bidding her arise as for espousal and come away, bidding her look forth, a spouse, from Amana and from the mountains of the leopards;[254] and the soul seemed to answer with the same inaudible voice, surrendering herself: *Inter ubera mea commorabitur.*[255]

This idea of surrender had a perilous attraction for his mind now that he felt his soul beset once again by the insistent voices of the flesh which began to murmur to him again during his prayers and meditations. It gave him an intense sense of power to know that he could, by a single act of consent, in a moment of thought, undo all that he had done. He seemed to feel a flood slowly advancing towards his naked feet and to be waiting for the first faint timid noiseless wavelet to touch his fevered skin. Then, almost at the instant of that touch, almost at the verge of sinful consent, he found himself standing far away from the flood upon a dry shore, saved by a sudden act of the will or a sudden ejaculation; and, seeing the silver line of the flood far away and beginning again its slow advance towards his feet, a new thrill of power and satisfaction shook his soul to know that he had not yielded nor undone all.

When he had eluded the flood of temptation many times in this way he grew troubled and wondered whether the grace which he had refused to lose was not being filched from him little by little. The clear certitude of his own immunity grew dim and to it succeeded a vague fear that his soul had really fallen unawares. It was with difficulty that he won back his old consciousness of his state of grace by telling himself that he had prayed to God at every temptation and that the grace which he had prayed for must have been given to him inasmuch as God was obliged to give it. The very frequency and violence of temptations showed him at last the truth of what he had heard about the trials of the saints. Frequent and violent temptations were a proof that the citadel of the soul had not fallen and that the devil raged to make it fall.

Often when he had confessed his doubts and scruples – some momentary inattention at prayer, a movement of trivial anger in his soul, or a subtle wilfulness in speech or act – he was bidden by his confessor to name some sin of his past life before absolution was given him. He named it with humility and shame and repented of it once more. It humiliated and shamed him to think that he would never be freed from it wholly, however holily he might live or whatever virtues or perfections he might attain. A restless feeling of guilt would always be present with him: he would confess and repent and be absolved, confess and repent again and be absolved again, fruitlessly. Perhaps that first hasty confession wrung from him by the fear of hell had not been good? Perhaps, concerned only for his imminent doom, he had not had sincere sorrow for his sin? But the surest sign that his confession had been good and that he had had sincere sorrow for his sin was, he knew, the amendment of his life.

– I have amended my life, have I not? he asked himself.

The director stood in the embrasure of the window, his back to the light, leaning an elbow on the brown crossblind, and, as he spoke and smiled, slowly dangling and looping the cord of the other blind, Stephen stood before him, following for a moment with his eyes the waning of the long summer daylight above the roofs or the slow deft movements of the priestly fingers. The priest's face was in total shadow, but the waning daylight from behind him touched the deeply grooved temples and the curves of the skull. Stephen followed also with his ears the accents and intervals of the priest's voice as he spoke gravely and cordially of indifferent themes, the vacation which had just ended, the colleges of the order abroad, the transference of masters. The grave and cordial voice went on easily with its tale and in the pauses Stephen felt bound to set it on again with respectful questions. He knew that the tale was a prelude and his mind waited for the sequel. Ever since the message of summons had come for him from the director his mind had struggled to find the meaning of the message; and, during the long restless time he had sat in the college parlour waiting for the director to come in, his eyes had wandered from one sober picture to another around the walls and his mind wandered from one guess to another until the meaning of the summons had almost become clear. Then, just as he was wishing that some unforeseen cause might prevent the director from coming, he had heard the handle of the door turning and the swish of a soutane.

The director had begun to speak of the dominican and franciscan orders and of the friendship between saint Thomas and saint Bonaventure.[256] The capuchin dress, he thought, was rather too . . .

Stephen's face gave back the priest's indulgent smile and, not being anxious to give an opinion, he made a slight dubitative movement with his lips.

– I believe, continued the director, that there is some talk now among the capuchins themselves of doing away with it and following the example of the other franciscans.[257]

– I suppose they would retain it in the cloisters? said Stephen.

– O certainly, said the director. For the cloister it is all right but for the street I really think it would be better to do away with it, don't you?

– It must be troublesome, I imagine.

– Of course it is, of course. Just imagine when I was in Belgium I used to see them out cycling in all kinds of weather with this thing up about their knees! It was really ridiculous. *Les jupes*,[258] they call them in Belgium.

The vowel was so modified as to be indistinct.

– What do they call them?

– *Les jupes.*

– O!

Stephen smiled again in answer to the smile which he could not see on the priest's shadowed face, its image or spectre only passing rapidly across his mind as the low discreet accent fell upon his ear. He gazed calmly before him at the waning sky, glad of the cool of the evening and of the faint yellow glow which hid the tiny flame kindling upon his cheek.

The names of articles of dress worn by women or of certain soft and delicate stuffs used in their making brought always to his mind a delicate and sinful perfume. As a boy he had imagined the reins by which horses are driven as slender silken bands and it shocked him to feel at Stradbrook the greasy leather of harness. It had shocked him, too, when he had felt for the first time beneath his tremulous fingers the brittle texture of a woman's stocking for, retaining nothing of all he read save that which seemed to him an echo or a prophecy of his own state, it was only amid soft-worded phrases or within rose-soft stuffs that he dared to conceive of the soul or body of a woman moving with tender life.

But the phrase on the priest's lips was disingenuous for he knew that a priest should not speak lightly on that theme. The phrase had been spoken lightly with design and he felt that his face was being searched by the eyes in the shadow. Whatever he had heard or read of the craft of jesuits[259] he had put aside frankly as not borne out by his own experience. His masters, even when they had not attracted him, had seemed to him always intelligent and serious priests, athletic and high-spirited prefects. He thought of them as men who washed their bodies briskly with cold water and wore clean cold linen. During all the years he had lived among them in Clongowes and in Belvedere he had received only two pandies and, though these had been dealt him in the wrong, he knew that he had often escaped punishment. During all those years he had never heard from any of his masters a flippant word: it was they who had taught him christian doctrine and urged him to live a good life and, when he had fallen into grievous sin, it was they who had led him back to grace. Their presence had made him diffident of himself when he was a muff[260] in Clongowes and it had made him diffident of himself also while he had held his equivocal position[261] in Belvedere. A constant sense of this had remained with him up to the last year of his school life. He had never once disobeyed or allowed turbulent companions to seduce him from his habit of quiet obedience; and, even when he doubted some statement of a master, he had never presumed to doubt openly. Lately some of their judgments had sounded a little childish in his ears and had made him feel a regret and pity as though he were slowly passing out of an accustomed world and were hearing its language for the last time. One day when some boys had gathered round a priest under the shed near the chapel, he had heard the priest say:

– I believe that Lord Macaulay[262] was a man who probably never committed a mortal sin in his life, that is to say, a deliberate mortal sin.

Some of the boys had then asked the priest if Victor Hugo were not the greatest French writer. The priest had answered that Victor Hugo had never written half so well when he had turned against the church as he had written when he was a catholic.[263]

– But there are many eminent French critics, said the priest, who consider that even Victor Hugo, great as he certainly was, had not so pure a French style as Louis Veuillot.[264]

The tiny flame which the priest's allusion had kindled upon Stephen's cheek had sunk down again and his eyes were still fixed calmly on the colourless sky. But an unresting doubt flew hither and thither before his mind. Masked memories passed quickly before him: he recognized scenes and persons yet he was conscious that he had failed to perceive some vital circumstance in them. He saw himself walking about the grounds watching the sports in Clongowes and eating slim jim out of his cricket cap. Some jesuits were walking round the cycle-track in the company of ladies. The echoes of certain expressions used in Clongowes sounded in remote caves of his mind.

His ears were listening to these distant echoes amid the silence of the parlour when he became aware that the priest was addressing him in a different voice.

– I sent for you today, Stephen, because I wished to speak to you on a very important subject.

– Yes, sir.

– Have you ever felt that you had a vocation?

Stephen parted his lips to answer yes and then withheld the word suddenly. The priest waited for the answer and added:

– I mean, have you ever felt within yourself, in your soul, a desire to join the order? Think.

– I have sometimes thought of it, said Stephen.

The priest let the blindcord fall to one side and, uniting his hands, leaned his chin gravely upon them, communing with himself.

– In a college like this, he said at length, there is one boy or perhaps two or three boys whom God calls to the religious life. Such a boy is marked off from his companions by his piety, by the good example he shows to others. He is looked up to by them; he is chosen perhaps as prefect by his fellow sodalists. And you, Stephen, have been such a boy in this college, prefect of Our Blessed Lady's sodality. Perhaps you are the boy in this college whom God designs to call to Himself.

A strong note of pride reinforcing the gravity of the priest's voice made Stephen's heart quicken in response.

To receive that call, Stephen, said the priest, is the greatest honour that the Almighty God can bestow upon a man. No king or emperor on this earth has the power of the priest of God. No angel or archangel in heaven, no saint, not even the Blessed Virgin herself, has the power of a priest of God: the power of the keys, the power to bind and to loose from sin, the power of exorcism,[265] the power to cast out from the creatures of God the evil spirits that have power over them; the power, the authority, to make the great God of Heaven come down upon the altar and take the form of bread and wine. What an awful power, Stephen!

A flame began to flutter again on Stephen's cheek as he heard in this proud address an echo of his own proud musings. How often had he seen himself as a priest wielding calmly and humbly the awful power of which angels and saints stood in reverence! His soul had loved to muse in secret on this desire. He had seen himself, a young and silent-mannered priest, entering a confessional swiftly, ascending the altarsteps, incensing, genuflecting, accomplishing the vague acts of the priesthood which pleased him by reason of their semblance of reality and of their distance from it. In that dim life which he had lived through in his musings he had assumed the voices and gestures which he had noted with various priests. He had bent his knee sideways like such a one, he had shaken the thurible[266] only slightly like such a one, his chasuble[267] had swung open like that of such another as he turned to the altar again after having blessed the people. And above all it had pleased him to fill the second place in those dim scenes of his imagining. He shrank from the dignity of celebrant[268] because it displeased him to imagine that all the vague pomp should end in his own person or that the ritual should assign to him so clear and final an office. He longed for the minor sacred offices, to be vested with the tunicle of subdeacon at high mass, to stand aloof from the altar, forgotten by the people, his shoulders covered with a humeral veil, holding the paten within its folds or, when the sacrifice had been accomplished, to stand as deacon in a dalmatic of cloth of gold on the step below the celebrant, his hands joined and his face towards the people, and sing the chant *Ite missa est*.[269] If ever he had seen himself celebrant it was as in the pictures of the mass in his child's massbook, in a church without worshippers, save for the angel of the sacrifice, at a bare altar, and served by an acolite scarcely more boyish than himself. In vague sacrificial or sacramental acts alone his will seemed drawn to go forth to encounter reality; and it was partly the absence of an appointed rite which had always constrained him to inaction whether he had allowed silence to cover his anger or pride or had suffered only an embrace he longed to give.

He listened in reverent silence now to the priest's appeal and through the words he heard even more distinctly a voice bidding him approach, offering him secret knowledge and secret power. He would know then what was the sin of Simon Magus and what the sin against the Holy Ghost for which there was no forgiveness.[270] He would know obscure things, hidden from others, from those who were conceived and born children of wrath. He would know the sins, the sinful longings and sinful thoughts and sinful acts, of others, hearing them murmured into his ears in the confessional under the shame of a darkened chapel by the lips of women and of girls; but rendered immune mysteriously at his ordination by the imposition of hands,[271] his soul would pass again uncontaminated to the white peace of the altar. No touch of sin would linger upon the hands with which he would elevate and break the host; no touch of sin would linger on his lips in prayer to make him eat and drink damnation to himself not discerning the body of the Lord.[272] He would hold his secret knowledge and secret power, being as sinless as the innocent, and he would be a priest for ever according to the order of Melchisedec.[273]

– I will offer up my mass tomorrow morning, said the director, that Almighty God may reveal to you His holy will. And let you, Stephen, make a novena to your holy patron saint, the first martyr,[274] who is very powerful with God, that God may enlighten your mind. But you must be quite sure, Stephen, that you have a vocation because it would be terrible if you found afterwards that you had none. Once a priest always a priest, remember. Your catechism tells you that the sacrament of Holy Orders is one of those which can be received only once because it imprints on the soul an indelible spiritual mark which can never be effaced. It is before you must weigh well, not after. It is a solemn question, Stephen, because on it may depend the salvation of your eternal soul. But we will pray to God together.

He held open the heavy hall door and gave his hand as if already to a companion in the spiritual life. Stephen passed out on to the wide platform above the steps and was conscious of the caress of mild evening air. Towards Findlater's church[275] a quartet of young men were striding along with linked arms, swaying their heads and stepping to the agile melody of their leader's concertina. The music passed in an instant, as the first bars of sudden music always did, over the fantastic fabrics of his mind, dissolving them painlessly and noiselessly as a sudden wave dissolves the sand-built turrets of children. Smiling at the trivial air he raised his eyes to the priest's face and, seeing in it a mirthless rejection of the sunken day, detached his hand slowly which had acquiesced faintly in the companionship.

As he descended the steps the impression which effaced his troubled self-communion was that of a mirthless mask reflecting a sunken day from the threshold of the college. The shadow, then, of the life of the college passed gravely over his consciousness. It was a grave and ordered and passionless life that awaited him, a life without material cares. He wondered how he would pass the first night in the novitiate[276] and with what dismay he would wake the first morning in the dormitory. The troubling odour of the long corridors of Clongowes came back to him and he heard the discreet murmur of the burning gas-flames. At once from every part of his being unrest began to irradiate. A feverish quickening of his pulses followed, and a din of meaningless words drove his reasoned thoughts hither and thither confusedly. His lungs dilated and sank as if he were inhaling a warm moist unsustaining air and he smelt again the moist warm air which hung in the bath in Clongowes above the sluggish turf-coloured water.

Some instinct, waking at these memories, stronger than education or piety, quickened within him at every near approach to that life, an instinct subtle and hostile, and armed him against acquiescence. The chill and order of the life repelled him. He saw himself rising in the cold of the morning and filing down with the others to early mass and trying vainly to struggle with his prayers against the fainting sickness of his stomach. He saw himself sitting at dinner with the community of a college. What, then, had become of that deep-rooted shyness of his which had made him loth to eat or drink under a strange roof? What had come of the pride of his spirit which had always made him conceive himself as a being apart in every order?

The Reverend Stephen Dedalus, s.j.[277]

His name in that new life leaped into characters before his eyes and to it there followed a mental sensation of an undefined face or colour of a face. The colour faded and became strong like a changing glow of pallid brick red. Was it the raw reddish glow he had so often seen on wintry mornings on the shaven gills of the priests? The face was eyeless and sour-favoured and devout, shot with pink tinges of suffocated anger. Was it not a mental spectre of the face of one of the jesuits whom some of the boys called Lantern Jaws and others Foxy Campbell?

He was passing at that moment before the jesuit house in Gardiner Street[278] and wondered vaguely which window would be his if he ever joined the order. Then he wondered at the vagueness of his wonder, at the remoteness of his own soul from what he had hitherto imagined her sanctuary, at the frail hold which so many years of order and obedience had of him when once a definite and irrevocable act of his threatened to end for ever, in time and in eternity, his freedom. The voice of the director urging upon him the proud claims of the church and the mystery and power of the priestly office repeated itself idly in his memory. His soul was not there to hear and greet it and he knew now that the exhortation he had listened to had already fallen into an idle formal tale. He would never swing the thurible before the tabernacle as priest. His destiny was to be elusive of social or religious orders. The wisdom of the priest's appeal did not touch him to the quick. He was destined to learn his own wisdom apart from others or to learn the wisdom of others himself wandering among the snares of the world.

The snares of the world were its ways of sin. He would fall. He had not yet fallen but he would fall silently, in an instant. Not to fall was too hard, too hard; and he felt the silent lapse of his soul, as it would be at some instant to come, falling, falling, but not yet fallen, still unfallen, but about to fall.

He crossed the bridge over the stream of the Tolka[279] and turned his eyes coldly for an instant towards the faded blue shrine of the Blessed

Virgin which stood fowl-wise on a pole in the middle of a ham-shaped encampment of poor cottages. Then, bending to the left, he followed the lane which led up to his house. The faint sour stink of rotted cabbages came towards him from the kitchen gardens on the rising ground above the river. He smiled to think that it was this disorder, the misrule and confusion of his father's house and the stagnation of vegetable life, which was to win the day in his soul. Then a short laugh broke from his lips as he thought of that solitary farmhand in the kitchen gardens behind their house whom they had nicknamed the man with the hat. A second laugh, taking rise from the first after a pause, broke from him involuntarily as he thought of how the man with the hat worked, considering in turn the four points of the sky and then regretfully plunging his spade in the earth.

He pushed open the latchless door of the porch and passed through the naked hallway into the kitchen. A group of his brothers and sisters was sitting round the table. Tea was nearly over and only the last of the second watered tea remained in the bottoms of the small glass jars and jampots which did service for teacups. Discarded crusts and lumps of sugared bread, turned brown by the tea which had been poured over them, lay scattered on the table. Little wells of tea lay here and there on the board, and a knife with a broken ivory handle was stuck through the pith of a ravaged turnover.

The sad quiet grey-blue glow of the dying day came through the window and the open door, covering over and allaying quietly a sudden instinct of remorse in Stephen's heart. All that had been denied them had been freely given to him, the eldest; but the quiet glow of evening showed him in their faces no sign of rancour.

He sat near them at the table and asked where his father and mother were. One answered:

– Goneboro toboro lookboro atboro aboro houseboro.

Still another removal! A boy named Fallon in Belvedere had often asked him with a silly laugh why they moved so often. A frown of scorn darkened quickly his forehead as he heard again the silly laugh of the questioner.

He asked:

– Why are we on the move again if it's a fair question?

– Becauseboro theboro landboro lordboro willboro putboro usboro outboro.

The voice of his youngest brother from the farther side of the fireplace began to sing the air *Oft in the Stilly Night*.[280] One by one the others took up the air until a full choir of voices was singing. They would sing so for hours, melody after melody, glee after glee, till the last pale light died down on the horizon, till the first dark night clouds came forth and night fell.

He waited for some moments, listening, before he too took up the air with them. He was listening with pain of spirit to the overtone of weariness behind their frail fresh innocent voices. Even before they set out on life's journey they seemed weary already of the way.

He heard the choir of voices in the kitchen echoed and multiplied through an endless reverberation of the choirs of endless generations of children and heard in all the echoes an echo also of the recurring note of weariness and pain. All seemed weary of life even before entering upon it. And he remembered that Newman had heard this note also in the broken lines of Virgil, *giving utterance, like the voice of Nature herself, to that pain and weariness yet hope of better things which has been the experience of her children in every time.*[281]

He could wait no longer.

From the door of Byron's public-house to the gate of Clontarf Chapel, from the gate of Clontarf Chapel[282] to the door of Byron's public-house and then back again to the chapel and then back again to the public-house he had paced slowly at first, planting his steps scrupulously in the spaces of the patchwork of the footpath, then timing their fall to the fall of verses. A full hour had passed since his father had gone in with Dan Crosby, the tutor, to find out for him something about the university.[283] For a full hour he had paced up and down, waiting: but he could wait no longer.

He set off abruptly for the Bull,[284] walking rapidly lest his father's shrill whistle might call him back; and in a few moments he had rounded the curve at the police barrack and was safe.

Yes, his mother was hostile to the idea, as he had read from her listless silence. Yet her mistrust pricked him more keenly than his father's pride and he thought coldly how he had watched the faith which was fading down in his soul ageing and strengthening in her eyes. A dim antagonism gathered force within him and darkened his mind as a cloud against her disloyalty and when it passed, cloud-like, leaving his mind serene and dutiful towards her again, he was made aware dimly and without regret of a first noiseless sundering of their lives.

The university! So he had passed beyond the challenge of the sentries who had stood as guardians of his boyhood and had sought to keep him among them that he might be subject to them and serve their

ends. Pride after satisfaction uplifted him like long slow waves. The
end he had been born to serve yet did not see had led him to escape by
an unseen path and now it beckoned to him once more and a new
adventure was about to be opened to him. It seemed to him that he
heard notes of fitful music leaping upwards a tone and downwards a
diminished fourth, upwards a tone and downwards a major third, like
triple-branching flames leaping fitfully, flame after flame, out of a
midnight wood. It was an elfin prelude, endless and formless; and, as it
grew wilder and faster, the flames leaping out of time, he seemed to
hear from under the boughs and grasses wild creatures racing, their
feet pattering like rain upon the leaves. Their feet passed in pattering
tumult over his mind, the feet of hares and rabbits, the feet of harts and
hinds and antelopes, until he heard them no more and remembered
only a proud cadence from Newman:

– Whose feet are as the feet of harts and underneath the everlasting
arms.[285]

The pride of that dim image brought back to his mind the dignity of
the office he had refused. All through his boyhood he had mused upon
that which he had so often thought to be his destiny and when the
moment had come for him to obey the call he had turned aside,
obeying a wayward instinct. Now time lay between: the oils of
ordination would never anoint his body. He had refused. Why?

He turned seaward from the road at Dollymount[286] and as he passed
on to the thin wooden bridge he felt the planks shaking with the tramp
of heavily shod feet. A squad of christian brothers was on its way back
from the Bull and had begun to pass, two by two, across the bridge.
Soon the whole bridge was trembling and resounding. The uncouth
faces passed him two by two, stained yellow or red or livid by the sea,
and, as he strove to look at them with ease and indifference, a faint stain
of personal shame and commiseration rose to his own face. Angry with
himself he tried to hide his face from their eyes by gazing down
sideways into the shallow swirling water under the bridge but he still
saw a reflection therein of their top-heavy silk hats and humble tape-
like collars and loosely-hanging clerical clothes.

– Brother Hickey.
Brother Quaid.
Brother MacArdle.
Brother Keogh. –

Their piety would be like their names, like their faces, like their
clothes, and it was idle for him to tell himself that their humble and
contrite hearts, it might be, paid a far richer tribute of devotion than

his had ever been, a gift tenfold more acceptable than his elaborate adoration. It was idle for him to move himself to be generous towards them, to tell himself that if he ever came to their gates, stripped of his pride, beaten and in beggar's weeds, that they would be generous towards him, loving him as themselves. Idle and embittering, finally, to argue, against his own dispassionate certitude, that the commandment of love bade us not to love our neighbour as ourselves with the same amount and intensity of love but to love him as ourselves with the same kind of love.

He drew forth a phrase from his treasure and spoke it softly to himself:

– A day of dappled seaborne clouds.[287]

The phrase and the day and the scene harmonised in a chord. Words. Was it their colours? He allowed them to glow and fade, hue after hue: sunrise gold, the russet and green of apple orchards, azure of waves, the grey-fringed fleece of clouds. No, it was not their colours: it was the poise and balance of the period itself. Did he then love the rhythmic rise and fall of words better than their associations of legend and colour? Or was it that, being as weak of sight as he was shy of mind, he drew less pleasure from the reflection of the glowing sensible world through the prism of a language many-coloured and richly storied than from the contemplation of an inner world of individual emotions mirrored perfectly in a lucid supple periodic prose?

He passed from the trembling bridge on to firm land again. At that instant, as it seemed to him, the air was chilled and, looking askance towards the water, he saw a flying squall darkening and crisping suddenly the tide. A faint click at his heart, a faint throb in his throat told him once more of how his flesh dreaded the cold infrahuman odour of the sea; yet he did not strike across the downs on his left but held straight on along the spine of rocks that pointed against the river's mouth.

A veiled sunlight lit up faintly the grey sheet of water where the river was embayed. In the distance along the course of the slow-flowing Liffey[288] slender masts flecked the sky and, more distant still, the dim fabric of the city lay prone in haze. Like a scene on some vague arras, old as man's weariness, the image of the seventh city of christendom was visible to him across the timeless air, no older nor more weary nor less patient of subjection than in the days of the thingmote.[289]

Disheartened, he raised his eyes towards the slow-drifting clouds, dappled and seaborne. They were voyaging across the deserts of the sky, a host of nomads on the march, voyaging high over Ireland, westward bound. The Europe they had come from lay out there beyond the Irish Sea, Europe of strange tongues and valleyed and woodbegirt and citadelled and of entrenched and marshalled races. He heard a confused music within him as of memories and names which he was almost conscious of but could not capture even for an instant; then the music seemed to recede, to recede, to recede, and from each receding trail of nebulous music there fell always one longdrawn calling note, piercing like a star the dusk of silence. Again! Again! Again! A voice from beyond the world was calling.

– Hello, Stephanos![290]

– Here comes The Dedalus!

– Ao! . . . Eh, give it over, Dwyer, I'm telling you, or I'll give you a stuff in the kisser[291] for yourself . . . Ao!

– Good man, Towser! Duck him!

– Come along, Dedalus! Bous Stephanoumenos! Bous Stephaneforos![292]

– Duck him! Guzzle[293] him now, Towser!

– Help! Help! . . . Ao!

He recognized their speech collectively before he distinguished their faces. The mere sight of that medley of wet nakedness chilled him to the bone. Their bodies, corpse-white or suffused with a pallid golden light or rawly tanned by the sun, gleamed with the wet of the sea. Their diving-stone, poised on its rude supports and rocking under their plunges, and the rough-hewn stones of the sloping breakwater over which they scrambled in their horseplay gleamed with cold wet lustre. The towels with which they smacked their bodies were heavy with cold seawater; and drenched with cold brine was their matted hair.

He stood still in deference to their calls and parried their banter with easy words. How characterless they looked: Shuley without his deep unbuttoned collar, Ennis without his scarlet belt with the snaky clasp, and Connolly without his Norfolk coat[294] with the flapless side-pockets! It was a pain to see them, and a sword-like pain to see the signs of adolescence that made repellent their pitiable nakedness. Perhaps they had taken refuge in number and noise from the secret dread in their souls.

But he, apart from them and in silence, remembered in what dread he stood of the mystery of his own body.

– Stephanos Dedalos! Bous Stephanoumenos! Bous Stephaneforos!

Their banter was not new to him and now it flattered his mild proud sovereignty. Now, as never before, his strange name seemed to him a prophecy. So timeless seemed the grey warm air, so fluid and impersonal his own mood, that all ages were as one to him. A moment before the ghost of the ancient kingdom of the Danes[295] had looked forth through the vesture of the haze-wrapped city. Now, at the name of the fabulous artificer,[296] he seemed to hear the noise of dim waves and to see a winged form flying above the waves and slowly climbing the air. What did it mean? Was it a quaint device opening a page of some medieval book of prophecies and symbols, a hawk-like man flying sunward above the sea, a prophecy of the end he had been born to serve and had been following through the mists of childhood and boyhood, a symbol of the artist forging anew in his workshop out of the sluggish matter of the earth a new soaring impalpable imperishable being?

His heart trembled; his breath came faster and a wild spirit passed over his limbs as though he was soaring sunward. His heart trembled in an ecstasy of fear and his soul was in flight. His soul was soaring in an air beyond the world and the body he knew was purified in a breath and delivered of incertitude and made radiant and commingled with the element of the spirit. An ecstasy of flight made radiant his eyes and wild his breath and tremulous and wild and radiant his windswept limbs.

– One! Two! . . . Look out!

– Oh, Cripes, I'm drownded!

– One! Two! Three and away!

– The next! The next!

– One! . . . Uk!

– Stephaneforos!

His throat ached with a desire to cry aloud, the cry of a hawk or eagle on high, to cry piercingly of his deliverance to the winds. This was the call of life to his soul not the dull gross voice of the world of duties and despair, not the inhuman voice that had called him to the pale service of the altar. An instant of wild flight had delivered him and the cry of triumph which his lips withheld cleft his brain.

– Stephaneforos!

What were they now but cerements shaken from the body of death – the fear he had walked in night and day, the incertitude that had ringed him round, the shame that had abased him within and without – cerements, the linens of the grave?

His soul had arisen from the grave of boyhood, spurning her grave-clothes. Yes! Yes! Yes! He would create proudly out of the freedom and power of his soul, as the great artificer whose name he bore, a living thing, new and soaring and beautiful, impalpable, imperishable.

He started up nervously from the stone-block for he could no longer quench the flame in his blood. He felt his cheeks aflame and his throat throbbing with song. There was a lust of wandering in his feet that burned to set out for the ends of the earth. On! On! his heart seemed to cry. Evening would deepen above the sea, night fall upon the plains, dawn glimmer before the wanderer and show him strange fields and hills and faces. Where?

He looked northward towards Howth.[297] The sea had fallen below the line of seawrack on the shallow side of the breakwater and already the tide was running out fast along the foreshore. Already one long oval bank of sand lay warm and dry amid the wavelets. Here and there warm isles of sand gleamed above the shallow tide and about the isles and around the long bank and amid the shallow currents of the beach were lightclad figures, wading and delving.

In a few moments he was barefoot, his stockings folded in his pockets and his canvas shoes dangling by their knotted laces over his shoulders and, picking a pointed salt-eaten stick out of the jetsam among the rocks, he clambered down the slope of the breakwater.

There was a long rivulet in the strand and, as he waded slowly up its course, he wondered at the endless drift of seaweed. Emerald and black and russet and olive, it moved beneath the current, swaying and turning. The water of the rivulet was dark with endless drift and mirrored the high-drifting clouds. The clouds were drifting above him silently and silently the sea-tangle was drifting below him and the grey warm air was still and a new wild life was singing in his veins.

Where was his boyhood now? Where was the soul that had hung back from her destiny, to brood alone upon the shame of her wounds and in her house of squalor and subterfuge to queen it in faded cerements and in wreaths that withered at the touch? Or where was he?

He was alone. He was unheeded, happy and near to the wild heart of life. He was alone and young and wilful and wild-hearted, alone amid a waste of wild air and brackish waters and the sea-harvest of shells and tangle and veiled grey sunlight and gayclad lightclad figures of children and girls and voices childish and girlish in the air.

A girl stood before him in midstream, alone and still, gazing out to sea. She seemed like one whom magic had changed into the likeness of a strange and beautiful seabird. Her long slender bare legs were delicate as a crane's and pure save where an emerald trail of seaweed had fashioned itself as a sign upon the flesh. Her thighs, fuller and soft-hued as ivory, were bared almost to the hips, where the white fringes of her drawers were like feathering of soft white down. Her slate-blue skirts were kilted boldly about her waist and dovetailed behind her.

Her bosom was as a bird's, soft and slight, slight and soft as the breast of some dark-plumaged dove. But her long fair hair was girlish: and girlish, and touched with the wonder of mortal beauty, her face.

She was alone and still, gazing out to sea; and when she felt his presence and the worship of his eyes her eyes turned to him in quiet sufferance of his gaze, without shame or wantonness. Long, long she suffered his gaze and then quietly withdrew her eyes from his and bent them towards the stream, gently stirring the water with her foot hither and thither. The first faint noise of gently moving water broke the silence, low and faint and whispering, faint as the bells of sleep; hither and thither, hither and thither; and a faint flame trembled on her cheek.

– Heavenly God! cried Stephen's soul, in an outburst of profane joy.

He turned away from her suddenly and set off across the strand. His cheeks were aflame; his body was aglow; his limbs were trembling. On and on and on and on he strode, far out over the sands, singing wildly to the sea, crying to greet the advent of the life that had cried to him.

Her image had passed into his soul for ever and no word had broken the holy silence of his ecstasy. Her eyes had called him and his soul had leaped at the call. To live, to err, to fall, to triumph, to recreate life out of life! A wild angel had appeared to him, the angel of mortal youth and beauty, an envoy from the fair courts of life, to throw open before him in an instant of ecstasy the gates of all the ways of error and glory. On and on and on and on!

He halted suddenly and heard his heart in the silence. How far had he walked? What hour was it?

There was no human figure near him nor any sound borne to him over the air. But the tide was near the turn and already the day was on the wane. He turned landward and ran towards the shore and, running up the sloping beach, reckless of the sharp shingle, found a sandy nook amid a ring of tufted sandknolls and lay down there that the peace and silence of the evening might still the riot of his blood.

He felt above him the vast indifferent dome and the calm processes of the heavenly bodies; and the earth beneath him, the earth that had borne him, had taken him to her breast.

He closed his eyes in the languor of sleep. His eyelids trembled as if they felt the vast cyclic movement of the earth and her watchers, trembled as if they felt the strange light of some new world. His soul was swooning into some new world, fantastic, dim, uncertain as under sea, traversed by cloudy shapes and beings. A world, a glimmer or a flower? Glimmering and trembling, trembling and unfolding, a breaking light, an opening flower, it spread in endless succession to itself,

breaking in full crimson and unfolding and fading to palest rose, leaf by
leaf and wave of light by wave of light, flooding all the heavens with its
soft flushes, every flush deeper than the other.

Evening had fallen when he woke and the sand and arid grasses of his
bed glowed no longer. He rose slowly and, recalling the rapture of his
sleep, sighed at its joy.

He climbed to the crest of the sandhill and gazed about him.
Evening had fallen. A rim of the young moon cleft the pale waste of
skyline, the rim of a silver hoop embedded in grey sand; and the tide
was flowing in fast to the land with a low whisper of her waves,
islanding a few last figures in distant pools.

Chapter 5

HE DRAINED HIS THIRD CUP of watery tea to the dregs and set to chewing the crusts of fried bread that were scattered near him, staring into the dark pool of the jar. The yellow dripping had been scooped out like a boghole and the pool under it brought back to his memory the dark turf-coloured water of the bath in Clongowes. The box of pawn tickets at his elbow had just been rifled and he took up idly one after another in his greasy fingers the blue and white dockets, scrawled and sanded and creased and bearing the name of the pledger as Daly or MacEvoy.

1 Pair Buskins.

1 D. Coat.

3 Articles and White.

1 Man's Pants.

Then he put them aside and gazed thoughtfully at the lid of the box, speckled with louse marks, and asked vaguely:

– How much is the clock fast now?

His mother straightened the battered alarm clock that was lying on its side in the middle of the mantelpiece until its dial showed a quarter to twelve and then laid it once more on its side.

– An hour and twenty-five minutes, she said. The right time now is twenty past ten. The dear knows[298] you might try to be in time for your lectures.

– Fill out the place for me to wash, said Stephen.

– Katey, fill out the place for Stephen to wash.

– Boody, fill out the place for Stephen to wash.

– I can't, I'm going for blue.[299] Fill it out, you, Maggy.

When the enamelled basin had been fitted into the well of the sink and the old washing glove flung on the side of it he allowed his mother to scrub his neck and root into the folds of his ears and into the interstices at the wings of his nose.

– Well, it's a poor case, she said, when a university student is so dirty that his mother has to wash him.

– But it gives you pleasure, said Stephen calmly.

An ear-splitting whistle was heard from upstairs and his mother thrust a damp overall into his hands, saying:

– Dry yourself and hurry out for the love of goodness.

A second shrill whistle, prolonged angrily, brought one of the girls to the foot of the staircase.

– Yes, father?

– Is your lazy bitch of a brother gone out yet?

– Yes, father.

– Sure?

– Yes, father.

– Hm!

The girl came back, making signs to him to be quick and go out quietly by the back. Stephen laughed and said:

– He has a curious idea of genders if he thinks a bitch is masculine.

– Ah, it's a scandalous shame for you, Stephen, said his mother, and you'll live to rue the day you set your foot in that place. I know how it has changed you.

– Good morning, everybody, said Stephen, smiling and kissing the tips of his fingers in adieu.

The lane behind the terrace was waterlogged and as he went down it slowly, choosing his steps amid heaps of wet rubbish, he heard a mad nun screeching in the nuns' madhouse[300] beyond the wall.

– Jesus! O Jesus! Jesus!

He shook the sound out of his ears by an angry toss of his head and hurried on, stumbling through the mouldering offal, his heart already bitten by an ache of loathing and bitterness. His father's whistle, his mother's mutterings, the screech of an unseen maniac were to him now so many voices offending and threatening to humble the pride of his youth. He drove their echoes even out of his heart with an execration; but, as he walked down the avenue and felt the grey morning light falling about him through the dripping trees and smelt the strange wild smell of the wet leaves and bark, his soul was loosed of her miseries.

The rain-laden trees of the avenue evoked in him, as always, memories of the girls and women in the plays of Gerhart Hauptmann;[301] and the memory of their pale sorrows and the fragrance falling from the wet branches mingled in a mood of quiet joy. His morning walk across the city had begun, and he foreknew that as he passed the sloblands of Fairview he would think of the cloistral silver-veined prose of Newman;[302] that as he walked along the North Strand Road, glancing idly at the windows of the provision shops, he would recall the dark humour of Guido Cavalcanti[303] and smile; that as he went by Baird's stonecutting works in Talbot Place the spirit of Ibsen[304] would blow through him like a keen wind, a spirit of wayward boyish beauty; and that passing a grimy marine dealer's shop beyond the Liffey he would repeat the song by Ben Jonson which begins:

I was not wearier where I lay.[305]

His mind when wearied of its search for the essence of beauty amid the spectral words of Aristotle or Aquinas turned often for its pleasure to the dainty songs of the Elizabethans. His mind, in the vesture of a doubting monk, stood often in shadow under the windows of that age, to hear the grave and mocking music of the lutenists or the frank laughter of waist-coateers[306] until a laugh too low, a phrase, tarnished by time, of chambering[307] and false honour stung his monkish pride and drove him on from his lurking-place.

The lore which he was believed to pass his days brooding upon so that it had rapt him from the companionship of youth was only a garner of slender sentences from Aristotle's poetics and psychology[308] and a *Synopsis Philosophiae Scholasticae ad mentem divi Thomae.*[309] His thinking was a dusk of doubt and self-mistrust, lit up at moments by the lightnings of intuition, but lightnings of so clear a splendour that in those moment the world perished about his feet as if it had been fire-consumed; and thereafter his tongue grew heavy and he met the eyes of others with unanswering eyes, for he felt that the spirit of beauty had folded him round like a mantle and that in revery at least he had been acquainted with nobility. But when this brief pride of silence upheld him no longer he was glad to find himself still in the midst of common lives, passing on his way amid the squalor and noise and sloth of the city fearlessly and with a light heart.

Near the hoardings on the canal he met the consumptive man with the doll's face and the brimless hat coming towards him town the slope of the bridge with little steps, tightly buttoned into his chocolate overcoat, and holding his furled umbrella a span or two from him like a divining rod. It must be eleven, he thought, and peered into a dairy to see the time. The clock in the dairy told him that it was five minutes to five but, as he turned away, he heard a clock somewhere near him, but unseen, beating eleven strokes in swift precision. He laughed as he heard it for it made him think of McCann, and he saw him a squat figure in a shooting jacket and breeches and with a fair goatee, standing in the wind at Hopkins' corner,[310] and heard him say:

– Dedalus, you're an antisocial being, wrapped up in yourself. I'm not. I'm a democrat and I'll work and act for social liberty and equality among all classes and sexes in the United States of the Europe[311] of the future.

Eleven! Then he was late for that lecture too. What day of the week was it? He stopped at a newsagent's to read the headline of a placard. Thursday. Ten to eleven, English; eleven to twelve, French; twelve to one, physics. He fancied to himself the English lecture and felt, even at that distance, restless and helpless. He saw the heads of his classmates meekly bent as they wrote in their notebooks the points they were bidden to note, nominal definitions, essential definitions[312] and examples or dates of birth or death, chief works, a favourable and an unfavourable criticism side by side. His own head was unbent for his thoughts wandered abroad and whether he looked around the little class of students or out of the window across the desolate gardens of the green an odour assailed him of cheerless cellar-damp and decay. Another head than his, right before him in the first benches, was poised squarely above its bending fellows like the head of a priest appealing without humility to the tabernacle for the humble worshippers about him. Why was it that when he thought of Cranly he could never raise before his mind the entire image of his body but only the image of the head and face? Even now against the grey curtain of the morning he saw it before him like the phantom of a dream, the face of a severed head or death-mask, crowned on the brows by its stiff black upright hair as by an iron crown. It was a priest-like face, priestlike in its palor, in the wide winged nose, in the shadowings below the eyes and along the jaws, priest-like in the lips that were long and bloodless and faintly smiling; and Stephen, remembering swiftly how he had told Cranly of all the tumults and unrest and longings in his soul, day after day and night by night, only to be answered by his friend's listening silence, would have told himself that it was the face of a guilty priest who heard confessions of those whom he had not power to absolve but that he felt again in memory the gaze of its dark womanish eyes.

Through this image he had a glimpse of a strange dark cavern of speculation but at once turned away from it, feeling that it was not yet the hour to enter it. But the nightshade of his friend's listlessness seemed to be diffusing in the air around him a tenuous and deadly exhalation and he found himself glancing from one casual word to another on his right or left in stolid wonder that they had been so silently emptied of instantaneous sense until every mean shop legend bound his mind like the words of a spell and his soul shrivelled up sighing with age as he walked on in a lane among heaps of dead language. His own consciousness of language was ebbing from his brain and trickling into the very words themselves which set to band and disband themselves in wayward rhythms:

> *The ivy whines upon the wall,*
> *And whines and twines upon the wall,*
> *The yellow ivy upon the wall,*
> *Ivy, ivy up the wall.*

Did anyone ever hear such drivel? Lord Almighty! Who ever heard of ivy whining on a wall? Yellow ivy; that was all right. Yellow ivory also. And what about ivory ivy?

The word now shone in his brain, clearer and brighter than any ivory sawn from the mottled tusks of elephants. *Ivory, ivoire, avorio, ebur.*[313] One of the first examples that he had learnt in Latin had run: *India mittit ebur;*[314] and he recalled the shrewd northern face of the rector who had taught him to construe the Metamorphoses of Ovid[315] in a courtly English, made whimsical by the mention of porkers and potsherds and chines of bacon. He had learnt what little he knew of the laws of Latin verse from a ragged book written by a Portuguese priest.[316]

Contrahit orator, variant in carmine vates.[317]

The crises and victories and secessions in Roman history were handed on to him in the trite words *in tanto discrimine*[318] and he had tried to peer into the social life of the city of cities through the words *implere ollam denariorum*[319] which the rector had rendered sonorously as the filling of a pot with denaries. The pages of his time-worn Horace[320] never felt cold to the touch even when his own fingers were cold; they were human pages and fifty years before they had been turned by the human fingers of John Duncan Inverarity and by his brother, William Malcolm Inverarity. Yes, those were noble names on the dusky flyleaf and, even for so poor a Latinist as he, the dusky verses were as fragrant as though they had lain all those years in myrtle and lavender and vervain; but yet it wounded him to think that he would never be but a shy guest at the feast of the world's culture and that the monkish learning, in terms of which he was striving to forge out an esthetic philosophy, was held no higher by the age he lived in than the subtle and curious jargons of heraldry and falconry.

The grey block of Trinity[321] on his left, set heavily in the city's ignorance like a dull stone set in a cumbrous ring, pulled his mind downward and while he was striving this way and that to free his feet from the fetters of the reformed conscience he came upon the droll statue of the national poet of Ireland.[322]

He looked at it without anger; for, though sloth of the body and of the soul crept over it like unseen vermin, over the shuffling feet and up the folds of the cloak and around the servile head, it seemed humbly conscious of its indignity. It was a Firbolg in the borrowed cloak of a Milesian;[323] and he thought of his friend Davin, the peasant student. It was a jesting name between them, but the young peasant bore with it lightly:

– Go on, Stevie, I have a hard head, you tell me. Call me what you will.

The homely version of his christian name on the lips of his friend had touched Stephen pleasantly when first heard for he was as formal in speech with others as they were with him. Often, as he sat in Davin's rooms in Grantham Street, wondering at his friend's well-made boots that flanked the wall pair by pair and repeating for his friend's simple ear the verses and cadences of others which were the veils of his own longing and dejection, the rude Firbolg mind of his listener had drawn his mind towards it and flung it back again, drawing it by a quiet inbred courtesy of attention or by a quaint turn of old English speech or by the force of its delight in rude bodily skill – for Davin had sat at the feet of Michael Cusack, the Gael[324] – repelling swiftly and suddenly by a grossness of intelligence or by a bluntness of feeling or by a dull stare of terror in the eyes, the terror of soul of a starving Irish village in which the curfew[325] was still a nightly fear.

Side by side with his memory of the deeds of prowess of his uncle Mat Davin, the athlete,[326] the young peasant worshipped the sorrowful legend of Ireland. The gossip of his fellow-students which strove to render the flat life of the college significant at any cost loved to think of him as a young fenian.[327] His nurse had taught him Irish and shaped his rude imagination by the broken lights of Irish myth. He stood towards this myth upon which no individual mind had ever drawn out a line of beauty and to its unwieldy tales that divided against themselves as they moved down the cycles[328] in the same attitude as towards the Roman catholic religion, the attitude of a dull-witted loyal serf. Whatsoever of thought or of feeling came to him from England or by way of English culture his mind stood armed against in obedience to a password; and of the world that lay beyond England he knew only the foreign legion of France in which he spoke of serving.

Coupling this ambition with the young man's humour Stephen had often called him one of the tame geese[329] and there was even a point of irritation in the name pointed against that very reluctance of speech and deed in his friend which seemed so often to stand between Stephen's mind, eager of speculation, and the hidden ways of Irish life.

One night the young peasant, his spirit stung by the violent or luxurious language in which Stephen escaped from the cold silence of intellectual revolt, had called up before Stephen's mind a strange vision. The two were walking slowly towards Davin's rooms through the dark narrow streets of the poorer jews.[330]

– A thing happened to myself, Stevie, last autumn, coming on winter, and I never told it to a living soul and you are the first person now I ever told it to. I disremember if it was October or November. It was October because it was before I came up here to join the matriculation class.

Stephen had turned his smiling eyes towards his friend's face, flattered by his confidence and won over to sympathy by the speaker's simple accent.

– I was away all that day from my own place over in Buttevant[331] – I don't know if you know where that is – at a hurling match between the Croke's Own Boys and the Fearless Thurles[332] and by God, Stevie, that was the hard fight. My first cousin, Fonsy Davin, was stripped to his buff[333] that day minding cool for the Limericks[334] but he was up with the forwards half the time and shouting like mad. I never will forget that day. One of the Crokes made a woeful wipe at him one time with his camann[335] and I declare to God he was within an aim's ace of getting it at the side of his temple. Oh, honest to God, if the crook of it caught him that time he was done for.

– I am glad he escaped, Stephen had said with a laugh, but surely that's not the strange thing that happened you?

– Well, I suppose that doesn't interest you, but leastways there was such noise after the match that I missed the train home and I couldn't get any kind of a yoke[336] to give me a lift for, as luck would have it, there was a mass meeting that same day over in Castletownroche[337] and all the cars in the country were there. So there was nothing for it only to stay the night or to foot it out. Well, I started to walk and on I went and it was coming on night when I got into the Ballyhoura hills, that's better than ten miles from Kilmallock[338] and there's a long lonely road after that. You wouldn't see the sign of a christian house along the road or hear a sound. It was pitch dark almost. Once or twice I stopped by the way under a bush to redden my pipe and only for the dew was thick I'd have stretched out there and slept. At last, after a bend of the road, I spied a little cottage with a light in the window. I went up and knocked at the door. A voice asked who was there and I answered I was over at the match in Buttevant and was walking back and that I'd be thankful for a glass of water. After a while a young woman opened the door and brought me out a big mug of milk. She was half undressed as if she was going to bed when I knocked and she had her hair hanging and I thought by her figure and by something in the look of her eyes that she must be carrying a child. She kept me in talk a long while at the door, and I thought it strange because her breast and her shoulders were bare. She asked me was I tired and would I like to stop the night there. She said she was all alone in the house and that her husband had gone that morning to Queenstown[339] with his sister to see her off. And all the time she was talking, Stevie, she had her eyes fixed on my face and she stood so close to me I could hear her breathing. When I handed her back the mug at last she took my hand to draw me in over the threshold and said: '*Come in and stay the night here. You've no call to be frightened. There's no one in it but ourselves*[340]. . . ' I didn't go in, Stevie. I thanked her and went on my way again, all in a fever. At the first bend of the road I looked back and she was standing at the door.

The last words of Davin's story sang in his memory and the figure of the woman in the story stood forth reflected in other figures of the peasant women whom he had seen standing in the doorways at Clane as the college cars drove by, as a type of her race and of his own, a bat-like soul waking to the consciousness of itself in darkness and secrecy and loneliness and, through the eyes and voice and gesture of a woman without guile, calling the stranger to her bed.

A hand was laid on his arm and a young voice cried:

– Ah, gentleman, your own girl, sir! The first handsel today, gentleman. Buy that lovely bunch. Will you, gentleman?

The blue flowers which she lifted towards him and her young blue eyes seemed to him at that instant images of guilelessness, and he halted till the image had vanished and he saw only her ragged dress and damp coarse hair and hoydenish face.

– Do, gentleman! Don't forget your own girl, sir!

– I have no money, said Stephen.

– Buy them lovely ones, will you, sir? Only a penny.

– Did you hear what I said? asked Stephen, bending towards her. I told you I had no money. I tell you again now.

– Well, sure, you will some day, sir, please God, the girl answered after an instant.

– Possibly, said Stephen, but I don't think it likely.

He left her quickly, fearing that her intimacy might turn to jibing and wishing to be out of the way before she offered her ware to another, a tourist from England or a student of Trinity. Grafton

Street,[341] along which he walked, prolonged that moment of discouraged poverty. In the roadway at the head of the street a slab was set to the memory of Wolfe Tone[342] and he remembered having been present with his father at its laying. He remembered with bitterness that scene of tawdry tribute. There were four French delegates in a brake and one, a plump smiling young man, held, wedged on a stick, a card on which were printed the words: *Vive l'Irlande!* [343]

But the trees in Stephen's Green[344] were fragrant of rain and the rain-sodden earth gave forth its mortal odour, a faint incense rising upward through the mould from many hearts. The soul of the gallant venal city which his elders had told him of had shrunk with time to a faint mortal odour rising from the earth and he knew that in a moment when he entered the sombre college he would be conscious of a corruption other than that of Buck Egan and Burnchapel Whaley.[345]

It was too late to go upstairs to the French class. He crossed the hall and took the corridor to the left which led to the physics theatre. The corridor was dark and silent but not unwatchful. Why did he feel that it was not unwatchful? Was it because he had heard that in Buck Whaley's time there was a secret staircase there? Or was the jesuit house extra-territorial and was he walking among aliens?[346] The Ireland of Tone and of Parnell[347] seemed to have receded in space.

He opened the door of the theatre and halted in the chilly grey light that struggled through the dusty windows. A figure was crouching before the large grate and by its leanness and greyness he knew that it was the dean of studies lighting the fire. Stephen closed the door quietly and approached the fireplace.

– Good morning, sir! Can I help you?

The priest looked up quickly and said:

– One moment now, Mr Dedalus, and you will see. There is an art in lighting a fire. We have the liberal arts and we have the useful arts. This is one of the useful arts.

– I will try to learn it, said Stephen.

– Not too much coal, said the dean, working briskly at his task, that is one of the secrets.

He produced four candle-butts from the side-pockets of his soutane and placed them deftly among the coals and twisted papers. Stephen watched him in silence. Kneeling thus on the flagstone to kindle the fire and busied with the disposition of his wisps of paper and candle-butts he seemed more than ever a humble server making ready the place of sacrifice in an empty temple, a levite of the Lord.[348] Like a levite's robe of plain linen the faded worn soutane draped the kneeling figure of one whom the canonicals or the bell-bordered ephod[349] would irk and trouble. His very body had waxed old in lowly service of the Lord – in tending the fire upon the altar, in bearing tidings secretly, in waiting upon worldlings, in striking swiftly when bidden – and yet had remained ungraced by aught of saintly or of prelatic beauty. Nay, his very soul had waxed old in that service without growing towards light and beauty or spreading abroad a sweet odour of her sanctity – a mortified will no more responsive to the thrill of its obedience than was to the thrill of love or combat his ageing body, spare and sinewy, greyed with a silver-pointed down.

The dean rested back on his hunkers and watched the sticks catch. Stephen, to fill the silence, said:

– I am sure I could not light a fire.

– You are an artist, are you not, Mr Dedalus? said the dean, glancing up and blinking his pale eyes. The object of the artist is the creation of the beautiful. What the beautiful is is another question.

He rubbed his hands slowly and drily over the difficulty.

– Can you solve that question now? he asked.

– Aquinas, answered Stephen, says *pulcra sunt quae visa placent*.[350]

– This fire before us, said the dean, will be pleasing to the eye. Will it therefore be beautiful?

– In so far as it is apprehended by the sight, which I suppose means here esthetic intellection, it will be beautiful. But Aquinas also says *Bonum est in quod tendit appetitus*.[351] In so far as it satisfies the animal craving for warmth fire is a good. In hell, however, it is an evil.

– Quite so, said the dean, you have certainly hit the nail on the head.

He rose nimbly and went towards the door, set it ajar and said:

– A draught is said to be a help in these matters.

As he came back to the hearth, limping slightly but with a brisk step, Stephen saw the silent soul of a jesuit look out at him from the pale loveless eyes. Like Ignatius he was lame[352] but in his eyes burned no spark of Ignatius's enthusiasm. Even the legendary craft of the company, a craft subtler and more secret than its fabled books of secret subtle wisdom, had not fired his soul with the energy of apostleship. It seemed as if he used the shifts and lore and cunning of the world, as bidden to do, for the greater glory of God, without joy in their handling or hatred of that in them which was evil but turning them, with a firm gesture of obedience back upon themselves and for all this silent service it seemed as if he loved not at all the master and little, if at all, the ends he served. *Similiter atque senis baculus*,[353] he was, as the founder would have had him, like a staff in an old man's hand, to be leaned on in the road at nightfall or in stress of weather, to lie with a lady's nosegay on a garden seat, to be raised in menace.

The dean returned to the hearth and began to stroke his chin.

– When may we expect to have something from you on the esthetic question? he asked.

– From me! said Stephen in astonishment. I stumble on an idea once a fortnight if I am lucky.

– These questions are very profound, Mr Dedalus, said the dean. It is like looking down from the cliffs of Moher[354] into the depths. Many go down into the depths and never come up. Only the trained diver can go down into those depths and explore them and come to the surface again.

– If you mean speculation, sir, said Stephen, I also am sure that there is no such thing as free thinking inasmuch as all thinking must be bound by its own laws.

– Ha!

– For my purpose I can work on at present by the light of one or two ideas of Aristotle and Aquinas.

– I see. I quite see your point.

– I need them only for my own use and guidance until I have done something for myself by their light. If the lamp smokes or smells I shall try to trim it. If it does not give light enough I shall sell it and buy another.

– Epictetus also had a lamp,[355] said the dean, which was sold for a fancy price after his death. It was the lamp he wrote his philosophical dissertations by. You know Epictetus?

– An old gentleman, said Stephen coarsely, who said that the soul is very like a bucketful of water.

– He tells us in his homely way, the dean went on, that he put an iron lamp before a statue of one of the gods and that a thief stole the lamp. What did the philosopher do? He reflected that it was in the character of a thief to steal and determined to buy an earthen lamp next day instead of the iron lamp.

A smell of molten tallow came up from the dean's candle butts and fused itself in Stephen's consciousness with the jingle of the words, bucket and lamp and lamp and bucket. The priest's voice, too, had a hard jingling tone. Stephen's mind halted by instinct, checked by the strange tone and the imagery and by the priest's face which seemed like an unlit lamp or a reflector hung in a false focus. What lay behind it or within it? A dull torpor of the soul or the dullness of the thundercloud, charged with intellection and capable of the gloom of God?

– I meant a different kind of lamp, sir, said Stephen.

– Undoubtedly, said the dean.

– One difficulty, said Stephen, in esthetic discussion is to know whether words are being used according to the literary tradition or according to the tradition of the marketplace. I remember a sentence of Newman's in which he says of the Blessed Virgin that she was detained in the full company of the saints.[356] The use of the word in the marketplace is quite different. *I hope I am not detaining you.*

– Not in the least, said the dean politely.

– No, no, said Stephen, smiling, I mean –

– Yes, yes; I see, said the dean quickly, I quite catch the point: *detain.* He thrust forward his under jaw and uttered a dry short cough.

– To return to the lamp, he said, the feeding of it is also a nice problem. You must choose the pure oil and you must be careful when you pour it in not to overflow it, not to pour in more than the funnel can hold.

– What funnel? asked Stephen.

– The funnel through which you pour the oil into your lamp.

– That? said Stephen. Is that called a funnel? Is it not a tundish?[357]

– What is a tundish?

– That. The . . . funnel.

– Is that called a tundish in Ireland? asked the dean. I never heard the word in my life.

– It is called a tundish in Lower Drumcondra,[358] said Stephen, laughing, where they speak the best English.

– A tundish, said the dean reflectively. That is a most interesting word. I must look that word up. Upon my word I must.

His courtesy of manner rang a little false and Stephen looked at the English convert with the same eyes as the elder brother in the parable may have turned on the prodigal.[359] A humble follower in the wake of clamorous-conversions,[360] a poor Englishman in Ireland, he seemed to have entered on the stage of jesuit history when that strange play of intrigue and suffering and envy and struggle and indignity had been all but given through – a late-comer, a tardy spirit. From what had he set out? Perhaps he had been born and bred among serious dissenters, seeing salvation in Jesus only and abhorring the vain pomps of the establishment. Had he felt the need of an implicit faith amid the welter of sectarianism and the jargon of its turbulent schisms, six principle men, peculiar people, seed and snake baptists, supralapsarian dogmatists?[361] Had he found the true church all of a sudden in winding up to the end like a reel of cotton some fine-spun line of reasoning upon insufflation or the imposition of hands or the procession of the Holy Ghost?[362] Or had Lord Christ touched him and bidden him follow, like that disciple who had sat at the receipt of custom, as he sat by the door of some zinc-roofed chapel,[363] yawning and telling over his church pence?

The dean repeated the word yet again.

– Tundish! Well now, that is interesting!

– The question you asked me a moment ago seems to me more interesting. What is that beauty which the artist struggles to express from lumps of earth, said Stephen coldly.

The little word seemed to have turned a rapier point of his sensitiveness against this courteous and vigilant foe. He felt with a smart of dejection that the man to whom he was speaking was a countryman of Ben Jonson. He thought:

– The language in which we are speaking is his before it is mine. How different are the words *home, Christ, ale, master*, on his lips and on mine! I cannot speak or write these words without unrest of spirit. His language, so familiar and so foreign, will always be for me an acquired speech. I have not made or accepted its words. My voice holds them at bay. My soul frets in the shadow of his language.

– And to distinguish between the beautiful and the sublime, the dean added, to distinguish between moral beauty and material beauty. And to inquire what kind of beauty is proper to each of the various arts. These are some interesting points we might take up.

Stephen, disheartened suddenly by the dean's firm, dry tone, was silent; and through the silence a distant noise of many boots and confused voices came up the staircase.

– In pursuing these speculations, said the dean conclusively, there is, however, the danger of perishing of inanition. First you must take your degree. Set that before you as your first aim. Then, little by little, you will see your way. I mean in every sense, your way in life and in thinking. It may be uphill pedalling at first. Take Mr Moonan. He was a long time before he got to the top. But he got there.

– I may not have his talent, said Stephen quietly.

– You never know, said the dean brightly. We never can say what is in us. I most certainly should not be despondent. *Per aspera ad astra.*[364]

He left the hearth quickly and went towards the landing to oversee the arrival of the first arts' class.

Leaning against the fireplace Stephen heard him greet briskly and impartially every student of the class and could almost see the frank smiles of the coarser students. A desolating pity began to fall like dew upon his easily embittered heart for this faithful serving man of the knightly Loyola, for this half brother of the clergy,[365] more venal than they in speech, more steadfast of soul than they, one whom he would never call his ghostly father;[366] and he thought how this man and his companions had earned the name of worldlings at the hands not of the unworldly only but of the worldly also for having pleaded, during all their history, at the bar of God's justice for the souls of the lax and the lukewarm and the prudent.

The entry of the professor was signalled by a few rounds of Kentish fire[367] from the heavy boots of those students who sat on the highest tier of the gloomy theatre under the grey cobwebbed windows. The calling of the roll began and the responses to the names were given out in all tones until the name of Peter Byrne was reached.

– Here!

A deep bass note in response came from the upper tier, followed by coughs of protest along the other benches.

The professor paused in his reading and called the next name:

– Cranly!

No answer.

– Mr Cranly!

A smile flew across Stephen's face as he thought of his friend's studies.

– Try Leopardstown![368] said a voice from the bench behind.

Stephen glanced up quickly but Moynihan's snoutish face, outlined on the grey light, was impassive. A formula was given out. Amid the rustling of the notebooks Stephen turned back again and said:

– Give me some paper for God's sake.

– Are you as bad as that? asked Moynihan with a broad grin.

He tore a sheet from his scribbler and passed it down, whispering:

– In case of necessity any layman or woman can do it.[369]

The formula which he wrote obediently on the sheet of paper, the coiling and uncoiling calculations of the professor, the spectre-like symbols of force and velocity fascinated and jaded Stephen's mind. He had heard some say that the old professor was an atheist freemason. O the grey dull day! It seemed a limbo of painless patient consciousness through which souls of mathematicians might wander, projecting long slender fabrics from plane to plane of ever rarer and paler twilight, radiating swift eddies to the last verges of a universe ever vaster, farther and more impalpable.

– So we must distinguish between elliptical and ellipsoidal. Perhaps some of you gentlemen may be familiar with the works of Mr W. S.

Gilbert.[370] In one of his songs he speaks of the billiard sharp who is condemned to play:

> *On a cloth untrue*
> *With a twisted cue*
> *And elliptical billiard balls.*[371]

– He means a ball having the form of the ellipsoid of the principal axes of which I spoke a moment ago.

Moynihan leaned down towards Stephen's ear and murmured:

– What price ellipsoidal balls! chase me, ladies, I'm in the cavalry!

His fellow student's rude humour ran like a gust through the cloister of Stephen's mind, shaking into gay life limp priestly vestments that hung upon the walls, setting them to sway and caper in a sabbath of misrule. The forms of the community emerged from the gust-blown vestments, the dean of studies, the portly florid bursar with his cap of grey hair, the president, the little priest with feather hair who wrote devout verses, the squat peasant form of the professor of economics, the tall form of the young professor of mental science discussing on the landing a case of conscience with his class like a giraffe cropping high leafage among a herd of antelopes, the grave troubled prefect of the sodality, the plump round-headed professor of Italian with his rogue's eyes. They came ambling and stumbling, tumbling and capering, kilting their gowns for leap frog, holding one another back, shaken with deep false laughter, smacking one another behind and laughing at their rude malice, calling to one another by familiar nicknames, protesting with sudden dignity at some rough usage, whispering two and two behind their hands.

The professor had gone to the glass cases on the side wall, from a shelf of which he took down a set of coils, blew away the dust from many points and, bearing it carefully to the table, held a finger on it while he proceeded with his lecture. He explained that the wires in modern coils were of a compound called platinoid lately discovered by F. W. Martino.[372]

He spoke clearly the initials and surname of the discovered. Moynihan whispered from behind:

– Good old Fresh Water Martin!

– Ask him, Stephen whispered back with weary humour, if he wants a subject for electrocution. He can have me.

Moynihan, seeing the professor bend over the coils, rose in his bench and, clacking noiselessly the fingers of his right hand, began to call with the voice of a slobbering urchin.

– Please, teacher! This boy is after saying a bad word, teacher.

– Platinoid, the professor said solemnly, is preferred to German silver because it has a lower coefficient of resistance by changes of temperature. The platinoid wire is insulated and the covering of silk that insulates it is wound on the ebonite bobbins just where my finger is. If it were wound single an extra current would be induced in the coils. The bobbins are saturated in hot paraffin wax . . .

A sharp Ulster voice said from the bench below Stephen:

– Are we likely to be asked questions on applied science?

The professor began to juggle gravely with the terms pure science and applied science. A heavy-built student, wearing gold spectacles, stared with some wonder at the questioner. Moynihan murmured from behind in his natural voice:

– Isn't MacAlister a devil for his pound of flesh?

Stephen looked coldly on the oblong skull beneath him overgrown with tangled twine-coloured hair. The voice, the accent, the mind of the questioner offended him and he allowed the offence to carry him towards wilful unkindness, bidding his mind think that the student's father would have done better had he sent his son to Belfast[373] to study and have saved something on the train fare by so doing.

The oblong skull beneath did not turn to meet this shaft of thought and yet the shaft came back to its bowstring; for he saw in a moment the student's whey-pale face.

– That thought is not mine, he said to himself quickly. It came from the comic Irishman in the bench behind. Patience. Can you say with certitude by whom the soul of your race was bartered and its elect betrayed – by the questioner or by the mocker? Patience. Remember Epictetus. It is probably in his character to ask such a question at such a moment in such a tone and to pronounce the word *science* as a monosyllable.

The droning voice of the professor continued to wind itself slowly round and round the coils it spoke of, doubling, trebling, quadrupling its somnolent energy as the coil multiplied its ohms of resistance.

Moynihan's voice called from behind in echo to a distant bell:

– Closing time, gents!

The entrance hall was crowded and loud with talk. On a table near the door were two photographs in frames and between them a long roll of paper bearing an irregular tail of signatures.[374] MacCann went briskly to and fro among the students, talking rapidly, answering rebuffs and leading one after another to the table. In the inner hall the dean of studies stood talking to a young professor, stroking his chin gravely and nodding his head.

Stephen, checked by the crowd at the door, halted irresolutely. From under the wide falling leaf of a soft hat Cranly's dark eyes were watching him.

– Have you signed? Stephen asked.

Cranly closed his long thin-lipped mouth, communed with himself an instant and answered:

– *Ego habeo.*[375]

– What is it for?

– *Quod.*[376]

– What is it for?

Cranly turned his pale face to Stephen and said blandly and bitterly:

– *Per pax universalis.*[377]

Stephen pointed to the Tsar's photograph and said:

– He has the face of a besotted Christ.

The scorn and anger in his voice brought Cranly's eyes back from a calm survey of the walls of the hall.

– Are you annoyed? he asked.

– No, answered Stephen.

– Are you in bad humour?

– No.

– *Credo ut vos sanguinarius mendax estis,* said Cranly, *quia facies vostra monstrat ut vos in damno malo humore estis.*[378]

Moynihan, on his way to the table, said in Stephen's ear:

– MacCann is in tiptop form. Ready to shed the last drop. Brand new world. No stimulants and votes for the bitches.[379]

Stephen smiled at the manner of this confidence and, when Moynihan had passed, turned again to meet Cranly's eyes.

– Perhaps you can tell me, he said, why he pours his soul so freely into my ear. Can you?

A dull scowl appeared on Cranly's forehead. He stared at the table where Moynihan had bent to write his name on the roll, and then said flatly:

– A sugar![380]

– *Quis est in malo humore,* said Stephen, *ego aut vos?*[381]

Cranly did not take up the taunt. He brooded sourly on his judgment and repeated with the same flat force:

– A flaming bloody sugar, that's what he is!

It was his epitaph for all dead friendships and Stephen wondered whether it would ever be spoken in the same tone over his memory. The heavy lumpish phrase sank slowly out of hearing like a stone through a quagmire. Stephen saw it sink as he had seen many another, feeling its heaviness depress his heart. Cranly's speech, unlike that of Davin, had neither rare phrases of Elizabethan English nor quaintly turned versions of Irish idioms. Its drawl was an echo of the quays of Dublin given back by a bleak decaying seaport, its energy an echo of the sacred eloquence of Dublin given back flatly by a Wicklow pulpit.[382]

The heavy scowl faded from Cranly's face as MacCann marched briskly towards them from the other side of the hall.

– Here you are! said MacCann cheerily.

– Here I am! said Stephen.

– Late as usual. Can you not combine the progressive tendency with a respect for punctuality?

– That question is out of order, said Stephen. Next business.

His smiling eyes were fixed on a silver-wrapped tablet of milk chocolate which peeped out of the propagandist's breastpocket. A little ring of listeners closed round to hear the war of wits. A lean student with olive skin and lank black hair thrust his face between the two, glancing from one to the other at each phrase and seeming to try to catch each flying phrase in his open moist mouth. Cranly took a small grey handball from his pocket and began to examine it closely, turning it over and over.

– Next business? said MacCann. Hom!

He gave a loud cough of laughter, smiled broadly and tugged twice at the straw-coloured goatee which hung from his blunt chin.

– The next business is to sign the testimonial.

– Will you pay me anything if I sign? asked Stephen.

– I thought you were an idealist, said MacCann.

The gipsy-like student looked about him and addressed the onlookers in an indistinct bleating voice.

– By hell, that's a queer notion. I consider that notion to be a mercenary notion.

His voice faded into silence. No heed was paid to his words. He turned his olive face, equine in expression, towards Stephen, inviting him to speak again.

MacCann began to speak with fluent energy of the Tsar's rescript, of Stead, of general disarmament arbitration in cases of international disputes,[383] of the signs of the times, of the new humanity and the new gospel of life which would make it the business of the community to secure as cheaply as possible the greatest possible happiness of the greatest possible number.

The gipsy student responded to the close of the period by crying:

– Three cheers for universal brotherhood!

– Go on, Temple, said a stout ruddy student near him. I'll stand you a pint after.

– I'm a believer in universal brotherhood, said Temple, glancing about him out of his dark oval eyes. Marx is only a bloody cod.[384]

Cranly gripped his arm tightly to check his tongue, smiling uneasily, and repeated:

– Easy, easy, easy!

Temple struggled to free his arm but continued, his mouth flecked by a thin foam:

– Socialism was founded by an Irishman[385] and the first man in Europe who preached the freedom of thought was Collins. Two hundred years ago. He denounced priestcraft, the philosopher of Middlesex. Three cheers for John Anthony Collins![386]

A thin voice from the verge of the ring replied:

– Pip! pip!

Moynihan murmured beside Stephen's ear:

– And what about John Anthony's poor little sister:

> *Lottie Collins lost her drawers;*
> *Won't you kindly lend her yours?*[387]

Stephen laughed and Moynihan, pleased with the result, murmured again:

– We'll have five bob each way on John Anthony Collins.

– I am waiting for your answer, said MacCann briefly.

– The affair doesn't interest me in the least, said Stephen wearily. You know that well. Why do you make a scene about it?

– Good! said MacCann, smacking his lips. You are a reactionary, then?

– Do you think you impress me, Stephen asked, when you flourish your wooden sword?

– Metaphors! said MacCann bluntly. Come to facts.

Stephen blushed and turned aside. MacCann stood his ground and said with hostile humour:

– Minor poets, I suppose, are above such trivial questions as the question of universal peace.

Cranly raised his head and held the handball between the two students by way of a peace-offering, saying:

– *Pax super totum sanguinarium globum.*[388]

Stephen, moving away the bystanders, jerked his shoulder angrily in the direction of the Tsar's image, saying:

– Keep your icon. If we must have a Jesus let us have a legitimate Jesus.

– By hell, that's a good one! said the gipsy student to those about him, that's a fine expression. I like that expression immensely.

He gulped down the spittle in his throat as if he were gulping down the phrase and, fumbling at the peak of his tweed cap, turned to Stephen, saying:

– Excuse me, sir, what do you mean by that expression you uttered just now?

Feeling himself jostled by the students near him, he said to them:

– I am curious to know now what he meant by that expression.

He turned again to Stephen and said in a whisper:

– Do you believe in Jesus? I believe in man. Of course, I don't know if you believe in man. I admire you, sir. I admire the mind of man independent of all religions. Is that your opinion about the mind of Jesus?

– Go on, Temple, said the stout ruddy student, returning, as was his wont, to his first idea, that pint is waiting for you.

– He thinks I'm an imbecile, Temple explained to Stephen, because I'm a believer in the power of mind.

Cranly linked his arms into those of Stephen and his admirer and said:

– *Nos ad manum ballum jocabimus.*[389]

Stephen, in the act of being led away, caught sight of MacCann's flushed blunt-featured face.

– My signature is of no account, he said politely. You are right to go your way. Leave me to go mine.

– Dedalus, said MacCann crisply, I believe you're a good fellow but you have yet to learn the dignity of altruism and the responsibility of the human individual.

A voice said:

– Intellectual crankery is better out of this movement than in it.

Stephen, recognising the harsh tone of MacAlister's voice, did not turn in the direction of the voice. Cranly pushed solemnly through the throng of students, linking Stephen and Temple like a celebrant attended by his ministers on his way to the altar.

Temple bent eagerly across Cranly's breast and said:

– Did you hear MacAlister what he said? That youth is jealous of you. Did you see that? I bet Cranly didn't see that. By hell, I saw that at once.

As they crossed the inner hall, the dean of studies was in the act of escaping from the student with whom he had been conversing. He stood at the foot of the staircase, a foot on the lowest step, his threadbare soutane gathered about him for the ascent with womanish care, nodding his head often and repeating:

– Not a doubt of it, Mr Hackett! Very fine! Not a doubt of it!

In the middle of the hall the prefect of the college sodality was speaking earnestly, in a soft querulous voice, with a boarder. As he spoke he wrinkled a little his freckled brow and bit, between his phrases, at a tiny bone pencil.

– I hope the matric men will all come. The first arts' men are pretty sure. Second arts, too.[390] We must make sure of the newcomers.

Temple bent again across Cranly, as they were passing through the doorway, and said in a swift whisper:

– Do you know that he is a married man? He was a married man before they converted him. He has a wife and children somewhere. By hell, I think that's the queerest notion I ever heard! Eh!

His whisper trailed off into sly cackling laughter. The moment they were through the doorway Cranly seized him rudely by the neck and shook him, saying:

– You flaming floundering fool! I'll take my dying bible there isn't a bigger bloody ape, do you know, than you in the whole flaming bloody world!

Temple wriggled in his grip, laughing still with sly content, while Cranly repeated flatly at every rude shake:

– A flaming flaring bloody idiot!

They crossed the weedy garden together. The president, wrapped in a heavy loose cloak, was coming towards them along one of the walks, reading his office.[391] At the end of the walk he halted before turning and raised his eyes. The students saluted, Temple fumbling as before at the peak of his cap. They walked forward in silence. As they neared the alley Stephen could hear the thuds of the players' hands and the wet smacks of the ball and Davin's voice crying out excitedly at each stroke.

The three students halted round the box on which Davin sat to follow the game. Temple, after a few moments, sidled across to Stephen and said:

– Excuse me, I wanted to ask you, do you believe that Jean-Jacques Rousseau[392] was a sincere man?

Stephen laughed outright. Cranly, picking up the broken stave of a cask from the grass at his feet, turned swiftly and said sternly:

– Temple, I declare to the living God if you say another word, do you know, to anybody on any subject, I'll kill you *super spottum*.[393]

– He was like you, I fancy, said Stephen, an emotional man.

– Blast him, curse him! said Cranly broadly. Don't talk to him at all. Sure, you might as well be talking, do you know, to a flaming chamber-pot as talking to Temple. Go home, Temple. For God's sake, go home.

– I don't care a damn about you, Cranly, answered Temple, moving out of reach of the uplifted stave and pointing at Stephen. He's the only man I see in this institution that has an individual mind.

– Institution! Individual! cried Cranly. Go home, blast you, for you're a hopeless bloody man.

– I'm an emotional man, said Temple. That's quite rightly expressed. And I'm proud that I'm an emotionalist.

He sidled out of the alley, smiling slyly. Cranly watched him with a blank expressionless face.

– Look at him! he said. Did you ever see such a go-by-the-wall?[394] His phrase was greeted by a strange laugh from a student who lounged against the wall, his peaked cap down on his eyes. The laugh, pitched in a high key and coming from a so muscular frame, seemed like the whinny of an elephant. The student's body shook all over and, to ease his mirth, he rubbed both his hands delightedly over his groins.

– Lynch is awake, said Cranly.

Lynch, for answer, straightened himself and thrust forward his chest.

– Lynch puts out his chest, said Stephen, as a criticism of life.

Lynch smote himself sonorously on the chest and said:

– Who has anything to say about my girth?

Cranly took him at the word and the two began to tussle. When their faces had flushed with the struggle they drew apart, panting. Stephen bent down towards Davin who, intent on the game, had paid no heed to the talk of the others.

– And how is my little tame goose? he asked. Did he sign, too?

Davin nodded and said:

– And you, Stevie?

Stephen shook his head.

– You're a terrible man, Stevie, said Davin, taking the short pipe from his mouth, always alone.

– Now that you have signed the petition for universal peace, said Stephen, I suppose you will burn that little copybook I saw in your room.

As Davin did not answer, Stephen began to quote:

– Long pace, fianna! Right incline, fianna! Fianna, by numbers, salute, one, two![395]

– That's a different question, said Davin. I'm an Irish nationalist, first and foremost. But that's you all out. You're a born sneerer, Stevie.

– When you make the next rebellion with hurleysticks,[396] said Stephen, and want the indispensable informer, tell me. I can find you a few in this college.

– I can't understand you, said Davin. One time I hear you talk against English literature. Now you talk against the Irish informers. What with your name and your ideas – Are you Irish at all?

– Come with me now to the office of arms[397] and I will show you the tree of my family, said Stephen.

– Then be one of us, said Davin. Why don't you learn Irish? Why did you drop out of the league class[398] after the first lesson?

– You know one reason why, answered Stephen.

Davin tossed his head and laughed.

– Oh, come now, he said. Is it on account of that certain young lady and Father Moran? But that's all in your own mind, Stevie. They were only talking and laughing.

Stephen paused and laid a friendly hand upon Davin's shoulder.

– Do you remember, he said, when we knew each other first? The first morning we met you asked me to show you the way to the matriculation class, putting a very strong stress on the first syllable. You remember? Then you used to address the jesuits as father,[399] you remember? I ask myself about you: *Is he as innocent as his speech?*

– I'm a simple person, said Davin. You know that. When you told me that night in Harcourt Street those things about your private life, honest to God, Stevie, I was not able to eat my dinner. I was quite bad. I was awake a long time that night. Why did you tell me those things?

– Thanks, said Stephen. You mean I am a monster.

– No, said Davin. But I wish you had not told me.

A tide began to surge beneath the calm surface of Stephen's friendliness.

– This race and this country and this life produced me, he said. I shall express myself as I am.

– Try to be one of us, repeated Davin. In heart you are an Irishman but your pride is too powerful.

– My ancestors threw off their language and took another, Stephen said. They allowed a handful of foreigners to subject them. Do you fancy I am going to pay in my own life and person debts they made? What for?

– For our freedom, said Davin.

– No honourable and sincere man, said Stephen, has given up to you his life and his youth and his affections from the days of Tone to those of Parnell, but you sold him to the enemy or failed him in need or reviled him and left him for another. And you invite me to be one of you. I'd see you damned first.

– They died for their ideals, Stevie, said Davin. Our day will come yet, believe me.

Stephen, following his own thought, was silent for an instant.

– The soul is born, he said vaguely, first in those moments I told you of. It has a slow and dark birth, more mysterious than the birth of the body. When the soul of a man is born in this country there are nets flung at it to hold it back from flight. You talk to me of nationality, language, religion. I shall try to fly by those nets.

Davin knocked the ashes from his pipe.

– Too deep for me, Stevie, he said. But a man's country comes first. Ireland first, Stevie. You can be a poet or a mystic after.

– Do you know what Ireland is? asked Stephen with cold violence. Ireland is the old sow that eats her farrow.

Davin rose from his box and went towards the players, shaking his head sadly. But in a moment his sadness left him and he was hotly disputing with Cranly and the two players who had finished their game. A match of four was arranged, Cranly insisting, however, that his ball should be used. He let it rebound twice or thrice to his hand and struck it strongly and swiftly towards the base of the alley, exclaiming in answer to its thud:

– Your soul!

Stephen stood with Lynch till the score began to rise. Then he plucked him by the sleeve to come away. Lynch obeyed, saying:

– Let us eke go, as Cranly has it.

Stephen smiled at this side-thrust.

They passed back through the garden and out through the hall where the doddering porter was pinning up a hall notice in the frame. At the foot of the steps they halted and Stephen took a packet of cigarettes from his pocket and offered it to his companion.

– I know you are poor, he said.

– Damn your yellow insolence, answered Lynch.

This second proof of Lynch's culture[400] made Stephen smile again.

– It was a great day for European culture, he said, when you made up your mind to swear in yellow.

They lit their cigarettes and turned to the right. After a pause Stephen began:

– Aristotle has not defined pity and terror.[401] I have. I say –

Lynch halted and said bluntly:

– Stop! I won't listen! I am sick. I was out last night on a yellow drunk with Horan and Goggins.

Stephen went on:

– Pity is the feeling which arrests the mind in the presence of whatsoever is grave and constant in human sufferings and unites it with the human sufferer. Terror is the feeling which arrests the mind in the presence of whatsoever is grave and constant in human sufferings and unites it with the secret cause.

– Repeat, said Lynch.

Stephen repeated the definitions slowly.

– A girl got into a hansom[402] a few days ago, he went on, in London. She was on her way to meet her mother whom she had not seen for many years. At the corner of a street the shaft of a lorry shivered the window of the hansom in the shape of a star. A long fine needle of the shivered glass pierced her heart. She died on the instant. The reporter called it a tragic death. It is not. It is remote from terror and pity according to the terms of my definitions.

– The tragic emotion, in fact, is a face looking two ways, towards terror and towards pity, both of which are phases of it. You see I use the word *arrest*. I mean that the tragic emotion is static. Or rather the dramatic emotion is. The feelings excited by improper art are kinetic, desire or loathing. Desire urges us to possess, to go to something; loathing urges us to abandon, to go from something. The arts which excite them, pornographical or didactic, are therefore improper arts. The esthetic emotion (I used the general term) is therefore static. The mind is arrested and raised above desire and loathing.

– You say that art must not excite desire, said Lynch. I told you that one day I wrote my name in pencil on the backside of the Venus of Praxiteles in the Museum.[403] Was that not desire?

– I speak of normal natures, said Stephen. You also told me that when you were a boy in that charming carmelite school[404] you ate pieces of dried cowdung.

Lynch broke again into a whinny of laughter and again rubbed both his hands over his groins but without taking them from his pockets.

– O, I did! I did! he cried.

Stephen turned towards his companion and looked at him for a moment boldly in the eyes. Lynch, recovering from his laughter, answered his look from his humbled eyes. The long slender flattened skull beneath the long pointed cap brought before Stephen's mind the image of a hooded reptile. The eyes, too, were reptile-like in glint and gaze. Yet at that instant, humbled and alert in their look, they were lit by one tiny human point, the window of a shrivelled soul, poignant and self-embittered.

– As for that, Stephen said in polite parenthesis, we are all animals. I also am an animal.

– You are, said Lynch.

– But we are just now in a mental world, Stephen continued. The desire and loathing excited by improper esthetic means are really not esthetic emotions not only because they are kinetic in character but also because they are not more than physical. Our flesh shrinks from what it dreads and responds to the stimulus of what it desires by a purely reflex action of the nervous system. Our eyelid closes before we are aware that the fly is about to enter our eye.

– Not always, said Lynch critically.

– In the same way, said Stephen, your flesh responded to the stimulus of a naked statue, but it was, I say, simply a reflex action of the nerves. Beauty expressed by the artist cannot awaken in us an emotion which is kinetic or a sensation which is purely physical. It awakens, or ought to awaken, or induces, or ought to induce, an esthetic stasis, an ideal pity or an ideal terror, a stasis called forth, prolonged, and at last dissolved by what I call the rhythm of beauty.

– What is that exactly? asked Lynch.

– Rhythm, said Stephen, is the first formal esthetic relation of part to part in any esthetic whole or of an esthetic whole to its part or parts or of any part to the esthetic whole of which it is a part.

– If that is rhythm, said Lynch, let me hear what you call beauty; and, please remember, though I did eat a cake of cowdung once, that I admire only beauty.

Stephen raised his cap as if in greeting. Then, blushing slightly, he laid his hand on Lynch's thick tweed sleeve.

– We are right, he said, and the others are wrong. To speak of these things and to try to understand their nature and, having understood it, to try slowly and humbly and constantly to express, to press out again, from the gross earth or what it brings forth, from sound and shape and colour which are the prison gates of our soul, an image of the beauty we have come to understand – that is art.

They had reached the canal bridge and, turning from their course, went on by the trees. A crude grey light, mirrored in the sluggish water and a smell of wet branches over their head seemed to war against the course of Stephen's thought.

– But you have not answered my question, said Lynch. What is art? What is the beauty it expresses?

– That was the first definition I gave you, you sleepy-headed wretch, said Stephen, when I began to try to think out the matter for myself. Do you remember the night? Cranly lost his temper and began to talk about Wicklow bacon.

– I remember, said Lynch. He told us about them flaming fat devils of pigs.

– Art, said Stephen, is the human disposition of sensible or intelligible matter for an esthetic end. You remember the pigs and forget that. You are a distressing pair, you and Cranly.

Lynch made a grimace at the raw grey sky and said:

– If I am to listen to your esthetic philosophy give me at least another cigarette. I don't care about it. I don't even care about women. Damn you and damn everything. I want a job of five hundred a year. You can't get me one.

Stephen handed him the packet of cigarettes. Lynch took the last one that remained, saying simply:

– Proceed!

– Aquinas, said Stephen, says that is beautiful the apprehension or which pleases.

Lynch nodded.

– I remember that, he said, *Pulcra sunt quae visa placent.*[405]

– He uses the word *visa*, said Stephen, to cover esthetic apprehensions of all kinds, whether through sight or hearing or through any other avenue of apprehension. This word, though it is vague, is clear enough to keep away good and evil which excite desire and loathing. It means certainly a stasis and not a kinesis. How about the true? It produces also a stasis of the mind. You would not write your name in pencil across the hypotenuse of a right-angled triangle.

– No, said Lynch, give me the hypotenuse of the Venus of Praxiteles.

– Static therefore, said Stephen. Plato, I believe, said that beauty is the splendour of truth.[406] I don't think that it has a meaning, but the true and the beautiful are akin. Truth is beheld by the intellect which is appeased by the most satisfying relations of the intelligible; beauty is beheld by the imagination which is appeased by the most satisfying relations of the sensible. The first step in the direction of truth is to understand the frame and scope of the intellect itself, to comprehend the act itself of intellection. Aristotle's entire system of philosophy rests upon his book of psychology and that, I think, rests on his statement that the same attribute cannot at the same time and in the same connexion belong to and not belong to the same subject.[407] The first step in the direction of beauty is to understand the frame and scope of the imagination, to comprehend the act itself of esthetic apprehension. Is that clear?

– But what is beauty? asked Lynch impatiently. Out with an other definition. Something we see and like! Is that the best you and Aquinas can do?

– Let us take woman, said Stephen.

– Let us take her! said Lynch fervently.

– The Greek, the Turk, the Chinese, the Copt, the Hottentot, said Stephen, all admire a different type of female beauty. That seems to be a maze out of which we cannot escape. I see, however, two ways out. One is this hypothesis: that every physical quality admired by men in women is in direct connexion with the manifold functions of women for the propagation of the species. It may be so. The world, it seems, is drearier than even you, Lynch, imagined. For my part I dislike that way out. It leads to eugenics rather than to esthetic. It leads you out of the maze into a new gaudy lecture-room where MacCann, with one hand on *The Origin of Species*[408] and the other hand on the new testament, tells you that you admired the great flanks of Venus because you felt that she would bear you burly offspring and admired her great breasts because you felt that she would give good milk to her children and yours.

– Then MacCann is a sulphur-yellow liar, said Lynch energetically.

– There remains another way out, said Stephen, laughing.

– To wit? said Lynch.

– This hypothesis, Stephen began.

A long dray laden with old iron came round the corner of Sir Patrick Dun's hospital[409] covering the end of Stephen's speech with the harsh roar of jangled and rattling metal. Lynch closed his ears and gave out oath after oath till the dray had passed. Then he turned on his heel rudely. Stephen turned also and waited for a few moments till his companion's ill-humour had had its vent.

– This hypothesis, Stephen repeated, is the other way out: that, though the same object may not seem beautiful to all people, all people who admire a beautiful object find in it certain relations which satisfy and coincide with the stages themselves of all esthetic apprehension. These relations of the sensible, visible to you through one form and to me through another, must be therefore the necessary qualities of beauty. Now, we can return to our old friend saint Thomas for another pennyworth of wisdom.

Lynch laughed.

– It amuses me vastly, he said, to hear you quoting him time after time like a jolly round friar. Are you laughing in your sleeve?

– MacAlister, answered Stephen, would call my esthetic theory applied Aquinas. So far as this side of esthetic philosophy extends, Aquinas will carry me all along the line. When we come to the phenomena of artistic conception, artistic gestation, and artistic reproduction I require a new terminology and a new personal experience.

– Of course, said Lynch. After all Aquinas, in spite of his intellect, was exactly a good round friar. But you will tell me about the new personal experience and new terminology some other day. Hurry up and finish the first part.

– Who knows? said Stephen, smiling. Perhaps Aquinas would understand me better than you. He was a poet himself. He wrote a hymn for Maundy Thursday. It begins with the words *Pange lingua gloriosi.*[410] They say it is the highest glory of the hymnal. It is an intricate and soothing hymn. I like it; but there is no hymn that can be put beside that mournful and majestic processional song, the *Vexilla Regis* of Venantius Fortunatus.[411]

Lynch began to sing softly and solemnly in a deep bass voice:

> *Impleta sunt quae concinit*
> *David fideli carmine*
> *Dicendo nationibus*
> *Regnavit a ligno Deus.*[412]

– That's great! he said, well pleased. Great music!

They turned into Lower Mount Street. A few steps from the corner a fat young man, wearing a silk neckcloth, saluted them and stopped.

– Did you hear the results of the exams? he asked. Griffin was plucked. Halpin and O'Flynn are through the home civil. Moonan got fifth place in the Indian.[413] O'Shaughnessy got fourteenth. The Irish fellows in Clark's gave them a feed last night. They all ate curry.

His pallid bloated face expressed benevolent malice and, as he had advanced through his tidings of success, his small fat-encircled eyes vanished out of sight and his weak wheezing voice out of hearing.

In reply to a question of Stephen's his eyes and his voice came forth again from their lurking-places.

– Yes, MacCullagh and I, he said. He's taking pure mathematics and I'm taking constitutional history. There are twenty subjects. I'm taking botany too. You know I'm a member of the field club.

He drew back from the other two in a stately fashion and placed a plump woollen-gloved hand on his breast from which muttered wheezing laughter at once broke forth.

– Bring us a few turnips and onions the next time you go out, said Stephen drily, to make a stew.

The fat student laughed indulgently and said:

– We are all highly respectable people in the field club. Last Saturday we went out to Glenmalure,[414] seven of us.

– With women, Donovan? said Lynch.

Donovan again laid his hand on his chest and said:

– Our end is the acquisition of knowledge.

Then he said quickly:

– I hear you are writing some essays about esthetics.

Stephen made a vague gesture of denial.

– Goethe and Lessing,[415] said Donovan, have written a lot on that subject, the classical school and the romantic school and all that. The Laocoon interested me very much when I read it. Of course it is idealistic, German, ultra-profound.[416]

Neither of the others spoke. Donovan took leave of them urbanely.

– I must go, he said softly and benevolently, I have a strong suspicion, amounting almost to a conviction, that my sister intended to make pancakes today for the dinner of the Donovan family.

– Goodbye, Stephen said in his wake. Don't forget the turnips for me and my mate.

Lynch gazed after him, his lip curling in slow scorn till his face resembled a devil's mask:

– To think that that yellow pancake-eating excrement can get a good job, he said at length, and I have to smoke cheap cigarettes!

They turned their faces towards Merrion Square[417] and went for a little in silence.

– To finish what I was saying about beauty, said Stephen, the most satisfying relations of the sensible must therefore correspond to the necessary phases of artistic apprehension. Find these and you find the qualities of universal beauty. Aquinas says: *Ad pulcritudinem tria requiruntur integritas, consonantia, claritas.* I translate it so: *Three things are needed for beauty, wholeness, harmony, and radiance.*[418] Do these correspond to the phases of apprehension? Are you following?

– Of course, I am, said Lynch. If you think I have an excrementitious intelligence run after Donovan and ask him to listen to you.

Stephen pointed to a basket which a butcher's boy had slung inverted on his head.

– Look at that basket, he said.

– I see it, said Lynch.

– In order to see that basket, said Stephen, your mind first of all separates the basket from the rest of the visible universe which is not the basket. The first phase of apprehension is a bounding line drawn about the object to be apprehended. An esthetic image is presented to us either in space or in time. What is audible is presented in time, what is visible is presented in space.[419] But, temporal or spatial, the esthetic image is first luminously apprehended as selfbounded and selfcontained upon the immeasurable background of space or time which is not it. You apprehended it as *one* thing. You see it as one whole. You apprehend its wholeness. That is *integritas*.

– Bull's eye! said Lynch, laughing. Go on.

– Then, said Stephen, you pass from point to point, led by its formal lines; you apprehend it as balanced part against part within its limits; you feel the rhythm of its structure. In other words, the synthesis of immediate perception is followed by the analysis of apprehension. Having first felt that it is *one* thing you feel now that it is a *thing*. You apprehend it as complex, multiple, divisible, separable, made up of its parts, the result of its parts and their sum, harmonious. That is *consonantia*.

– Bull's eye again! said Lynch wittily. Tell me now what is *claritas* and you win the cigar.

– The connotation of the word, Stephen said, is rather vague. Aquinas uses a term which seems to be inexact. It baffled me for a long time. It would lead you to believe that he had in mind symbolism or idealism,[420] the supreme quality of beauty being a light from some other world, the idea of which the matter is but the shadow, the reality of which it is but the symbol. I thought he might mean that *claritas* is the artistic discovery and representation of the divine purpose in anything or a force of generalisation which would make the esthetic image a universal one, make it outshine its proper conditions. But that is literary talk. I understand it so. When you have apprehended that basket as one thing and have then analysed it according to its form and apprehended it as a thing you make the only synthesis which is logically and esthetically permissible. You see that it is that thing which it is and no other thing. The radiance of which he speaks in the scholastic *quidditas*, the *whatness* of a thing.[421] This supreme quality is felt by the artist when the esthetic image is first conceived in his imagination. The mind in that mysterious instant Shelley likened beautifully to a fading coal.[422] The instant wherein that supreme quality of beauty, the dear radiance of the esthetic image, is apprehended luminously by the mind which has been arrested by its wholeness and fascinated by its harmony in the luminous silent stasis of esthetic pleasure, a spiritual state very like to that cardiac condition which the Italian physiologist Luigi Galvani, using a phrase almost as beautiful as Shelley's, called the enchantment of the heart.[423]

Stephen paused and, though his companion did not speak, felt that his words had called up around them a thought-enchanted silence.

– What I have said, he began again, refers to beauty in the wider sense of the word, in the sense which the word has in the literary tradition. In the marketplace it has another sense. When we speak of beauty in the second sense of the term our judgment is influenced in the first place by the art itself and by the form of that art. The image, it is clear, must be set between the mind or senses of the artist himself and the mind or senses of others. If you bear this in memory you will see that art necessarily divides itself into three forms progressing from one to the next. These forms are: the lyrical form, the form wherein the artist presents his image in immediate relation to himself; the epical form, the form wherein he presents his image in mediate relation to himself and to others; the dramatic form, the form wherein he presents his image in immediate relation to others.

– That you told me a few nights ago, said Lynch, and we began the famous discussion.

– I have a book at home, said Stephen, in which I have written down questions which are more amusing than yours were. In finding the answers to them I found the theory of esthetic which I am trying to explain. Here are some questions I set myself: *Is a chair finely made tragic or comic? Is the portrait of Mona Lisa good if I desire to see it? Is the bust of Sir Philip Crampton*[424] *lyrical, epical or dramatic? If not, why not?*

– Why not, indeed? said Lynch, laughing.

– *If a man hacking in fury at a block of wood, Stephen continued, make there an image of a cow, is that image a work of art? If not why not?*

– That's a lovely one, said Lynch, laughing again. That has the true scholastic stink.

– Lessing, said Stephen, should not have taken a group of statues to write of.[425] The art, being inferior, does not present the forms I spoke of distinguished clearly one from another. Even in literature, the highest and most spiritual art, the forms are often confused. The lyrical form is in fact the simplest verbal vesture of an instant of emotion, a rhythmical cry such as ages ago cheered on the man who pulled at the oar or dragged stones up a slope. He who utters it is more conscious of the instant of emotion than of himself as feeling emotion. The simplest epical form is seen emerging out of lyrical literature when the artist prolongs and broods upon himself as the centre of an epical event and this form progresses till the centre of emotional gravity is equidistant from the artist himself and from others. The narrative is no longer purely personal. The personality of the artist passes into the narration itself, flowing round and round the persons and the action like a vital sea. This progress you will see easily in that old English ballad *Turpin Hero*[426] which begins in the first person and ends in the third person. The dramatic form is reached when the vitality which has flowed and eddied round each person fills every person with such vital force that he or she assumes a proper and intangible esthetic life. The personality of the artist, at first a cry or a cadence or a mood and then a fluid and lambent narrative, finally refines itself out of existence, impersonalizes itself, so to speak. The esthetic image in the dramatic form is life purified in and reprojected from the human imagination. The mystery of esthetic, like that of material creation, is accomplished. The artist, like the God of creation, remains within or behind or beyond or above his handiwork, invisible, refined out of existence, indifferent, paring his fingernails.

– Trying to refine them also out of existence, said Lynch.

A fine rain began to fall from the high veiled sky and they turned into the duke's lawn to reach the national library[427] before the shower came.

– What do you mean, Lynch asked surlily, by prating about beauty and the imagination in this miserable Godforsaken island? No wonder the artist retired within or behind his handiwork after having perpetrated this country.

The rain fell faster. When they passed through the passage beside the royal Irish academy[428] they found many students sheltering under the arcade of the library. Cranly, leaning against a pillar, was picking his teeth with a sharpened match, listening to some companions. Some girls stood near the entrance door. Lynch whispered to Stephen:

– Your beloved is here.

Stephen took his place silently on the step below the group of students, heedless of the rain which fell fast, turning his eyes towards her from time to time. She too stood silently among her companions. She has no priest to flirt with, he thought with conscious bitterness, remembering how he had seen her last. Lynch was right. His mind, emptied of theory and courage, lapsed back into a listless peace.

He heard the students talking among themselves. They spoke of two friends who had passed the final medical examination, of the chances of getting places on ocean liners, of poor and rich practices.

– That's all a bubble. An Irish country practice is better.

– Hynes was two years in Liverpool and he says the same. A frightful hole he said it was. Nothing but midwifery cases.

– Do you mean to say it is better to have a job here in the country than in a rich city like that? I know a fellow . . .

– Hynes has no brains. He got through by stewing,[429] pure stewing.

– Don't mind him. There's plenty of money to be made in a big commercial city.

– Depends on the practice.

– *Ego credo ut vita pauperum est simpliciter atrox, simpliciter sanguinarius atrox, in Liverpoolio.*[430]

Their voices reached his ears as if from a distance in interrupted pulsation. She was preparing to go away with her companions.

The quick light shower had drawn off, tarrying in clusters of diamonds among the shrubs of the quadrangle where an exhalation was breathed forth by the blackened earth. Their trim boots prattled as they stood on the steps of the colonnade, talking quietly and gaily, glancing at the clouds, holding their unbrellas at cunning angles against the few last raindrops, closing them again, holding their skirts demurely.

And if he had judged her harshly? If her life were a simple rosary of hours, her life simple and strange as a bird's life, gay in the morning, restless all day, tired at sundown? Her heart simple and wilful as a bird's heart?

Towards dawn he awoke. O what sweet music! His soul was all dewy wet. Over his limbs in sleep pale cool waves of light had passed. He lay still, as if his soul lay amid cool waters, conscious of faint sweet music. His mind was waking slowly to a tremulous morning knowledge, a morning inspiration. A spirit filled him, pure as the purest water, sweet as dew, moving as music. But how faintly it was inbreathed, how passionlessly, as if the seraphim themselves were breathing upon him! His soul was waking slowly, fearing to awake wholly. It was that windless hour of dawn when madness wakes and strange plants open to the light and the moth flies forth silently.

An enchantment of the heart! The night had been enchanted. In a dream or vision he had known the ecstasy of seraphic life. Was it an instant of enchantment only or long hours and years and ages?

The instant of inspiration seemed now to be reflected from all sides at once from a multitude of cloudy circumstances of what had happened or of what might have happened. The instant flashed forth like a point of light and now from cloud on cloud of vague circumstance confused form was veiling softly in afterglow. O! In the virgin womb of the imagination the word was made flesh. Gabriel the seraph had come to the virgin's chamber.[431] An afterglow deepened within his spirit, whence the white flame had passed, deepening to a rose and ardent light. That rose and ardent light was her strange wilful heart, strange that no man had known or would know, wilful from before the beginning of the world; and lured by that ardent rose-like glow the choirs of the seraphim were falling from heaven.

> *Are you not weary of ardent ways,*
> *Lure of the fallen seraphim?*
> *Tell no more of enchanted days.*

The verses passed from his mind to his lips and, murmuring them over, he felt the rhythmic movement of a villanelle[432] pass through them. The rose-like glow sent forth its rays of rhyme; ways, days, blaze, praise, raise. Its rays burned up the world, consumed the hearts of men and angels: the rays from the rose that was her wilful heart.

> *Your eyes have set man's heart ablaze*
> *And you have had your will of him.*
> *Are you not weary of ardent ways?*

And then? The rhythm died away, ceased, began again to move and beat. And then? Smoke, incense ascending from the altar of the world.

> *Above the flame the smoke of praise*
> *Goes up from ocean rim to rim*
> *Tell no more of enchanted days.*

Smoke went up from the whole earth, from the vapoury oceans, smoke of her praise. The earth was like a swinging swaying censer, a ball of incense, an ellipsoidal fall. The rhythm died out at once; the cry of his heart was broken. His lip began to murmur the first verses over and over; then went on stumbling through half verses, stammering and baffled; then stopped. The heart's cry was broken.

The veiled windless hour had passed and behind the panes of the naked window the morning light was gathering. A bell beat faintly very far away. A bird twittered; two birds, three. The bell and the bird ceased; and the dull white light spread itself east and west, covering the world, covering the roselight in his heart.

Fearing to lose all, he raised himself suddenly on his elbow to look for paper and pencil. There was neither on the table; only the soup plate he had eaten the rice from for supper and the candlestick with its tendrils of tallow and its paper socket, singed by the last flame. He stretched his arm wearily towards the foot of the bed, groping with his hand in the pockets of the coat that hung there. His fingers found a pencil and then a cigarette packet. He lay back and, tearing open the packet, placed the last cigarette on the window ledge and began to write out the stanzas of the villanelle in small neat letters on the rough cardboard surface.

Having written them out he lay back on the lumpy pillow, murmuring them again. The lumps of knotted flock under his head reminded him of the lumps of knotted horsehair in the sofa of her parlour on which he used to sit, smiling or serious, asking himself why he had come, displeased with her and with himself, confounded by the print of the Sacred Heart above the untenanted sideboard.[433] He saw her approach him in a lull of the talk and beg him to sing one of his curious songs. Then he saw himself sitting at the old piano, striking chords softly from its speckled keys and singing, amid the talk which had risen again in the room, to her who leaned beside the mantelpiece a dainty song of the Elizabethans, a sad and sweet loth to depart,[434] the victory chant of Agincourt,[435] the happy air of Greensleeves.[436] While he sang and she listened, or feigned to listen, his heart was at rest but when the quaint old songs had ended and he heard again the voices in the room he remembered his own sarcasm: the house where young men are called by their christian names a little too soon.[437]

At certain instants her eyes seemed about to trust him but he had waited in vain. She passed now dancing lightly across his memory as she had been that night at the carnival ball, her white dress a little lifted, a white spray nodding in her hair. She danced lightly in the round. She was dancing towards him and, as she came, her eyes were a little averted and a faint glow was on her cheek. At the pause in the chain of hands her hand had lain in his an instant, a soft merchandise.

– You are a great stranger now.

– Yes. I was born to be a monk.

– I am afraid you are a heretic.

– Are you much afraid?

For answer she had danced away from him along the chain of hands, dancing lightly and discreetly, giving herself to none. The white spray nodded to her dancing and when she was in shadow the glow was deeper on her cheek.

A monk! His own image started forth a profaner of the cloister, a heretic franciscan, willing and willing not to serve, spinning like Gherardino da Borgo San Donnino,[438] a lithe web of sophistry and whispering in her ear.

No, it was not his image. It was like the image of the young priest in whose company he had seen her last, looking at him out of dove's eyes, toying with the pages of her Irish phrasebook.

– Yes, yes, the ladies are coming round to us. I can see it every day. The ladies are with us. The best helpers the language has.

– And the church, Father Moran?

– The church too. Coming round too. The work is going ahead there too. Don't fret about the church.

Bah! he had done well to leave the room in disdain. He had done well not to salute her on the steps of the library! He had done well to leave her to flirt with her priest, to toy with a church which was the scullery-maid of christendom.

Rude brutal anger routed the last lingering instant of ecstasy from his soul. It broke up violently her fair image and flung the fragments on all sides. On all sides distorted reflections of her image started from his memory: the flower girl in the ragged dress with damp coarse hair and a hoyden's face who had called herself his own girl and begged his handsel, the kitchen-girl in the next house who sang over the clatter of her plates, with the drawl of a country singer, the first bars of *By Killarney's Lakes and Fells*,[439] a girl who had laughed gaily to see him stumble when the iron grating in the footpath near Cork Hill had caught the broken sole of his shoe, a girl he had glanced at, attracted by her small ripe mouth, as she passed out of Jacob's biscuit factory,[440] who had cried to him over her shoulder:

– Do you like what you seen of me, straight hair and curly eyebrows?

And yet he felt that, however he might revile and mock her image, his anger was also a form of homage. He had left the classroom in disdain that was not wholly sincere, feeling that perhaps the secret of her race lay behind those dark eyes upon which her long lashes flung a quick shadow. He had told himself bitterly as he walked through the streets that she was a figure of the womanhood of her country, a bat-like soul waking to the consciousness of itself in darkness and secrecy and loneliness, tarrying awhile, loveless and sinless, with her mild lover and leaving him to whisper of innocent transgressions in the latticed ear of a priest.[441] His anger against her found vent in coarse railing at her paramour, whose name and, voice and features offended his baffled pride: a priested peasant, with a brother a policeman in Dublin and a brother a potboy in Moycullen.[442] To him she would unveil her soul's shy nakedness, to one who was but schooled in the discharging of a formal rite rather than to him, a priest of the eternal imagination, transmuting the daily bread of experience into the radiant body of everliving life.

The radiant image of the eucharist united again in an instant his bitter and despairing thoughts, their cries arising unbroken in a hymn of thanksgiving.

> *Our broken cries and mournful lays*
> *Rise in one eucharistic hymn*
> *Are you not weary of ardent ways?*
>
> *While sacrificing hands upraise*
> *The chalice flowing to the brim.*
> *Tell no more of enchanted days.*

He spoke the verses aloud from the first lines till the music and rhythm suffused his mind, turning it to quiet indulgence; then copied them painfully to feel them the better by seeing them; then lay back on his bolster.

The full morning light had come. No sound was to be heard; but he knew that all around him life was about to awaken in common noises, hoarse voices, sleepy prayers. Shrinking from that life he turned towards the wall, making a cowl of the blanket and staring at the great overblown scarlet flowers of the tattered wallpaper. He tried to warm his perishing joy in their scarlet glow, imagining a roseway from where he lay upwards to heaven all strewn with scarlet flowers. Weary! Weary! He too was weary of ardent ways.

A gradual warmth, a languorous weariness passed over him descending along his spine from his closely cowled head. He felt it descend and, seeing himself as he lay, smiled. Soon he would sleep.

He had written verses for her again after ten years. Ten years before she had worn her shawl cowlwise about her head, sending sprays of her warm breath into the night air, tapping her foot upon the glassy road. It was the last tram; the lank brown horses knew it and shook their bells to the clear night in admonition. The conductor talked with the driver, both nodding often in the green light of the lamp. They stood on the steps of the tram, he on the upper, she on the lower. She came up to his step many times between their phrases and went down again and once or twice remained beside him forgetting to go down and then went down. Let be! Let be!

Ten years from that wisdom of children to his folly. If he sent her the verses? They would be read out at breakfast amid the tapping of egg-shells. Folly indeed! Her brothers would laugh and try to wrest the page from each other with their strong hard fingers. The suave priest, her uncle, seated in his arm-chair, would hold the page at arm's length, read it smiling and approve of the literary form.

No, no; that was folly. Even if he sent her the verses she would not show them to others. No, no; she could not.

He began to feel that he had wronged her. A sense of her innocence moved him almost to pity her, an innocence he had never understood till he had come to the knowledge of it through sin, an innocence which she too had not understood while she was innocent or before the strange humiliation of her nature had first come upon her. Then first her soul had begun to live as his soul had when he had first sinned, and a tender compassion filled his heart as he remembered her frail pallor and her eyes, humbled and saddened by the dark shame of womanhood.

While his soul had passed from ecstasy to languor where had she been? Might it be, in the mysterious ways of spiritual life, that her soul at those same moments had been conscious of his homage? It might be.

A glow of desire kindled again his soul and fired and fulfilled all his body. Conscious of his desire she was waking from odorous sleep, the temptress of his villanelle. Her eyes, dark and with a look of languor, were opening to his eyes. Her nakedness yielded to him, radiant, warm, odorous and lavish-limbed, enfolded him like a shining cloud, enfolded him like water with a liquid life; and like a cloud of vapour or like water circumfluent in space the liquid letters of speech, symbols of the element of mystery, flowed forth over his brain.

Are you not weary of ardent ways,
Lure of the fallen seraphim?
Tell no more of enchanted days.

Your eyes have set man's heart ablaze
And you have had your will of him.
Are you not weary of ardent ways?

Above the flame the smoke of praise
Goes up from ocean rim to rim.
Tell no more of enchanted days.

Our broken cries and mournful lays
Rise in one eucharistic hymn.
Are you not weary of ardent ways?

While sacrificing hands upraise
The chalice flowing to the brim.
Tell no more of enchanted days.

And still you hold our longing gaze
With languorous look and lavish limb!
Are you not weary of ardent ways?
Tell no more of enchanted days.

What birds were they? He stood on the steps of the library to look at them, leaning wearily on his ashplant.[443] They flew round and round the jutting shoulder of a house in Molesworth Street. The air of the late March evening made clear their flight, their dark quivering bodies flying clearly against the sky as against a limp-hung cloth of smoky tenuous blue.

He watched their flight; bird after bird: a dark flash, a swerve, a flutter of wings. He tried to count them before all their darting quivering bodies passed: six, ten, eleven: and wondered were they odd or even in number. Twelve, thirteen: for two came wheeling down from the upper sky. They were flying high and low but ever round and round in straight and curving lines and ever flying from left to right, circling about a temple of air.[444]

He listened to the cries: like the squeak of mice behind the wainscot: a shrill twofold note. But the notes were long and shrill and whirring, unlike the cry of vermin, falling a third or a fourth and trilled as the flying beaks clove the air. Their cry was shrill and clear and fine and falling like threads of silken light unwound from whirring spools.

The inhuman clamour soothed his ears in which his mother's sobs and reproaches murmured insistently and the dark frail quivering bodies wheeling and fluttering and swerving round an airy temple of the tenuous sky soothed his eyes which still saw the image of his mother's face.

Why was he gazing upwards from the steps of the porch, hearing their shrill twofold cry, watching their flight? For an augury of good or evil? A phrase of Cornelius Agrippa[445] flew through his mind and then there flew hither and thither shapeless thoughts from Swedenborg on the correspondence of birds to things of the intellect and of how the creatures of the air have their knowledge and know their times and seasons because they, unlike man, are in the order of their life and have not perverted that order by reason.[446]

And for ages men had gazed upward as he was gazing at birds in flight. The colonnade above him made him think vaguely of an ancient temple and the ashplant on which he leaned wearily of the curved stick of an augur.[447] A sense of fear of the unknown moved in the heart of his weariness, a fear of symbols and portents, of the hawk-like man whose name he bore soaring out of his captivity on osier-woven wings, of Thoth,[448] the god of writers, writing with a reed upon a tablet and bearing on his narrow ibis head the cusped moon.

He smiled as he thought of the god's image for it made him think of a bottle-nosed judge in a wig, putting commas into a document which he held at arm's length, and he knew that he would not have remembered the god's name but that it was like an Irish oath.[449] It was folly. But was it for this folly that he was about to leave for ever the house of prayer and prudence into which he had been born and the order of life out of which he had come?

They came back with shrill cries over the jutting shoulder of the house, flying darkly against the fading air. What birds were they? He thought that they must be swallows who had come back from the south. Then he was to go away for they were birds ever going and coming, building ever an unlasting home under the eaves of men's houses and ever leaving the homes they had built to wander.

> *Bend down your faces, Oona and Aleel.*
> *I gaze upon them as the swallow gazes*
> *Upon the nest under the eave before*
> *He wander the loud waters.*[450]

A soft liquid joy like the noise of many waters flowed over his memory and he felt in his heart the soft peace of silent spaces of fading tenuous sky above the waters, of oceanic silence, of swallows flying through the sea-dusk over the flowing waters.

A soft liquid joy flowed through the words where the soft long vowels hurtled noiselessly and fell away, lapping and flowing back and ever shaking the white bells of their waves in mute chime and mute peal, and soft low swooning cry; and he felt that the augury he had sought in the wheeling darting birds and in the pale space of sky above him had come forth from his heart like a bird from a turret, quietly and swiftly.

Symbol of departure or of loneliness? The verses crooned in the ear of his memory composed slowly before his remembering eyes the scene of the hall on the night of the opening of the national theatre.[451] He was alone at the side of the balcony, looking out of jaded eyes at the culture of Dublin in the stalls and at the tawdry scene-cloths and human dolls framed by the garish lamps of the stage. A burly policeman sweated behind him and seemed at every moment about to act. The catcalls and hisses and mocking cries ran in rude gusts round the hall from his scattered fellow students.

– A libel on Ireland!

– Made in Germany.[452]

– Blasphemy!

– We never sold our faith!

– No Irish woman ever did it!

– We want no amateur atheists.

– We want no budding buddhists.[453]

A sudden swift hiss fell from the windows above him and he knew that the electric lamps had been switched on in the reader's room.[454] He turned into the pillared hall, now calmly lit, went up the staircase and passed in through the clicking turnstile.

Cranly was sitting over near the dictionaries. A thick book, opened at the frontispiece, lay before him on the wooden rest. He leaned back in his chair, inclining his ear like that of a confessor to the face of the medical student who was reading to him a problem from the chess page of a journal. Stephen sat down at his right and the priest at the other side of the table closed his copy of *The Tablet*[455] with an angry snap and stood up.

Cranly gazed after him blandly and vaguely. The medical student went on in a softer voice:

– Pawn to king's fourth.

– We had better go, Dixon, said Stephen in warning. He has gone to complain.

Dixon folded the journal and rose with dignity, saying:

– Our men retired in good order.

– With guns and cattle, added Stephen, pointing to the title page of Cranly's book on which was printed *Diseases of the Ox*.

As they passed through a lane of the tables Stephen said:

– Cranly, I want to speak to you.

Cranly did not answer or turn. He laid his book on the counter and passed out, his well-shod feet sounding flatly on the floor. On the staircase he paused and gazing absently at Dixon repeated:

– Pawn to king's bloody fourth.

– Put it that way if you like, Dixon said.

He had a quiet toneless voice and urbane manners and on a finger of his plump clean hand he displayed at moments a signet ring.

As they crossed the hall a man of dwarfish stature came towards them. Under the dome of his tiny hat his unshaven face began to smile with pleasure and he was heard to murmur. The eyes were melancholy as those of a monkey.

– Good evening, gentlemen, said the stubble-grown monkeyish face.

– Warm weather for March, said Cranly. They have the windows open upstairs.

Dixon smiled and turned his ring. The blackish, monkey-puckered face pursed its human mouth with gentle pleasure and its voice purred:

– Delightful weather for March. Simply delightful.

– There are two nice young ladies upstairs, captain, tired of waiting, Dixon said.

Cranly smiled and said kindly:

– The captain has only one love: sir Walter Scott. Isn't that so, captain?

– What are you reading now, captain? Dixon asked. *The Bride of Lammermoor*?[456]

– I love old Scott, the flexible lips said, I think he writes something lovely. There is no writer can touch sir Walter Scott.

He moved a thin shrunken brown hand gently in the air in time to his praise and his thin quick eyelids beat often over his sad eyes.

Sadder to Stephen's ear was his speech: a genteel accent, low and moist, marred by errors, and, listening to it, he wondered was the story true and was the thin blood that flowed in his shrunken frame noble and come of an incestuous love?

The park trees were heavy with rain; and rain fell still and ever in the lake, lying grey like a shield. A game of swans[457] flew there and the water and the shore beneath were fouled with their green-white slime. They embraced softly, impelled by the grey rainy light, the wet silent trees, the shield-like witnessing lake, the swans. They embraced without joy or passion, his arm about his sister's neck. A grey woollen cloak was wrapped athwart her from her shoulder to her waist and her fair head was bent in willing shame. He had loose red-brown hair and tender shapely strong freckled hands. Face? There was no face seen. The brother's face was bent upon her fair rain-fragrant hair. The hand freckled and strong and shapely and caressing was Davin's hand.

He frowned angrily upon his thought and on the shrivelled mannikin who had called it forth. His father's jibes at the Bantry gang[458] leaped out of his memory. He held them at a distance and brooded uneasily on his own thought again. Why were they not Cranly's hands? Had Davin's simplicity and innocence stung him more secretly?

He walked on across the hall with Dixon, leaving Cranly to take leave elaborately of the dwarf.

Under the colonnade Temple was standing in the midst of a little group of students. One of them cried:

– Dixon, come over till you hear. Temple is in grand form.

Temple turned on him his dark gipsy eyes.

– You're a hypocrite, O'Keeffe, he said. And Dixon is a smiler. By hell, I think that's a good literary expression.

He laughed slyly, looking in Stephen's face, repeating:

– By hell, I'm delighted with that name. A smiler.

A stout student who stood below them on the steps said:

– Come back to the mistress, Temple. We want to hear about that.

– He had, faith, Temple said. And he was a married man too. And all the priests used to be dining there. By hell, I think they all had a touch.[459]

– We shall call it riding a hack to spare the hunter, said Dixon.

– Tell us, Temple, O'Keeffe said, how may quarts of porter have you in you?

– All your intellectual soul is in that phrase, O'Keeffe, said Temple with open scorn.

He moved with a shambling gait round the group and spoke to Stephen.

– Did you know that the Forsters are the kings of Belgium? he asked.

Cranly came out through the door of the entrance hall, his hat thrust back on the nape of his neck and picking his teeth with care.

– And here's the wiseacre, said Temple. Do you know that about the Forsters?

He paused for an answer. Cranly dislodged a figseed from his teeth on the point of his rude toothpick and gazed at it intently.

– The Forster family, Temple said, is descended from Baldwin the first, king of Flanders. He was called the Forester. Forester and Forster are the same name. A descendant of Baldwin the First, captain Francis Forster, settled in Ireland and married the daughter of the last chieftain of Clanbrassil. Then there are the Blake Forsters. That's a different branch.[460]

– From Baldhead, king of Flanders, Cranly repeated, rooting again deliberately at his gleaming uncovered teeth.

– Where did you pick up all that history? O'Keeffe asked.

– I know all the history of your family, too, Temple said, turning to Stephen. Do you know what Giraldus Cambrensis[461] says about your family?

– Is he descended from Baldwin too? asked a tall consumptive student with dark eyes.

– Baldhead, Cranly repeated, sucking at a crevice in his teeth.

– *Pernobilis et pervetusta familia*,[462] Temple said to Stephen.

The stout student who stood below them on the steps farted briefly. Dixon turned towards him, saying in a soft voice:

– Did an angel speak?

Cranly turned also and said vehemently but without anger:

– Goggins, you're the flamingest dirty devil I ever met, do you know.

– I had it on my mind to say that, Goggins answered firmly. It did no one any harm, did it?

– We hope, Dixon said suavely, that it was not of the kind known to science as a *paulo post futurum*.[463]

– Didn't I tell you he was a smiler? said Temple, turning right and left. Didn't I give him that name?

– You did. We're not deaf, said the tall consumptive.

Cranly still frowned at the stout student below him. Then, with a snort of disgust, he shoved him violently down the steps.

– Go away from here, he said rudely. Go away, you stinkpot. And you are a stinkpot.

Goggins skipped down on to the gravel and at once returned to his place with good humour. Temple turned back to Stephen and asked:

– Do you believe in the law of heredity?

– Are you drunk or what are you or what are you trying to say? asked Cranly, facing round on him with an expression of wonder.

– The most profound sentence ever written, Temple said with enthusiasm, is the sentence at the end of the zoology. Reproduction is the beginning of death.

He touched Stephen timidly at the elbow and said eagerly:

– Do you feel how profound that is because you are a poet?

Cranly pointed his long forefinger.

– Look at him! he said with scorn to the others. Look at Ireland's hope!

They laughed at his words and gesture. Temple turned on him bravely, saying:

– Cranly, you're always sneering at me. I can see that. But I am as good as you any day. Do you know what I think about you now as compared with myself?

– My dear man, said Cranly urbanely, you are incapable, do you know, absolutely incapable of thinking.

– But do you know, Temple went on, what I think of you and of myself compared together?

– Out with it, Temple! the stout student cried from the steps. Get it out in bits!

Temple turned right and left, making sudden feeble gestures as he spoke.

– I'm a ballocks, he said, shaking his head in despair. I am and I know I am. And I admit it that I am.

Dixon patted him lightly on the shoulder and said mildly:

– And it does you every credit, Temple.

– But he, Temple said, pointing to Cranly, he is a ballocks, too, like me. Only he doesn't know it. And that's the only difference I see.

A burst of laughter covered his words. But he turned again to Stephen and said with a sudden eagerness:

– That word is a most interesting word. That's the only English dual number.[464] Did you know?

– Is it? Stephen said vaguely.

He was watching Cranly's firm-featured suffering face, lit up now by a smile of false patience. The gross name had passed over it like foul water poured over an old stone image, patient of injuries; and, as he watched him, he saw him raise his hat in salute and uncover the black hair that stood stiffly from his fore head like an iron crown.

She passed out from the porch of the library and bowed across Stephen in reply to Cranly's greeting. He also? Was there not a slight flush on Cranly's cheek? Or had it come forth at Temple's words? The light had waned. He could not see.

Did that explain his friend's listless silence, his harsh comments, the sudden intrusions of rude speech with which he had shattered so often Stephen's ardent wayward confessions? Stephen had forgiven freely for he had found this rudeness also in himself. And he remembered an evening when he had dismounted from a borrowed creaking bicycle to pray to God in a wood near Malahide. He had lifted up his arms and spoken in ecstasy to the sombre nave of the trees, knowing that he stood on holy ground and in a holy hour. And when two constabulary men had come into sight round a bend in the gloomy road he had broken off his prayer to whistle loudly an air from the last pantomime.

He began to beat the frayed end of his ashplant against the base of a pillar. Had Cranly not heard him? Yet he could wait. The talk about him ceased for a moment and a soft hiss fell again from a window above. But no other sound was in the air and the swallows whose flight he had followed with idle eyes were sleeping.

She had passed through the dusk. And therefore the air was silent save for one soft hiss that fell. And therefore the tongues about him had ceased their babble. Darkness was falling.

Darkness falls from the air.[465]

A trembling joy, lambent as a faint light, played like a fairy host around him. But why? Her passage through the darkening air or the verse with its black vowels and its opening sound, rich and lutelike?

He walked away slowly towards the deeper shadows at the end of the colonnade, beating the stone softly with his stick to hide his revery from the students whom he had left: and allowed his mind to summon back to itself the age of Dowland and Byrd and Nash.[466]

Eyes, opening from the darkness of desire, eyes that dimmed the breaking east. What was their languid grace but the softness of chambering?[467] And what was their shimmer but the shimmer of the scum that mantled the cesspool of the court of a slobbering Stuart.[468] And he tasted in the language of memory ambered wines, dying fallings of sweet airs, the proud pavan,[469] and saw with the eyes of memory kind gentlewomen in Covent Garden wooing from their balconies with sucking mouths and the pox-fouled wenches of the taverns and young wives that, gaily yielding to their ravishers, clipped[470] and clipped again.

The images he had summoned gave him no pleasure. They were secret and inflaming but her image was not entangled by them. That was not the way to think of her. It was not even the way in which he thought of her. Could his mind then not trust itself? Old phrases, sweet only with a disinterred sweetness like the figseeds Cranly rooted out of his gleaming teeth.

It was not thought nor vision though he knew vaguely that her figure was passing homeward through the city. Vaguely first and then more sharply he smelt her body. A conscious unrest seethed in his blood. Yes, it was her body he smelt, a wild and languid smell, the tepid limbs over which his music had flowed desirously and the secret soft linen upon which her flesh distilled odour and a dew.

A louse crawled over the nape of his neck and, putting his thumb and forefinger deftly beneath his loose collar, he caught it. He rolled its body, tender yet brittle as a grain of rice, between thumb and finger for an instant before he let it fall from him and wondered would it live or die. There came to his mind a curious phrase from Cornelius à Lapide[471] which said that the lice born of human sweat were not created by God with the other animals on the sixth day. But the tickling of the skin of his neck made his mind raw and red. The life of his body, ill clad, ill fed, louse-eaten, made him close his eyelids in a sudden spasm of despair and in the darkness he saw the brittle bright bodies of lice falling from the air and turning often as they fell. Yes, and it was not darkness that fell from the air. It was brightness.

Brightness falls from the air.

He had not even remembered rightly Nash's line. All the images it had awakened were false. His mind bred vermin. His thoughts were lice born of the sweat of sloth.

He came back quickly along the colonnade towards the group of students. Well then, let her go and be damned to her! She could love some clean athlete who washed himself every morning to the waist and had black hair on his chest. Let her.

Cranly had taken another dried fig from the supply in his pocket and was eating it slowly and noisily. Temple sat on the pediment of a pillar, leaning back, his cap pulled down on his sleepy eyes. A squat young man came out of the porch, a leather portfolio tucked under his armpit. He marched towards the group, striking the flags with the heels of his boots and with the ferrule of his heavy umbrella. Then, raising the umbrella in salute, he said to all:

– Good evening, sirs.

He struck the flags again and tittered while his head trembled with a slight nervous movement. The tall consumptive student and Dixon and O'Keeffe were speaking in Irish and did not answer him. Then, turning to Cranly, he said:

– Good evening, particularly to you.

He moved the umbrella in indication and tittered again. Cranly, who was still chewing the fig, answered with loud movements of his jaws.

– Good? Yes. It is a good evening.

The squat student looked at him seriously and shook his umbrella gently and reprovingly.

– I can see, he said, that you are about to make obvious remarks.

– Um, Cranly answered, holding out what remained of the half chewed fig and jerking it towards the squat student's mouth in sign that he should eat.

The squat student did not eat it but, indulging his special humour, said gravely, still tittering and prodding his phrase with his umbrella:

– Do you intend that . . . ?

He broke off, pointed bluntly to the munched pulp of the fig, and said loudly:

– I allude to that.

– Um, Cranly said as before.

– Do you intend that now, the squat student said, as *ipso facto* or, let us say, as so to speak?

Dixon turned aside from his group, saying:

– Goggins was waiting for you, Glynn. He has gone round to the Adelphi[472] to look for you and Moynihan. What have you there? he asked, tapping the portfolio under Glynn's arm.

– Examination papers, Glynn answered. I give them monthly examinations to see that they are profiting by my tuition.

He also tapped the portfolio and coughed gently and smiled.

– Tuition! said Cranly rudely. I suppose you mean the barefooted children that are taught by a bloody ape like you. God help them!

He bit off the rest of the fig and flung away the butt.

– I suffer little children to come unto me,[473] Glynn said amiably.

– A bloody ape, Cranly repeated with emphasis, and a blasphemous bloody ape!

Temple stood up and, pushing past Cranly, addressed Glynn:

– That phrase you said now, he said, is from the new testament about suffer the children to come to me.

– Go to sleep again, Temple, said O'Keeffe.

– Very well, then, Temple continued, still addressing Glynn, and if Jesus suffered the children to come why does the church send them all to hell if they die unbaptized?[474] Why is that?

– Were you baptized yourself, Temple? the consumptive student asked.

– But why are they sent to hell if Jesus said they were all to come? Temple said, his eyes searching Glynn's eyes.

Glynn coughed and said gently, holding back with difficulty the nervous titter in his voice and moving his umbrella at every word:

– And, as you remark, if it is thus, I ask emphatically whence comes this thusness.

– Because the church is cruel like all old sinners, Temple said.

– Are you quite orthodox on that point, Temple? Dixon said suavely.

– Saint Augustine says that about unbaptized children[475] going to hell, Temple answered, because he was a cruel old sinner too.

– I bow to you, Dixon said, but I had the impression that limbo existed for such cases.

– Don't argue with him, Dixon, Cranly said brutally. Don't talk to him or look at him. Lead him home with a sugan[476] the way you'd lead a bleating goat.

– Limbo! Temple cried. That's a fine invention too. Like hell.

– But with the unpleasantness left out, Dixon said.

He turned smiling to the others and said:

– I think I am voicing the opinions of all present in saying so much.

– You are, Glynn said in a firm tone. On that point Ireland is united.

He struck the ferrule of his umbrella on the stone floor of the colonnade.

– Hell, Temple said. I can respect that invention of the grey spouse of Satan.[477] Hell is Roman, like the walls of the Romans, strong and ugly. But what is limbo?

– Put him back into the perambulator, Cranly, O'Keeffe called out.

Cranly made a swift step towards Temple, halted, stamping his foot, crying as if to a fowl:

– Hoosh!

Temple moved away nimbly.

– Do you know what limbo is? he cried. Do you know what we call a notion like that in Roscommon?[478]

– Hoosh! Blast you! Cranly cried, clapping his hands.

– Neither my arse nor my elbow! Temple cried out scornfully. And that's what I call limbo.

– Give us that stick here, Cranly said.

He snatched the ashplant roughly from Stephen's hand and sprang down the steps: but Temple, hearing him move in pursuit, fled through the dusk like a wild creature, nimble and fleet-footed. Cranly's heavy boots were heard loudly charging across the quadrangle and then returning heavily, foiled and spurning the gravel at each step.

His step was angry and with an angry abrupt gesture he thrust the stick back into Stephen's hand. Stephen felt that his anger had another cause but, feigning patience, touched his arm slightly and said quietly:

– Cranly, I told you I wanted to speak to you. Come away.

Cranly looked at him for a few moments and asked:

– Now?

– Yes, now, Stephen said. We can't speak here. Come away.

They crossed the quadrangle together without speaking. The bird call from *Siegfried*[479] whistled softly followed them from the steps of the porch. Cranly turned, and Dixon, who had whistled, called out:

– Where are you fellows off to? What about that game, Cranly?

They parleyed in shouts across the still air about a game of billiards to be played in the Adelphi hotel. Stephen walked on alone and out into the quiet of Kildare Street opposite Maple's hotel[480] he stood to wait, patient again. The name of the hotel, a colourless polished wood, and its colourless front stung him like a glance of polite disdain. He stared angrily back at the softly lit drawing-room of the hotel in which he imagined the sleek lives of the patricians of Ireland housed in calm. They thought of army commissions and land agents: peasants greeted them along the roads in the country; they knew the names of certain French dishes and gave orders to jarvies[481] in high-pitched provincial voices which pierced through their skin-tight accents .

How could he hit their conscience or how cast his shadow over the imaginations of their daughters, before their squires begat upon them, that they might breed a race less ignoble than their own? And under the deepened dusk he felt the thoughts and desires of the race to which he belonged flitting like bats across the dark country lanes, under trees by the edges of streams and near the pool-mottled bogs. A woman had waited in the doorway as Davin had passed by at night and, offering him a cup of milk, had all but wooed him to her bed; for Davin had the mild eyes of one who could be secret. But him no woman's eyes had wooed.

His arm was taken in a strong grip and Cranly's voice said:

– Let us eke go.

They walked southward in silence. Then Cranly said:

– That blithering idiot, Temple! I swear to Moses, do you know, that I'll be the death of that fellow one time.

But his voice was no longer angry and Stephen wondered was he thinking of her greeting to him under the porch.

They turned to the left and walked on as before. When they had gone on so for some time Stephen said:

– Cranly, I had an unpleasant quarrel this evening.

– With your people? Cranly asked.

– With my mother.

– About religion?

– Yes, Stephen answered.

After a pause Cranly asked:

– What age is your mother?

– Not old, Stephen said. She wishes me to make my easter duty.[482]

– And will you?

– I will not, Stephen said.

– Why not? Cranly said.

– I will not serve, answered Stephen.

– That remark was made before, Cranly said calmly.

– It is made behind now, said Stephen hotly.

Cranly pressed Stephen's arm, saying:

– Go easy, my dear man. You're an excitable bloody man, do you know.

He laughed nervously as he spoke and, looking up into Stephen's face with moved and friendly eyes, said:

– Do you know that you are an excitable man?

– I daresay I am, said Stephen, laughing also.

Their minds, lately estranged, seemed suddenly to have been drawn closer, one to the other.

– Do you believe in the eucharist?[483] Cranly asked.

– I do not, Stephen said.

– Do you disbelieve then?

– I neither believe in it nor disbelieve in it, Stephen answered.

– Many persons have doubts, even religious persons, yet they over-come them or put them aside, Cranly said. Are your doubts on that point too strong?

– I do not wish to overcome them, Stephen answered.

Cranly, embarrassed for a moment, took another fig from his pocket and was about to eat it when Stephen said:

– Don't, please. You cannot discuss this question with your mouth full of chewed fig.

Cranly examined the fig by the light of a lamp under which he halted. Then he smelt it with both nostrils, bit a tiny piece, spat it out and threw the fig rudely into the gutter.

Addressing it as it lay, he said:

– Depart from me, ye cursed, into everlasting fire![484]

Taking Stephen's arm, he went on again and said:

– Do you not fear that those words may be spoken to you on the day of Judgment?

– What is offered me on the other hand? Stephen asked. An eternity of bliss in the company of the dean of studies?

– Remember, Cranly said, that he would be glorified.

– Ay, Stephen said somewhat bitterly, bright, agile, impassible and, above all, subtle.[485]

– It is a curious thing, do you know, Cranly said dispassionately, how your mind is supersaturated with the religion in which you say you disbelieve. Did you believe in it when you were at school? I bet you did.

– I did, Stephen answered.

– And were you happier then? Cranly asked softly, happier than you are now, for instance?

– Often happy, Stephen said, and often unhappy. I was someone else then.

– How someone else? What do you mean by that statement?

– I mean, said Stephen, that I was not myself as I am now, as I had to become.

– Not as you are now, not as you had to become, Cranly repeated. Let me ask you a question. Do you love your mother?

Stephen shook his head slowly.

– I don't know what your words mean, he said simply.

– Have you never loved anyone? Cranly asked.

– Do you mean women?

– I am not speaking of that, Cranly said in a colder tone. I ask you if you ever felt love towards anyone or anything?

Stephen walked on beside his friend, staring gloomily at the footpath.

– I tried to love God, he said at length. It seems now I failed. It is very difficult. I tried to unite my will with the will of God instant by instant. In that I did not always fail. I could perhaps do that still –

Cranly cut him short by asking:

– Has your mother had a happy life?

– How do I know? Stephen said.

– How many children had she?

– Nine or ten, Stephen answered. Some died.

– Was your father . . . Cranly interrupted himself for an instant, and then said: I don't want to pry into your family affairs. But was your father what is called well-to-do? I mean, when you were growing up?

– Yes, Stephen said.

– What was he? Cranly asked after a pause

Stephen began to enumerate glibly his father's attributes.

– A medical student, all oarsman, a tenor, an amateur actor, a shouting politician, a small landlord, a small investor, a drinker, a good fellow, a story-teller, somebody's secretary, something in a distillery, a tax-gatherer, a bankrupt and at present a praiser of his own past.

Cranly laughed, tightening his grip on Stephen's arm, and said:

– The distillery is damn good.

– Is there anything else you want to know? Stephen asked.

– Are you in good circumstances at present?

– Do I look it? Stephen asked bluntly.

– So then, Cranly went on musingly, you were born in the lap of luxury.

He used the phrase broadly and loudly as he often used technical expressions, as if he wished his hearer to understand that they were used by him without conviction.

– Your mother must have gone through a good deal of suffering, he said then. Would you not try to save her from suffering more even if . . . or would you?

– If I could, Stephen said, that would cost me very little.

– Then do so, Cranly said. Do as she wishes you to do. What is it for you? You disbelieve in it. It is a form: nothing else. And you will set her mind at rest.

He ceased and, as Stephen did not reply, remained silent. Then, as if giving utterance to the process of his own thought, he said:

– Whatever else is unsure in this stinking dunghill of a world a mother's love is not. Your mother brings you into the world, carries you first in her body. What do we know about what she feels? But whatever she feels, it, at least, must be real. It must be. What are our ideas or ambitions? Play. Ideas! Why, this bloody bleating goat Temple has ideas. MacCann has ideas too. Every jackass going the roads thinks he has ideas.

Stephen, who had been listening to the unspoken speech behind the words, said with assumed carelessness:

– Pascal, if I remember rightly, would not suffer his mother to kiss him[486] as he feared the contact of her sex.

– Pascal was a pig, said Cranly.

– Aloysius Gonzaga, I think, was of the same mind, Stephen said.

– And he was another pig then, said Cranly.

– The church calls him a saint, Stephen objected.

– I don't care a flaming damn what anyone calls him, Cranly said rudely and flatly. I call him a pig.

Stephen, preparing the words neatly in his mind, continued:

– Jesus, too, seems to have treated his mother with scant courtesy in public but Suarez, a jesuit theologian and Spanish gentleman, has apologized for him.[487]

– Did the idea ever occur to you, Cranly asked, that Jesus was not what he pretended to be?

– The first person to whom that idea occurred, Stephen answered, was Jesus himself.

– I mean, Cranly said, hardening in his speech, did the idea ever occur to you that he was himself a conscious hypocrite, what he called the jews of his time, a whited sepulchre?[488] Or, to put it more plainly, that he was a blackguard?

– That idea never occurred to me, Stephen answered. But I am curious to know are you trying to make a convert of me or a pervert of yourself?

He turned towards his friend's face and saw there a raw smile which some force of will strove to make finely significant.

Cranly asked suddenly in a plain sensible tone:

– Tell me the truth. Were you at all shocked by what I said?

– Somewhat, Stephen said.

– And why were you shocked, Cranly pressed on in the same tone, if you feel sure that our religion is false and that Jesus was not the son of God?

– I am not at all sure of it, Stephen said. He is more like a son of God than a son of Mary.

– And is that why you will not communicate, Cranly asked, because you are not sure of that too, because you feel that the host, too, may be the body and blood of the son of God and not a wafer of bread? And because you fear that it may be?

– Yes, Stephen said quietly, I feel that and I also fear it.

– I see, Cranly said

Stephen, struck by his tone of closure, reopened the discussion at once by saying:

– I fear many things: dogs, horses, fire-arms, the sea, thunderstorms, machinery, the country roads at night.

– But why do you fear a bit of bread?

– I imagine, Stephen said, that there is a malevolent reality behind those things I say I fear.

– Do you fear then, Cranly asked, that the God of the Roman catholics would strike you dead and damn you if you made a sacrilegious communion?[489]

– The God of the Roman catholics could do that now, Stephen said. I fear more than that the chemical action which would be set up in my soul by a false homage to a symbol behind which are massed twenty centuries of authority and veneration.

– Would you, Cranly asked, in extreme danger, commit that particular sacrilege? For instance, if you lived in the penal days?[490]

– I cannot answer for the past, Stephen replied. Possibly not.

– Then, said Cranby, you do not intend to become a protestant?

– I said that I had lost the faith, Stephen answered, but not that I had lost self-respect. What kind of liberation would that be to forsake an absurdity which is logical and coherent and to embrace one which is illogical and incoherent?

They had walked on towards the township of Pembroke[491] and now, as they went on slowly along the avenues, the trees and the scattered lights in the villas soothed their minds. The air of wealth and repose diffused about them seemed to comfort their neediness. Behind a hedge of laurel a light glimmered in the window of a kitchen and the voice of a servant was heard singing as she sharpened knives. She sang, in short broken bars, *Rosie O'Grady*.[492]

Cranly stopped to listen, saying:

– *Mulier cantat.*[493]

The soft beauty of the Latin word touched with an enchanting touch the dark of the evening, with a touch fainter and more persuading than the touch of music or of a woman's hand. The strife of their minds was quelled. The figure of a woman as she appears in the liturgy of the church passed silently through the darkness: a white-robed figure, small and slender as a boy, and with a falling girdle. Her voice, frail and high as a boy's, was heard intoning from a distant choir the first words of a woman which pierce the gloom and clamour of the first chanting of the passion:

– *Et tu cum Jesu Galilaeo eras.*[494]

And all hearts were touched and turned to her voice, shining like a young star, shining clearer as the voice intoned the proparoxyton[495] and more faintly as the cadence died.

The singing ceased. They went on together, Cranly repeating in strongly stressed rhythm the end of the refrain:

> *And when we are married,*
> *O, how happy we'll be*
> *For I love sweet Rosie O'Grady*
> *And Rosie O'Grady loves me.*

– There's real poetry for you, he said. There's real love.

He glanced sideways at Stephen with a strange smile and said:

– Do you consider that poetry? Or do you know what the words mean?

– I want to see Rosie first, said Stephen

– She's easy to find, Cranly said.

His hat had come down on his forehead. He shoved it back and in the shadow of the trees Stephen saw his pale face, framed by the dark, and his large dark eyes. Yes. His face was handsome and his body was strong and hard. He had spoken of a mother's love. He felt then the sufferings of women, the weaknesses of their bodies and souls; and would shield them with a strong and resolute arm and bow his mind to them.

Away then: it is time to go. A voice spoke softly to Stephen's lonely heart, bidding him go and telling him that his friendship was coming to an end. Yes; he would go. He could not strive against another. He knew his part.

– Probably I shall go away, he said.

– Where? Cranly asked.

– Where I can, Stephen said.

– Yes, Cranly said. It might be difficult for you to live here now. But is it that makes you go?

– I have to go, Stephen answered.

– Because, Cranly continued, you need not look upon yourself as driven away if you do not wish to go or as a heretic or an outlaw. There are many good believers who think as you do. Would that surprise you? The church is not the stone building nor even the clergy and their dogmas. It is the whole mass of those born into it. I don't know what you wish to do in life. Is it what you told me the night we were standing outside Harcourt Street station?[496]

– Yes, Stephen said, smiling in spite of himself at Cranly's way of remembering thoughts in connexion with places. The night you spent half an hour wrangling with Doherty about the shortest way from Sallygap to Larras.

– Pothead! Cranly said with calm contempt. What does he know about the way from Sallygap to Larras?[497] Or what does he know about anything for that matter? And the big slobbering washing-pot head of him!

He broke into a loud long laugh.

– Well? Stephen said. Do you remember the rest?

– What you said, is it? Cranly asked. Yes, I remember it. To discover the mode of life or of art whereby your spirit could express itself in unfettered freedom.

Stephen raised his hat in acknowledgement.

– Freedom! Cranly repeated. But you are not free enough yet to commit a sacrilege. Tell me would you rob?

– I would beg first, Stephen said.

– And if you got nothing, would you rob?

– You wish me to say, Stephen answered, that the rights of property are provisional, and that in certain circumstances it is not unlawful to rob. Everyone would act in that belief. So I will not make you that answer. Apply to the jesuit theologian, Juan Mariana de Talavera,[498] who will also explain to you in what circumstances you may lawfully kill your king and whether you had better hand him his poison in a goblet or smear it for him upon his robe or his saddlebow. Ask me rather would I suffer others to rob me, or if they did, would I call down upon them what I believe is called the chastisement of the secular arm?[499]

– And would you?

– I think, Stephen said, it would pain me as much to do so as to be robbed.

– I see, Cranly said.

He produced his match and began to clean the crevice between two teeth. Then he said carelessly:

– Tell me, for example, would you deflower a virgin?

– Excuse me, Stephen said politely, is that not the ambition of most young gentlemen?

– What then is your point of view? Cranly asked.

His last phrase, sour smelling as the smoke of charcoal and disheartening, excited Stephen's brain, over which its fumes seemed to brood.

– Look here, Cranly, he said. You have asked me what I would do and what I would not do. I will tell you what I will do and what I will not do. I will not serve that in which I no longer believe, whether it call itself my home, my fatherland, or my church: and I will try to express myself in some mode of life or art as freely as I can and as wholly as I can, using for my defence the only arms I allow myself to use – silence, exile, and cunning.

Cranly seized his arm and steered him round so as to lead him back towards Leeson Park. He laughed almost slyly and pressed Stephen's arm with an elder's affection.

– Cunning indeed! he said. Is it you? You poor poet, you!

– And you made me confess to you, Stephen said, thrilled by his touch, as I have confessed to you so many other things, have I not?

– Yes, my child, Cranly said, still gaily.

– You made me confess the fears that I have. But I will tell you also what I do not fear. I do not fear to be alone or to be spurned for another or to leave whatever I have to leave. And I am not afraid to make a mistake, even a great mistake, a lifelong mistake, and perhaps as long as eternity too.

Cranly, now grave again, slowed his pace and said:

– Alone, quite alone. You have no fear of that. And you know what that word means? Not only to be separate from all others but to have not even one friend.

– I will take the risk, said Stephen.

– And not to have any one person, Cranly said, who would be more than a friend, more even than the noblest and truest friend a man ever had.

His words seemed to have struck some deep chord in his own nature. Had he spoken of himself, of himself as he was or wished to be? Stephen watched his face for some moments in silence. A cold sadness was there. He had spoken of himself, of his own loneliness which he feared.

– Of whom are you speaking? Stephen asked at length.

Cranly did not answer.

MARCH 20. Long talk with Cranly on the subject of my revolt. He had his grand manner on. I supple and suave. Attacked me on the score of love for one's mother. Tried to imagine his mother: cannot. Told me once, in a moment of thoughtlessness, his father was sixty-one when he was born. Can see him. Strong farmer type. Pepper and salt suit. Square feet. Unkempt, grizzled beard. Probably attends coursing matches. Pays his dues regularly but not plentifully to Father Dwyer of Larras. Sometimes talks to girls after nightfall. But his mother? Very young or very old? Hardly the first. If so, Cranly would not have spoken as he did. Old then. Probably, and neglected. Hence Cranly's despair of soul: the child of exhausted loins.

March 21, morning. Thought this in bed last night but was too lazy and free to add to it. Free, yes. The exhausted loins are those of Elizabeth and Zacchary.[500] Then he is the precursor. Item: he eats chiefly belly bacon and dried figs. Read locusts and wild honey.[501] Also, when thinking of him, saw always a stern severed head or death mask as if outlined on a grey curtain or veronica. Decollation they call it in the fold.[502] Puzzled for the moment by saint John at the Latin gate.[503] What do I see? A decollated precursor trying to pick the lock.

March 21, night. Free. Soul free and fancy free. Let the dead bury the dead.[504] Ay. And let the dead marry the dead.

MARCH 22. In company with Lynch followed a sizeable hospital nurse. Lynch's idea. Dislike it. Two lean hungry greyhounds walking after a heifer.

MARCH 23. Have not seen her since that night. Unwell? Sits at the fire perhaps with mamma's shawl on her shoulders. But not peevish. A nice bowl of gruel? Won't you now?

MARCH 24. Began with a discussion with my mother. Subject: B.V.M.[505] Handicapped by my sex and youth. To escape held up relations between Jesus and Papa against those between Mary and her son.[506] Said religion was not a lying-in hospital. Mother indulgent. Said I have a queer mind and have read too much. Not true. Have read little and understood less. Then she said I would come back to faith because I had a restless mind. This means to leave church by back door of sin and re-enter through the skylight of repentance. Cannot repent. Told her so and asked for sixpence. Got threepence.

Then went to college. Other wrangle with little round head rogue's eye Ghezzi.[507] This time about Bruno the Nolan.[508] Began in Italian and ended in pidgin English. He said Bruno was a terrible heretic. I said he was terribly burned. He agreed to this with some sorrow. Then gave me recipe for what he calls *risotto alla bergamasca*.[509] When he pronounces a soft *o* he protrudes his full carnal lips as if he kissed the vowel. Has he? And could he repent? Yes, he could: and cry two round rogue's tears, one from each eye.

Crossing Stephen's, that is, my green, remembered that his countrymen and not mine had invented what Cranly the other night called our religion. A quartet of them, soldiers of the ninety-seventh infantry regiment, sat at the foot of the cross and tossed up dice for the overcoat of the crucified.[510]

Went to library. Tried to read three reviews. Useless. She is not out yet. Am I alarmed? About what? That she will never be out again.

Blake wrote:

> *I wonder if William Bond will die*
> *For assuredly he is very ill.*[511]

Alas, poor William![512]

I was once at a diorama in Rotunda.[513] At the end were pictures of big nobs. Among them William Ewart Gladstone,[514] just then dead. Orchestra played *O Willie, we have missed you.*[515]

A race of clodhoppers!

MARCH 25, MORNING. A troubled night of dreams. Want to get them off my chest.

A long curving gallery. From the floor ascend pillars of dark vapours. It is peopled by the images of fabulous kings, set in stone. Their hands are folded upon their knees in token of weariness and their eyes are darkened for the errors of men go up before them for ever as dark vapours.

Strange figures advance as from a cave. They are not as tall as men. One does not seem to stand quite apart from another. Their faces are phosphorescent, with darker streaks. They peer at me and their faces seem to ask me something. They do not speak.

MARCH 30. This evening Cranly was in the porch of the library, proposing a problem to Dixon and her brother. A mother let her child fall into the Nile. Still harping on the mother.[516] A crocodile seized the child. Mother asked it back. Crocodile said all right if she told him what he was going to do with the child, eat it or not eat it.

This mentality, Lepidus would say, is indeed bred out of your mud by the operation of your sun.[517]

And mine? Is it not too? Then into Nile mud with it!

APRIL 1. Disapprove of this last phase.

APRIL 2. Saw her drinking tea and eating cakes in Johnston's, Mooney and O'Brien's.[518] Rather, lynx-eyed Lynch saw her as we passed. He tells me Cranly was invited there by brother. Did he bring his crocodile? Is he the shining light now? Well, I discovered him. I protest I did. Shining quietly behind a bushel of Wicklow bran.[519]

APRIL 3. Met Davin at the cigar shop opposite Findlater's church.[520] He was in a black sweater and had a hurley stick. Asked me was it true I was going away and why. Told him the shortest way to Tara was *via* Holyhead.[521] Just then my father came up. Introduction. Father polite and observant. Asked Davin if he might offer him some refreshment. Davin could not, was going to a meeting. When we came away father told me he had a good honest eye. Asked me why I did join a rowing club. I pretended to think it over. Told me then how he broke Pennyfeather's heart.[522] Wants me to read law. Says I was cut out for that. More mud, more crocodiles.

APRIL 5. Wild spring. Scudding clouds. O life! Dark stream of swirling bogwater on which apple-trees have cast down their delicate flowers. Eyes of girls among the leaves. Girls demure and romping. All fair or auburn: no dark ones. They blush better. Houpla!

APRIL 6. Certainly she remembers the past. Lynch says all women do. Then she remembers the time of her childhood – and mine, if I was ever a child. The past is consumed in the present and the present is living only because it brings forth the future. Statues of women, if Lynch be right, should always be fully draped, one hand of the woman feeling regretfully her own hinder parts.

APRIL 6, LATER. Michael Robartes remembers forgotten beauty and, when his arms wrap her round, he presses in his arms the loveliness which has long faded from the world.[523] Not this. Not at all. I desire to press in my arms the loveliness which has not yet come into the world.

APRIL 10. Faintly, under the heavy night, through the silence of the city which has turned from dreams to dreamless sleep as a weary lover whom no caresses move, the sound of hoofs upon the road. Not so faintly now as they come near the bridge; and in a moment, as they pass the darkened windows, the silence is cloven by alarm as by an arrow. They are heard now far away, hoofs that shine amid the heavy night as gems, hurrying beyond the sleeping fields to what journey's end – what heart? – bearing what tidings?

APRIL 11. Read what I wrote last night. Vague words for a vague emotion. Would she like it? I think so. Then I should have to like it also.

APRIL 13. That tundish has been on my mind for a long time. I looked it up and find it English and good old blunt English too. Damn the dean of studies and his funnel! What did he come here for to teach us his own language or to learn it from us. Damn him one way or the other!

April 14. John Alphonsus Mulrennan has just returned from the west of Ireland. European and Asiatic papers please copy. He told us he met an old man there in a mountain cabin. Old man had red eyed and short pipe. Old man spoke Irish. Mulrennan spoke Irish. Then old man and Mulrennan spoke English. Mulrennan spoke to him about universe and stars. Old man sat, listened, smoked, spat. Then said:

– Ah, there must be terrible queer creatures at the latter end of the world.[524]

I fear him. I fear his red-rimmed horny eyes. It is with him I must struggle all through this night till day come, till he or I lie dead, gripping him by the sinewy throat till . . . Till what? Till he yield to me? No. I mean no harm.

APRIL 15. Met her today point blank in Grafton Street. The crowd brought us together. We both stopped. She asked me why I never came, said she had heard all sorts of stories about me. This was only to gain time. Asked me was I writing poems? About whom? I asked her. This confused her more and I felt sorry and mean. Turned off that valve at once and opened the spiritual-heroic refrigerating apparatus, invented and patented in all countries by Dante Alighieri.[525] Talked rapidly of myself and my plans. In the midst of it unluckily I made a sudden gesture of a revolutionary nature. I must have looked like a fellow throwing a handful of peas into the air. People began to look at us. She shook hands a moment after and, in going away, said she hoped I would do what I said.

Now I call that friendly, don't you?

Yes, I liked her today. A little or much? Don't know. I liked her and it seems a new feeling to me. Then, in that case, all the rest, all that I thought I thought and all that I felt I felt, all the rest before now, in fact . . . O, give it up old chap! Sleep it off!

APRIL 16. Away! Away!

The spell of arms and voices: the white arms of roads, the promise of close embraces and the black arms of tall ships that stand against the moon, their tale of distant nations. They are held out to say: We are alone – come. And the voices say with them: We are your kinsmen. And the air is thick with their company as they call to me, their kinsman, making ready to go, shaking the wings of their exultant and terrible youth.

APRIL 26. Mother is putting my new secondhand clothes in order. She prays now, she says, that I may learn in my own life and away from home and friends what the heart is and what it feels. Amen. So be it.

Welcome, O life! I go to encounter for the millionth time the reality of experience and to forge in the smithy of my soul the uncreated conscience of my race.

APRIL 27. Old father, old artificer,[526] stand me now and ever in good stead.

Dublin, 1904
Trieste, 1914

NOTES TO THE TEXT

When I have been unable to identify the source of a reference myself, I have relied on Don Gifford's *Joyce Annotated: Notes for 'Dubliners' and 'A Portrait of the Artist as a Young Man'*, second edition (University of California Press, Berkeley and Los Angeles 1982). References to this work will be given as (G) in the notes. *Joyce Annotated* is the most comprehensive source of references for *Portrait* and can be consulted for further information about the individual references given below or about the novel in general. When I have been unable to locate a reference in Gifford or elsewhere, I have consulted the edition of *A Portrait of the Artist as a Young Man* edited by Seamus Deane (Penguin Books, London 1992). References to this text will be given as (D) in the notes. For full references to the first and second editions of Ellmann's *James Joyce*, see the Bibliography following the Introduction. The full reference for Joyce's *Letters* is *Letters of James Joyce*, 3 vols, (eds) Stuart Gilbert and Richard Ellmann (Faber, London 1957–66). All biblical quotations are from the King James Version of the Bible (abbreviated KJV), unless otherwise noted.

1 (p. 2) *Et ignotas animum dimittit in artes*   Latin: 'And he applies his mind to unknown arts . . . ' The passage, from a description of Daedalus's creation of wings for himself and his son Icarus (see Introduction, pp. xv–xvi and Note 7) in Ovid's *Metamorphoses*, viii, 188, continues ' . . . and changes the laws of nature.' The *Metamorphoses* is a series of linked verse narratives on the theme of transformation in Greek and Roman mythology by the Roman poet Publius Ovidius Naso (43BC–AD18).

2 (p. 3) *lemon platt*   plaited lemon candy stick

3 (p. 3) *Michael Davitt*   (1846–1906) Irish nationalist who joined the militant group the Fenians (see Note 70) in 1865. Imprisoned for treason from 1870 to 1877, in 1879 he co-founded the Land League with Charles Stewart Parnell. Jailed intermittently for his political activities, he won a seat in the British Parliament in 1882; he did not, however, actually sit in Parliament until 1895–9, during which time he encouraged reconciliation between various factions of Irish nationalism.

4 (p. 3) *Parnell*   Charles Stewart Parnell (1846–91), leader in the British Parliament of the Irish Home Rule Movement from 1877. Son of a Protestant landowner, he was the most powerful and popular Irish politician of his time. His power at Westminster as leader of the Irish Parliamentary Party caused British Prime Minister Gladstone to move towards granting some measure of limited independence (or 'Home Rule') to Ireland. His political career ended in 1890, and with it hopes for Home Rule, when he was named in the divorce case of Katherine O'Shea, as this led to his denouncement by the Irish Catholic clergy and his abandonment by his own political party.

5 (p. 3) *cachou*   a sweetmeat, usually in the form of a pill, used to sweeten the breath

6 (p. 4) *Apologise . . . pull out his eyes*   from Isaac Watts (1674–1748), *Divine Songs Attempted in Easy Language for the Use of Children*, song XXIII. The song is based on Proverbs 30:17. (G)

7 (p. 4) *Dedalus*   figure from Greek mythology; sculptor, architect, and inventor of mechanical devices. He constructed the Labyrinth for King Minos, which housed the Minotaur; he was later imprisoned in the Labyrinth with his son Icarus and fashioned wings to aid their escape (see Introduction pp. xv–xvi). The correct spelling is actually Daedalus, which was the spelling of Stephen's surname in *Stephen Hero*; Joyce changed the spelling for *Portrait*.

8 (p. 5) *peach*   inform on (slang)

9 (p. 5) *Hamilton Rowan*   Archibald Hamilton Rowan (1751–1834), member of the revolutionary group the United Irishmen (founded in 1791 and inspired by French Republican ideals). He escaped to France after being tried and sentenced for sedition in 1794, but returned to Ireland after being pardoned in 1803. In 1794 he supposedly hid in the castle (Clongowes Wood College was originally a medieval castle) while fleeing from British soldiers, throwing his hat on a bank (a ha-ha is a bank or dry moat) as a decoy.

10 (p. 5) *Leicester Abbey*   the Abbey of St Mary Pré, located about a hundred miles from London. Cardinal Wolsey died there in 1530 while in transit to London to face trial for treason (see Note 12).

11 (p. 5) *Doctor Cornwell's Spelling Book*   James Cornwell (1812–1902), English educationalist and author of numerous schoolbooks used throughout the nineteenth century. With Alexander Allen, he wrote *A Grammar for Beginners: Being an Introduction to Allen and Cornwell's English School Grammar* (London 1838), the text referred to here.

12 (p. 5) *Wolsey*   Cardinal Thomas Wolsey (*c.*1475–1530), powerful statesman during the reign of Henry VIII. He was made Lord Chancellor of England in 1515, but when he was unable to secure the annulment of

Henry's marriage to Catherine of Aragon, he was dismissed in 1529. He died while travelling to face charges of treason (see Note 10).

13 (p. 6) *square ditch*   the Clongowes cesspool

14 (p. 6) *hacking chestnut*   game in which two chestnuts are each tied to a short piece of string. Two players swing them at each other and the one that does not crack is the winning chestnut.

15 (p. 6) *suck*   servile flatterer (slang)

16 (p. 6) *Wicklow Hotel*   on Wicklow Street in central Dublin

17 (p. 7) *York . . . Lancaster*   The boys are divided into teams based on the two opposing sides in the Wars of the Roses (1445–85). The House of York was the ruling dynasty of England from 1461 to 1485; the House of Lancaster was the English royal family deposed by the House of York during the Wars of the Roses. Henry Tudor re-established the claims of Lancaster in 1485 and became Henry VII. The symbol of the House of York was the white rose, that of Lancaster the red rose.

18 (p. 7) *in a wax*   fit of anger (slang)

19 (p. 7) *elements*   spelling and grammar, Latin, mathematics, history, geography

20 (p. 8) *Dalkey*   village on the Irish coast eight miles south of Dublin; on the railway journey from Bray to Dublin

21 (p. 8) *Tullabeg*   Fifty-five miles west of Dublin, this was the site of St Stanislaus College, founded like Clongowes by Father Peter Kenny. The site became the Jesuit Novitiate in Ireland after the two colleges were merged at the Clongowes site.

22 (p. 9) *Clongowes Wood College*   a Jesuit private boarding school for boys founded in 1814 by Father Peter Kenny. Joyce attended Clongowes Wood from 1888 to 1891.

23 (p. 10) *Sallins/County Kildare*   County Kildare, west of Dublin; Sallins is a few miles south of Clongowes.

24 (p. 10) *for a cod*   for a joke (slang)

25 (p. 11) *O Lord, open our lips . . . help us!*   initial prayer for the hour of Matins in the Divine Office. The first two lines are taken from the book of Psalms 51:15.

26 (p. 11) *Clane*   a village a mile and a half south of Clongowes

27 (p. 12) *Visit, we beseech Thee . . . through Christ our Lord*   penultimate prayer for the hour of Compline, the final hour in the Divine Office

28 (p. 13) *Their master . . . cloak of a marshal*   Born in Austria, Maximilian Ulysses, Count von Browne, was the son of an Irish Jacobite. A marshal in the Austrian army, he was killed in 1757 at the Battle of Prague.

Clongowes Wood was owned by the Browne family in the eighteenth century, and it was said that Count von Browne's ghost appeared there on the day he died. (G)

29 (p. 13) *Bodenstown*   Theobald Wolfe Tone (see Note 342) is buried in Bodenstown, and Sallins is part of the parish.

30 (p. 13) *Hill of Allen*   a hill of 676 feet, west of Sallins in Co. Kildare

31 (p. 15) *foxing*   faking (slang)

32 (p. 15) *Brother Michael*   A brother is a novitiate accepted as a lay member of the order to conduct domestic/temporal duties but not to be ordained as a priest.

33 (p. 15) *Hayfoot! Strawfoot!*   In order to teach them how to march, army recruits in the country had hay attached to their left feet and straw attached to their right feet.

34 (p. 16) *catafalque*   A temporary structure, often decorated, erected to hold a coffin during the funeral mass. The colours worn by the priest would be black and gold.

35 (p. 16–17) *Dingdong . . . soul away*   anonymous nursery rhyme (G)

36 (p. 17) *Athy*   a town forty-three miles southwest of Dublin, in Co. Kildare

37 (p. 18) *The liberator*   Daniel O'Connell (1775–1847), Irish statesman known as 'the Liberator' for his central role in bringing about the passing of the Catholic Emancipation Act (1829). He founded the Catholic Association in 1823 and was elected to the British Parliament in 1828 but refused to take up his seat until Emancipation was granted. After this, he agitated for the repeal of the Act of Union between Britain and Ireland. He died in Genoa on a pilgrimage to Rome.

38 (p. 19) *toasted boss*   A boss is a type of foot-rest ('toasted' because it is in front of the hearth).

39 (p. 19) *three cramped fingers making a birthday present for Queen Victoria*   Mr Casey has got his 'three cramped fingers' from picking oakum (a loose fibre obtained by picking old rope to pieces), one form of hard labour in British nineteenth-century prisons. (G)   The implication is that Mr Casey was a Fenian and imprisoned for his nationalist activities (see Note 70).

40 (p. 20) *round the Head*   Bray Head, the promontory that overlooks the town of Bray, south-east of Dublin near the County Wicklow border

41 (p. 20) *manufacturing . . . champagne*   'Champagne' possibly means explosives. (G)

42 (p. 20) *dewlaps*   the loose skin hanging from the necks of cattle; derogatory term for the folds on the human neck

43 (p. 21) *Bless us, O Lord . . . Amen*   common Catholic mealtime prayer

44 (p. 21) *Dunn's of D'Olier Street*   fashionable shop selling poultry, game and fish on D'Olier Street in central Dublin (G)

45 (p. 21) *Ally Daly*   Dublin slang for something of the highest quality

46 (p. 21) *pandybat*   reinforced leather strap used to punish schoolboys by striking them on the palms; called a turkey because punishment with it turns the hands red

47 (p. 21) *Eton jacket*   short jacket pointed at the back, made of black broadcloth

48 (p. 22) *I'll pay your dues . . . polling-booth*   refers to the role of the Irish Catholic Church in bringing down Parnell and in using its influence in Irish political matters

49 (p. 23) *Were we . . . English people?*   After Parnell was implicated in the O'Shea divorce case, Gladstone and his Liberal Party distanced themselves from any association with the disgraced leader; it was after this occurred that sections of the Irish public began to denounce Parnell.

50 (p. 23) *Woe be to the man . . . Holy Ghost*   Luke 17:1–2: 'Then said he unto the disciples, It is impossible but that offences will come, but woe unto him through whom they come . . . It were better for him that a millstone were hanged about his neck, and he cast into the sea, then that he should offend one of these little ones.' Dante changes 'offences' and 'offend' to 'scandal' and 'scandalise'.

51 (p. 23) *pope's nose*   (also parson's nose) the piece of fatty flesh from the turkey's rump

52 (p. 24) *Is it for Billy with the Lip . . . tub of guts up in Armagh?*   Billy the Lip is the Revd William Joseph Walsh (1841–1921), the Catholic Archbishop of Dublin, who initially supported Parnell but then encouraged the Irish Parliamentary Party to remove him from the leadership; 'tub of guts' refers to Revd Michael Logue (1839–1924), the Archbishop of Armagh (1887–1924) and patron of the Gaelic League. He opposed Parnell's continuing leadership of the party after the divorce case.

53 (p. 24) *Lord Leitrim's coachman*   Lord Leitrim (1806–78) was a notably harsh English absentee landlord assassinated in 1878 in Donegal. His coachman supposedly attempted to save him, and the term became one of abuse for any Irishman thought to be supporting the British. (D)

54 (p. 25) *County Wicklow*   on Ireland's east coast, south of County Dublin

55 (p. 25) *Alleghanies*   the Allegheny Mountains, a US mountain range in the central Appalachians extending over parts of Virginia, Maryland and Pennsylvania

56 (p. 25) *chainies*   flawed or spoiled chinaware

57 (p. 25) *Tower of Ivory . . . House of Gold*   from the Catholic Litany of Our Lady, epithets for the Virgin Mary

58 (p. 26) *tig*   a children's game similar to hide-and-seek

59 (p. 26) *Arklow*   a town in County Wicklow

60 (p. 26) *The chief*   Charles Stewart Parnell (see Note 4)

61 (p. 26) *Priest-hunter!*   After sections of the Catholic clergy denounced him for his involvement in the O'Shea case, Parnell went on the counter-attack against them.

62 (p. 26) *The Paris Funds! Mr Fox! Kitty O'Shea!*   all refer to charges against Parnell in the wake of the O'Shea divorce trial. Funds of the Irish Parliamentary Party were kept in Paris to avoid any interference from the British government. Parnell was accused of using these to support his affair with Katherine O'Shea. Fox was a false name Parnell used in his correspondence with her, and the diminutive form of Katherine, 'Kitty', had insulting sexual connotations at the time.

63 (p. 26) *quid of Tullamore*   a pound's worth of a brand of chewing tobacco made in the town of Tullamore, west of Dublin

64 (p. 27) *Canbinteely Road*   road on an inland route from Bray to Dublin; the route would have been little used and therefore safer for Mr Casey (who is possibly trying to avoid arrest for political activities) to escape by to Dublin. (G)

65 (p. 27) *whiteboy*   The 'Whiteboys' were an Irish agrarian secret society active in the eighteenth and nineteenth centuries. Formed initially in protest against the enclosure of land, they also protested against tithes and rents. So-called because they wore white smocks over their clothes during their illegal night-time raids, which involved the destruction of property and livestock. Participation in Whiteboy activities was deemed a capital offence by Parliament in 1765.

66 (p. 27) *he would never let one of them put his two feet under his mahogany*   He would never allow one of them to sit at his dining-room table; that is, he would never extend his hospitality to them.

67 (p. 27) *Touch them not . . . the apple of My eye*   Zechariah 2:8: 'For thus saith the Lord of hosts; After the glory hath he sent me unto the nations which spoiled you: for he that toucheth you toucheth the apple of his eye.'

68 (p. 28) *Didn't the bishops of Ireland betray us . . . Marquess Cornwallis?*   Charles Cornwallis (1738–1805) became viceroy and com-mander-in-chief in Ireland in 1798, and it was under his leadership that the Union between Britain and Ireland occurred, dissolving the independent Irish parliament. Bishop Lanigan (d. 1812), Catholic bishop of Ossory, supposedly paid court to Cornwallis after the Union. Many Catholic bishops were bribed into voting for the Union on the promise that

Catholic Emancipation would be granted with the Union; when Emancipation was not granted, Cornwallis resigned from his post as Irish Lord-Lieutenant.

69 (p. 28) *Didn't the bishops . . . catholic emancipation*   While the Catholic hierarchy supported Daniel O'Connell's campaign for Catholic Emancipation, once this act was passed in 1829, the Catholic Church's support of O'Connell's efforts to have the Act of Union repealed was less wholehearted. Catholic Emancipation granted certain rights to Catholics, such as a limited franchise and the right to hold public office.

70 (p. 28) *Didn't they denounce the fenian movement from the pulpit and in the confession box?*   The Fenians (formally known as the Irish Republican Brotherhood or IRB) were an Irish nationalist organisation, founded in 1858 and reaching their high point of activity in the 1860s. They often used violent means of protest and were supported by Irish Americans. The name 'Fenian' derives from the Fianna (Irish for 'warrior') army of an Irish medieval saga. The Fenians argued that the Catholic Church had no place in Irish politics, while the church condemned the Fenians as an anti-governmental and anti-clerical secret society.

71 (p. 28) *Terence Bellew MacManus*   (1823–60) joined the nationalist Young Ireland movement and was arrested for his political activities. He escaped to America, where he died in poverty. His funeral was the occasion for a public demonstration on the part of the Fenian movement in Ireland. Archbishop Paul Cullen refused MacManus a lying-in-state at the city's main cathedral in the belief that it would develop into a political event for nationalists. This, as well as those events and individuals mentioned in the preceding notes, represent, for Stephen's father, examples of the Catholic clergy's betrayal of Irish nationalism.

72 (p. 28) *Paul Cullen*   (1803–78) Archbishop of Dublin, 1852–78; first Irishman to become a cardinal, 1866. Opposed radical nationalist movements like the Fenians. A dominant figure in Irish Catholicism in the mid-nineteenth century, he founded the National Association in 1864 to forge links between Irish nationalism and the Catholic Church.

73 (p. 29) *Hill of Lyons*   about eleven miles west of Dublin and six miles east of Clongowes Wood College

74 (p. 29) *fecked cash*   stolen cash

75 (p. 29) *the altar wine they keep in the press in the sacristy*   'Press' is a term used particularly in Scotland and Ireland for a shelved cupboard found in a recess; the sacristy is the church room where vestments, sacred vessels and other objects used during the service are kept; also the room where the priest prepares for the service.

76 (p. 30) *boatbearer . . . the wood*   Before the incense is placed in the censer for use in the Benediction, it is carried in an incense-holder by the

boatbearer; there is an altar in Clongowes wood where Benediction would have been performed. (G)

77 (p. 30) *sprinter*   bicycle racer

78 (p. 30) *prof*   captain of a cricket team

79 (p. 30) *playing rounders and bowling twisters and lobs*   Rounders is a British variant of baseball; twisters and lobs are types of bowling in cricket.

80 (p. 31) *Smugging*   schoolboy homosexual activity (G)

81 (p. 31) *Bective Rangers*   one of the leading Irish football clubs

82 (p. 32) *Balbus was building a wall*   In Cicero's *Letters to Atticus* (47 BC), Balbus is mentioned as an example of a Roman citizen who pursues pleasure (in Balbus's case, building new villas) instead of attending to more serious affairs of state. (G)

83 (p. 32) *Julius Caesar wrote The Calico Belly*   Caesar wrote *Commentarii de Bello Gallico* ('Commentaries on the Gallic Wars'); the *Calico Belly* is meant to be a pun.

84 (p. 32) *six and eight*   the number of smacks intended for each hand administered in corporal punishment. This number can vary (see 'twice nine', below) and so 'twisting the note' prevents the student from reading his punishment in advance. (G)

85 (p. 32) *how many ferulae*   how many smacks with the *ferula* (plural, *ferulae*), an instrument of corporal punishment, such as a rod or cane

86 (p. 33) *twice nine*   nine strokes per hand; the most severe punishment to be given per day (G)

87 (p. 34) *monstrance*   an open vessel somewhat like a chalice in which the Host (the communion bread) is displayed for veneration by the congregation

88 (p. 35) *mare*   the sea (Latin)

89 (p. 35) *rector . . . provincial . . . general*   The general is the highest authority in the Jesuits; next in authority are the provincials, who oversee a country or large region; following these are local superiors, with rectors being included in this category.

90 (p. 36) *tomorrow and tomorrow and tomorrow*   Macbeth, 5, 5, 19

91 (p. 39) *Senate and the Roman people*   the form of a Roman senatorial decree (G)

92 (p. 40) *Magnall's Questions*   Richmal Mangnall (1769–1820), a schoolmistress whose *Historical and Miscellaneous Questions for the Use of Young People* (1800) was reissued continually in the nineteenth century. Joyce misspells her name in the novel.

93 (p. 40) *Peter Parley's Tales about Greece and Rome*   Peter Parley was the *nom de plume* of the American Samuel Griswold Goodrich (1793–1860)

who wrote *Peter Parley's Tales about Ancient and Modern Greece* (1832) and *Peter Parley's Tales about Ancient and Modern Rome* (1833).

94 (p. 41) *Ignatius Loyola* St Ignatius Loyola (1491–1556), a Basque nobleman who was a soldier until his conversion to the religious life in 1521. He wrote *Spiritual Exercises* in 1522–3 and, with Francis Xavier, founded in 1534 the Society of Jesus (the Jesuits), organising the order along military lines. The Jesuits are particularly dedicated to foreign missions and education. The order became one of the most powerful in the Roman Catholic Church, which led to the society's dissolution by Pope Clement XIV in 1773 over fears that it had become too powerful. The society was restored in 1814.

95 (p. 41) *Ad Majorem Dei Gloriam* Latin: 'For the Greater Glory of God', the Jesuit motto

96 (p. 41) *Saint Francis Xavier pointing to his chest* (1506–52) Spanish co-founder of the Jesuit order (with Ignatius Loyola). From 1541 he travelled widely in South Asia and Japan as a missionary for the Jesuits. He died *en route* to China, where he intended to continue his missionary work. He is conventionally represented pointing to his chest (or, more accurately, pointing to the crucifix on his chest), as 'the central emphasis of his missionary sermons is reported to have been the cross'. (G)

97 (p. 41) *Lorenzo Ricci with his berretta on his head* Lorenzo Ricci (1703–75) was elected a Jesuit general in 1758; the berretta was worn as a symbol of his rank.

98 (p. 41) *three patrons . . . saint Stanislaus Kostka, saint Aloysius Gonzaga, and Blessed John Berchmans* Stanislaus Kostka (1550–68), Jesuit novice born in Poland who walked 350 miles from Vienna to Rome to be received into the Jesuit order, but who died after only nine months in the order. Aloysius Gonzaga (1568–91), son of a Spanish noble family, became a Jesuit in 1587. He nursed plague victims and died of the plague himself in 1591 at the age of twenty-three. St John Berchmans (1599–1621), born at Diest in Brabant, entered the Jesuit order and was known for kindness and piety. He died of fever, aged twenty-two, and was declared 'Blessed' in 1865 and canonised in 1888.

99 (p. 42) *Father Peter Kenny* (1779–1841) Irish Jesuit, founded Clongowes Wood College in May 1814

100 (p. 42) *skull on the desk* a *memento mori* (Latin: 'remember that you have to die'), designed to remind one of the transience of earthly life

101 (p. 44) *Major Barton's* the estate of Bertram F. Barton (a local dignitary and magistrate), about two miles east of Clongowes (G)

102 (p. 44) *gallnuts* an excrescence produced on trees, especially oaks

103 (p. 45) *black twist* a strong cord of twisted tobacco

104 (p. 45) *O, twine me a bower* or *Blue Eyes and Golden Hair* or *The Groves of Blarney* 'O, Twine Me a Bower' is by Irish antiquarian Thomas Crofton Croker (1798–1854) and 'The Groves of Blarney' is by J. Alfred Milliken (1767–1815). 'Blue Eyes and Golden Hair' might refer either to 'Blue Eyes' by James L. Molloy (1837–1909) or 'I Would not Give My Irish Wife' by Thomas D'Arcy McGee (1825–68). (D)

105 (p. 45) *Blackrock* a south Dublin suburb on Dublin Bay

106 (p. 46) *the font . . . the floor of the porch* The font is a basin containing holy water at the church entrance; those entering and leaving the church sprinkle the water over themselves as a form of blessing.

107 (p. 46) *Cork* now Ireland's second city, in County Cork on the southern coast

108 (p. 46) *Stillorgan . . . Dundrum . . . Sandyford* villages within a few miles of Blackrock

109 (p. 46) *Munster* the southernmost of the four provinces of Ireland (Leinster, Connaught and Ulster are the others). Cork is its main city.

110 (p. 47) *The Count of Monte Cristo* Novel by Alexandre Dumas ('Dumas père', 1802–70), published in 1845, in which Edmund Dantes (the 'dark avenger' Stephen refers to) attempts to avenge his wrongful imprisonment and consequent loss of his fiancée to a rival using treasure found on the island of Monte Cristo, from which Dantes takes his assumed name.

111 (p. 47) *island cave* the cave on the island of Monte Cristo in which Dantes discovers treasure and which he later transforms into a hideout

112 (p. 47) *Marseille . . . Mercedes* Dantes was originally from Marseille in the South of France; Mercedes was Dantes's fiancée. Believing him to be dead, she married his rival, with whom she had a son.

113 (p. 47) *Madame, I never eat muscatel grapes* Dantes says this to Mercedes twice in order to disguise the fact that he will not eat in the house of the man upon whom he wishes to take his vengeance.

114 (p. 47) *castle* one of the numerous Martello towers dotted along the coastline of Dublin Bay. The towers were built between 1803 and 1806 to defend Ireland against French invasion; Stephen briefly resides in one of these towers at the start of *Ulysses*.

115 (p. 47) *seawrack* seaweed washed up along the shore by the tide. When the tide recedes, the seawrack is left behind forming a rough line on the shore.

116 (p. 47) *Carrickmines . . . Stradbrook* villages south of Blackrock

117 (p. 49) *Merrion Road* main road from Blackrock to Dublin; indicating the Dedalus family's move from the suburb to the city

118 (p. 50) *custom-house*   completed in 1791, the Custom House stands on a quay on the north side of the River Liffey

119 (p. 50) *Mabel Hunter*   possibly a stage actress (G)

120 (p. 51) *Harold's Cross*   a south Dublin inner suburb

121 (p. 52) *A.M.D.G.*   The Jesuit motto *Ad Majorem Dei Gloriam* ('For the Greater Glory of God') is often abbreviated to AMDG.

122 (p. 52) *E— C—*   In Chapter 3 her name is given as Emma; she is not fully named in *Portrait*, but in *Stephen Hero* she is called Emma Cleary.

123 (p. 52) *Lord Byron*   George Gordon, Lord Byron (1788–1824), British Romantic poet who gained unprecedented celebrity with the publication of *Childe Harold's Pilgrimage*. Self-exiled from Britain from 1816, he died while attempting to join the Greek struggle for independence. The 'Byronic hero' (generally represented as a melancholy, brooding and often tragic figure) is derived equally from Byron's artistic creations and his own personal reputation.

124 (p. 53) *moiety notices*   half-year notices of monies due

125 (p. 53) *L.D.S.*   an abbreviation of *Laus Deo Semper* (Latin: 'Praise to God Always'), a Jesuit motto 'traditionally placed at the end of school exercises' (G)

126 (p. 53) *Belvedere*   Jesuit school in north Dublin

127 (p. 53) *Christian brothers*   teaching brotherhood of Catholic laymen interested in practical (as opposed to academic) education

128 (p. 54) *the corporation*   the municipal authorities of Dublin, called the Dublin corporation

129 (p. 55) *Whitsuntide*   the seventh week after Easter, commencing with Pentecost Sunday and celebrating the Holy Spirit's descent upon the Apostles (Acts 2:1–4)

130 (p. 55) *Blessed Sacrament had been removed*   refers to the display of the Blessed Sacrament (the Eucharist, particularly the bread) on the altar. It would not be appropriate to display the Eucharist in the context of such events as the school play.

131 (p. 55) *Indian clubs*   two bottle-shaped clubs swung in gymnastics as a form of exercise for the arms

132 (p. 57) *He that will not hear . . . publicana*   Matthew 18:17. In 1898 Joyce performed such an impersonation of the rector during a school play (Ellmann, *James Joyce*, 2nd edn, p. 56).

133 (p. 57) *after beads*   i.e., after the Rosary prayer, which is recited on beads

134 (p. 58) *one sure five*   a sure thing (G)

135 (p. 59) *Confiteor*   the prayer with which the supplicant prepares for Confession

136 (p. 60) *without a possibility of . . . ever reaching*   Catholic doctrine states that the individual's soul is provided with 'sufficient grace' to approach the communion it desires with God. Stephen's essay suggests that this approach can never take place; he corrects his supposed heresy by saying 'reaching' instead, with its acceptable implication that, while able to approach God, the soul will never achieve absolute communion with Him. (G)

137 (p. 60) *Captain Marryat*   Frederick Marryat (1792–1848), novelist and navy captain. He was the author of numerous children's books and naval adventure novels, such as *The Naval Officer, or Scenes and Adventures in the Life of Frank Mildmay* (1829).

138 (p. 60) *Cardinal Newman*   John Henry Newman (1801–90), English clergyman, co-founder of the Oxford Movement (which attempted to revitalise the Anglican Church through the reintroduction of Catholic practices). Newman converted to Catholicism in 1845, became a cardinal in 1879, and became the first rector of the newly-founded University College Dublin in 1854. Writings such as the autobiographical work *Apologia Pro Vita Sua* (1864) displayed the elegant prose style for which he was well known. Critics generally agree, however, that this is an odd choice for a schoolboy of Stephen's age.

139 (p. 61) *Lord Tennyson*   Alfred, Lord Tennyson (1809–92), English Poet Laureate from 1850 to 1892. He was made a peer in 1884. *The Charge of the Light Brigade* (1855) and *The Idylls of the King* (1842–85) are his most well-known works.

140 (p. 61) *As Tyson . . . Kafoozelum*   after the anonymous ballad 'The Daughter of Jerusalem', which had a number of bawdy variations (G)

141 (p. 61) *trans*   a translation or crib

142 (p. 63) *national revival*   the movement to revive Gaelic culture and language, especially as represented by organisations such as the Gaelic League and the Gaelic Athletic Association (see Notes 324 and 398)

143 (p. 64) *The Lily of Killarney*   the overture to the opera *The Lily of Killarney* (1862) by Sir Julius Benedict and based on Dion Boucicault's play *The Colleen Bawn* (1861), which was based on Gerald Griffin's novel, *The Collegians* (1829)

144 (p. 65) *Kingsbridge*   The former Kingsbridge Station is now Heuston Station and serves southern and western travel from Dublin.

145 (p. 66) *Maryborough . . . Mallow*   towns lying on the train route between Dublin and Cork

146 (p. 66) *jingle*   covered two-wheeled car

147 (p. 66) *Victoria Hotel* fashionable hotel in what was at that time the main shopping district in Cork (G)

148 (pp. 66–7) ' *'Tis youth and folly . . . The mountain dew'* possibly a version of the ballad 'Love is Pleasin' '

149 (p. 67) *come-all-yous* street-ballads

150 (p. 67) *drisheens* a regional Cork pudding made from sheep's intestines and blood

151 (p. 67) *Queen's College* Queen's College, Cork (now University College, Cork); one of three Queen's Colleges (along with Belfast and Galway) established in 1845

152 (p. 67) *Mardyke* commercial row leading west from the centre of Cork that had once been a fashionable promenade (G)

153 (p. 68) *Groceries* a store selling foodstuffs and other household items, but which is also a pub (G)

154 (p. 69) *street arabs* poor or gypsy children

155 (p. 69) *maneens* diminutive form of 'man', used to indicate boys attempting to behave like adults (D)

156 (p. 70) *slim jim* a long, slender marshmallow candy

157 (p. 71) *lob* slang in Cork for a penny (G)

158 (p. 71) *Dublin jackeen* likely deriving from the term 'jackanapes', a pert or insolent Dubliner, usually lower class or working class (G)

159 (p. 71) *Lee* the river on which Cork city is situated

160 (p. 71) *Dilectus* 'a phrase book of Latin quotations' (G)

161 (p. 71) *Tempora mutantur nos et mutamur in illis* or *Tempora mutantur et nos mutamur in illis.* The first translates: 'Circumstances change and we change in them,' and the second: 'Circumstances change and we change with them.' While they are both grammatically correct, only the second is metrically correct.

162 (p. 72) *Sunday's Well* a fashionable area of Cork city

163 (p. 72) *Kerry Boy* Kerry is the county to the west of Cork in southern Ireland.

164 (p. 73) *Art thou pale for weariness . . . / . . . Wandering companionless . . . ?* from the unfinished poem, 'To the Moon' (1824) by Percy Bysshe Shelley (1792–1822). The first stanza in full is: 'Art thou pale for weariness / Of climbing heaven and gazing on the earth, / Wandering companionless / Among the stars that have a different birth, / And ever changing, like a joyless eye / That finds no object worth its constancy?'

165 (p. 73) *the house of commons of the old Irish parliament* After the Act of Union dissolved the Irish parliament in 1801, the former House of Commons building was taken over by the Bank of Ireland.

166 (p. 73) *Hely Hutchinson . . . Flood . . . Henry Grattan . . . Charles Kendal Bushe* John Hely-Hutchinson (1724–94), a member of the Irish parliament for over thirty years, began his career in opposition but then switched allegiances to join the government. He opposed the Union between Britain and Ireland, favoured Catholic Emancipation and was known for his thirst for government favour and places. Henry Flood (1732–91), Irish politician and orator, became a member of the Irish parliament in 1759 and was Vice Treasurer of Ireland in 1775, for which he was criticised by nationalists, as this was a British imperial position. Flood and Henry Grattan were allies in attempting to establish legislative independence for Ireland, but in 1783 Flood became a member of the British Parliament. Henry Grattan (1746–1820) became a member of the Irish parliament in 1775. Despite winning free trade (1779) and legislative independence (1782) for Ireland, he failed to prevent the Act of Union between Britain and Ireland, after which he became a member of the British Parliament where he fought for Catholic Emancipation. Charles Kendal Bushe (1767–1843) was elected to the Irish parliament in 1796. He opposed the Union between Britain and Ireland; he was offered a government place in return for his support for the Union, but refused the place; he was also an advocate of Catholic Emancipation.

167 (p. 73) *they are only as I roved out . . . sweet July* from the numerous songs beginning with 'As I roved out . . . '; it indicates that the persons referred to are not worthy of consideration. In this case, it is being claimed that the current Irish leadership does not live up to its predecessors. (D)

168 (p. 73) *Barnardo's* J. M. Barnardo & Son, furriers, on Grafton Street (G)

169 (p. 74) *Underdone's* Jammet's French restaurant. Ellmann suggests that 'Underdone's' was the Joyce family's nickname for the restaurant (*James Joyce*, 1st edn, p. 40).

170 (p. 74) *Ingomar . . . The Lady of Lyons* Maria Anne Lovell's *Ingomar the Barbarian* (1851) is adapted from the play *Der Sohn der Wildnis* (*The Son of the Wilderness*, 1842) by Austrian dramatist Baron E. F. J. von Munch-Bellinghausen (pseudonym, Friedrich Halm). *The Lady of Lyons or Love and Pride* (1838) by Edward Bulwer-Lytton (1803–73), British politician, poet and novelist.

171 (p. 75) *Claude Melnotte* character from Bulwer-Lytton's *The Lady of Lyons*. Melnotte pays suit to Pauline Deschappelles, is rejected, assumes a false identity and marries her, then leaves her to join the French army. He eventually returns, reveals his true identity and settles happily with Pauline.

172 (p. 78) *Shelley's fragment . . . weariness* See Note 164

173 (p. 79) *sanctifying . . . actual grace* Actual grace is the awareness of the grace of eternal salvation granted by God as an impulse to do good; it lasts only for the duration of the good act itself. Sanctifying grace is a permanent (also known as 'habitual') state of grace; the aim of actual grace is the attainment and retention of sanctifying grace.

174 (p. 79) *morally present . . . see nor hear* Despite not being in the church, they are considered to be in the presence of the Eucharist and thus present at the mass. (G)

175 (pp. 79–80) *prefecture . . . Virgin Mary* Stephen has been granted the distinction of being made student prefect of one of the two confraternities at Belvedere, the Congregation of the Blessed Virgin Mary. A sodality is an association of Catholics providing its members with a programme for religious service and prayer.

176 (p. 80) *little office* a liturgical devotion to the Blessed Virgin Mary

177 (p. 80) *psalms of prophecy* In Roman Catholicism, many of the Psalms are taken to be prophecies of the coming of the Messiah, His passion, death and resurrection.

178 (p. 80) *Quasi cedrus . . . suavitatem odoris* Ecclesiasticus 24:13–15, 'I was exalted like a cedar in Libanus, and as a cypress tree upon the mountains of Hermon. I was exalted like a palm tree in En-gaddi, and as a rose plant in Jericho, as a fair olive tree in a pleasant field, and grew up as a plane tree by the water. I gave a sweet smell like cinnamon and aspalathus, and I yielded a pleasant odour like the best myrrh . . . '

179 (p. 80) *bright and musical, telling of heaven and infusing peace* Cardinal Newman, 'The Glories of Mary for the Sake of Her Son', *Discourses Addressed to Mixed Congregations* (London 1849), Discourse XVII, p. 380. This discourse is particularly relevant to the 'retreat' section of *Portrait*, because in it Newman argues that 'to understand the full consistency and harmony of Catholic teaching requires study and meditation' (p. 363). This discourse also focuses on the intercessional powers of Mary. Father Arnall repeats a fuller version of this quotation on page 89: 'And now thy very face and form, sweet mother, speak to us of the Eternal, not like earthly beauty, dangerous to look upon, but like the morning star, which is thy emblem, bright and musical, breathing purity, telling of heaven, and infusing peace.'

180 (p. 80) *sums and cuts* geometry problems set for the class

181 (p. 80) *My excellent friend Bombados* possibly from a Dublin pantomime but exact source is unknown (G)

182 (p. 80) *game ball . . . scut* That's excellent. We can skip the whole hour. (slang)

183 (p. 81) *Don't make such a bally racket!* Don't make so much noise ('bally' is a euphemism for 'bloody').

184 (p. 81) *The sentence of saint James . . . guilty of all*   James 2:10, 'For whosoever shall keep the whole law, and yet offend in one point, he is guilty of all.'

185 (p. 82) *saint Francis Xavier whose feast day is Saturday*   See Note 96. The feast day is 3 December.

186 (p. 82) *saint Ignatius*   St Ignatius Loyola. See Note 94.

187 (p. 82) *great fisher of souls!*   When Jesus calls the first apostles to follow him, he says that he will make them 'fishers of men' (Matthew 4:19).

188 (p. 83) *Remember only thy last things . . . the book of Ecclesiastes, seventh chapter, fortieth verse*   Not from Ecclesiastes, but Ecclesiasticus (the Apocrypha in the KJV). In the KJV, the quote is from Ecclesiasticus 7:36, but the Roman Catholic Douay Bible (which was the first official English translation of the Bible for use in the Roman Catholic Church) on occasion differs from the KJV in chapter and verse numbering, as here. In the KJV the quote is: 'Whatsoever thou takest in hand, remember the end [thy last things], and thou shalt never do amiss.' The four last things, according to the Catholic Church, are death, judgment, hell and heaven. (G)

189 (p. 84) *What doth it profit . . . soul?*   Matthew 16:26: 'For what is a man profited if he shall gain the whole world, and lose his own soul?'

190 (p. 85) *He who remembers . . . sin for ever*   the reference is to Ecclesiasticus (G)

191 (p. 85) *bovine god*   the golden calf made and worshipped by the Israelites while Moses was on Mt Sinai receiving the Ten Commandments. See Exodus 32:1–6.

192 (p. 86) *particular . . . general judgment*   Particular judgment is of the individual when they die; general judgment is the Last Judgment, that of mankind.

193 (p. 86) *The stars of heaven . . . rolled away*   Revelation 6:12–14

194 (p. 86) *The archangel Michael . . . death of time*   Revelation 10:1–6 describes an angel with one foot on the sea and one on the land, but this passage does not name the angel. According to Catholic doctrine it is Michael who will proclaim the arrival of the Last Judgment, and thus he would be the angel described in Revelation.

195 (p. 87) *Jehoshaphat*   Joel 3:2 and 12, 'I will also gather all nations, and will bring them down into the valley of Jehoshaphat' (3:2); 'Let the heathen be wakened, and come up to the valley of Jehoshaphat: for there will I sit to judge all the heathen round about' (3:12); site of the Last Judgment.

196 (p. 87) *attended by nine choirs . . . God Everlasting*   This follows Jesus's description of the Last Judgment in Matthew 25:31 and the tradition that

the host of angels is made up of nine choirs, with angels in the lowest choir and seraphim in the highest.

197 (p. 87) *Depart from me . . . his angels* Matthew 25:41

198 (p. 87) *whited sepulchres* Matthew 23:27, 'Woe unto you, scribes and Pharisees, hypocrites! For ye are like unto whited sepulchres, which indeed appear beautiful outward, but are within full of dead [men's] bones, and of all uncleanness.'

199 (p. 88) *Addison . . . the wicked young earl of Warwick* Joseph Addison (1672–1719), English poet, essayist and statesman, married the Countess of Warwick in 1716, and supposedly sent for his stepson on his deathbed and said to him, 'See in what peace a Christian can die.' Addison was 'a Tory and an apparently staunch supporter of William of Orange . . . and his anti-Catholic, anti-Irish policies'. (G)

200 (p. 88) *O grave, where is thy victory?/O death, where is thy sting?* from I Corinthians 15:55, where the questions are in the reverse order. The next verse of Corinthians is, 'The sting of death is sin; and the strength of sin is the law.' Alexander Pope (1688–1744) uses these verses in his poem 'The Dying Christian to His Soul'.

201 (p. 89) *not like earthly beauty . . . musical* See Note 179.

202 (p. 89) *Forty days and forty nights* Genesis 7:4

203 (p. 89) *Hell has enlarged . . . Isaias, fifth chapter, fourteenth verse* 'Therefore hell hath enlarged herself, and opened her mouth without measure: and their glory, and their multitude, and their pomp, and he that rejoiceth, shall descend into it' (KJV). This passage is part of Isaiah's prophecy to the 'inhabitants of Jerusalem, and men of Judah' (5:3) of the consequences of their sinful behaviour.

204 (p. 90) *Lucifer . . . son of the morning* Isaiah 14:12

205 (p. 90) *non serviam: I will not serve* St Thomas Aquinas (see Note 225) is one such theologian who believed that pride was responsible for Satan's downfall. *Non serviam* is Latin for 'I will not serve' and derives from Jeremiah 2:20, in which God reproaches the people of Judah for abandoning Him: 'For of old time I have broken thy yoke, and burst thy bands; and thou saidst, I will not transgress [serve].'

206 (p. 90) *serpent . . . field* Genesis 3:1; much of the material in this and the following paragraph is drawn from Genesis 3.

207 (p. 90) *weaker vessel* I Peter 3:7

208 (p. 91) *He was born . . . Judea* Luke 2:7

209 (p. 91) *And then . . . new gospel* John 1:17, 'For the law was given by Moses, but grace and truth came by Jesus Christ.'

210 (p. 91) *Did they listen . . . issued continually* traditional elements of the Passion taken from various passages in the four Gospels

211 (p. 91) *the hill of Calvary*   according to Luke 23:33, the place where Jesus was crucified. The name comes from the Latin word for 'skull' (*calvaria*) as used in the Vulgate Bible, following the earlier use of the Aramaic 'Golgotha' meaning 'the skull'.

212 (p. 91) *He founded the holy catholic church*   Matthew 16:18–19, Jesus says ' . . . thou art Peter, and upon this rock I will build my church . . . '. The name Peter means 'the rock'.

213 (p. 91) *founded it upon the rock of ages*   See note above; 'Rock of Ages' is also an eighteenth-century Protestant hymn. (G)

214 (p. 91) *saint Anselm . . . De Similitudinibus*   by (or based on the ideas of) St Anselm (*c.*1033–1109), Benedictine theologian and Archbishop of Canterbury. The passage is actually taken from a paraphrase of *De Similitudinibus* by Giovanni Pietro Pinamonti (1632–1703), an Italian Jesuit whose work *Hell Opened to Christians, To Caution Them from Entering into It* (1688) Joyce draws on extensively for the language and texture of Father Arnall's sermons. (G)

215 (p. 92) *Babylonian furnace*   Daniel 3:19–30

216 (p. 92) *Of all the plagues . . . called horrible*   The plagues inflicted on Egypt are described in Exodus 7–12. Darkness is the ninth of the ten plagues.

217 (p. 92) *saint Bonaventure*   (1221–1274) Italian theologian and scholastic philosopher. He entered the Franciscan order *c.*1243, and became general of the order in 1256; he was known as the 'Seraphic Doctor'.

218 (p. 94) *In olden times . . . and a serpent*   from the Roman *Lex Pompeia de Parricidiis* in which the animals mentioned are those noted plus a dog and an ape (G)

219 (p. 94) *Saint Catherine of Siena once saw a devil*   St Catherine of Sienna (1347–80), Italian mystic known for her asceticism and her visions; influenced Pope Gregory XI's decision to return the papacy to Rome from Avignon, thus ending the Babylonian Captivity. She composed *The Dialogue* to convey her beliefs to her disciples. The passage is from Pinamonti, citing St Catherine. (G)

220 (p. 95) *Depart from me . . . his angels!*   See Note 197.

221 (p. 96) *blue funk*   extreme nervousness or dread (slang)

222 (p. 96) *Malahide*   seaside village nearly ten miles north of Dublin

223 (p. 97) *I am cast away . . . twenty-third verse*   The chapter and verse is from the Douay Bible; in the KJV the passage is in Psalm 31:22.

224 (p. 97) *what our holy founder calls . . . the composition of place*   from the first exercise, Item 47 of *The Spiritual Exercises* (1548) by St Ignatius Loyola (G)

225 (p. 97) *Saint Thomas . . . angelic doctor* St Thomas Aquinas (*c.*1225–74), a Dominican theologian and philosopher whose work attempted to reconcile Christian beliefs and rational thought. His *Summa Theologica* uses Aristotelian logic to examine God's existence. His extremely influential writings became basic texts in Roman Catholic theology. 'Doctors' of the church are so designated because of their contribution to Catholic doctrine and teaching; in the middle ages the most celebrated doctors of the church were given epithets that expressed their special characteristics – St Thomas is 'angelic' because of his purity and intellect.

226 (p. 98) *poena damni, the pain of loss* the loss of the possibility of loving God or knowing his presence. These divisions of spiritual pains (pains resulting from the loss of God's presence) are derived from Pinamonti. (G)

227 (p. 98) *the sting of conscience . . . triple sting* This is a paraphrase of Pinamonti quoting Pope Innocent III. The triple sting is the affliction of memory, the disquiet of late repentance and the torment of the lack of time. (G)

228 (p. 99) *saint Augustine* St Augustine of Hippo (354–430), major early Christian theologian and writer. His works include his *Confessions* and the Christian philosophy of history, *The City of God*.

229 (p. 102) *mortal sin . . . venial sin* While it affects the soul, a venial sin admits of pardon or forgiveness; a mortal sin destroys the soul.

230 (p. 102) *made Lucifer and a third part . . . fall from their glory* Not so much from Catholic doctrine as from John Milton's (1608–1674) *Paradise Lost* II: 689–95 ('Art thou that Traitor-Angel, art thou he, / Who first broke peace in Heaven and faith, till then / Unbroken, and in proud rebellious arms / Drew after him the third part of Heaven's sons, / Conjured against the Highest – for which both thou / And they, outcast from God, are here condemned / To waste eternal days in woe and pain?'); see also *Paradise Lost* V: 708–10 and for Milton's source, Revelation 12:3–4.

231 (p. 102) *hanging for three hours on the cross* Matthew 27:45 and Luke 23:44

232 (p. 103) *act of contrition* What follows is a traditional Act of Contrition. During absolution, the penitent is meant to contemplate Jesus's sacrifice on the cross and declare their sorrow.

233 (p. 106) *He once had meant . . . guide us home* From Cardinal Newman, 'The Glories of Mary for the Sake of Her Son', *Discourses to Mixed Congregations* (London 1849), Discourse XVII (pp. 379–80).

234 (p. 108) *Church Street chapel* in the Capuchin Friary on Church Street, north of the Liffey

235 (p. 109) *brown habit of a capuchin* The Capuchins are a branch of the Franciscan order; the habit consists of a brown robe belted with white rope and a cowl.

236 (p. 109) *God's yoke was sweet and light*   Matthew 11:29–30

237 (p. 109) *God loved little children . . . come to Him*   Mark 10:14 and Luke 18:16

238 (p. 112) *ciborium*   vessel used to hold the Eucharist

239 (p. 112) *Corpus Domini nostri . . . In vitam eternam. Amen*   'The Body of our Lord . . . to everlasting life. Amen . . .' (Latin) The beginning and end of the priest's words as he gives the Body to each person taking communion. (G)

240 (p. 113) *Sunday was dedicated . . . Virgin Mary*   Drawn from 'Devotions for Every Day of the Week' in *The Sodality Manual; or a Collection of Prayers and Spiritual Exercises for Members of the Sodality of the Blessed Virgin Mary* (Dublin 1896). (G)

241 (p. 113) *heroic offering . . . for the intentions of the sovereign pontiff*   Offering a lifetime's worth of good works to God for the sake of another, such as, in this case, the Pope. A daily prayer for the Pope is traditionally made by devout Catholics.

242 (p. 113) *interleaved prayer-book*   a prayer book marked with cards to remind one of important personal occasions for prayer (G)

243 (p. 113) *two candles . . . new testaments*   The altar candles on either side of the crucifix represent the Old and New Testaments.

244 (p. 113) *catacombs*   The early Christians in Rome were forced to worship in the catacombs to avoid detection during the years of their persecution.

245 (p. 113) *By means of ejaculations . . . canonical penances*   Following Catholic doctrine, the duration of the punishment suffered by souls in Purgatory would be shortened by Stephen's acts. 'Ejaculations' are short prayers and 'quarantines' are strictly observed forty-day fasts. (G)

246 (p. 113) *supererogation*   In the Roman Catholic Church, actions beyond what duty requires that create a fund of merit that can be drawn on for sinners through prayer.

247 (p. 114) *He offered up each of his three daily chaplets . . . sanctified him*   A chaplet is a string of fifty-five beads that forms one third of the rosary. The three virtues are named in I Corinthians 13:13: 'And now abideth faith, hope, charity, these three; but the greatest of these is charity.'

248 (p. 114) *the seven gifts of the Holy Ghost*   The seven gifts are derived from Isaiah 11:2–3 and are wisdom, understanding, counsel, fortitude, knowledge, piety and fear of the Lord.

249 (p. 114) *the unseen Paraclete . . . mass once a year*   Paraclete, from the Greek for 'called in aid', is another term for the Holy Ghost. The dove is the symbol of the Holy Ghost used in the Gospels and the wind the symbol used in Acts 2:2. The mass for Pentecost is held on the seventh

Sunday after Easter to celebrate the Holy Ghost descending upon the Apostles, in Acts 2:3.

250 (p. 116) *twigging* sweeping with a stiff broom

251 (p. 116) *visit to the Blessed Sacrament* a solitary visit to church when mass is not taking place (see Note 130)

252 (p. 117) *an old neglected book written by saint Alphonsus Liguori* Liguori (1696–1787) was ordained in 1726. In 1732 he founded the missionary order of the Congregation of the Holy Redeemer, dedicated to the rural poor. Major works are *Moral Theology* and *The Glories of Mary*. Gifford suggests that the book referred to here is *Visits to the Most Blessed Sacrament*.

253 (p. 117) *canticles* the Song of Solomon in the King James Bible; Canticle of Canticles in the Douay Bible

254 (p. 117) *Amana . . . mountains of the leopards* *amana*: 'firm, constant' (Hebrew); the name of a mountain in the Song of Solomon 4:8, 'Come with me from Lebanon, my spouse, with me from Lebanon: look from the top of Amana, from the top of Shenir and Hermon, from the lions' dens, from the mountains of the leopards.'

255 (p. 117) *Inter ubera mea commorabitur* 'He shall lie betwixt my breasts' (Latin), from the Song of Solomon 1:13.

256 (p. 118) *friendship between saint Thomas and saint Bonaventure* St Dominic (1170–1221) founded the Dominicans c.1205; St Francis (c.1181–1226) founded the Franciscans in the early thirteenth century. Thomas was a Dominican, Bonaventure a Franciscan; they became friends while teaching at the University of Paris.

257 (p. 119) *the example of the other franciscans* The other Franciscans only wear the traditional habit in cloisters and in public wear dark suits with clerical collars, whereas the Capuchins wear the traditional brown, cowled habit at all times.

258 (p. 119) *Les jupes* The skirts (French)

259 (p. 119) *the craft of the jesuits* Jesuit zeal gained the order a reputation as sometimes willing to allow the end to justify the means in their approach to the counter-Reformation; thus, Protestants had a particular mistrust of the Jesuits. (G)

260 (p. 120) *muff* slang for an awkward or clumsy person, particularly in sport

261 (p. 120) *his equivocal position* i.e., as a non-fee paying student

262 (p. 120) *Lord Macaulay* Thomas Babington Macaulay (1800–59), historian and essayist; he gave up a political career to write a five-volume *History of England* (1849–61), but died before its completion.

263 (p. 120) *Victor Hugo . . . when he was a catholic* Victor Hugo (1802–85), French writer of central importance to French Romanticism. Hugo's

mother was a royalist and a Catholic who tried to impress these beliefs upon her son, but his later work abandoned some of the religiosity of his earlier writings.

264 (p. 120) *Louis Veuillot* (1813–83), French author who professed ultramontane Catholicism; he used poetry, novels and journalism to criticise liberal ideas.

265 (p. 121) *the power of a priest of God . . . exorcism* The power of the keys is taken to mean the general powers and authority of the priesthood; the powers to hear confession and absolve from sin ('to bind and loose from sin') are granted to the priesthood in Matthew 16:18–19. Exorcism is also considered by most to be the exclusive power of the priesthood (following Matthew 10:1).

266 (p. 122) *thurible*   a censer

267 (p. 122) *chasuble*   outer vestment worn by a priest celebrating mass or the Eucharist

268 (p. 122) *celebrant*   the person performing the rite – in this case, the priest at the Eucharist

269 (p. 122) *the tunicle of subdeacon . . . Ite missa est*   The subdeacon assists the deacon at the altar, while the deacon assists the priest leading the service; these positions are almost exclusively held by priests. A tunicle is a short vestment, a humeral veil is worn over the shoulders, the paten holds the communion bread, and a dalmatic is a long, loose vestment with wide sleeves. *Ite, missa est* is said at the end of the mass to dismiss the congregation.

270 (p. 122) *the sin of Simon Magus . . . no forgiveness*   Simon Magus was known for his magic arts (Magus meaning 'magician'). Simon offered the Apostles Peter and John money so that he could bestow the Holy Ghost through the laying on of hands, which he regarded as a magical power. Peter rebuked him and urged him to do penance (Acts 8:9–24). Simon is regarded by the early writers of the church as the first heretic.

271 (p. 122) *imposition of hands*   As Jesus laid hands upon Peter, so it is considered that the powers of the priesthood are passed on through the imposition of hands.

272 (p. 122) *No touch of sin . . . body of the Lord*   I Corinthians 11:29

273 (p. 122) *the order of Melchisedec*   Arising from Genesis 14:18: 'And Melchizedek king of Salem brought forth bread and wine: and he was the priest of the most high God.' Hebrews 5:5–10 and 6:20 allude to this passage in naming Christ as the high priest of God 'after the order of Melchisedec'. Because Jesus is of the order of Melchisedec and is believed to have ordained Peter, the priesthood is considered to be of the order as well.

274 (p. 123) *a novena to your holy patron saint, the first martyr* A novena is a devotion that consists of special prayers offered on nine successive days. St Stephen was the first Christian martyr, found guilty of blasphemy and stoned to death.

275 (p. 123) *Findlater's church* The Abbey Church, endowed by Alexander Findlater, is located in Rutland Square (now Parnell Square).

276 (p. 123) *novitiate* refers to both the probationary period before the novice takes religious vows and the house occupied by the novices during this period

277 (p. 124) *S.J.* abbreviation for the Society of Jesus (the Jesuits)

278 (p. 124) *jesuit house in Gardiner Street* the Jesuit presbytery for the Church of St Francis Xavier, north-east of the Dublin city centre (G)

279 (p. 124) *Tolka* river that flowed through what was at that time the northern outskirts of the city of Dublin

280 (p. 125) *Oft in the Stilly Night* poem (set to music) by Thomas Moore (see Note 322)

281 (p. 126) *giving utterance . . . in every time* from Cardinal Newman, *An Essay in Aid of a Grammar of Assent* (1881) (G)

282 (p. 126) *Byron's public-house . . . Clontarf Chapel* Byron's appears to be fictional; Clontarf Chapel is the Roman Catholic Church of St John the Baptist. Clontarf is about four miles north-east of the centre of Dublin.

283 (p. 126) *the university* University College, Dublin

284 (p. 126) *the Bull* Bull Wall is a sea wall stretching from the shore of Clontarf into Dublin Bay, running along one end of North Bull Island to the North Bull lighthouse.

285 (p. 127) *Whose feet . . . everlasting arms* From Cardinal Newman's *The Idea of a University Defined and Illustrated* (1852) in the Introductory Discourse: 'What grey hairs are on the head of Judah, whose youth is renewed like the eagle's, whose feet are like the feet of harts, and underneath the Everlasting arms?' (3rd edn, 1873, p. 14). As far as the cadence is concerned, the line is in nine perfect iambic feet.

286 (p. 127) *Dollymount* north of Clontarf (see Note 282)

287 (p. 128) *A day of dappled seaborne clouds* a misquotation from *The Testimony of the Rocks; or, Geology in Its Bearings on the Two Theologies, Natural and Revealed* (1857) by Hugh Miller (G)

288 (p. 128) *Liffey* the main river in Dublin, flowing through the centre of the city

289 (p. 128) *the seventh city of christendom . . . thingmote* The phrase 'seventh city of christendom' seems to be Joyce's own but perhaps relates to the sacred or mystical associations with the number seven. (G) A thingmote is a mound where medieval Scandinavians held their councils of

law; the thingmote in Dublin would have been the location from which the Danes ruled Dublin from 852 to 1014.

290 (p. 129) *Stephanos*   crown or garland (Greek)

291 (p. 129) *a stuff in the kisser*   a punch in the mouth (slang)

292 (p. 129) *Bous Stephanoumenos! Bous Stephaneforos!*   'Garland-bearing ox of the sacrifice!' and 'Ox-soul of Stephen!' (Greek) (G)

293 (p. 129) *Guzzle*   seize by the throat, throttle

294 (p. 129) *Norfolk coat*   a box-pleated jacket with a loose belt

295 (p. 130) *the ancient kingdom of the Danes*   The Danes held Dublin from the ninth century until the Battle of Clontarf in 1014.

296 (p. 130) *the name of the fabulous artificer*   Daedalus (see Note 7)

297 (p. 131) *Howth*   the headland to the north-east of Dublin Bay

298 (p. 134) *The dear knows*   A translation from an Irish phrase in which the Irish word for 'deer' is substituted for the word for 'God' (the words being similar in Irish); thus this becomes a mild oath to avoid taking God's name in vain. (G)

299 (p. 134) *I'm going for blue*   possibly means that she is in a rush, working as fast as she can; or, more literally, she is going for 'blue', meaning laundry powder

300 (p. 135) *the nuns' madhouse*   The nuns were in charge of St Vincent's Lunatic Asylum on Convent Avenue. (G)

301 (p. 135) *Gerhart Hauptmann*   (1862–1946) German playwright and novelist who inaugurated the naturalist movement in German theatre. His heroines often are seen as romantically tragic or pathetic figures.

302 (p. 135) *the sloblands of Fairview . . . silver-veined prose of Newman*   The tidal flats where the Tolka enters Dublin Bay were used as a dumping ground and called 'Mud Island'; 'silver-veined prose' perhaps suggests the rivulets in the tidal flats. (G)   In all of the juxtapositions that follow, there seem to be only tenuous connections between the places and authors mentioned.

303 (p. 135) *North Strand Road . . . the dark humour of Guido Cavalcanti*   North Strand Road is a main road on the north side of Dublin. Cavalcanti (*c.*1255–1300), Italian poet and friend of Dante. Guido's 'dark humour' emerges in an episode from *The Decameron* (VI, 9) in which he uses his wit to defeat his antagonists.

304 (p. 135) *Baird's stonecutting works in Talbot Place . . . Ibsen*   Baird's was an actual business located in Talbot Place, just north of the Liffey. Henrik Ibsen (1828–1906) was a Norwegian dramatist best known for his realistic social plays such as *A Doll's House* (1879) and *Hedda Gabler* (1890). See Gifford for a possible explanation of the links between the stonecutting works and Ibsen (p. 226).

305 (p. 136) *a grimy marine dealer's shop . . . I was not wearier where I lay* Ben Jonson (1572–1637), English playwright and poet. The quote is from the epilogue to Jonson's *The Vision of Delight* (1617), lines 237–42: 'I was not wearier where I lay /By frozen *Tythons* side to night; /Then I am willing now to stay, /And be a part of your delight. /But I am urged by the Day, /Against my will to bid you come away.'

306 (p. 136) *waist-coateers* prostitutes

307 (p. 136) *chambering* sexual promiscuity

308 (p. 136) *Aristotle's poetics and psychology* The 'slender sentences' are likely to be from selections from works of Aristotle's (384–322BC): *Poetics* (his lectures on tragedy), *De Sensu* (*Of the Senses*) and *De Anima* (*Of the Soul*).

309 (p. 136) *Synopsis Philosophiae ad mentem divi Thomae* This appears to be a reference to *Elementa Philosophiae ad mentem D. Thomae Aquinatis*, a selection of Thomas Aquinas's writings edited and published by G. M. Mancini in 1898. (G)

310 (p. 136) *Hopkins' corner* a jeweller's on Lower Sackville Street (now O'Connell Street) (G)

311 (p. 136) *the United States of . . . Europe* the title of a book (published in 1899) by William Thomas Stead, an English journalist

312 (p. 137) *nominal definitions, essential definitions* This distinction is taken from Aristotle's *Posterior Analytics*. The 'nominal' refers to descriptions of effects, and the 'essential' refers to an analysis of causes. (G)

313 (p. 138) *Ivory, ivoire, avorio, ebur* 'ivory' repeated in English, French, Italian and Latin

314 (p. 138) *India mittit ebur* India exports ivory. (Latin)

315 (p. 138) *the Metamorphoses of Ovid* See Note 1.

316 (p. 138) *the laws of Latin verse . . . by a Portuguese priest* versification rules in *Prosodia* by the Portuguese Jesuit, Emmanuel Alvarez (1526–82) (G)

317 (p. 138) *Contrahit orator, variant in carmine vates* 'The orator summarises; the poet-prophets transform [elaborate] in their verses.' (Latin) This is from *Prosodia* and in context forms part of a rule for scansion. (G)

318 (p. 138) *in tanto discrimine* in such a great crisis (Latin)

319 (p. 138) *implere ollam denariorum* the filling of a pot with *denaries* (Latin), *denaries* being Roman coins

320 (p. 138) *Horace* Quintus Horatius Flaccus (65–8BC), Roman satirist and lyric poet, famous for his *Odes*, *Satires*, *Epistles* and *Epodes*

321 (p. 138) *grey block of Trinity* Trinity College, Dublin, founded by Queen Elizabeth in 1591. Catholics were banned from attending until 1873. Once Trinity allowed Catholics to attend, the Catholic Church in

Ireland then forbade them to do so; Catholics would instead have attended University College Dublin, as Stephen does.

322 (p. 138) *the droll statue of the national poet of Ireland*   The Irish poet Thomas Moore (1779–1852) was famous for *The Irish Melodies* (1808–34), a series of Irish airs rendered into English. His efforts to appeal to English audiences by popularising aspects of Irish history and culture in the *Melodies*, and the sort of sentimental nationalist tradition he represents within Ireland, make him an object of derision for Stephen, who is being ironic here – Moore was not the 'national poet of Ireland'.

323 (p. 139) *Firbolg . . . Milesian*   It was believed that the Firbolgs were the inhabitants of prehistoric Ireland, and the Milesians were later invaders. Firbolgs were seen as uncultured compared to the more artistic, poetic Milesians. The ironic suggestion here is that the statue shows Moore as a Milesian, when he is merely a Firbolg.

324 (p. 139) *Michael Cusack, the Gael*   (1847–1907) one of the founders of the Gaelic Athletic Association, a nationalist organisation founded in 1884 that encouraged the revival of traditional Irish sports such as hurling (see Note 332) and that placed a ban on 'foreign' (or English) sports such as cricket. Joyce used Cusack as a model for the bigoted nationalist character of 'the Citizen' in *Ulysses*.

325 (p. 139) *the curfew*   The British Parliament passed over a hundred Coercion Acts in the period from 1800 to 1921, some of which allowed for the imposition of curfews.

326 (p. 139) *Mat Davin, the athlete*   This name comes from mixing the forenames of the brothers Maurice and Pat Davin. Maurice was one of the founders of the Gaelic Athletic Association, while Pat was himself an athlete. (G)

327 (p. 139) *fenian*   See Note 70.

328 (p. 139) *the cycles*   the epic mythical tales of ancient Ireland, such as those concerning the heroes Cuchulain and Finn MacCool, which were repopularised at the turn of the century by the Irish Literary Revival

329 (p. 139) *tame geese*   Ironic reference to the 'Wild Geese', an epithet that originally referred to those Irish Catholics allowed to go into exile in France after William III reconquered Ireland in 1690. Many of the Catholic soldiers who left Ireland in the 1690s went on to serve in continental armies, cementing the links between Ireland and other Catholic European countries (hence Davin's wish to serve in the 'foreign legion of France'). The 'Wild Geese' later became a general term for Ireland's self-exiled.

330 (p. 140) *the dark narrow streets of the poorer jews*   an area of south Dublin slightly north of Grantham Street (G)

331 (p. 140) *Buttevant* a market town about thirty miles north-east of Cork

332 (p. 140) *hurling match between the Croke's Own Boys and the Fearless Thurles* Hurling is an Irish sport revived by the Gaelic Athletic Association and resembling both field hockey and rugby. Archbishop Croke of Cashel was the first patron of the association; Thurles is a town located about halfway between Dublin and Cork.

333 (p. 140) *stripped to the buff* not naked, but merely wearing no shirt (G)

334 (p. 140) *minding cool for the Limericks* 'minding cool' comes from the Irish *cùl*, meaning 'the back', and the person doing this guards the goal or gap while his teammates are forward, attempting to score. (G) Limerick is a city in the west of Ireland, south of Galway.

335 (p. 140) *camann* (or *camaun*) the hurling stick, somewhat similar to a hockey stick but shorter

336 (p. 140) *any kind of a yoke* A yoke is any equipment, device, used in work; Davin means that he could not find any mode of transport.

337 (p. 140) *a mass meeting . . . in Castletownroche* A 'mass meeting' is a political demonstration or rally. Castletownroche is five miles east of Buttevant in Co. Cork.

338 (p. 140) *Ballyhoura Hills . . . Kilmallock* Hills extending along the north of Buttevant; Kilmallock is a market town north of Buttevant.

339 (p. 141) *Queenstown* a Cork Harbour seaport now called Cobh

340 (p. 141) *There's no one in it but ourselves* Hiberno-English: There's no one here but you and I.

341 (p. 142) *Grafton Street* The main shopping street in Dublin, connecting the front of Trinity College/College Green with the north-west corner of St Stephen's Green.

342 (p. 142) *a slab was set to the memory of Wolfe Tone* Theobald Wolfe Tone (1763–98), Irish nationalist and founding member of the United Irishmen. During the 1798 Uprising, he was captured by the British while accompanying a small invasion force provided by France. Tone was condemned to death but committed suicide before his execution could take place. The slab mentioned was placed in the north-west corner of St Stephen's Green on 15 August 1898 for the hundredth anniversary of the Uprising, marking the spot where a sculpture was originally intended to be placed. This sculpture never materialised and the slab was removed with the later widening of the streets at that corner of the Green. The four French delegates are presumably at the ceremony to mark Tone's enlisting of French support during the 1798 Rising.

343 (p. 142) *Vive l'Irlande!* Long Live Ireland! (French)

344 (p. 142) *Stephen's Green*   St Stephen's Green is a park filling a city square in south Dublin. Trinity College is to the north of it and University College is to the south.

345 (p. 142) *Buck Egan and Burnchapel Whaley*   John Egan (*c.*1750–1810) was a politician with a penchant for duelling. 'Burnchapel Whaley' is Richard Whaley, whom Stephen confuses with his son, Thomas ('Buck' or 'Jerusalem') Whaley (1766–1800). Richard Whaley, a staunch Protestant, became known as 'Burnchapel' because of his role in burning a number of Catholic chapels in the wake of the 1798 United Irishmen uprising. His son Thomas was a politician (he was bribed first into voting for the Union in 1800 and then bribed into voting against it) renowned for gambling and betting and his extravagant lifestyle. Egan supposedly celebrated black masses with Thomas Whaley in buildings that later became part of University College.

346 (p. 142) *jesuit house . . . among aliens?*   i.e., because the Jesuits' ultimate allegiance is to the Pope, is Stephen in papal territory rather than Irish territory?

347 (p. 142) *The Ireland of Tone and of Parnell*   This would be an independent Ireland of civil and religious liberties for all; but, for Stephen, this possibility has receded through extra-territorial interference, whether from Britain or from Rome.

348 (p. 142) *a levite of the Lord*   a subordinate priest

349 (p. 143) *canonicals . . . ephod*   the dress prescribed by canon law for officiating ministers at particular church occasions; associated with the High Priest in the Old Testament, an ephod is a sleeveless vestment with slits at the sides below the armpits, a girdle at the waist and buckles at the shoulders

350 (p. 143) *Aquinas . . . pulcra sunt quae visa placent*   'We call that beautiful which pleases the sight' (Latin); Stephen is misquoting Aquinas's, 'We call a thing beautiful when it pleases the eye of the beholder' (*Summa Theologica*, Part 1, Question 5, Article 4). (G)

351 (p. 143) *Bonum est in quod tendit appetitus*   'That is good toward which the appetite [or desire] is moved' (Latin); Stephen is again paraphrasing a passage from *Summa Theologica*. (G)

352 (p. 143) *Like Ignatius he was lame*   Loyola's conversion to the religious life was initiated in the aftermath of his being rendered lame in battle.

353 (p. 143) *Similiter atque senis baculus*   'Similar to an old man's walking stick' (Latin). This is what the good Jesuit should be for his superiors in the order. (G)

354 (p. 144) *cliffs of Moher*   cliffs of over six hundred feet in Co. Clare in the west of Ireland

355 (p. 144) *Epictetus also had a lamp . . . after his death* Epictetus, first-century-AD Greek Stoic philosopher who believed that individual will was the only thing in man's power to control. Epictetus's lamp was supposedly purchased by a follower after his death. Epictetus's sayings were collected by his pupil Arrian in the *Discourses*, the work to which Stephen and the Dean of Studies refer in the sentences that follow.

356 (p. 145) *a sentence of Newman's . . . of the saints* Newman's translation of a passage from Ecclesiasticus 24 in 'The Glories of Mary for the Sake of Her Son', in *Discourses to Mixed Congregations* (London 1849): ' . . . and I *took root* in an honourable people, and in the fulness of the saints was I *detained . . .*' (p. 379)

357 (p. 145) *tundish* an English, not an Irish, word; a wooden bowl with a tube at the bottom that fits into a cask or other receptacle; used as a type of funnel in brewing

358 (p. 145) *Lower Drumcondra* suburban village in north Dublin

359 (p. 145) *the elder brother in the parable . . . prodigal* The story of the prodigal son is told by Jesus in Luke 15:11–32; the elder, dutiful son is angry when his father welcomes back his wayward younger brother.

360 (p. 145) *A humble follower in the wake of clamorous-conversions* The Oxford Movement inspired a number of conversions to Catholicism, perhaps the most well known being that of Cardinal Newman (see Note 138).

361 (p. 145) *six principle men . . . supralapsarian dogmatists* All sects of the Baptist Church. The Six-Principle Baptists were founded in 1690 in London and followed the six principles of Hebrews 6. The 'peculiar people' are Original Freewill Baptists; founded in North Carolina in the second half of the eighteenth century, they refused all medical assistance. The 'seed and snake baptists' are Two-Seed-in-the-Spirit Baptists; founded in Tennessee in the first half of the nineteenth century, they believed some of Eve's children were the seed of God and the rest the seed of the Devil (the snake). The 'supralapsarian dogmatists' are Baptists who believed that no human effort could affect God's will, and so they saw no need for the formal institutions of religion. (G)

362 (p. 146) *insufflation . . . imposition of hands . . . procession of the Holy Ghost* Insufflation is breathing on or over someone as a sign of the coming of the Holy Spirit; for imposition of hands, see Note 271; both can be employed in the expulsion of evil from a person. The procession of the Holy Ghost refers to the belief that the Holy Spirit, as part of the Holy Trinity, proceeds from God the Father and God the Son.

363 (p. 146) *that disciple who had sat at the receipt of custom . . . zinc-roofed chapel* The disciple is Matthew, who was a tax collector before being

called by Jesus (Matthew 9:9). 'Chapel' is used to distinguish a place of worship of a dissenting sect from a 'church' of the established Church of England.

364 (p. 146) *Per aspera ad astra*   By rough paths to the stars (Latin)

365 (p. 147) *half brother of the clergy*   possibly because he is a late convert to Catholicism or because he is a teacher and not a parish priest (G)

366 (p. 147) *ghostly father*   The powers of the priesthood were first considered to be conferred by a laying on of hands that bestowed the Holy Ghost upon the priest (see Note 271); Stephen does not see the dean of studies as 'ghostly', i.e. as possessing the spirit of the Holy Ghost that enables him to perform sacramental duties such as confession, thus throughout this scene Stephen addresses him as 'sir' rather than as 'father'.

367 (p. 147) *Kentish fire*   extended rhythmic applause with hands and feet intended as an expression of dissent or displeasure, deriving its name from demonstrations held in Kent in opposition to the Catholic Relief Bill (1829)

368 (p. 147) *Leopardstown*   a racecourse south of Dublin

369 (p. 147) *In case of necessity . . . can do it*   According to Catholic doctrine, baptism can be administered validly by any person in cases of necessity.

370 (pp. 147–8) *Mr W. S. Gilbert*   Sir William Schwenck Gilbert (1836–1911), English librettist of the Gilbert and Sullivan partnership.

371 (p. 148) *On a cloth untrue . . . And elliptical billiard balls*   from Act 2 of *The Mikado* by Gilbert and Sullivan (1885)

372 (p. 148) *platinoid . . . F. W. Martino*   American chemist (b. 1863) Fernando Wood Martin. Platinoid is an alloy composed of copper, nickel, tungsten and zinc.

373 (p. 149) *Belfast*   Queen's University, Belfast (established 1849)

374 (p. 149) *two photographs . . . signatures*   The photographs are of the Russian Tsar Nicholas II (1868–1918) and the Tsarina Alexandra Fyodorovna (1872–1918), who were assassinated during the Russian Revolution; Nicholas issued a 'Peace Rescript' in 1898 to encourage world peace, and the long roll of paper is part of this petition.

375 (p. 150) *Ego habeo*   literal Latin translation of 'I have'. All of the 'Latin' in the conversation that follows is a form of dog-Latin that translates English literally.

376 (p. 150) *Quod?*   What? (dog-Latin)

377 (p. 150) *Per pax universalis*   For universal peace (dog-Latin)

378 (p. 150) *Credo . . . malo humore estis*   I believe you are a bloody liar . . . because your face shows that you are in a damned bad humour. (dog-Latin)

379 (p. 150) *No stimulants and votes for the bitches* referring to temperance campaigns and the campaign for women's rights (including voting rights)

380 (p. 150) *A sugar!* Anglicisation of the Irish use of 'a sugan' for 'a weakling', deriving more properly from the Irish word 'sugán' for 'straw rope' (G)

381 (p. 150) *Quis est in malo humore . . . ego aut vos?* Who is in bad humour . . . you or I? (dog-Latin)

382 (p. 151) *Elizabethan English . . . Wicklow pulpit* It was a conventional idea that English spoken in Ireland was a more pure form of English, like that spoken in Elizabethan times. Stephen laments that Cranly's modern Dublin speech bears little resemblance to this 'Elizabethan English', or to rural Gaelic-inflected speech. The 'sacred eloquence of Dublin' refers to the language of eighteenth-century Irish politicians such as Edmund Burke (1729–97) and Henry Grattan (see Note 166). The exact reference to 'Wicklow pulpit' is unknown, but the general thrust of the passage would indicate that the speeches delivered in such a place would be a pale reflection of the great rhetoric of the eighteenth-century orators.

383 (p. 151) *Tsar's rescript . . . Stead . . . disarmament . . . international disputes* For Stead, see Note 311; general disarmament and international arbitration were issues raised (to little effect) at the Hague Peace Conference of 1899, itself a product of Nicholas II's 'Peace Rescript', see Note 374.

384 (p. 152) *Marx is only a bloody cod* i.e., Marx is just a joker (for 'cod', see Note 24). Karl Marx (1818–83), German social and economic theorist, was author (with Frederich Engels) of *The Communist Manifesto* (1848).

385 (p. 152) *Socialism was founded by an Irishman* Pioneering socialist, atheist, and vegetarian William Thompson (1775–1833) is the most likely candidate for this title; he published *An Inquiry into the Distribution of Wealth* (1824) and was quoted by Marx. James Bronterre O'Brien (1804–64) is the other possible candidate; he was a reformer and activist considered the 'schoolmaster' of the Chartist Movement.

386 (p. 152) *John Anthony Collins!* Anthony Collins (1676–1729), free-thinking theologian and philosopher whose *Discourse on Freethinking* (1713) was attacked in a pamphlet by Jonathan Swift. He also wrote *Discourse on the Grounds and Reasons of the Christian Religion*, which controversially sought to undermine 'factual' aspects of the Old Testament.

387 (p. 152) *Lottie Collins . . . yours?* a street rhyme referring to the 1890s English music-hall star Lottie Collins (G)

388 (p. 152) *Pax super totum sanguinarium globum* Peace over this whole bloody globe (dog-Latin)

389 (p. 153) *Nos ad manum ballum jocabimus* Let's go play handball. (dog-Latin)

390 (p. 154) *the second matric men . . . The first arts men . . . Second arts . . .*
'Matric' – matriculation – refers to the qualification examination for joining First Arts; First Arts and Second Arts are first- and second-year humanities students, respectively.

391 (p. 154) *reading his office*   prayers of the Divine Office, that is, the prescribed prayers for the different canonical hours of the day

392 (p. 154) *Jean-Jacques Rousseau*   (1712–78), Swiss-born writer and philosopher. His *Social Contract* (1762) examines the relationship between society and government and was influential in the French Revolution. Both his enormously popular novel *Émile* (1762) and his *Confessions* (1782) had a significant effect on the development of Romanticism.

393 (p. 154) *super spottum*   on the spot (dog-Latin)

394 (p. 155) *go-by-the-wall*   a creeping, slippery or helpless person

395 (p. 155) *Long pace, fianna . . . one, two!*   Stephen is mocking the language of the military drills of the Fenians (see Note 70); 'Fianna' is their rallying cry. (G)

396 (p. 156) *Hurleysticks*   hurling stick or *camann* (see Note 335)

397 (p. 156) *the office of arms*   genealogical records of Irish families held in Dublin Castle

398 (p. 156) *league class*   Irish-language classes run by the Gaelic League (founded 1893)

399 (p. 156) *address the jesuits as father*   Possibly Stephen ridicules this because he makes the distinction between those priests who have educational duties and those who perform sacramental duties (see Note 366) – only those performing the latter duties would be called 'father'.

400 (p. 157) *second proof of Lynch's culture*   Joyce writes 'Cranly misuses words. Thus he says "let us eke go" where he means to say "let us e'en go" that is "let us even go," eke meaning also and having no sense in the phrase, whereas even or e'en is a slight adverbial embellishment. By quoting Cranly's misquotation Lynch gives the first proof of his culture. The word yellow . . . is his personal substitution for the more sanguine hued adjective, bloody.' (Joyce, *Letters*, Vol. 3, p. 130)

401 (p. 157) *Aristotle has not defined pity and terror*   from Aristotle's *Poetics*, where he refers to the use of pity and terror in tragedy (in order to achieve catharsis), without actually defining the terms 'pity' or 'terror' (or, indeed, 'catharsis')

402 (p. 158) *hansom*   two-wheeled horsedrawn carriage

403 (p. 158) *the Venus of Praxiteles in the Museum*   Praxiteles, a Greek sculptor active in the period 370–330BC. His Venus (of Cnidus) only survived in Roman copies, of which a reproduction (since removed) stood in the Irish National Museum in Kildare Street.

404 (p. 158) *carmelite school*   school administered by the Roman Catholic order, Our Lady of Mount Carmel

405 (p. 160) *Aquinas . . . Pulcra sunt quae visa placent*   See Note 350.

406 (p. 160) *Plato . . . beauty is the splendour of truth*   Plato (*c.*427–347BC), Greek philosopher who studied under Socrates and founded the school at which Aristotle studied. Both Plato's *Phaedrus* and *Symposium* contain statements such as this. (G)

407 (p. 160) *Aristotle's entire system . . . same subject*   There is no 'book of psychology'; this refers to Aristotle's *Metaphysics* – psychology forms part of the subject of this work. The statement is from book gamma, III, 1005b, 19–20. (G)

408 (p. 161) *The Origin of Species*   published in 1859 by naturalist Charles Darwin (1809–82), it first brought Darwin's theory of evolution to public attention and sparked numerous religious and social debates and controversies

409 (p. 161) *Sir Patrick Dun's hospital*   between Lower Mount Street and Grand Canal Street. The estate of Sir Patrick Dun (1642–1713), president of the Irish Royal College of Physicians and an Irish MP, financed its building.

410 (p. 162) *a hymn for Maundy Thursday . . . Pange lingua gloriosi*   Maundy Thursday is the day before Good Friday. The words are Latin for 'Tell, my tongue, in glorious . . . ' and are the first words of a processional hymn by Thomas Aquinas.

411 (p. 162) *the Vexilla Regis of Venantius Fortunatus*   The hymn 'Vexilla Regis Prodeunt' (Latin for 'The Banners of the King Advance') is also sung on Maundy Thursday (as well as at other times). Venantius Fortunatus (*c.*530–600) was a bishop and Latin poet.

412 (p. 162) *Impleta sunt quae concinit . . . / . . . Regnavit a ligno Deus*   from 'Vexilla Regis Prodeunt' (see Note above), translated as, 'Fulfilled is all that David told / In true prophetic song of old, / Amidst the nations, God, saith he, / Hath reigned and triumphed from the Tree.'

413 (p. 162) *Griffin was plucked . . . the home civil . . . in the Indian*   'plucked': failed; 'through the home civil': passed the civil service examinations; 'fifth place in the Indian': fifth place in the British Colonial service examinations for service in India

414 (p. 163) *Glenmalure*   a valley in the Wicklow Mountains

415 (p. 163) *Goethe and Lessing*   Johann Wolfgang von Goethe (1749–1832), German poet, playwright and novelist; a dominant figure in German Romanticism, his most famous works include *Faust* and *The Sorrows of Young Werther* (1774), a work that exerted a strong influence on European Romantic literatures. Gotthold Ephraim Lessing (1729–81),

German playwright and critic, pioneered German Classicism (although he would not have used that term, as 'Classical' and 'Romantic' were terms that only emerged later in the nineteenth century). Broadly speaking, the 'Classical school' refers to art that is concerned with formal rules and tradition; while the 'Romantic school' stressed innovation and formal experimentation.

416 (p. 163) *The Laocoon . . . ultra-profound*   The *Laocoön* is a 1766 essay by Lessing contrasting the natures of poetry and painting; however, it predates the philosophical theories of German 'ultra-profound' idealism by at least two decades, which indicates that Donovan does not actually know much on the subject.

417 (p. 163) *Merrion Square*   fashionable Georgian square in south Dublin

418 (p. 163) *Ad pulcritudinem . . . radiance*   a paraphrase of a section from Part I, Question 39 of Aquinas's *Summa Theologica* (G)

419 (p. 164) *What is audible . . . presented in space*   taken from Lessing's *Laocoön*

420 (p. 164) *symbolism or idealism*   'Symbolism' is used in terms of nineteenth-century transcendental idealism, in which physical 'reality' is considered to be symbolic of a spiritual reality.

421 (p. 164) *the scholastic quidditas, the whatness of a thing*   This 'whatness' is the thing's essence, or what its place is in God's scheme, a characteristic concern in medieval philosophy. The moment of understanding 'the whatness of a thing' is like the experience of an epiphany.

422 (p. 164) *The mind . . . fading coal*   Percy Bysshe Shelley (see Note 164), from 'A Defence of Poetry' (1840): 'the mind in creation is as a fading coal which some invisible influence, like an inconstant wind, awakens to transitory brightness . . .' *Shelley's Poetry and Prose* (Norton, New York 1977) pp. 503–4

423 (p. 165) *Luigi Galvani . . . enchantment of the heart*   The Italian physiologist and physicist Galvani (1737–98) used this phrase to describe the momentary pause in the heartbeat of a frog when a needle was inserted into its spinal cord. (G)

424 (p. 165) *the bust of Sir Philip Crampton*   (1777–1858) renowned Dublin surgeon. The bust stood above a public drinking fountain. (G)

425 (p. 165) *Lessing . . . statues to write of*   The Laocoön is a sculpture from the Hellenistic period (first century BC) depicting the figures of Laocoön and his sons entwined by serpents. For Lessing's essay on this sculpture, see Notes 415 and 416.

426 (p. 166) *Turpin Hero*   The original title of *Portrait*, *Stephen Hero*, was meant to recall this English ballad, which tells the story of the eighteenth-

century highwayman Dick Turpin. *Portrait* reverses the order of the narrative voice of *Turpin Hero*, beginning in the third person and ending in the first.

427 (p. 166) *the duke's lawn . . . national library*   The lawn is to the east of Leinster House, once the residence of the Duke of Leinster but now housing the Irish parliament. Leinster House forms a horseshoe-shaped trio of public buildings with the National Museum and the National Library of Ireland.

428 (p. 166) *royal Irish academy*   Founded in 1785 to promote the study of antiquities, science and literature, the Royal Irish Academy has (since the mid-nineteenth century) been located on Dawson Street, which is actually one street away from the National Library.

429 (p. 167) *stewing*   through forced, hard study, as opposed to natural intelligence

430 (p. 167) *Ego credo . . . in Liverpoolio*   I believe the life of the poor is simply atrocious, simply bloody atrocious, in Liverpool. (dog-Latin)

431 (p. 167) *Gabriel . . . the virgin's chamber*   The angel Gabriel appears to Mary to tell her of the coming birth of Christ in Luke 1:26–38.

432 (p. 168) *villanelle*   A nineteen-line poem of six stanzas, five tercets and the final stanza a quatrain. The rhyme scheme of each of the tercets is *aba*, while that of the quatrain is *abaa*, so that only two different rhymes are used throughout. The first line is repeated in lines 6, 12 and 18, and the third line is repeated in lines 9, 15 and 19. An example of a villanelle is Dylan Thomas's 'Do Not Go Gentle Into That Good Night'.

433 (p. 169) *the print of the Sacred Heart above the untenanted sideboard*   St Margaret Mary Alacoque (1647–90) was a French mystic who founded the devotion to the 'Sacred Heart of Jesus' after she saw visions of Jesus in which she was told about his loving heart. She was beatified in 1864 and canonised in 1920; after her beatification these prints became very popular for display in Catholic households. The sideboard is 'untenanted' because no alcoholic drinks have been placed upon it.

434 (p. 169) *loth to depart*   a song that expresses regret for departure

435 (p. 169) *the victory chant of Agincourt*   fifteenth-century song celebrating the English victory under Henry V over the French at Agincourt (in north-west France) in 1415

436 (p. 169) *Greensleeves*   Though probably older than this, this ballad of inconstant love first appeared in print in 1584, with the title 'A New Courtly Sonnet, of the Lady Greensleeves'. (G)

437 (p. 169) *called by their christian names a little too soon*   their first names, at this time normally only used by family and close friends

438 (p. 169) *Gherardino da Borgo San Donnino*   Condemned as a heretic, he died in prison in 1276. He led the 'Spirituals' wing of the Franciscan order, which wished for a return to the order's original, more austere ways.

439 (p. 170) *By Killarney's Lakes and Fells*   a song from the opera *Innisfallen* by Michael William Balfe (1808–70).

440 (p. 170) *Jacob's biscuit factory*   W. and R. Jacob & Co, located west of St Stephen's Green (G)

441 (p. 170) *latticed ear of a priest*   refers to the lattice-work in the confessional

442 (p. 170) *a potboy in Moycullen*   a waiter who serves ale or beer. Moycullen is a small town north-west of Galway.

443 (p. 173) *ashplant*   a staff or walking-stick

444 (p. 173) *temple of air*   In Roman augury, the Latin term *templum* means a space in the sky or on earth marked out by the augur (the reader of omens) for the purpose of taking auspices; divination is then based on reading the movements of birds in the templum of the sky.

445 (p. 173) *Cornelius Agrippa*   Heinrich Cornelius Agrippa von Nettesheim (1486–1535), German philosopher, physician and occultist, whose work *De Occulta Philosophia* discusses divination. The phrase Stephen is thinking of is unidentified.

446 (p. 173) *Swedenborg . . . by reason*   Emanuel Swedenborg (1688–1772), Swedish scientist, theologian and mystic (called Daedalus Hyberboreus, the Daedalus of the North) who denied the Trinity and believed that Christ alone was God. The 'correspondence of birds to things' may refer to passages in *The True Christian Religion* (1771). (G)

447 (p. 173) *curved stick of an augur*   The *lituus* is the crooked staff used by the augur to mark out the templum.

448 (p. 173) *Thoth*   in ancient Egyptian mythology, the god of the moon, of wisdom, the measurer of time and the inventor of writing and numbers. Thoth is conventionally represented as having an ibis head with a crown formed of the horns of the moon.

449 (p. 174) *like an Irish oath*   'The original expression is *thauss* [Thoth] *ag Dhee* (given here phonetically), meaning *God knows*: but as this is too solemn and profane for most people they changed it to *thauss ag fee*, i.e., *the deer knows*.' (P. W. Joyce, quoted in G). See Note 298.

450 (p. 174) *Bend down your faces, Oona and Aleel . . . He wander the loud waters*   The beginning of the Countess's farewell speech, from Scene 5 of William Butler Yeats's play *The Countess Cathleen* (1892). Yeats (1865–1939), a central figure in the Irish Literary Revival, was a senator in the Irish Free State and was awarded the Nobel Prize for Literature in 1923.

451 (p. 174) *the opening of the national theatre*   The Irish Literary Theatre (known from 1904 as the Abbey Theatre) was founded in 1898 by Yeats, Lady Gregory and Edward Martyn; it was dedicated to the performance of 'Celtic and Irish plays'. The incident Stephen recalls involves the controversy accompanying the production of Yeats's play *The Countess Cathleen*, which was first performed on 8 May 1899 and criticised on moral and political grounds by Irish Nationalists. The play portrayed an Irish noblewoman who sold her soul to save her tenants from starvation – many Irish Catholic nationalists objected to this on religious grounds (hence the shouts of 'Blasphemy' and 'We never sold our faith').

452 (p. 174) *Made in Germany*   from Ernest Williams's *Made in Germany* (1896), an alarmist account of German industry. The phrase came to imply work that was either substandard or unfairly subsidised. (G)

453 (p. 175) *We want no budding buddhists*   reference to W. B. Yeats's interest in eastern religions and mysticism, particularly theosophy

454 (p. 175) *reader's room*   the reading room in the National Library of Ireland

455 (p. 175) *The Tablet*   a conservative Catholic weekly magazine

456 (p. 176) *Walter Scott . . . The Bride of Lammermoor*   Sir Walter Scott (1771–1832), Scottish poet and novelist. Best known for series of historical novels, such as *Waverley* (1814) and *The Bride of Lammermoor* (1819).

457 (p. 176) *game of swans*   a flock of swans, usually kept for pleasure

458 (p. 176) *Bantry gang*   members of an extended political family from Bantry (in the south-west of Ireland), including Timothy Sullivan (1827–1914), who owned the conservative anti-Fenian Dublin newspaper *The Daily Nation*, and his nephew Timothy Healy (1855–1931), who was a lieutenant of Parnell and came to be known as his 'betrayer' (G)

459 (p. 177) *a touch*   engaged in sexual intercourse (slang)

460 (p. 177) *Forsters are the kings of Belgium . . . a different branch*   Genealogical nonsense – there is no Irish connection. Baldwin I (1058–1118), though of the House of Flanders, was king of Jerusalem, not Flanders itself. Baldwin the Forester claimed to be Baldwin I of Constantinople (1171–c.1206), but was later executed after being exposed as an impostor. (G)

461 (p. 177) *Giraldus Cambrensis* (c.1146–c.1220) Welsh historian and chronicler; he took holy orders c.1172. He travelled to Ireland with Prince John in 1172, and wrote a history of Henry II's conquest of Ireland (*Expugnatio Hibernica*) and a book on the topography of Ireland (*Topographia Hibernica*), both of which were unsympathetic in their depictions of the Irish.

462 (p. 177) *Pernobilis et pervetusta familia*   A very noble and venerable family (Latin). Giraldus Cambrensis describes the Fitz-Stephen (sons of Stephen) family in this way. (G)

463 (p. 178) *paulo post futurum*   Latin term for a particular verb tense in Greek used for an event that is about to happen

464 (p. 179) *That's the only English dual number*   Referring to 'ballocks'; a dual number is a particular form of the plural that is used for nouns indicating a pair, of which there are effectively none in modern English.

465 (p. 179) *Darkness falls from the air*   a misquote of a line from 'A Litany in Time of Plague' (1592) by Thomas Nashe (1567–1601), English author of pamphlets, plays, poems, and what has been called the first picaresque novel in English, *The Unfortunate Traveller* (1594). The correct line is 'Brightness falls from the air'.

466 (p. 180) *Dowland and Byrd and Nash*   all English Elizabethan figures: John Dowland (1563–1626), composer best known for the lute pieces *Lachrimae* (1604); William Byrd (1543–1623), composer known as 'the Atlas of English music'. Nash is Thomas Nashe (see Note above).

467 (p. 180) *chambering*   See Note 307.

468 (p. 180) *the court of a slobbering Stuart*   James I (1566–1625), Elizabeth I's successor, whose tongue was described as being so large that it made him drool by forcing his lips apart.

469 (p. 180) *pavan*   (or pavane), a stately sixteenth-century dance with elaborate dress

470 (p. 180) *clipped*   embrace, or, in this context, engage in sexual intercourse

471 (p. 180) *Cornelius à Lapide*   (1567–1637) Flemish Jesuit who put forth the theory that maggots, flies and lice were not created by God directly, but arose by spontaneous generation from sweat or decaying meat, etc. (G)

472 (p. 181) *Adelphi*   a hotel south-west of the National Library on South Anne Street

473 (p. 182) *I suffer little children to come unto me*   Mark 10:14, 'But when Jesus saw it, he was much displeased, and said unto them, Suffer the little children to come unto me, and forbid them not: for of such is the kingdom of God.'

474 (p. 182) *why does the church send them all to hell if they die unbaptized?*   Catholic doctrine does not actually believe that such children go to Hell, but rather to Limbo, meant to be a place of sadness but without the eternal pain of those in Hell.

475 (p. 182) *Saint Augustine . . . unbaptized children*   Augustine, in *Admonition and Grace*, argues that unbaptised children are condemned to

Hell because of the mark of Original Sin that is left on an unbaptised child.

476 (p. 182) *sugan*   See Note 380.

477 (p. 182) *grey spouse of Satan*   'Sin' is named as Satan's daughter and wife in Book II of Milton's *Paradise Lost*, and their son is Death.

478 (p. 183) *Roscommon*   a town and county in central Ireland

479 (p. 183) *the bird call from Siegfried*   passages from *Siegfried* (1876), the third opera of the cycle *The Ring of the Nibelungs* by German composer Richard Wagner (1813–83)

480 (p. 183) *Kildare Street opposite Maple's hotel*   Maple's was a small hotel on the opposite side of Kildare Street from the National Library.

481 (p. 183) *jarvies*   hackney-coach drivers

482 (p. 184) *easter duty*   also called the 'Eucharistic Precept'; the requirement to receive communion (and, usually, to go to confession) within the Easter period from Ash Wednesday to Ascension Day

483 (p. 184) *Do you believe in the eucharist?*   i.e., Do you believe in transubstantiation, the conversion of the bread and wine into the body and blood of Christ?

484 (p. 185) *Depart from me, ye cursed, into everlasting fire!*   See Note 197.

485 (p. 185) *bright, agile, impassible and . . . subtle*   According to Catholic doctrine, these are the four qualities of the heavenly bodies of the saints. The body of the saint will shine ('bright'); will be able to move swiftly ('agile'); will not be subject to pain ('impassible'); and will be subject to the will of the soul ('subtle').

486 (p. 187) *Pascal . . . would not suffer his mother to kiss him*   It was alleged that the French religious philosopher, mathematician and physicist Blaise Pascal (1623–62) would not let his mother touch him. Pascal's works include *Provincial Letters* (1656–7) and *Pensées* (published posthumously).

487 (p. 187) *Suarez . . . has apologized for him*   The Spanish Jesuit Francisco Suarez (1548–1617) claimed that in the original Aramaic Jesus's words to his mother in John 2:4, 'Woman, what have I to do with Thee?' are in fact courteous. (G)

488 (p. 187) *whited sepulchre*   See Note 198.

489 (p. 188) *sacrilegious communion*   Taking communion falsely while knowingly in a state of mortal sin is a sacrilege.

490 (p. 188) *penal days*   the period of the Penal Laws, dating from the end of the seventeenth century until Catholic Emancipation in 1829, during which Roman Catholic religious practice was suppressed and Catholics were disenfranchised

491 (p. 188) *township of Pembroke*   south-east of Dublin

492 (p. 188) *Rosie O'Grady*   popular song by Maud Nugent (G)

493 (p. 188) *Mulier cantat*   The/a woman sings. (Latin)

494 (p. 189) *Et tu cum Jesu Galilaeo eras*   Latin translation of Matthew 26:69, 'Thou also wast with Jesus of Galilee.' Peter is so accused after the arrest of Jesus, and in denying this, he begins to fulfil Jesus's prophecy of 26:34, 'Verily I say unto thee, That this night, before the cock crow, thou shalt deny me thrice.' The Latin also forms the first words of the Passion of Saint Matthew, sung by a woman on Palm Sunday.

495 (p. 189) *proparoxyton*   a word in which the acute accent is on the last syllable but two – here, the third syllable of '*Galilaeo*': ga–li–lá–e–o

496 (p. 190) *Harcourt Street Station*   railway terminus near St Stephen's Green, now defunct

497 (p. 190) *Sallygap to Larras*   Sallygap is in the Wicklow Mountains; Larras is about eight miles south of Sallygap, connected most directly by a road straight over the mountains. (G)

498 (p. 190) *Juan Mariana de Talavera*   (1536?–1624) Spanish Jesuit whose *De Rege et Regis Insitutione* (*Of Tyrants and Tyrannical Institutions*, 1599) controversially defended the right to depose and kill tyrants. The work was publicly burned in France in 1610.

499 (p. 190) *chastisement of the secular arm*   refers to the common phraseology used during the Inquisition in turning heretics over to the civil authorities for punishment

500 (p. 192) *Elizabeth and Zacchary*   the parents of John the Baptist. Luke 1:7 states that when John was born 'they both were now well stricken in years', hence the reference to their 'exhausted loins'. John the Baptist is the 'precursor' of Jesus, in that he is 'to make ready a people prepared for the Lord' (Luke 1:17).

501 (p. 192) *Locusts and wild honey*   refers to John the Baptist's ascetic life in the wilderness, where 'his meat was locusts and wild honey' (Matthew 3:4)

502 (p. 192) *a stern severed head . . . veronica. Decollation . . . in the fold*   John the Baptist was beheaded on the orders of King Herod (Matthew 14:10); the celebration of the Decollation (beheading) of John the Baptist is held on 29 August; 'veronica' refers to the story of Veronica, who wiped Jesus's face with a cloth in the procession to Calvary and later found an image of Christ's face imprinted on the cloth.

503 (p. 192) *saint John at the Latin gate*   the place where St John the Evangelist (not St John the Baptist) was freed from his Roman captors by divine intervention. This event is celebrated on 6 May, the same day that commemorates the dedication of the Basilica of St John Lateran in Rome to both John the Baptist and John the Evangelist.

504 (p. 192) *Let the dead bury the dead*   Luke 9:60

505 (p. 192) *B.V.M.* Blessed Virgin Mary

506 (p. 192) *relations between Jesus and Papa . . . Mary and her son* an argument that the relationship between Jesus and God the Father should be given greater centrality than that between Jesus and Mary in Catholic teachings and faith

507 (p. 192) *Ghezzi* Father Charles Ghezzi, Joyce's Italian lecturer at University College, Dublin

508 (p. 192) *Bruno the Nolan* Giordano Bruno (1548–1600), Italian philosopher, born in Nola in the Kingdom of Naples (hence 'the Nolan'), entered the Dominican order in 1563; influenced by the theories of Copernicus, he was arrested by the Inquisition and burned at the stake for his heretical religious views.

509 (p. 192) *risotto alla bergamasca* Italian rice dish originating in Bergamo

510 (p. 193) *soldiers of the ninety-seventh infantry . . . crucified* John 19:23–4

511 (p. 193) *I wonder if . . . he is very ill* from 'William Bond' by William Blake (1757–1827), English radical printer, engraver and poet. The first stanza is, 'I wonder whether the Girls are mad / And I wonder whether they mean to kill / And I wonder if William Bond will die / For assuredly he is very ill.'

512 (p. 193) *Alas, poor William* refers to Hamlet's 'Alas, poor Yorrick! I knew him, Horatio – a fellow of infinite jest, of most excellent fancy' (*Hamlet*, 5, 1).

513 (p. 193) *Rotunda* building complex including a maternity hospital and theatre on Parnell (then Rutland) Square on the north side of central Dublin

514 (p. 193) *William Ewart Gladstone* (1809–98) Four times British prime minister he dominated the British Liberal Party. He oversaw the disestablishment of the Church of Ireland (1869) and cooperated with Parnell on the issue of Irish Home Rule, but later distanced himself from Parnell in the wake of the O'Shea divorce case.

515 (p. 193) *O Willie, we have missed you* song by the American Stephen Foster (1824–64)

516 (p. 193) *Still harping on the mother* Polonius says of Hamlet in his 'mad' state, 'Still harping on my daughter' (*Hamlet*, 2, 2).

517 (p. 193) *Lepidus would say . . . your sun* 'Your serpent of Egypt is bred now of your mud by the operation of your sun. So is your crocodile' (*Antony and Cleopatra*, 2, 7). Lepidus, one of the three rulers of Rome, says this while drunk.

518 (p. 193) *Johnston, Mooney and O'Brien's* chain of tearooms owned by these Dublin biscuit makers (G)

519 (p. 193) *bushel of Wicklow bran*   refers to Cranly's country origins in Co. Wicklow in terms of the Sermon on the Mount, Matthew 5:14–15, 'Ye are the light of the world. A city that is set on a hill cannot be hid. Neither do men light a candle, and put it under a bushel, but on a candlestick; and it giveth light unto all that are in the house.' See Joyce's *Letters*, Vol. 3, p. 130.

520 (p. 193) *cigar shop opposite Findlater's church*   A tobacconist's shop (C. S. M'Garvey's) was opposite Findlater's Church on Parnell (then Rutland) Square. (G)

521 (p. 194) *Tara was via Holyhead*   Tara was the seat of power of the ancient High Kings of Ireland and suggests a mythical Irish golden age. Holyhead is the seaport in north-west Wales through which most travellers from Dublin to England (and further, the Continent) passed. Although there are several glosses on this phrase it generally suggests that leaving Ireland is required in order to achieve success.

522 (p. 194) *Pennyfeather's heart*   The phrase 'suggests at once a disappointment in love, but men use it without explanation somewhat coquettishly . . . ' (Joyce, *Letters*, Vol. 3, p. 130).

523 (p. 194) *Michael Robartes . . . faded from the world*   lines 1–3 from Yeats's poem 'Michael Robartes Remembers Forgotten Beauty' (*The Wind Among the Reeds*, 1899; renamed 'He Remembers Forgotten Beauty' in the *Collected Poems* of 1956): 'When my arms wrap you round I press / My heart upon the loveliness / That has long faded from the world.'

524 (p. 195) *John Alphonsus Mulrennan . . . latter end of the world*   possibly a parody of the interest in – and the attempts to use for literary purposes – Irish peasant speech and culture amongst those involved in the Literary Revival (D)

525 (195) *spiritual-heroic refrigerating apparatus . . . Dante Alighieri*   an allusion to the platonic nature of Dante's love and admiration for Beatrice in *La Vita Nuova* (G)

526 (p. 196) *Old father, old artificer*   reference to the mythical Daedalus